TWO STRAIGHT-SHOOTIN'
WILL COOK WESTERNS
FOR ONE LOW PRICE!

TEXAS YANKEE

Taylor Blaine whirled, his expression slack with fear. "Pull yourself together," Dan Canby advised. "Keep your voice down. The walls are thin."

"Will they burn down my place?" Blaine asked.

"To the ground."

"I have a right to protection. Canby, this means as much to you as to me. You're my partner, and—"

"I'm not your damned partner," Canby snapped. "And you say it again and I'll open that door and call Kirby's men. Now shut up. I'm going back out there."

BULLETS FOR THE DOCTOR

"Get some help," I said to Mulligan. "A dozen men! Tear down some doors to carry these men! Get a wagon!"

There were at least thirty Spindle riders standing in the saloon, staring dumbly at the sudden destruction, and I shouted them into action. They tore off the tops of Mulligan's poker tables and we began to carry the wounded outside.

Christina Heidler was making up some beds in the hospital room when I rushed in. "There's been a shooting," I said, then further qualified that. "Get four beds ready. You'll have to help me the best you can. It's all we can do."

Other *Leisure* Double Westerns By Will Cook:
BADMAN'S HOLIDAY/THE WIND RIVER KID
FORT STARKE/FIRST COMMAND
LAST COMMAND/APACHE AMBUSH
BULLET RANGE/IRON MAN, IRON HORSE

TEXAS YANKEE/
BULLETS FOR THE DOCTOR

WILL COOK

LEISURE BOOKS   NEW YORK CITY

TEXAS YANKEE

1

As soon as she heard Hank Swain, Amy Leland put down her pen and closed the ledger over it, then picked up her "swear box" and walked out of the hot freight office. She went across the wagon yard, sidestepping manure piles and muddy spots; Hank Swain was trying to harness a six-up span of mules, and sweat ran off his face and soaked his shirt, and men stood around and watched him.

They watched Amy Leland coming and smiled, and Hank turned as she said, "All those unprintables will cost you a dollar. Pay now."

Swain threw down a mass of harness leather and took off his hat and angrily flogged dust off his clothes. "Now damn it—"

"Careful," she warned. "The price will go up." She was a small woman in her twenties, with a mass of naturally wavy brown hair and blue eyes that could stare right at a man and make him wish he hadn't said that.

"It seems to me with all the trouble—"

She held up her hand, and Hank Swain stopped talking; he dug into his dirty jeans and produced a dollar, dropping it in the box. "That was my last dollar," he said. "Meant to have a drink at Muller's crossin'." He wiped his sleeve across his sweaty face and began to mutter. "Workin' for a woman—it ain't natural, that's what."

"Hank, do you want to quit?"

He pawed a circle in the dirt with his toe. "I went to work for your pa the first day he rolled a wagon, and I guess I'll

5

stay on until they stop—which may not be long, the rate things are goin'."

"And in the meantime we'll learn how to talk without swearing, won't we?" She turned her head quickly and looked at the men standing about. "All caught up with your work?"

They were stirred to instant activity, and she smiled to herself and went back into the hot office. It wasn't much, board and batten, with a tin roof that turned it into an oven by midday. She rattled the swear box and decided to empty it; she took off the lid and dumped the money on her desk and counted it—nearly thirty dollars. She had a tin box in the safe, and she added this money to it and scratched the new total, a little over three hundred dollars, on the torn-out ledger sheet she kept in the box.

That certainly was a lot of swearing, she had to admit to herself. Expecially when it spanned only five months.

She planted her elbows on the desk and put her chin in her hands and looked out the window at the end of the main street, the buildings crowded cheek by jowl, and beyond, the endless rolling plains of Texas, unfenced from the Indian Nations to Matamoros.

It was a land of extremes: dust and wind in the summers and rain and mud in the winter and now and then snow and a bone-aching cold snap. It was the land of the Kiowa and the Comanche and the buffalo, and every man was a law unto himself.

And it was Amy Leland's land, although in five years she had nearly forgotten that.

Nothing in Texas was the same; the war fought a thousand miles away had reached out and changed everything, used up Texas resources and Texas men and Texas money, then left it like some sick and spent thing to gasp out its last breath.

There had been a time when Texas, after defeating Mexico, had grown until it just seemed never to find an end to it. The gulf ports were calls for vessels flying many flags, and Texas beef fattened the South.

Amy Leland could remember well how it was before the war. Largely populated by transplanted Southern men, the ties to Louisiana and Georgia and Alabama and Kentucky were strong; Texas lived and grew and played and never really thought about the North at all, and what trade goods managed to trickle in hardly caused a stir on the market.

Texas was an extension of the South; she carried on an immense trade, and when war was declared, she broke from the Union and gave her young men to the South.

Now it was almost over, and some of the men had already come back, but not to the Texas they had left. The town still stood, and the mansions the cattle barons had built still stood, but they were shells now, lived in but not really alive, for Texas was standing still, strangling because there was no one to trade with now, and the Yankees controlled the seaports with their blockades, and men just didn't know where to turn.

They looked for work, and when there wasn't any, they turned to stealing, from the Yankee Army at first, and when the pickings got lean, they started stealing from one another, and soon the terms "outlaw" and "renegade" didn't mean anything bad; it was just another way of making a living.

A fever had taken her mother in '59, and her father had decided that it was time for her to go East and get an education and marry some fine man who would never once in his life think seriously of going to Texas. She went because it was what he wanted, and a little bit of what she wanted, too, because she had already had eight grades of Abilene's one-teacher, one-room school, and she could play the pump organ and properly set a table; her mother had taught her those things, the commandments of a gentlewoman.

She had felt it was time to go on, to become a lady, and no age is finer than seventeen to begin.

St. Louis was not as fine a town as Boston or Baltimore or even Philadelphia for this purpose, but she had a maiden aunt there who knew a good school, and St. Louis had become Amy Leland's home for five years. A good five years. Not always happy, but not altogether sad, and the prospects of a good marriage were bright; the man was from a good family, big in the tannery and fur business, with a manufacturing branch that made all kinds of leather goods, from small men's clasp purses to harness and saddles and buggy dashboards.

His name was Taylor Blaine and his sympathy Southern, a dashing man of twenty-six, tall, athletic, and inclined to accept credit for things not quite accomplished. Amy Leland was not sure that she loved him, but if not, she had been willing to accept what she felt for love and was sure she could be happily married on it.

But that had never come to pass. Jake Leland, her father, had camped the night near the Peace, on his way to a buffalo hunters' camp near a place that would later be known as Adobe Walls. Sometime during the night a rattlesnake had joined Leland in his blankets. No one knew what happened, really, but Hank Swain figured that maybe Leland rolled on the snake, angered it; anyway, he was bitten, and he died out there on the prairie, bloated and alone, beyond help and hope.

Another freighter found him almost a week later, and since Leland left a will, Amy, aged twenty-two, was summoned from St. Louis and told that she had inherited a freight line, consisting of six heavy wagons, eighty mules, a freight yard, four way stations, and a payroll of thirty some men.

Taylor Blaine and all he represented faded into unimportance once Amy found herself back on home ground. She had a business without competition, but not without trouble; the Indians were a bother, and with the war on, renegades parading as loyal soldiers of the Confederacy stole everything they could get their hands on, and each success made them bolder, more aggressive.

Amy Leland opened the books she had been working on, glanced at the sums, and marveled that she could still be breaking even, let alone showing a little profit. She ran wagons to Austin, connecting there with the railroad, and serviced the towns and Ranger posts in between, a stretch of two hundred miles. And her wagons went north, into the Staked Plains country for the Indian and buffalo hunter trade; that was her profit, and she didn't want to lose it.

She closed the safe and locked it, then left the office and walked down the street to the square and the Mexican quarter beyond. Children and dogs chased each other, unmindful of the heat, and around the well curbing women pounded clothes with wooden paddles while their men slept in the shade.

The Martinez adobe was crowded in among the others, and Pablo Martinez was sleeping by the door; she stirred him gently with her foot, and he came awake, got to his feet when he saw who it was.

He swept off his hat and bowed, and Amy said, "Pablo, would you like work?"

"*Sí.*"

"I want you to build an adobe office for me, and another adobe building for the men to live in."

"*Sí*, it can be done."

"If you do good work, I'll pay you two hundred dollars."

"I am the best builder in the town," Pablo assured her. "When must I commence?"

"As soon as you can."

He grinned. "It will have thick walls to hold out the heat, and a roof of tile to keep out the rain. You will be pleased, senorita."

"Use the wood from the old buildings for beams and flooring," Amy Leland said. "I'll pay as the work goes along, Pablo. How many weeks will it take?"

He thought a moment. "Three at the most."

"Then I'll pay you a third each week."

He bowed again and smiled, and she turned and made her way through the heat back toward the freight yard. Waves danced from the dust in the street, and the sun bounced off the bleached wooden walls like a blow, making even the shade beneath the porches thick and stuffy.

Dan Canby was standing in his doorway, watching her progress along the street; he spoke as she drew even. "The heat'll get you if you don't wear a hat, Amy."

She stopped and squinted at him; he was a lanky man in a white shirt, with a bone-handled pistol stuck into his belt, butt to the front. He had a bold face and a dark mustache and even darker eyes; they always made her very alert, as though Canby were going to take advantage of her if she didn't watch him closely. He was a soft-spoken man and very dangerous; she had seen him shoot two men not far from the very spot where she stood.

"Do you worry about me?" she asked.

"Why, sure. With only six unmarried females in town, it's like me to worry." He smiled. "Still say you ought to throw your outfit in with mine."

"No. How many times does that make now?"

"Oh, forty or fifty. I never keep track of the noes. Just the yeses." He straightened. "Got some tea inside. I've got a cistern, the best in town, and—"

"Thank you, no."

"I'm not going to bite you," he said.

"Now I didn't say you were." She compressed her lips. "Don't think a dare will work with me, Dan Canby."

"Didn't expect it to." He smiled again. "But I guess it's just your way of flattering yourself."

"What's that supposed to mean?"

"Oh, I don't know how to tell you. But if you were fifty and fat, you'd come in and drink the tea, but since you're young and pretty, you've just got to figure that I'll chase you around the sugar barrels and—"

"Well, I like that!" she snapped and came onto the porch. When she reached the doorway, Canby put out his hand, touching her with his fingertips.

"Hold on now. I want you to know I deliberately boogered you into comin' in. If you don't want to, then don't."

She looked at him a moment then said, "That's honest of you to admit it. Are you always this way?"

"Try to be."

"Then I'll have some tea," she said and walked past him. His store was ten degrees cooler, choked with the flavors of spices and leather and coal oil. His rooms and office were in back, and she went there, and he wound the windlass on the cistern. She watched him, then said, "My, that's a way down, isn't it?"

"Over a hundred feet. Mexicans dug a well here nearly forty years ago. Went dry, so I use it for a cistern. 'Course it's got some water in it now, but it keeps things nice and cold." The hopper came up, and he poured from a glass jug.

Immediately her glass began to sweat, and she drank some of the tea. "My, that is good. Really cold."

"The best cistern in town," he admitted, sitting on the edge of the kitchen table. "How's business?"

"Well, still holding its own." She regarded him seriously. "May I ask you a question?"

"Sure."

"When Dad died, quite a few men in town came to me with bills that he owed them. I've been waiting for you to show up."

"He didn't owe me anything," Dan Canby said evenly. "Fact is, I owed him eighty dollars for some freight haulin'. I'd like to pay it now. You can give me a receipt when you get around to it."

"Why didn't you say something before?"

"What good would it have done? I didn't have the money. I do a lot of business on a swap basis, Amy. Besides, Confederate dollars just ain't as popular with some of those New Orleans merchants as Yankee gold. I'm payin' you in gold."

"I'd take Confederate money, Dan."

He shook his head. "Made the deal with your pa for Yankee gold, and that's what I'll pay." He got up and crossed to his desk and took the money out of the cashbox and counted it out for her. "It ain't my way to stick my nose in someone else's business, but I don't recollect your pa ever owing Pete Field and Doc Scully anything."

"How would you know?"

Canby shrugged his thin shoulders. "I hear 'most everything that goes on in Abilene, Amy. I just never heard about that."

"Well, I paid them, a total of four hundred dollars. And more than I could afford," she added.

"Scully never sold your pa any mules. Field never had a lien on the wagons, either."

She compressed her lips tightly. "That makes me look like a fool, doesn't it? I suppose everyone has been laughing at me?"

"Well, they were at the start," Canby said, "but they've learned a bit different. You've lasted."

"And what did you think?"

"Honestly?"

"Of course. I don't cry easily."

"Yeah, so I've learned. Well, I didn't think you'd last.

Most of us figured you'd sell out and go back to St. Louis. Now it seemed natural, didn't it? We heard you had a man back there you was thinking of marrying." He smiled, and he had a very pleasant face. "I'm happy to be wrong, though."

"Dan, are you positive about Scully and Field?"

He nodded. "Absolutely. However, it's not been my place to say or do anything, Amy. You'd have resented it, and—"

"That's right, I would have. Dan, will you lend me a pistol?" He started to take his .44 cap-and-ball Remington from his belt, but she shook her head. "I'd never be able to cock that."

"Come on," he said and went into his store, taking her behind the counter to a glass showcase of pistols. He took a .36 Remington pocket revolver out of the case, loaded it, seated caps on the nipples, and handed it to her.

"How much is this pistol?"

"Twenty-one dollars. Why don't you just take the loan of it?" He watched her steadily, and then she nodded and turned to the front door. When she left his porch, he stood in the doorway, watching her cross over and walk down a block to where Pete Field had his blacksmith shop.

Field was folding some red-hot strap iron over a round mandrel, making hinges, and he looked up with some surprise when Amy Leland stopped in his doorway. Field was a man of tremendous girth, but he had strength to go along with his beef, and some said that he had shod oxen, double shoe, without using a yoke and stall.

He saw the pistol and stood there, hammer hanging loose in his hand. "What you want, Miss Leland?"

"The money you said my father owed you," Amy said. "You were lying."

"I don't allow a man to say that to me, and I like it no less when a woman says it." He raised his hammer to go on working, then stopped when she cocked the pistol. "Put that away now."

"I paid you two hundred and nine dollars. Get it for me now."

Pete Field tipped his head back and laughed, then he let the humor vanish and looked past her. "Did you tell her this, Canby?"

Amy shot a glance behind her; Canby was leaning against

one of the support poles, and she saw that he was not carrying his gun. "I wouldn't lie to her, Pete. And I figure it was a mistake for you to."

"Now I see it," Field said. "You've come along to see that she gets it back."

"Nope. I came to watch her get it back." He slapped his plank of a stomach. "No gun, Pete. However, she's got one." He smiled and lit a cigar.

"I'm not scared of a woman," Pete Field said and dropped his hammer on his work. Amy Leland fired, bouncing the bullet off the anvil, making it ring and startling Field enough so that he dropped back a step. Powder smoke drifted in the still air, and he looked at Amy Leland, his mouth slack.

"I'll take what you owe me now," she said.

Field hesitated, and Dan Canby said, "Was I you, I'd get it, Pete."

Field kept his money in a leather sack, hidden in a stall, in a grain box, and he counted it out, dropping the gold pieces into her palm, slowly, as though they were drops of blood from his own veins. Then he looked at Dan Canby. "I figure you owe me this now, Dan."

"You figure wrong, but if you're a mind to collect, you know where I'll be." He turned then and walked back to his store and went inside.

Amy Leland stepped out of the blacksmith shop and cut across the street to where Doe Scully had a livery stable and corral. Scully had been standing in his doorway, and from the expression on his face, Amy Leland guessed that he had heard it all.

"I didn't mean no real harm," he said when she came up. He worked his jaws furiously on some burley twist and watched her with unwavering attention. "I sure don't want any trouble over this, Miss Leland."

"Just what do you think you have now?" she said. "You're a crook, Doe Scully, and everyone in town's going to know about it. Now get the money you weaseled out of me."

"Sure thing now." He bowed and grinned and ducked inside. She heard a door slam shut; he had quarters in a shack on one side of the barn, and she supposed he had gone there. Then she heard Scully yelp, and there was a heavy clatter of something falling; a moment later Scully came out, the money in his hand. A dribble of blood ran from the corner of his mouth, mingling with the tobacco juice in his beard.

"Fell," he said and gave her the money. "No hard feelin's, be there?"

"What do you think?"

She turned and walked back toward Dan Canby's store; he was inside, standing behind the counter, sorting through some sacked goods. She laid the pistol on the counter. "How much for firing it once?"

"Oh, I don't think it hurt it much," Canby said. "I'll clean it, and it'll be as good as new." He reached for the pistol, and she saw that he had two knuckles skinned.

Quickly she put out her hand, over his. "All right, honest man, how did it happen?" She looked at him, then smiled. "You went in the back way, didn't you? What was he going to do, Dan?"

"Well, he had some foolish idea. There wasn't time to talk him out of it, so—"

"—so you hit him in the mouth."

He grinned and ran his fingers through his hair. "Yeah, somethin' like that. You can keep on holding my hand if you like, though."

She pulled hers away quickly and put it behind her. "I'm not going to thank you."

"Didn't expect it."

"Then why'd you do it?"

He shrugged. "Scully's a mean old cuss. Maybe a little more than I wanted to see you handle. Fact is, you'd have had to shoot him, and I didn't want to see you do that. Too nice a day."

"Dan, I've got to take care of my own affairs."

"Sure you do."

She studied him, trying to understand him, then she turned and stepped to the door. "You've bought trouble for yourself, Dan."

"Well, it was so cheap I just couldn't turn it down. That's the bargain hunter in me."

"Then thank you."

He watched her go, then dropped the loading lever, pulled

the cylinder pin, and let the cylinder fall free. He pulled the loads with a corkscrew, cleaned the gun thoroughly, reassembled it, and returned it to the display case.

Pete Field and Doe Scully came in, stopping just inside the door. Scully carried a Sharps rifle, and Field had a .36 Colt jammed in the waistband of his leather apron.

"You shouldn't have stuck your nose in," Scully said. "It wasn't any business of yours anyway, Dan."

"Oh, I don't know; it never did set right with me." He looked from one to the other. "You want a little trouble over it?"

"You must have figured you had that when you told her," Field said. "That was the first hard money I'd seen in a year, Dan. Damn it all!"

"Cheatin' a woman—is that the way to get it?" Canby asked.

"What do you get out of this?" Scully asked. "Or don't you want me to guess?"

"I'd advise you not to," Canby told him. He walked down the length of the counter and came around the end, and then they saw the sawed-off eight-gauge Greener with the hammers eared back. He placed the shotgun on the counter but kept his fingers curled around the stock, and both men looked at it. "The trouble with both of you is that you're sore losers. Jake Leland wouldn't take you in as a partner, not even when he needed one. He had you figured out, Scully—a dirty little man with a big ambition and nothing else." He switched his glance to Pete Field. "You never put a shoe on Leland stock, and that galled you bad. And you never could beat Jake to anything, so you decided to take it out on the girl. That was a mistake."

"Who says so?"

"She does."

"She's just a woman," Field said. "If she was a man—"

Canby laughed. "Pete, if she was a man, you'd never have had the guts to cheat her."

Field thought about this, then said, "Are you throwin' in with her, Dan?"

He shook his head. "She won't have it."

"A man like you never picks up an ax unless he means to grind it," Scully said. "Known you too long to think otherwise. Maybe you want a part of that line. Never knew you to mix in another's fuss before."

"You learn somethin' new every day, don't you?"

"Yeah, and some things a man don't forget," Field declared.

"But I'll wait. I've got the time." He wheeled and stomped out, knocking back a man who was standing out there, listening to it all.

"Now how about you?" Dan Canby asked. "Ain't you goin' to threaten me and leave?"

"I don't figure it's worth shootin' over," Scully said. "She can't last. She's a woman. She just can't last. Ain't tough enough."

"Now you'd be a fool to bet on that, Doe."

Scully scratched his head and turned to spit; he splattered the boots of a man standing just outside the door; there was a good crowd now, and the man had no chance to jump back. This angered Scully, and he snapped, "What the hell you all want? Go on, get out of here!"

"You go," Canby said easily, and Scully's head came around quickly.

"Don't talk to me that way, Dan. You want to lose a friend —"

"You were never a friend of mine," Canby told him.

Scully hesitated. "Can't figure it. I just can't figure your game at all."

"Well, you work on it then." He stood there, and Scully turned and pushed his way through the men standing around the porch. They hesitated a moment and then moved on, and Dan Canby put the shotgun behind the counter and stood there, frowning a little.

It seemed odd to him that men like Scully and Field couldn't understand that a man did things just because they were the right things to do. Then he wondered if maybe they weren't a little right about him—that there was something behind it that he really didn't understand himself.

2

AUGUST was the hottest month anyone remembered, and through the ceaseless, blistering heat Pablo Martinez and four of his relatives labored to build the two buildings Amy Leland wanted. Martinez was a craftsman; he laid his blocks true and vertical, and each window and door was square, with the heavy timbers mortised into the adobe.

A saw pit was built, and the timbers of the old buildings were ripped for planks, and each one was carefully smoothed and oiled, then laid down, drilled and pegged in place. Martinez, who had a reputation for being a listless, idle man, worked from the first peek of the morning sun to the last view of it, and he completed the buildings in twenty-six days, took the last of his money, and went home.

The next day he resumed his siestas while his wife beat clothes at the well.

Hank Swain was summoned to the office, and Amy Leland laid down a few ground rules. There would be no spitting of tobacco on the floor, and because she knew the contrary nature of these men, she added the walls and ceiling to that rule. The barracks would be scrubbed once a week, each Saturday, and she would inspect it personally. The bathing facilities—a large metal tank installed at the west end—would be used frequently.

And any man who didn't like it could draw his pay and leave.

Hank Swain didn't like it, but he chewed his tobacco and

nodded, and because the only kind of job he knew how to do was a good one, the orders would be followed to the letter.

Mail was delivered by Amy Leland's drivers. That is, it was brought to Dan Canby's store, and people picked it up there when they came to town, and it was not unusual for letters and packages to go uncalled for for a month or more.

But any news of the war spread quickly because many of these people had kin fighting in the South; the country had almost been denuded of young men, some of them away for their third year now, and many had gone for good, fallen or died in Yankee prisons.

The war wasn't going well, and ideas of an early victory had vanished. No one said that the South was losing; they just stopped talking about the South winning, especially after the siege of Vicksburg. Once in a while men would come back, some riding, some walking, some with an empty sleeve or an eye gone; they went to their homes and stayed there as though they were hiding from something, and a few of them joined the renegades, thinking they could go on fighting that way.

The rains began in the early fall, heavy showers that soaked the land and swelled the creeks, and the buffalo hunting season came to an end, and Amy Leland put all her wagons on the southern run. Somehow the summer had been a good one; she bought four wagons from a man in Santa Fe who wanted out of the business, and she took thirty of his mules and six men he had working for him. It seemed incredible, but she paid cash, nearly eleven hundred dollars for the lot, delivered.

By careful management she was showing a profit, looking for every opportunity to put her hands on Yankee gold, and when she took Confederate money, she insisted that it be discounted, at first only ten percent, then later twenty, and now she'd only accept it at fifty cents on the dollar.

There was a lot of talk about this; some said that she was downright unpatriotic and that a body ought to have more faith in Jefferson Davis, but that was street talk. The merchants were shying away from Confederate money and more often would accept script, privately printed paper that in reality was only promissory notes backed by the large landowners and cattlemen.

Dan Canby came to her office one evening; it was early, but the sun was down, and she was working on the records by lamplight. He knocked, then stepped inside and unbuttoned his coat.

"Got a few minutes?"

"Well, since you're one of my biggest accounts, I guess I have. Sit down." She saw that he carried an unlighted cigar between his fingers. "Smoke if you like. Ordinarily I wouldn't allow it, but since you pay your bills on time—"

"I knew there was some reward in virtue," Canby said and scratched a match on the sole of his boot. "Thought we'd have a little talk about the business world and the way things are going."

She swiveled her chair and looked at him. "Talk. I'm listening."

"Well, as a practical man, I'd say it was just a matter of time before the South turns belly up. Not a pretty thing to say, but a man has to be smart enough to know when he's been licked. Agree?"

"I don't disagree."

"Looking at the whole situation from a business standpoint, things could be a lot better, and they could be one hell of a lot worse. The Yankee blockade of Texas ports two years ago was nothing at all. You could either buy your way clear or slip by; they just didn't have the picket ships to do a good job of it. Last year it was some different. Things began to tighten up, and getting through to New Orleans was a tough job." He rolled his cigar around in his mouth. "Right now you'd be lucky if you could sneak a rowboat through, the ports are so well blockaded. So there's no use in talking about doing business with New Orleans. Money is tight, and Confederate paper just isn't worth much; they want Yankee gold or nothing, and I don't blame them."

"What's your point, Dan?"

"That things are going to get worse before they get better. You and me, we may be out of business before this is over. Hate to see that. A lot of hard work going for nothing." He took a letter from his coat pocket and laid it on her desk. "The way I see it, we're just running out of everything— money, something to sell, and a place to sell it. Confederate goods are poor quality; everyone's in a hurry or short of this or that. Yankee goods will bring top dollar. They'll bring gold out of cookie jars and burial places, gold that's been saved for real tough times." He put his hand on the letter. "About eight months ago I sent a letter overland to a friend of mine in California, telling him to be on the lookout for something good to buy. Well, I got this in the last mail. He owned several stores in the gold country. Now he wants to sell out. The price is so good I can't afford to pass it up."

"Keep talking," Amy invited.

"I'm talking about all Yankee goods, Amy. First-class quality. Goods like Texas hasn't seen in three years. Wool blankets that will last fifteen years, and cotton shirts with real buttons, not wooden ones. Can you imagine it? Jeans with real copper rivets, and knives and forks that aren't tinplate?"

"If the stuff's so good, how come he can't sell it there?"

"The gold petered out, and the whole town, about fifteen thousand people, just packed up and took off."

"I was talking about San Francisco."

"San Francisco is glutted with hard goods, and the market's down. He can't give the stuff away there. That's why it's a good buy for me. I can get it at a price that's more than he could sell for in San Francisco, yet a lot less than he paid for it. He just wants to take as small a loss as possible."

"California's a long way, Dan. I take it you're asking me to haul for you?"

"Yes, if you'll go for the deal."

"How many wagons?"

"Twenty-five or more."

She laughed. "You know I don't have—"

"Better listen to the deal. Ore wagons are going begging; I can pick them up in California. Oxen, too."

"Now I don't want oxen."

"They're slow, but they're steady."

"My men won't drive them, and I won't ask them to."

"Mexicans will," Canby said. "Amy, I've got it all worked out. I'll take the men with me, and we'll go west and on up through Arizona—the Mexicans have been using those trails for years."

"A lot of miles, Dan. With wagons and oxen?" She shook her head.

"It can be done. And no blockade, either."

"There must be Yankee Army—"

"We'll have to duck the Army. It's a chance I'm willing to take."

"It's a big gamble," she said. "Dan, you could lose your shirt."

"If I sit here doing nothing, I'm going to lose it anyway. So are you. I can swing the whole deal for about four thousand in gold, but I don't have that much. Three thousand is my limit. I need to hire men, get them there, buy wagons and stock and the merchandise, and get back. It'll take seven months on the inside, and I'll need another two thousand."

"You're asking me for two thousand?"

"Yes."

"And what am I getting for my money?"

"Wagons and stock. All right, so you don't like oxen. Then sell them to the Mexicans and get back part of your investment. But these ore wagons will haul three times what your freight wagons carry. And they're built to last."

"There are a lot of gopher holes in this, Dan. You could stumble and break both legs in a dozen places."

"Sure, but it's do it or curl up your toes, and I don't want to do that. People have crossed the desert before, and they'll do it again. I figure it's a fighting chance, and I mean to take it."

"Why come to me?"

He shrugged and gnawed on his cigar. "Well, I've always held to the notion that one of these days you'd stop saying no to me and then we'd kind of merge everything. You've never really pushed me away, you know."

"That sounded almost like a proposal."

"It was. Although when a man's back is against the wall, it's a poor time to think of it. Keep it in mind, though."

"Why, of course. Who'll head this up, Dan?"

"I will if you'll run my store."

When she opened her mouth to object, he held up his hand. "It's just like any other business—profit and loss, and you understand that well enough." He put his cigar aside and leaned forward, his manner intense. "The Yankees let one passenger packet leave Galveston every fifteen days, and I could be on that with men and horses. We'd leave the packet at Vera Cruz, and then it's a four-day ride to a village on the coast called Acapulco. The Mexicans tell me it's no trouble at all to get a schooner to California from there."

"Is there a trail through there?"

"A good road, the way I hear it."

She thought a moment, tapping the pencil against her front teeth. "You know, Dan, it might not be a bad idea to ship south out of San Francisco. You figure the cost of men and animals for five months on the trail, and it comes to a big hunk. Before I really made up my mind to come back overland, I'd look into the availability of shipping."

"A good point. Still, there's the Yankee pickets." He mulled this over. "Of course, it might be possible to go northeast through Mexico and cross the Rio Grande. I don't think that's ever been done, though. The trail down through New Mexico is open; some goods have come in that way. I was just trying to eliminate as many of the risks as possible."

"It wouldn't be very funny to be stopped by a picket boat," Amy said.

"Mmm. No. That would be losing the hard way. I'll look into the shipping angle very carefully. And I suppose we can reduce the time by a good two and a half months this way."

"As well as eliminating Indian trouble. When did you want to start, Dan?"

"In the morning. I can get the men together and—"

"Then I'll have the money for you," she said. "Want to shake on it?"

"I kind of thought a kiss would—"

"Why, how nice of you to think of it," she said and stood up. He put his arms around her, looked at her for a moment, then kissed her, holding her against him for several minutes.

When he released her, she blew out a breath and laughed nervously. "Mr. Canby, that wasn't exactly a decent kiss."

"Want me to take it back?"

Dan Canby was too smart to leave town in the company of sixty Mexican drovers; he made his arrangements with them, and they left in twos and threes, and they met ten days later in Galveston, and there Canby secured passage on the packet *Argonaut*, destination Vera Cruz.

There was some talk around town about the way Amy Leland took over Canby's store. She got wind of it, pinned most of it to Doc Scully, and then took a new buggy whip out of the rack and danced Scully the length of the main street, cutting his legs and backside pretty badly in the process.

The talk stopped, and Scully ate his meals standing for ten days, and Pete Field, not wanting a taste of this, stayed close to his blacksmith shop, industriously pounding away.

Vera Cruz was not what Dan Canby expected; he'd thought it would be a hamlet in the sun, and he was surprised to find a hustling, busy port backed by a large town. As an American, particularly a Texan, he was viewed with a certain suspicion, but the Mexicans with him allayed the fears of the government officials, and they were given a travel permit and left the town without further delay.

The road was not bad; it cut its way through dense rain forest, thick undergrowth with a steaming humidity and bright birds wheeling and hawking and so many snakes that a man had to be very careful where he put down his bedding.

Rain in Canby's part of Texas was rare enough to draw considerable comment, but during the nine-day journey it rained each afternoon near enough to two o'clock for a man to tell time by it. And this was a special rain, with huge, fat drops, pelting down as though merely falling were not good enough. It thundered down, beating foliage, soaking them in seconds, falling so thickly that visibility was actually reduced. It would rain so for fifteen minutes, then abruptly cease, as though someone had turned it off. And then the heat would close in again, and the insects would bite furiously, and the land would steam and smolder and soak up the rain.

Acapulco was a small town crowded against the bluest of seas and sheltered by a crescent bay and a white sandy beach. Fishing boats snuggled against the shore, and in the roads, riding to anchor, a barkentine and a full-rigged ship waited for cargo or passengers.

Canby asked questions and found that the full-rigged ship had put in for repairs and was going around the Horn, destination Liverpool and the River Clyde. The barkentine was plying coastal trade—hides, hard goods, wines, and some passengers. The captain was an Australian, and he agreed on a price to sail with the next tide to San Francisco.

Canby brought his Mexicans and horses aboard, and before sunset the anchor was catted, sail set, and the barkentine heeled to a fresh breeze.

For six days they westered offshore, then the captain tacked about and set a northeasterly course. The weather was balmy with a good trade wind husking them along on the port tack, and Canby, who had never been to sea before, began to enjoy it, and he began to think that Amy was right—that this was better than shipping overland.

That kind of trip was always dangerous, for the Indians were troublesome and unpredictable, and he had never heard of a train getting through without some kind of attack. And there were renegades about who robbed anyone, and the desert was a menace, with water holes few and far between.

She was right; a ship was the fastest and safest way to bring back the goods.

When they sailed through the Golden Gate and passed under the cannon of the Yankee fort, Canby expected trouble from officials and was surprised to find none at all. An officious major asked him his name and destination; Canby told him, and then the major suggested one of the river steamers to Sacramento, even going so far as to point out the pier where the steamers berthed.

With his Mexicans in tow, Canby bought passage, and since there were no cabin accommodations for the Mexicans, Canby slept on deck with them. It was a pleasurable voyage in sheltered waters. Sacramento was a clapboard city with dusty streets and shady trees and a river bank that reminded Canby of the Mississippi and Louisiana. With their horses unloaded, Canby bought supplies and listened to the talk in the stores. All the merchants complained about how poor business was. The gold rush was over in California, and Nevada was getting it now; there had been quite a few silver strikes of late, and the population was migrating there.

Because they were all Yankees, Dan Canby paid particular attention to the people of Sacramento; it was a large town, populated now by farmers and merchants and fruit growers; the get-rich-in-a-hurry population had eased on. Canby was amazed to see a large police force and nice homes with watered lawns and a large section of the town almost totally Chinese.

Canby stayed at the Metropolitan Hotel on West I Street, and it cost him four dollars a day, but the room was splendid luxury and certainly as fine as any hotel in New Orleans. He had sent messages with the Hangtown stage driver to be given to his friend, and four days later Ken Buckley called at the desk, then went up to Canby's room.

They embraced and pounded each other on the back and poured drinks. Canby studied his friend and decided that ten years had brought a few changes. Buckley was tall and heavy through the shoulders, and he wore rough trail clothes, but he carried himself like a man of means.

"Why don't you come back to Texas with me?" Canby suggested.

Buckley laughed and shook his head. "Don't want to sound unkind, Dan, but California's got it all over Texas."

"They're all Yankees!"

"That's a matter of politics," Buckley said, "and a man must learn to live with politics." He sat down and flung an arm over the back of the chair. "So you're in the store business. Well, everyone's got to eat, don't they? I'm moving out of it. To me it was only an investment, and I made my poke. San Francisco's the place for me."

"Got something lined up?"

"Banking," Buckley said casually.

Dan Canby whistled softly. "Say, that appeals to me, but it takes a lot of money."

"I'm going into partnership," Buckley said. "The three of us are putting up half a million."

Canby couldn't help staring; he even swallowed hard. "Ken, you're just not joshing, are you? Half a million dollars? Gold?"

"Gold," Buckley said. "Rather simple. I gambled and made a stake, then moved into the gold fields when the rush started. Poker seemed the best way to make steady money, and I started buying up fractions for whatever small amount I had to pay—sometimes as low as thirty dollars."

"What's a fraction?"

"Odd bits and pieces left over from adjoining claims." He smiled. "I made enough off these pieces to put me into the store business. Had four places until the die-up came. I could sell anything I could get my hands on."

"And I came to buy everything I can get my hands on," Canby said. "When could we get started? I've got sixty Mexicans put up down in Chinee Town. I'm after wagons, mules, horses, oxen, and enough to load the wagons."

"No trouble there except for mules and horses. If a mule can stand, it's worth three hundred dollars. A horse will bring up to seven-fifty. Most of them have been taken over to Nevada. Ranchers around here have stock, but they won't sell. Oxen you can still buy, just like I said in my letter."

"You want to bunk here tonight?"

"I was hoping you'd ask," Buckley said. "And I trust you're treating me to dinner?"

They were enjoying cigars and coffee and brandy, and Buckley had his vest open, indicating that he couldn't hold another bite. "The war," he was saying, "hasn't concerned California much, except to make her rich. I don't suppose there's a businessman out here who hasn't sold Northern goods in Southern markets, with Texas getting a fair share of it. There are outfits freighting to Arizona and New Mexico on a regular basis, and of course from there it gets to Texas, and if you can get past the blockade, some of it finds its way to the Southern states. That's why I wrote you, Dan. I can't sell out here. First off, I'd have to move it all to Nevada or ship it back to San Francisco, and the market just isn't there."

"I thought things were booming."

"The wholesale market isn't," Buckley said. "Besides, I've got to move on this banking venture. There's a lot of talk about building a railroad into Nevada and Utah, and I want in on that. Time is of value to me." He stopped talking and looked past Dan Canby as a big, round-bellied man came up to the table. "Hello, Carver. Do you smell blood?"

The man laughed and sat down. "I smell horses." He offered Canby his hand. "Carver's the name. Do you want to sell your horses?" His glance touched Buckley. "Or have you already bought them?"

Buckley shook his head. "I'm selling, not buying. Besides, I don't have time to drive horses to Nevada and make my profit."

"Heard you were thinking about banking," Carver said. He scratched his muttonchops. "I'm a man of few words, Mr. Canby—I got your name from the clerk. I want to buy your horses, cash, in gold. Five hundred dollars a head, if they're sound."

"Sixty head?" Canby said. "That's thirty thousand dollars."

"I won't mince words," Carver admitted. "I run a stage line, fast mail between San Francisco and the Nevada diggings. I need horses. Good horses. And I'll pay cash."

"Well, I have business in Whiskey Flat," Canby said, "and I don't relish the idea of walking there."

"Understand you've got Mexicans with you, so I'll bend a little. Give me possession of the horses in Whiskey Flat, and I'll pay you then." He sat there, waiting, his heavy watch fob stirring with his breathing.

Finally Canby said, "All right, you've made a deal."

"A pleasure," Carver said, shaking hands. He got up. "Sorry to have disturbed your dinner. I'll see you in Whiskey Flat in—"

"Three days," Buckley said. "We're leaving in the morning."

"That's fine with me," Carver said and left the dining room.

Canby watched him leave, then looked at Buckley. "Did I make a mistake?"

"No more than I'm making selling out my stores. You could take the horses to Nevada and get nearly twice that for them, but it's the bother of doing it, especially when a man's in a hurry to do something else. We've each got to pick our own pie and eat it and let the other fellow have his. No, I'd say you made a good deal."

"And I can get oxen?"

"Oxen you can get," Buckley said, rising. "I'm for an early start. How about you?"

They left at dawn the next day, the entourage of Mexicans strung out behind them, and Canby was amused because they had collected a following of tearful sweethearts in the short time they had been in town.

From the flatlands of the Sacramento Valley they rode through scrub timber and wild olive trees, climbing gently toward the blue-veiled mountains that loomed many miles ahead. The road was well traveled, a good road, and they saw stages going both ways, the drivers whipping along, raising thick clouds of dust.

In two days they reached Dutchman's Flat and found a half dozen people remaining in a town built to house four thousand. The buildings stood empty, some locked, some boarded up, but the majority left open. Canby wanted to see this because he couldn't believe that people would go away and leave furniture and merchandise on the shelves. A lot of it had been looted by travelers, but enough remained to convince him that the owners had just up and left in a hurry.

"What a waste," he told Buckley, who just shrugged.

"You look at these buildings," Buckley said, "and you can see that they're good buildings with only one thing wrong with them."

"What's that?"

"They're in the wrong place."

"But to leave everything—"

"No way to take it along," Buckley said.

Canby was attracted by some abandoned wagons and four mudwagon stages. He and Buckley asked around and could find no one who claimed them, so Canby had horses hitched to the rigs, and they left town.

"It would bother me," Canby said as they moved along the road, "to see a town die like that."

"Depends on what you want. These people were after gold. The town meant nothing to them." He paused to light a cigar. "Someday, when people start farming this land, the town may come alive again. Who knows, and, I guess, who cares?"

"I'd care," Canby said. "I've got to be building, Ken. Growing is what a man does best. Someday I'm going to look back and see the things I've built. That's what I want."

"Do you care how you get there?"

"I'd step on a man if I had to," Canby said frankly.

Columbia was their destination, a substantial town with brick buildings and shady streets, and they, too, were empty now except for a few people who stayed behind because they had small farms or garden patches.

The arrival of the Mexicans caused a stir, but it was short-lived. Buckley's store was in the middle of the block, and they went inside. Dust lay thick on the counters, and Canby stopped and stared at the jungle vine of hanging harness and the shelves bowed under the weight of clothing and hardware.

One wall was covered with canned goods, and he examined them, reading the labels: peaches and apples and tomatoes and potatoes.

"About a hundred cases in all," Buckley said. "My office is in the back room, and I've got a complete inventory there. I have another store in Angel's Camp and one in Murphy's Flat. There was another in Whiskey Flat, but it's not worth bothering with."

"It is to me," Canby said, turning around again to look at the merchandise. "Can I find enough wagons? You wrote about ore wagons."

"They'll be pretty heavy on the Arizona trail," Buckley said. "You see, that's the rub, Dan, getting this stuff overland to Texas. Hell, it'll be winter before you make it back, and with the Indians—"

"I'll take it to San Francisco and ship it and cross Mexico," Canby said. "I've already made the arrangements."

"Can you do that?"

"I've got a better chance than overland. Now how about the ore wagons?"

"Hell, take anything you can find, in that case."

Carver arrived and bought the horses; he had ten men with him, and by late afternoon he had left with the herd, and Canby had three leather pouches of gold coin. The Mexicans were sent out to buy oxen; they were excellent judges of these animals, and in the four days that Canby remained in the town, the old stage corral was gradually filled with these slow, lolling beasts.

Buckley was a little irritated with Canby's methodical, planned manner, but each item was inventoried, accounted for, crated if fragile, and loaded onto a mounting string of ore wagons. Canby stripped the deserted blacksmith shop of shoes and nails and ironware; he knew that when he got back to Abilene, there wouldn't be any of the double shoes for oxen, and he didn't want to lose the battle for survival for want of a nail.

Canby bought out Buckley clean, even to the counters and glass showcases; these he stuffed with cloth and then crated so that the curved glass wouldn't be broken. The wagons were not merely loaded. Each load was precisely packed; then, with lumber taken from buildings, the load was sealed with a stout lid and the entire wagon box fastened with strap iron. When they reached the ship, it was Canby's intention to remove the loaded boxes from the wagon running gear and let them serve as their own containers.

Because Buckley was in a hurry, Mexicans and wagons were dispatched to Angel's Camp and Murphy's Flat and the contents of both stores brought back, there to be inventoried, crated, and put aside. Buckley and Canby haggled a bit over the price, and since Canby was getting a lot more than he had originally planned, he paid Buckley six thousand in gold, and Buckley left, leaving Canby to finish up by himself.

Canby, realizing that few Mexicans ever had enough money to buy firearms, opened two crates of double-barreled shotguns and gave one to each man, along with two boxes of brass shells. As he did this, he realized that the shotguns would have brought a good price in Texas, but he had seven cases of Sharps rifles and two cases of Remington pistols, along with powder, caps, and accouterments already packed and sealed in one wagon.

Each wagon had a code painted on all four sides, and from Canby's records he could instantly tell the contents of the wagon. His original intention had been to take perhaps thirty wagons; he had figured two men to a wagon, but the opportunity to increase this was too great, and finally he had them all loaded—sixty wagons.

It felt good to be ready to move, to pull out, yet he was a long way from Texas, and in Canby's mind there lurked the suspicion that since things had been going so well, they were due for a bad turn. He didn't know what it would be—weather, or something man dreamed up—but he was determined to be ready for it.

They left at dawn, taking the road back, and the oxen made a steady one mile an hour, which gave them about ten hours on the road, for darkness was coming a little earlier each day—not much, just a couple of minutes, but enough so a man could notice.

Each night he posted a heavy guard and kept fires burning, and he slept lightly, a pair of pistols always handy, but the trouble he watched for didn't show up, and in time he made Sacramento.

The wagons were taken to the river, and by nightfall they crowded the deck of a steamer for the journey to San Francisco. The desire to spend a few days in the hotel, sleeping in a good bed, was strong, but the desire to get moving again, to get back to Texas, was stronger, and Canby started down river late that night.

This California, Canby decided, was a wonderful place, and a man could get rich if he had a lick of sense and knew what to do with a dollar. He supposed that Ken Buckley would be worth a million dollars someday, yet the thought of all that money was not lure enough to woo Dan Canby away from Texas.

I'd rather be broke in Texas than rich here, he thought, and knew that this was the truth. He supposed that a man never really analyzed why he felt this way about a place, but the feeling was there, pure and strong, and he sure wouldn't fight it.

San Francisco was an irritation to Canby because he had to delay six days. The barkentine was up river, anchored off Benicia in one of the coves because the water was fresh there and lying to in it killed the barnacles. This was just one of those little details of seamanship that had to be attended to, and once the barnacles were dead, the ship was heeled on the mudflats, and at low tide the sailors scraped her clean.

In time, and on the captain's schedule, the barkentine arrived in San Francisco, and the process of loading began. The wagons were dismantled and loaded in the hold, and Canby was Buckley's guest at one of the fashionable hotels. Delays seemed endless, and this irritated Canby, yet he realized that as Buckley's friend he was making contacts for future business deals, and he was certain there would be more.

Canby was an opportunist in a land of opportunity; he didn't deny this or pretend to be anything else, and neither did Ken Buckley or any of his friends. They were a pleasant group of men who often found themselves jumping at the same chance and bumping heads, and once in a while they pulled some very sharp deals on each other, but they never took it personally.

The world was, they seemed to think, a prize, up for grabs to the man with the quickest hands, and Canby had to go along with that. He talked a lot about Texas, and while none of these men denied that opportunity was there, they didn't want to get involved because of the North-South political difference. Politics, Canby came to learn, was not conducive to good business. When politics entered, profit fled.

To make money, stay out of politics; he swore he would remember that.

Amy Leland received no word from Dan Canby and expected none; mail service was sketchy at best. It either came through the south or was brought in when the Army took a patrol south through the Indian Nations, and the war had put a stop to that.

Her days were spent at the store, and much as she admired Canby's business sense, she felt that there were a lot of things that he didn't stock and should have. It was a man's store, and other than food, there was nothing that appealed to women.

Goods of any kind were increasingly hard to get.

Hank Swain, who managed her freight line now, brought back word from Austin that the State of Texas was offering a mail contract in the spring, with a provision that a coach would arrive and depart each week from the capital. It was a plum, although the pay was in Confederate money. But this wasn't what Amy Leland was interested in; she found the prospect of getting mules and property for way stations very inviting, and the franchise itself was worth something, for it gave a foothold against competitors.

But she had no coaches and no prospect of getting any, while Scully and Field were busy working in a locked barn, building coaches. It made her sick to think of it and to hear Field at the anvil late at night.

Still, she couldn't give it up, not without trying, so she made application for the franchise and sent it to Austin with Hank Swain and hoped that somehow by spring she'd be able to get her hands on two coaches. Where, she had no idea, for Texas had been stripped of stages; every vehicle available was pressed into service with the Army fighting now on short rations and, if the latest rumor was true, short on ammunition.

The war, in spite of what people said and hoped, was drawing to a close. The Union troops were pushing the Southern army back on every front, and Yankee ships blockaded every port so that nothing went in or out.

It was a bad time, with bleak prospects for the future, and she wished that Dan Canby hadn't gone to California because she really didn't like being alone, making all the decisions and never sure that any of them were right.

Dan Canby was put ashore with his wagons in Acapulco, and the government officials were most cordial to him, and after a bit of wining and dining, he began to understand why. They felt that since so much merchandise was being transported through Mexico, a duty ought to be levied. Canby readily understood that this was going into their own pockets, and he remembered Buckley's advice about not fighting politics.

He offered them a proposition, outlining it carefully, about how he wanted to journey across Mexico and cross the Rio Grande at Piedras Negras. Of course, he would need a company of soldiers to guard the wagons.

Canby was assured that this was impossible, and a price was offered, which changed the melody of the song considerably, and after much wine and more talk he paid four hundred in gold and would pay another four hundred as the wagons crossed the river. In Mexican money this was a fortune, and the bargain was sealed.

They were talking about a distance of four hundred and seventy miles, across mountains and deserts, with the oxen making twelve miles a day in good terrain and five or six in bad. They were talking about sixty days of weather and heat and trouble, but when they crossed the river, there would be no Yankees waiting on the other side to take what had been so hard-earned.

Captain Christobal was in command of the soldiers, and Canby could not help but think about his position. He never fooled himself about how much any Mexican loved a Texan, and here he was, in the middle of some pretty lonely country with a hundred and thirty of them and sixty wagons loaded to the moaning axles.

The Mexican officials and Captain Christobal had already taken under-the-table money to make this journey possible, so Canby did not think for a moment that Christobal was above stealing the whole thing.

Alone, he was helpless and knew it and did not even bother to wear his pistols around the night camps. His weapon was words, and he spent his time talking.

"'There'll be five extra gold pieces for each of you when we reach Texas," he said to one group around the fire. This was a lot of money to them, and he knew it. "It is most important that we reach Texas, *amigos*. If we do not, there will be no money for you. Nothing for your families."

Canby would let this go around the camp; they were great talkers and discussed everything at length, important or not. And each night he would work on them. "When we get to Texas, each of you will have a job that pays well, in gold. It will feed your families and clothe your children. But we must reach Texas to do this."

They were all poor, and two pesos was a fortune; Canby was talking about dollar-a-day wages, and they listened carefully. "The goods on the wagons will bring much money in

Texas. And if I make the money, you will all have good jobs. We must guard the goods with our lives."

Day after day he kept this up, and he could not be sure whether or not he was making the impression he wanted to. The soldiers were doing some talking of their own, and Canby was sure they were trying to sway the drovers to their side.

"Each of you has a fine shotgun, a truly fine weapon," he pointed out. "With this weapon you can protect yourselves and the wagons so that when we get to Texas you will get your money and take it proudly to your wives."

Daily they moved eastward, relentlessly, paced by the plod of the oxen, which seemed to vary little, uphill or down. They crossed mountains and plains and rivers and endured the dust and the torrential rains, and the weeks stretched into a month, and he began to think that there would be no trouble from the soldiers.

Then a sergeant tried to break into one of the wagons, and a shotgun boomed, and the sergeant died there, and Christobal rushed to take charge of his troops. Canby, in his blankets when it happened, grabbed a long Green River knife and dashed toward the commotion.

Christobal had a squad lined up, and they covered the Mexican drovers, and Canby figured that the captain was making his move at last.

"What's going on here?" he said innocently and came up to Christobal, and before the captain could answer, Canby grabbed him around the throat and pressed the point of his knife against the flesh there. "Tell your men to put down their rifles, or I'll slit you from ear to ear!"

The captain started to struggle bravely, and Canby opened him up a little and made him bleed, and then Christobal gave the order. The Mexican drovers disarmed the soldiers, and the rifles and ammunition were distributed.

"We will have no more use for your services, captain," Canby said, shoving him away. "Take your horses and leave camp. Trouble us again and we'll leave you for the buzzards to pick clean."

The captain pressed a hand to the small gash on his throat. "It is a long way to Texas, *amigo*."

"We'll get there," Canby told him. "These men have families there, jobs there. Their children will go to school and learn to read there. You'd steal these wagons and the goods for a few gold pieces each because you don't know where your money is coming from tomorrow. Captain, these men earn money each week. They have work and honor, and they won't throw away tomorrow and all the other days to come for a few pieces of gold." He made a cutting motion with his hand. "Get out of this camp. Take your men and horses and get!"

"There are many *bandidos,*" Christobal said. "It is only the soldiers that keep them from attacking you."

"Why, I believe you're right there," Canby said. "Order your men to take their uniforms off. *Andale!*" He called to his wagon masters. "Sanchez! Cruz! Have your men dress in the uniforms."

In the firelight Christobal's complexion seemed to blanch. "Senor Canby, if we're without arms and dressed as peons, the *bandidos* will be on us before we travel a mile."

"Now you should have thought of that sooner," Canby told him. "When a man tries to be a thief, then he's got to take a few chances. Now strip!"

The first news that Amy Leland had that Dan Canby was in Texas was Hank Swain's hurried report the minute he got back from San Antonio. No, he hadn't seen Canby, but there was talk about the wagons and oxen that had crossed the river and were moving north. Likely they were on the San Antonio road right now.

This filled Amy Leland with a fluttery excitement, and she found that the days of waiting were incredibly slow. She hired a boy to watch the south road for them, and finally, weeks later, they were coming. The boy said they were only an hour away, but she didn't know about an oxen's slow, sure gait, so it was nearly two hours before they appeared at the end of the main street, coming on slowly, a sea of bowed, straining backs and rumbling wagons that left deep furrows in the soft earth.

Canby pulled up in front of his store and stopped, getting down carefully while a large crowd gathered. Amy Leland came out and looked up and down the street, and he watched her eyes as her gaze traveled from wagon to wagon.

Canby stepped up on the porch beside her, then signaled for one of the Mexicans to come over. He spoke fluent Spanish, and the Mexican nodded, went to one of the wagons, and broke open a case of canned peaches. He brought it to Canby, who took out the cans and tossed them into the air for the people there to catch.

"If you want more, you can buy at Canby's store," he said and laughed. Then he glanced at Amy Leland and saw that she was looking at the dismantled coaches in the last wagons. "I've got somethin' for you, Amy. A present from California."

"Are those mudwagons? Where did you get those mud-wagons?"

"California. Nobody wanted 'em, so I took the wheels off and loaded 'em on." He frowned. "I thought—"

"Dan, I've been praying for coaches."

"You have? Ain't you been prayin' for me?"

"Field and Scully are building some coaches. I know they're after a mail contract."

"What contract?"

"I'll explain it later," she said, touching him on the arm. She looked up and down the line of wagons. "My, they're big, aren't they?"

"Big, heavy, and slow. But I'll tell you one thing. I brought them across Mexico through the damnedest terrain you ever saw, and not even an axle broke. Any way you look at it, they're plain hell for strong." He thumbed a match alight for his cigar.

"Where are the horses?"

"Sold 'em."

"You what!"

He grinned. "For eight times what they'd have brought in Texas." He took a thick money belt from beneath his shirt. "There's enough gold in there to really set us up in business."

"Say, I put up half of those horses, you know."

"Sure, and we're going to split right down the middle." He kept watching her and smiling. "Do you suppose I could get a bath and a shave? Then we could talk it all over after we've had supper."

"Well, I can't think of a better excuse. And I suppose there are a lot of details."

"Oh, yeah, hundreds at least." He rubbed the dirty front of his buckskin shirt and shifted powder horn and pistols and his long knife to the back of his hip. "When I met Hank Swain down the line, he told me you'd about sold me out. Once we get these wagons unloaded, I expect to wait on the counter while you ring the cash register. Just wait until you see these goods."

"Every time I look at your sign," she said, "I'm struck by the fact that it ought to read Canby & Leland. It would look much better."

He stepped down and backed into the street and looked at it. "Doggone if you ain't right." He grinned. "We'll talk about it over supper."

"I thought you said after."

"How about over?"

"All right. Now don't you think you ought to get to unloading before something is stolen?"

3

On April 9, 1865, General Lee met General Grant at Appomattox and the war was over, but the news of it did not reach Texas until May 22, and it was like the death of a loved one who has suffered a long illness—expected, yet hard to take.

To most Texans it meant that their sons and husbands and fathers would be coming home, not as they would have liked, victorious, but coming home just the same.

To the freighting company of Leland & Canby it meant that the newly signed mail contract was worthless; Texas, as a government, was bankrupt and would soon be under Yankee military law.

Amy Leland and Dan Canby talked it over thoroughly, and the firm of Canby & Leland threw all their cash resources into the stage line, and it nearly drained them. The erection of stage stations, the salaries, and the cost of the equipment maintenance used most of their capital. They were ready to begin passenger schedules and regular mail service, but they needed working money.

To back out now would be to lose it all, and to continue meant to go on paying the bills with no real income in sight. Texas, broke, beaten, politically confused, could not help them, and they didn't bother to ask.

The store was clear, and they really had no outstanding debts, no loans to repay; their problem was getting enough money so they could operate for a year. To try to borrow money from friends in the South was out of the question; everything was chaos, money worthless, prices gone sky-high, and nothing to buy. In New Orleans a pound of brown sugar sold for a dollar and twelve cents, and a pair of cheap Georgia duck pants went for eighteen dollars, gold.

Dan Canby decided to ride overland to San Francisco and find Ken Buckley and, if he could, establish a line of credit. The blockade was lifted, and ships regularly plied the gulf ports, and there was a railroad near completion across that strip of Panama; a man could expect a shipment to arrive in three or four months.

Once Canby had made up his mind, there was no stopping him; he found a rancher who agreed to sell him two good horses, and with one bearing his pack, he left town, not expecting to be back until late summer or fall.

Alone again, Amy Leland moved to the store and pondered her idle stagecoaches. It seemed a shame that they should sit there; they were magnificent vehicles, high and boxy, built to travel light over the roughest roads in any weather. They would carry eight passengers and three hundred pounds of mail.

Everything hinged on Canby's being able to borrow money. Still, it was better to gamble now, run the coaches while she could, and then if they went broke, it wouldn't be because they hadn't tried. So she had some signs made and sent Hank Swain out to distribute them.

LELAND & CANBY STAGES
ANNOUNCING
Northbound leaving Austin
each Wednesday noon for:

Fredericksburg
San Saba
Comanche
Abilene
Tascosa

Southbound leaving Tascosa
each Monday for southern
towns.

FARE:	$31.00, gold
MAIL:	25¢
FREIGHT:	6¢ lb.

She dispatched a coach north to Tascosa, and the driver had some notices to put up. Another went south to Austin to post notices and wait for departure time. Leland & Canby had no stage offices in either town, so they parked in front of the largest hotel and made up for their run there. The hotels didn't mind, because the passengers usually stayed there and took their meals there.

When the southbound came through Abilene, Amy Leland was there to meet it. Eight passengers crowded together inside, and four of the heartier breed rode the top. Hank Swain drove this run personally, and he waddled into her office, his jaws rapidly kneading his tobacco. Hostlers changed the mules while the passengers went down the street to eat and cut the dust out of their throats.

"Six hundred pounds of freight and two sacks of mail," Hank Swain said. He dug into his pocket for a leather poke and counted out a hundred and forty-four dollars in gold for the fares, over thirty dollars in mail money, and thirty-six dollars in freight. Then he grinned. "Once I posted them notices, folks almost fought to be on that stage, even for a short run. You want I should send another coach north before I pull out?"

"No, I'll take care of it."

"I can't wait to meet the northbound," Swain said. "How were the crossings?"

"Up pretty high on the banks, but the worst is over. No Injun trouble at all." He scrubbed his uncombed hair. "Sure is lonely country. Those stations seem mighty few and far between. Ought to be closer than thirty miles."

"That takes money, and we haven't got it," Amy said. She went with Swain and watched him leave town, then walked back to her office in the store, trying to still a rising sense of excitement. She knew better than to count on this kind of revenue; it would soon taper off and cut into the profits.

Doc Scully and Pete Field were standing on the walk, and she didn't see them until she started onto the porch, then she stopped. Scully said, "Feelin' kind of big, ain't you?" He nudged Pete Field and grinned. "As soon as we get our hands on some horses or mules, we'll give you some competition. Got three coaches built now and workin' on the fourth."

"You've got a blabbermouth," Field said heavily. "That mail contract don't mean a thing now. We can carry mail as well as you can. Passengers, too."

"You get your livestock and then tell me about it," Amy said and went on into the store. She watched Scully and Field through the window; they had their heads together, talking; then they went on down the street.

Competition was something she expected, and she was content to let it be Scully and Field, because they had a talent for being just a little late in everything they did. Now Dan Canby was something else; he was a man who recognized opportunity and seized it, and even before he'd come back from his first California trip, she had decided that it was better to join him than to butt heads with him.

During the month of May and well into June Amy Leland began to understand that somehow she was going to have to double her service; each coach that came through was filled to capacity and then some, with men riding on top and baggage lashed onto the sides and overflowing the boot. Amy tried to understand this migration, this desire to travel; conditions were uncomfortable at best, yet people who had no money managed to scrape together the fare, and often a few weeks later they would take a returning stage.

Soldiers were coming back in increasing numbers, and the mail volume picked up, almost doubling in thirty days, while the stage freight was limited only by the amount that could be carried.

Stage relay stations held Amy Leland back; she figured this was an even weaker link than not enough coaches. Thirty miles between stations kept the drivers from running the mules. If she could build stations between them, cutting the distance to fifteen miles, with a fresh change of mules, she could double the service and not have to buy any more coaches.

It was something to work on, and she kept her drivers on the lookout for mules, but they never found any.

The Yankee Army came in late June, two companies under the command of a stern-faced major, and they started to build a fort on the Elm Fork of the Brazos, about ten miles northeast of town. The Texans were sullen about this intrusion, but they showed no reluctance to work for the Yankees and never missed a pay day, for the money was gold, and that was always pretty hard to come by.

There was considerable gossip as to just what the Army intended to do in that part of Texas, and Amy Leland listened to the gossip and withheld her opinion; they'd know when the Army told them and not before. The major's name was Bolton, and he came into town with a long-legged sergeant, and they tied up in front of the store, and the sergeant went in ahead of the major as though he intended to sweep aside anything that might be in the way.

The clerk went into the back office and told Amy Leland they were in the store, and she came out, walking the length of the counter to where the major stood, rocking back and forth on his heels and stripping off his gauntlets.

"I'd like to speak to Mr. Leland," the major said. "I was advised that he could be found here." He was a strongly built man with a square, stern face and a voice capable of shouting orders over the clamor of battle.

"I'm Amy Leland. I'm a partner in this store and in the stage company."

The major frowned, a hairy gathering of his eyebrows. "Is your partner Mr. Canby?"

"Yes."

"I'll speak with him then."

"Mr. Canby is in California on business." She glanced at the sergeant, a man touching thirty; he had a semblance of a smile half-hidden beneath his fawn-colored mustache. "What is it you want, major?"

"I'm not accustomed to conducting business with a woman."

"And I'm not used to Yankee officers," Amy said. "So we're starting even, aren't we?"

For a moment it seemed that he would take offense; then he

smiled and took off his hat and laid it on the counter. "You're quite right there, Miss Leland. It is 'Miss,' isn't it?"

"Yes."

"I heard the name of Leland & Canby when my command halted one of your southbound stages," he said. "My name, by the way, is Harry Bolton." He offered his hand briefly, a strong, sincere grip. "I know you won't like this, but I'm going to be the military governor. The fact that you were operating mail and passenger service impressed me. I'd like to talk to you about it."

"Well, I have an office in the back room."

"That would be fine. Come along, sergeant." They went in back, and Amy saw that they had chairs and invited Bolton to light his cigar. "This is Sgt. Maj. Ben Talon. If we can reach any kind of agreement, you'll be seeing him from time to time."

"An agreement on what, major?"

"Perhaps I've gotten ahead of myself," Bolton admitted. "The military function here is varied. We are going to try to reestablish local, county, and statewide government on a graft-free basis." His smile was wry. "That may be optimistic, but we're going to do it. We also intend to work to improve the economic condition; Texas is broke, peddling worthless money and script. Under separate command, police forces are being recruited to maintain law and order, although that's not my province, thank God."

"What's the matter with them?" Amy asked.

"Why," Bolton said, "they're colored."

"That's insane! There'll be another war!"

"We hope not," Bolton said. "However, I think we'll have more than our hands full. We're supposed to put down any Indian trouble, in addition to the other duties I've mentioned. Miss Leland, we will need the help of as many citizens as we can enlist. An army lives on line of supply. And as it stands, we're pretty thin. Men are being mustered out by the thousands, and I consider myself fortunate to have two companies. Equipment is lying fallow in some of the frontier posts because we don't have the manpower to use it." He paused to flick ash off his cigar with his little finger. "I've seen your stage line, and it's a shoestring operation."

"Not because I want it to be. We just can't get mules or stages."

"I can get you three hundred mules," Bolton said, "and twenty stages. They're Army mudwagons and ambulances, but they can be converted." He leaned forward and spoke confidentially. "Texans will work for you when they won't for me. Sure, we're hiring them, but they're quitting, too, when they get two twenty-dollar gold pieces in their pocket. Loyalty is something we'll have to learn to live without, so I'm not going to waste my time asking you to do anything for me. I'm going to buy it right down the line. Interested?"

"I'm in business," Amy said. "Keep talking."

"Fort Phantom Hill is going to need supplies, transportation, mail service. We haven't the men, and I wouldn't spare them to that duty if I had them, so I'll make you this offer: freight at half rates, passengers at twenty percent off, mail and dispatches free. In exchange I'll put Sergeant Talon in charge of the detail to get you your mules and coaches. I'll give you twenty men. You provide forty. You can leave for Camp Beecher when you're ready."

"Where's that?"

"More than four hundred miles, as the crow flies, and through the Indian Nations to Kansas." He straightened in his chair. "I'll provide mounts. You provision them out of the store."

She considered it, feeling that she should hold her breath. Then she said, "Major, I'll be ready to leave by noon tomorrow. But why Leland & Canby?"

"Because you exist. We'll need you, and believe me, Miss Leland, you're going to need us." He got up and offered his hand again. "You'll provide wagons for the journey?"

"Yes. I'll meet you at your fort site at noon with my men."

He nodded and drew on his gloves. "Of course, when you say you'll be there, you really mean one of your representatives."

"No, major. I mean *I'll* be there."

"Remarkable," Bolton said. "We don't have that kind of woman back East."

"Oh, yes, you do. And they walked to Texas when they first came here," Amy said. She went out with them and went behind the counter and opened a glass cigar case. She took out a handful and laid them down. "Good Havana cigars from California, sergeant. I'd suggest they'd go best after evening mess."

Ben Talon glanced at Bolton, then picked up the cigars and put them in his pocket. "That's very thoughtful," he said and stepped back, again taking his place in the military system.

The major and the sergeant rode out of town, passing on down the street while everyone stood there and stared suspiciously, and Amy Leland watched them go, holding back the urge to dance on the porch in plain view of everyone.

She had many plans to make and set to them. There were two clerks in the store, and she could trust them to manage while she was gone. She sent a boy to the freight yard for Hank Swain. She told Hank of the offer and left him in charge. He would round up the men, the mules, and the wagons and bring them around back for loading after dark.

The store closed at nine, and it was a half hour later, while she was going over the books, that someone rattled the front door. She picked up a lamp and a sawed-off shotgun and went to see who it was. Raising the shade, she saw Sgt. Ben Talon standing there, grinning, with a huge fistful of wild flowers.

Amy opened the door, and Talon stepped inside, taking off his hat. Wheat-colored hair lay heavy over his ears. He handed her the flowers.

"For you," he said and then acted as though he didn't know what to do with his hands.

"Sergeant, did you ride to the post and then back to bring me these?"

"Yes, I did."

She smiled. "That was foolish. But very nice."

"Yep. But that was the way I felt about the cigars—foolish but nice." He stood there and looked at her, still smiling. "The major smokes cheap stogies, and you give me Havanas. That was foolish. But the thought behind it was nice."

"I didn't like the idea of one man smoking when another wanted to and couldn't," Amy said.

"All things can't be equal," Talon said. "There's always majors, and there's always sergeants. The two don't mix, not very good, anyway. How come you don't talk like the rest of these people? You got Yankee blood in you or something?" He held up his hand quickly. "Now don't get sore. I just can't get used to everyone talking so slow. Why, if they was to yell fire, the town would be burned down before they got it out."

"Sergeant, would you like some coffee and something to eat?"

"For a fact, I would."

"Just help yourself to whatever you want off the shelves. I'll stoke up a fire and make the coffee." She took the flowers and put them in a vase, then filled the coffeepot.

Talon came back, spearing peaches from a can with his knife. "Now I haven't had anything like this for a year," he said, leaning against the door. "Ain't you a little young to be in charge of so much?"

"Now what kind of a question is that?" She looked at him, studying him.

He shrugged. "Well, a man don't expect to find a pretty woman running a store and a freight line, that's all. It kind of staggered the major a little, although he didn't let it show. He's got a wife and daughters back in Indiana, and he's got some firm ideas on what a woman should do."

"And shouldn't?"

Ben Talon grinned. "Why, a man gets those first. Didn't you know?" He ate the last of the peaches, licked his knife, and then folded it and put it in his pocket.

Amy Leland watched him carefully. "Sergeant, sit down." He took a chair, and she leaned back against the wall and crossed her arms. "Illinois?"

"How did you know?"

"The way you talk. I went to school in St. Louis for five years." The coffeepot began to bump on the stove, and she pulled it back from the hot spot. "Aren't you a little young to be a sergeant major?"

"Yep." He tapped his head. "But I've got it here. Don't know what it is, but I've got it."

"I notice you limp and carry your left arm a little stiffly."

He let his eyes widen and smiled. "Now that's some looking, I'll say. Is there anything you miss?" He laughed softly.

"Minie ball in '62, and a sniper in '64. Just never did learn to zig when I should zag."

She let her expression change, and there was a sadness in her eyes. "The war seemed a long way from here, sergeant, then men came back, with an arm or a leg or an eye gone. It's hard to understand how it really happened, because you feel no pain, and they no longer remember it. All it means is waste. A terrible waste."

"Sure, that's all it is. To tell you the truth, I never thought I was fighting for anything. The rebels was out there, and they'd shoot first if they got the chance, so you tried to beat 'em to it. Now that never made much sense, because if both sides would have held their fire, the damned war would have been over before it started." He got up and felt of the coffee-pot, and she got two cups so he could pour. "I have two brothers. They didn't want to go to war any more than I did. Earl, the oldest, bought out for three hundred dollars; he got some poor devil on the other side of town to take his place. He was killed at the first Battle of Bull Run. Marvin, my other brother, didn't want to go, and Pa didn't have the money to buy him out, so I sold myself to someone else so Marvin could buy out." He shook his head sadly. "He died that fall of fever. Pa, too." He looked at her and found her gravely watching him. "That ain't something you'll get many Yankees to tell you about, how they bought out of going to war by paying someone else to take their place. But somehow I've lost my shame of it. It's all right with me if us Yankees didn't want to go to war and the Southern fellas all ran to sign up. There's enough room in this country for all them heroes."

"They didn't want to go, either," Amy said. "Not really. But the band plays, and politicians make speeches, and you go, and then you come back if you're lucky."

"Or maybe the lucky don't come back," Talon said. "You make good coffee. Is your man nice?"

"My man?"

"Sure, Mr. Canby."

"Now wait a minute, he's not my man!" She was on the edge of losing her temper and drew back. "Around town they'll tell you I've whipped a man raw for saying that out loud. You're new here, so I'll just tell you once."

"Didn't know you felt that strong about men," Ben Talon said.

"Not about men, but I'll choose when I'm ready."

"Well, I've got nothing against a woman taking her time. How about putting me on the considering list?"

"Women put *all* men on the list," Amy said. "Some are just eliminated quickly. Besides, you don't know me, Ben."

"I'll know you time we get back. You'll know me, too."

"What kind of country is it? Wild?"

He rolled his eyes. "Renegade border bandits and Injuns. We'll fight before we get back. Fight plenty. A man don't ride across; he shoots his way." He paused to drink some more of his coffee. "Everybody wants what the other guy's got. You take those mules and wagons, for instance. They're sitting there, and they'd rot there, and no one would buy 'em. But once we start back, the border gangs will gather, and they'll kill us for the wagons and mules. Lord knows what they'd do with 'em once they got 'em, but they'd kill us just the same."

"And the Indians?"

Ben Talon shrugged. "Who knows about 'em? You can't talk to 'em because you can't speak their language. I've known some scouts who claimed they could, but they were lying. A few words, maybe, but no more. The trouble is, Amy, we're just not nice to people, and as time goes by, we build up a flock of enemies that way. Indians are what we've made 'em, I guess. You just can't push a man around and expect him to appreciate it."

"Ben, the major said something about Negro police. Is that so?"

He nodded. "You've got some Yankees in Washington who think it's a downright shame you went and put us to the trouble of a war. I guess they've been thinking real hard, trying to figure out some way to make you pay for it."

"There's going to be a lot of trouble," Amy said softly. "And I don't want any part of it."

Talon finished his coffee and put the cup aside. "Trouble is something we all have plenty of. Mixing in it seems natural

enough. You might say that's our first talent, finding trouble."
He touched his fingers to the beak of his forager cap. "I'll be
looking for you around noon. You're not going to disappoint
me now and stay home, are you?"

"No," she said. "I won't disappoint you."

He turned and went out through the front of the store, and
after she heard his horse leave, she went and locked up, then
stood there in the darkness, remembering clearly how he'd
looked at her, and the prospect of forty days with this man
held shards of excitement for her.

"I'll have to keep you on the list," she said and went back
and got ready for bed.

4

KEN BUCKLEY enjoyed money. He didn't care to save it; rather he enjoyed the challenge of making it, and with the proceeds from the sale of his store, and other investments, he joined with two other men and formed a bank in San Francisco.

The war, the town, the location, the foreign trade, and the constant influx of people all blended to make it very malleable, and Buckley's partnership flourished at a surprising rate. Land prices rose steadily; a lot bought on Powell Street for a thousand dollars tripled in months, and everywhere new buildings were going up; there seemed to be no end to the money coming into the city.

Dan Canby had no difficulty establishing credit at the Bank of San Francisco; his friendship and reputation with Ken Buckley assured that. Canby was looking for three thousand dollars, but after two luncheons and an afternoon in Buckley's office, with his partners present, they rejected the loan of so small an amount. Texas was in for some difficult years, and the man who was solvent would end up on top, and they had no intention of backing a man who was destined to lose because he was shortsighted.

Buckley pointed out that Dan Canby was in trouble because he had always paid cash or borrowed no more than he needed, which left him eventually with the chore of getting more or losing what he had. They would, Buckley felt, extend him a line of credit, in gold, up to thirty thousand dollars, at ten percent, and as he needed more to keep up with a growing economy, they could extend the line to fifty thousand, sixty, and on up.

The Bank of San Francisco just did not want to back a loser.

With letters of credit in his pocket, Dan Canby sailed with four thousand dollars' worth of merchandise in the hold and had made arrangements to have another shipment follow within sixty days—firearms and ammunition and clothing and dried fruit and bulk flour and three tons of tinned stuffs. Behind him in San Francisco he was leaving Ken Buckley as his agent; a lot of arrangements had been made, and there was some hope in Canby's mind that shipments could be made overland, with his own wagons picking up the merchandise in Lawrence or Kansas City, and in that way reduce drastically the cost of the merchandise.

This time Dan did not enjoy the sea travel, but he endured it, and when he landed at Galveston, he found the Yankee Army in charge of everything. Two days were wasted in endless inspections, but he dispatched a rider to Austin with word that he wanted thirty wagons, and sixteen days later he was ready to load for the long drive north.

Impatient to get back, he took the stage from Austin and left the wagon train to follow, and when he arrived in Abilene and found that Amy Leland had been gone for nearly twenty-five days, he felt angry and depressed, and for several days the clerks steered a course around him until his normally good-humored disposition returned.

Camp Beecher was a wind-blown, nearly deserted post; the soldiers remaining spent their time on guard duty to keep looters from stealing everything that wasn't deeply planted. A weary captain was in charge, and he detailed men to provide all possible assistance to Sergeant Talon; the sooner he got rid of everything, the sooner he would be mustered out, which was his sole, consuming desire.

Amy Leland had her pick of the mules; she took ninety, and seven Army mudwagons, and all the spare parts she could find in the farrier's yard. The captain invited her to inspect the post and to take anything else she wanted, and she thought of the way stations she would have to build, so she took the stoves from three mess buildings and packed the coaches with pots and pans and boxes of knives and forks and tin dishes.

Over the evening cook fire, Amy Leland said, "I feel so guilty, taking all these things. Why, I must have two hundred blankets and good wooden bunks and furniture."

Ben Talon laughed softly. "After a war it's the junkman who gets rich." He shrugged and made an open-palm gesture. "What's the government going to do with all this stuff besides let it sit? There aren't enough men to fill the bunks, let alone take 'em apart and ship 'em back East to some warehouse. Hell, the war wasn't hardly over when some outfit in New York—ah—Bannerman—was in there buying up everything he could get his hands on. And I mean everything. Cannon, observation balloons—everything. So you take what you want, load as many wagons as you want. The captain will be pulling out one of these days with his company, and I'll lay you odds that within a week there won't be a stick standing." He paused to fill his tin cup from the coffeepot. "All the lumber you see will go into building new front porches or picket fences. You wouldn't want to be here when the captain leaves. People will fight like dogs for what they can pick up. Some good men are going to get killed. That's the way it goes."

"It doesn't seem right, Ben."

"Didn't say it was, but that's the way it'll be. Man isn't much, Amy. Just a dangerous animal that's been highly trained. Once in a while they forget the training and you've got war." He swished the coffee around to pick up the grounds in the cup, then splashed it into the fire, raising steam. "You asked me once how come I was a sergeant major at my age. Major Bolton was General Bolton four months ago. I was Captain Talon then. You see how things are? Same way here." He stood up and stretched. "We ought to leave in the morning. I'm taking four of the light artillery pieces with me."

"Why?"

"The border raiders let us pass through because we didn't have anything to steal. But goin' south it'll be different, and I figure the cannon loaded with grape will go a long way to discourage 'em." He grinned. "Besides, you can put one on each corner of the courthouse lawn when you get back, and they'll give a dinner in your honor for your civic pride."

"Sometimes I don't know when you're joking," she said.

They assembled at dawn, when the sky was barely turning light, and the wagons were all hitched with an eight-mule span although they would normally do with six; it was Ben Talon's way of handling the mules without having to herd them along.

A day took them thirty miles to the southwest, for the land was rolling and grassy and traveling was easy. They made close camp the first night with a heavy guard, and the next day they traveled with scouts out, and when one came back, it was as Ben Talon expected; the border bandits were flanking them each step of the way, keeping down just below the crown of the low, rounded hills.

"They're looking us over," he said to Amy Leland.

Six days took them to the Cimarron, six days of being watched and paced, and when they reached the crossing, Ben Talon knew they were going to have to fight. The border bandits needed the crossing; it would slow the wagons and mules down, pin them against the river so they could be cut to pieces and have no avenue of retreat.

"Get the cannon out of the wagons and mount 'em on the carriages." Talon passed this order back and at the same time ordered the drivers to start getting the mules and wagons across; it would take all of that day and perhaps a part of the next.

The approach to the crossing was a swale flanked by low hills, and the bandits appeared, mounted, at least a hundred and fifty of them, and they stood their high ground as though waiting for a signal.

Ben Talon didn't hesitate. "Fire some grape in there for effect," he said, and a fieldpiece boomed and reared on its trails, and suddenly a gap was rent among the mounted men.

"Fire! . . . Fire! . . . Fire!" Talon yelled, spacing his commands so that one artillery piece was always loaded. The grape shot tore into the hill, spouting geysers of earth but doing little damage because the bandits wheeled and passed out of sight and into safety.

The artillery was loaded and hooked onto the wagons and remained on the north bank, protecting the crossing, which went on through the night, following lanterns hung on rope strung from bank to bank.

Amy Leland was not sure what she thought of Ben Talon's opening fire on the bandits; a part of her mind told her that he was attacking first, a sound military move, and another part of her mind kept bringing her to the fact that the first burst had killed and maimed a dozen men.

Talon said nothing to her—no explanation, no apology; he acted as though it had never happened, although he never once relaxed his guard during the remainder of the trip.

They saw Indians and buffalo—many Indians but not so many buffalo—and Talon fired on the Indians to keep them back, but he had the cannon stuffed with powder and used dried mud balls for shot so that no real harm came to the Indians.

Amy Leland wasn't sure she understood that, either; Talon was a complex man, with rigid personal codes which he lived by. There was no mercy in him, yet he was merciful.

He'll take some figuring out, Amy thought to herself.

Forty-seven days after she left Abilene, Amy Leland returned. She had so many mules that a temporary corral had to be built to hold them, and the mudwagons crowded the freight yard. Nearly everyone in town came to see them, and she looked around for Dan Canby, expecting to find him, for she was sure he had returned by now.

But she didn't see him.

Major Bolton and a squad were in town; he rode up and dismounted and stood with his hands on his hips, looking at the crowded yard. Sergeant Talon rode up and swung off, and the major said, "What the devil did you bring the cannon for?"

"Going to put them in the courthouse yard, sir."

"You're joking, sergeant."

"No, sir, I think they'll look real nice there." He grinned at Amy Leland. "I've brought you this far, so I guess it's all right for me to walk you to the store."

"I've been waiting for the offer," she said. "There's a few things I want to tell Hank Swain—"

"Go ahead," Talon invited. "I'll chew the fat with the major."

Bolton brought out a cigar, then offered one to Talon. "I was beginning to worry about you, Ben. You took a long time."

"Well, we didn't push very hard. Get the post finished?"

"Just about. Some roofing to be done on one or two sheds." He frowned. "The police unit moved in on us—three squads. White officer, but the troopers are colored. None of us like it, but what can we do?" He puffed nervously on his cigar. "I feel sorry for the troopers; they don't want to be here. They're not trained, and they don't want trouble. You haven't met Canby yet, have you?"

"No, sir."

"I'll be interested in your opinion, Ben. Will you be coming back to the post tonight?"

"Yes, sir, I probably will."

"Stop at my quarters then," Bolton said and mounted his horse.

Amy Leland came out with Swain; she introduced him, and Swain grinned and wiped his hand on his pants before offering it.

"Nice to meet you there, saajint. Heard your name mentioned here and there." He turned his head and looked at the crowded yard. "We sure are set up in business now. Sure are."

"How's your ox freight coming along?"

"Hate 'em," Swain said. "But the Mexicans can handle 'em just fine. It takes some doin'. Man, they get to fightin' and gorin' one another, and I'd as soon be in another county. But the Mexicans do all right. Must have forty or more workin' the freight wagons now." He turned and looked again at the mules. "Some of them is for the freight wagons, ain't they?"

"Stages," Amy said. She glanced at Ben Talon. "I'm ready."

"And I've been waiting. It's been some years since I've walked a pretty woman up the street." He offered his arm, and she took it; they moved along the walk, and the sun beat down, bounced from the dusty street, and reflected harshly off the walls of the buildings.

Halfway down, a painter was working on a sign: Abilene Citizens' Bank. D. Can—

Amy stopped and looked at the sign, then said, "Well, what do you know!"

They mounted the porch of the store and stepped inside; Dan Canby was behind the counter, reading a newspaper, and he didn't put it down until Amy stepped up and rattled a tin canister. "Hey," she said, "what are you sore about?"

"When I leave a partner in charge of something," he said, "then I expect her to be here when I come back."

"I couldn't pass this up, Dan. You ought to understand that."

"Well, I don't care to talk about business in front of strangers."

"Ben's not a stranger," Amy said.

"He is to me," Canby snapped. "But I guess you two got to know each other right well."

Ben Talon took off his cap and mopped his face with his neckerchief. "Tell you what, Canby, it's a hot day, and we're all worn to a frazzle, and likely we're ready to lose our tempers at everyone. So why don't I just say good day and—"

"You can make it good-bye as far as I'm concerned!"

"Dan, that's no way to be," Amy snapped.

"It's the way I am—take it or leave it."

She held her temper. "Dan, I don't think we ought to be giving each other choices to make. Now why don't you crank up the cistern and get us all something cold to drink?" She waited, but he made no move away from the counter. "Why didn't you come to the freight yard and meet me, Dan? What were you doing? Standing here, sulking?"

"Don't talk to me like that," he said quickly.

"Why don't we all change the subject?" Talon invited pleasantly. "I think we'll get rain this summer."

"When I want your bell to ring," Canby said, "I'll pull your rope."

"That sounds fair enough," Talon said, replacing his cap. He smiled and looked around the store. "I've got a hankering for some more of those peaches. Like to take a couple of cans back to the post with me."

"I've never sold you any pea—" Canby closed his mouth as Amy Leland went around the counter, got two cans, and set them in front of Ben Talon. Canby put out his hand and kept Talon from picking them up. "Twenty cents apiece."

"Take it out of my share," Amy said.

"I want him to pay for 'em."

"And I want him to have them. What's it going to be, Dan? Make up your mind in a hurry now because you won't get a chance to change it later."

He looked at her, saw that set of the jaw and the unwavering eyes, then laughed and pushed the cans toward Ben Talon. Then he smiled, and the irritation drained away from him, and he said, "Talon, you've just seen Dan Canby give his impersonation of a jackass."

"My ears were beginning to feel a little long myself," Talon admitted. "To be real honest with you, I knew I wasn't going to like you the minute I looked at her. But I've learned that she isn't mine, and she isn't yours."

"You learn quicker than I do," Canby said. "And I'll have to remember that. How about some chilled cider?" He went on in back, leading the way, and cranked up the cistern.

They talked and drank nearly a gallon of cider. "—Buckley's really struck it rich in California," Canby was saying. "Lord knows how much money he made in the store business, but if I know him, he salted most of it. Anyway, he's in the banking business with two other men, and he established a line of credit for me."

"Is that why you're opening a bank down the street?" Amy asked.

"Sure. Makes sense, doesn't it? With thirty thousand dollars in credit, I'd be a fool not to make it work for me. Look at it this way: I've got thirty thousand put aside in Buckley's bank for me to use, as much as I want, when I want; I just draw against the account and pay ten percent interest on what I use. All right, that means that here in Texas I'm sitting on one big pile of Yankee dollars. So with just a few thousand in cash, which will cost me ten percent, and the credit to back me, I'm in the banking business, making loans, accepting deposits, which in turn I'll loan on the right security so that in the long run I can use Buckley's money for nothing, profit here canceling out the interest. And unless things go really bust, I may get enough ahead until I have my own finances, my own credit."

"Well, now, partner," Amy said, "how about financing the building of ten way stations so I can expand my service?" She glanced at Ben Talon and winked. "Because you're such a sorehead, you didn't see the mudwagons and eighty mules I got off the Army. All the way back I've been figuring out how best to use the mules and coaches, and I think I'd be a fool not to expand."

"To where?" Talon asked.

"Well, there's Cameron and Waco and Dallas and on up through Paris to Fort Smith, Arkansas." She looked from one to the other. "What's wrong with that? Scare you a little?"

"That's a lot of territory," Ben Talon said gravely. "It's being spread mighty thin."

"I think we ought to move before anyone else does," Dan Canby said. "You're shortsighted, Talon. There's a tide to everything."

"It's a gamble I wouldn't take," Talon said. "Personal opinion."

"But it's one I'll take," Dan Canby said. "By golly, yes. We'll get started on it right away, just as soon as we get the line from Austin running on increased schedule."

"And I've been thinking about that, too," Amy admitted. "Scully and Field have four coaches. Why couldn't we make a deal with them? Let them run as independents and use our stations. We'll charge for it. It's either that or nothing at all for them. They're too late for anything else."

"I don't know about hooking up with those two," Canby said.

Talon, with his chair tipped back and cold cider in his glass, said, "Did I hear you right? Did you disagree with her about something?"

"He knows I'm right," Amy said. "Scully and Field can be pests. My way they'll be too busy to be a bother. And we can use the added service and collect a station stop fee. I'll even rent them the mules to get started."

"Good point there," Canby said. He heard the bell jangle over his front door and got up and went out.

They could hear him talking, and there was the soft melody run of a woman's voice, and Amy Leland started to get up, but Ben Talon put out his hand and pushed her back.

"Don't do that, Ben. I want to see."

"You get to see too much as it is," he said. "Drink some more cider."

"You can be pretty bossy at times. I don't know whether I like it or not."

"Something a woman has to get used to. A man, too. Each one needs a little telling off now and then."

"And you know just when that time is?"

"Yep. Figure I've got that much sense."

She studied him at length over the rim of her glass. "You don't approve of me doing all this, do you?"

"I see no harm in it. But there'll come a day when you'll give it up."

"Ben, I just can't see that day."

"It'll come. You're a woman, and what a woman needs she can't get out of ledgers or a fat bank account."

"My, that's pretty smug, Ben."

"Well, it's the truth. Coat it any way you like."

He looked around as a woman spoke from the doorway. "I thought I heard voices back here." She was in her mid-twenties, very fair, and quite tall. Her face was squarish, but she had good eyes and lips that smiled nicely. She looked at Amy Leland, saying, "When Daddy drove me into town and I saw all those mules, I just knew you were back, Amy. You look so nice tanned."

"Ben, this is Emily Vale. Sgt. Ben Talon."

He got up, and Emily gave him her hand. "I heard about you, sergeant. You must pay us a visit at the ranch. It's eleven miles due south. You can't miss it."

"If my duties permit," he said.

"Surely they must give you time off, sergeant." She turned when Canby came up. "If you'll have the clerk set everything out back, we'll pick it up before leaving town."

"Would you like some cold cider?" Canby asked.

"Is it hard?"

"No, but it's got a tang." He poured a cup and handed it to her. She drank some and wrinkled her nose and smiled. "I had some hard cider once, when I was twelve. Grandfather used to make it, and I found where he hid it. Everyone was properly disgraced." She finished the cup and handed it back.

Ben Talon blew out his breath and put on his cap. "Like it or not, I've got to get back to the post. It's been a pleasure, Miss Vale."

"My daddy says you Yankees are going to rub our noses in the dirt. Is that so, sergeant?"

"No, that's not so," Talon said.

"Daddy won't believe that."

"If I see your daddy, I'll tell him that," Ben Talon said. "And if he's got a lick of sense, he'll believe it. I'm as sick of the war as you are. Do you believe that?"

"I lost kin. Two brothers. Another came back with one arm. Who pays for that, sergeant?"

"Nobody. How could they?" He watched her carefully, then asked, "Why do you want me to come out to your ranch?"

"So my daddy and all the men there can beat your Yankee head off," she snapped. He continued to study her, no expression on his face, then she started to wheel away, but he caught her by the arm and held her.

"You've had your say," Talon said softly. "Now you stand pat and hear what I've got to say. Didn't your daddy get his craw full of fighting? Wasn't losing two of his boys enough? Or is it just a girl talking? A girl who's hurt and wants to hit out and don't quite know who to hit?"

"I—let me go!" She started to cry.

"So you can run? Where are you going to run to? Where can any of us go now? We killed each other, and now we've got to live together. Maybe we can't, but we have to try." He let go of her arm. "I'll be out to see you one of these days. Maybe you'll play the spinet for me, and we'll sit in the shade and talk, and maybe out of it all will be something to take the place of what we have now."

She dried her eyes with the back of her hand and watched him. "I—have to go." She started to turn, and then looked back at him. "It hurts to lose. It really hurts."

"I know."

She left the store, and Dan Canby gnawed on a cold cigar, his expression grave. Then he said, "Talon, you've fooled me. I'll have to watch you."

"If you want to waste your time," Ben Talon said, then went out and walked down the street to his horse.

5

LELAND & CANBY began stage service to Fort Smith, Arkansas, in September, when the steady rains began and the buffalo started to move south and the Indians were too busy hunting to bother the stages.

One of the first southbound passengers was a tall man with dark hair and a clipped mustache and carrying a silver-headed cane. He endured the tedious days of jolting and suffered the indifferent meals in the stage way stations, and in time—although he thought that time would never come—he arrived in Abilene.

Without delay he ordered a room at the hotel and instructed the clerk to have tub and water brought up for his bath, a thing that gave him away immediately as a dude. An hour later, dressed in a fresh suit, he left the hotel and walked toward the adobe office of Leland & Canby, knocking with his cane on the heavy door.

A clerk let him in. "I would like to see Miss Leland," he said crisply.

There was another clerk; he looked up, then a door farther down opened, and Amy Leland said, "Sam, I want you to go over these freight manif—" She saw the man standing there, and she smiled and hurried to him. "Taylor. Taylor Blaine. Why, what on earth are you doing in Texas?" She took his arm and led him into her office and closed the door.

He looked around, at the rich furniture and tapestries and ornate lamps. "Very plush," he said, removing his hat and gloves. "Very."

"Oh, this." She laughed and sat down, smoothing her

skirt. "My partner brought them from California, for my house. But I never got around to building one." She nodded to another door leading back. "When I had the office built, I had the room added. That's where I live. This is a combination living room and parlor." She bent forward, her hands clasped together, her expression warm. "Taylor, it's so good to see you."

"Why, I believe you mean that."

"Of course I do. Why shouldn't I? Did you come here on business?"

"In a way. Business, yes, but I could have sent someone." He had a gaunt face, darkened a bit from the sun, and strong eyes that looked at everything directly. "A month and a half ago I had occasion to ship some cutting equipment to Paris, Texas. I routed it on one of your freight wagons, Amy, and it struck me that much too much time had passed since your last letter, and since there are certain opportunities here that I want to investigate, I decided to come myself." He spread his hands and smiled. "Really very simple."

"But very nice," she said. "Will you be staying here in Abilene?"

"A good part of the time," Blaine said. "I want to open an office here and another in Tascosa, if suitable personnel can be found."

"What kind of office?"

"Hide buying. Buffalo and cowhide."

She pursed her lips. "Most of the buffalo hunters sell their hides at Fort Larned. I don't run wagons there, Taylor."

"Yes, I know. I was thinking of shipping to Fort Smith. If my hide buying is successful, I'd like to talk about a contract."

"You mentioned cowhide. Are you in the cattle buying business?"

"Hide buying," he said. "There's a tremendous market for beef in the North, but unfortunately I have no way of shipping it there. Hides are an entirely different matter. I don't suppose I'll have any trouble renting office space?"

"No. Several business places have gone broke. They'd be glad to rent."

He got up and took her hand. "Amy, I'm staying at the hotel. Will you have dinner with me?"

"Tonight?"

"Yes. About seven?"

"That would be fine," she said and walked to the front door with him. He bent and kissed her hand and then walked on, passing Dan Canby, who was walking toward the freight office.

"Now who the devil was that dude?" Canby asked Amy.

"A gentleman I knew in St. Louis."

"Yeah, just how well?"

"We were once engaged," she said.

He turned and had a final look before Blaine turned into the hotel. "Taylor Blaine?"

"In person. Come on inside; I don't want you to display your temper on the street." She went back into the office and closed the door; he sat down and lit a cigar. "Taylor's family is pretty big in the leather goods business. He wants to set up an office and buy hides and ship them to Fort Smith."

"He's too far south for buffalo," Canby said.

"Cowhide, too, Dan."

Canby laughed. "The country may be way overstocked with cattle, but these ranchers won't sell hides and leave the beef to rot. What would he offer a head? A dollar?"

"Twenty-five cents," Taylor Blaine said evenly and became the first carpetbagger these people had ever seen. They were in his office—George Vale with his enormous frown, and Owen Kirby with nearly fifteen thousand head of beef that he couldn't give away, and Fred Early who owned nearly a whole county to the south.

Dan Canby was there, and several other people who had a passing interest in Blaine & Co., St. Louis.

Owen Kirby spoke for all of them. "If you meant that as a joke, sir, I'll laugh, even though it's a bad one. But if it was not a joke—"

"I never joke about business," Blaine said. "My offer, gentlemen, is twenty-five cents a hide, delivered to the freight yard for baling and shipment."

George Vale said, "Even if I would, I couldn't afford to

have my steers slaughtered for that price. And I'm not about to leave meat to rot on the prairie."

"Very well," Blaine said evenly. "But I pay cash, in gold, in case any of you want to change your mind. I would like to ship four thousand hides by the end of this month."

"None of mine," Fred Early said and left, stamping his boots angrily. Blaine looked at the others; they shook their heads and walked out.

Dan Canby remained, gently puffing his cigar and rolling it between his lips. "A quarter is damned little, Mr. Blaine. I'm surprised that you'd offer it."

"Oh, I'd have gone up," Blaine said. "But unfortunately they didn't care to discuss it." He tipped back his chair. "I haven't thanked you properly for getting me this office and finding the men to repaint it."

"Since you bought the paint from my store and I kept ten percent of the rent, I figure there is no need to thank me."

Taylor Blaine laughed. "I can appreciate a man who is ready to grab every dime that comes his way. There are a lot of opportunities. Be a shame to miss any of them." He took a bottle from his desk drawer, and two shot glasses; filling them, he handed one to Dan Canby. "In the two weeks I've been here, I've learned a good deal about your—situation. These cattlemen are against the wall, Canby. The market is simply too far away."

"Seems like it, but I hear that a fella named Goodnight is talking about driving north."

"I expect he's going to stop off at the moon while he's at it," Blaine said, and they both laughed. "Why, if they could make it, it would take eight months to get there and get back." He shook his head. "I'm afraid they're going to have to wait for the railroads, and that, my friend, is a long way away." He paused to light a cigar. "I hear that the Negro police are having a devil of a time with these Texans."

Canby nodded. "During the war there were some outlaw bands stealing in the name of the Confederacy. By the time the war ended, some of them were wanted by so many sheriffs that they couldn't come home. Now, since one man is just about as poor as another, they've got nothing to steal. So they fight the police. Not much trouble around here, but I hear that up near the border there's been several police killed."

"It's too bad these men don't have gainful employment," Blaine said. "How many of these—outlaws do you think there are?"

Dan Canby thought a moment, then said, "There was close to fifty or sixty in one gang that used to come into town."

"I don't suppose you ever see any of these men any more."

"Now and then I do. They try not to draw attention to themselves." He studied the end of his cigar a moment. "Mr. Blaine, you're talking like a man with business on his mind. Why don't you just come out with it? I'm not a man who's surprised easily."

Taylor Blaine laughed. "I should have known you were a liberal-minded man. Naturally, in the leather business, I can't help but think of a cow as anything more than hide. I suppose, because there's no place to sell the beef, that these —ah—independent businessmen never bother with stealing them."

"What's the use?"

"Exactly. But I am interested in buying hides."

"Just how much is a hide really worth?" Canby asked.

"At the railhead in St. Louis about four dollars and fifty cents. Tanned, about ten dollars. On the prairie, right here, about a dollar seventy-five."

"More like two dollars and seventy-five cents," Canby said. "Don't try to fool me, Blaine. I like straight talk, straight dealing."

Taylor Blaine shrugged. "Very well. My company would pay two seventy-five right here in Abilene." He drew deeply on his cigar and partially screened his face with smoke. "The range is crowded with unbranded cattle. How many would you say, Mr. Canby? Ten thousand head?"

"Twice that, if you wanted to be fussy and take only the unbranded ones. That's what you're trying to say, isn't it? That we ought to start a little business?"

"It was a thought. Interested?"

"How much profit is in it?"

"A dollar for you and a dollar for me and seventy-five cents for the gentlemen who kill and skin. Providing, of course, that you can make the arrangements with the—independent businessmen."

"I can do that," Canby said. "But it'll take organization. The hides will have to be brought here and—"

"I'll take complete charge of that," Blaine said. "When can we get started?"

"This weekend. One is bound to come in for supplies. I'll talk to him then." He took a final drag on his cigar and dropped it into the spittoon. "Blaine, I'd like to suggest that you be very careful and take only unbranded hides. It's going to be risky as it is, and there'll be some trouble."

"Why, to be expected. Any time a man sets out to make twenty thousand dollars, there's going to be trouble over it. Amy Leland will freight the hides, won't she?"

"Why ask me?"

"Because you're her partner."

"Hell, you were engaged to her!"

"Some time ago," Blaine said. "I would rather rely on your influence than mine."

"All right, I'll guarantee that she'll haul the hides."

"Then I rather think we have a business deal," Blaine said. "Shake on it?"

"Sure. I'm sure you can count accurately."

"But of course. This is a legitimate business, Canby. Everything aboveboard. We are in the business of buying hides, and each one is inspected, and since there are no brands or other marks of ownership, we must assume that the hide is the property of the seller. Right?"

"Right as rain," Canby admitted, getting up. "I'll be in touch."

That evening Taylor Blaine tried very hard not to complain about the bill of fare at the hotel, but the beef was Texas beef, tough as a cinch strap, and the potatoes tasted of dirt, and the greens lacked a certain leafy tastiness to which he was accustomed. The pie, his remaining hope, was a dismal affair —canned peaches wedged between a burned crust and a soggy one.

He gave up and settled for coffee stout enough to float an

eight-penny nail. Cream cut it a little, and sugar killed the gall of it, which made it fit for him to drink.

"You certainly don't have much of an appetite," Amy Leland observed.

"I'm just not hungry." He sighed and leaned back in the chair. "I suppose you heard that I had no luck at all with the cattlemen."

"Twenty-five cents a hide—why, you insulted them, Taylor! What did you really expect?"

"Well, to bargain at least."

She shook her head. "You're not in St. Louis now, Taylor. Men bargain only when they can afford it. These men are on their heels, and they're mighty run over. They've lost their taste for haggling. They took your price as a final offer. I thought you understood that."

"Well, I'm sorry. I didn't. I could go to a dollar."

"If you want, I can see that word gets passed around."

"Certainly appreciate it," he said. "After all, if I can't buy hides, then my venture is a failure." Then he laughed. "But surely they'll sell. In time they'll have to. Money is money, Amy." He reached out and patted her hand. "I would say, on the surface of things, that you're in a very good business, and I'll be surprised if you don't make a lot of money."

"I don't think it's just the money," she said.

"It would be with me, and I'm not ashamed to admit it. Surely you don't intend to stay here, Amy."

"Why not?"

"Well, you weren't overjoyed at the prospect of coming back."

"I know, but I'll stay now."

"There certainly are a lot of opportunities here, if a man had some investment capital. After all, these big ranchers can't expect to hold onto all their land. They'll have to let some of it go, and there are farmers who would pay ten dollars an acre for it if a man held out for it."

"Taylor, let me give you some good advice. Don't talk about farmers here, or joke about them, or refer to them, or suggest that you even know what a farm is."

He reared his head, surprised. "Why, for heaven's sake?"

"Because it sets the Indians off on a rampage. They see a

plow and know that some mucklehead is going to turn the grass over and kill off the buffalo. And it makes a cattleman see red because a farmer doesn't have much land, and to protect it, he builds a fence."

He nodded. "Advice well taken. I'll stick to hide buying."

Doe Scully and Pete Field owned four wagons, and Canby persuaded Amy Leland to sell them the oxen because they were going into the hide-hauling business. She thought that was ridiculous, because Taylor Blaine hadn't contracted for any hides, but to get the two men out of her way, she went along with Dan Canby.

They left town and weren't seen for nearly a month, mid-October, but when they returned, they had ninety bales of hides, ten to a bale. This caused a stir in town, and Blaine put them into his warehouse, then made arrangements to ship them north immediately.

Sgt. Maj. Ben Talon returned to town, one arm in a sling; he had been doing battle with some renegade Kiowas over on the Brazos, but that was done now, and he was given twenty days' leave while his wound healed.

The wagons were in Amy Leland's freight yard, making up for the trip north, when Talon swung down, looked them over, then went inside. The weather was nippy and the sky gray overcast, and a chill wind was whipping up dust on the street. He knocked at Amy Leland's office and then went in. She had the stove going, and he took off his coat, carefully moving it around his bad arm.

"Ben Talon, what happened to you?"

"The Kiowas are learning to shoot some better," he said, smiling. "Is that coffee there or Hank Swain's mud?"

"Coffee, made by myself. I'll get a cup."

When she handed it to him, he said, "I've missed you, Amy. When those Kiowas were trying to do me in, I thought of you, and it kept me going."

"Oh, you're lying." She moved a chair around for him. "I suppose you're going to be in and out again?"

"Nope. Got twenty days this time. Seems kind of fortunate, too." He scratched his mustache. "I couldn't help noticing those hides you're getting ready to ship. They represent a lot of steers rotting on the prairie."

"Yes, but it's not my responsibility, Ben. I contracted to haul them, that's all."

"They also represent some pretty mad Texans," Talon mentioned. "Kirby and Vale and Early went to see the major about it. Someone's cleaning the range of unbranded stock, butchering it for the hides, and leaving the carcasses. They want the Army to step in."

"Is the major going to do that?"

Talon shrugged. "Don't see how he can. The stock is unbranded. Hell of it is, the cattlemen could round it up, brand it, and claim it for themselves if they had the money to pay the wages of a roundup. Vale and the others didn't like being turned away. Can't blame them. They have no market, but it goes against everything they believe to see beef killed for hides."

"There are a lot of things going on, Ben, that we don't like. Dan opened a bank."

"Heard about it. Very enterprising fella, Dan is. He'll either end up owning it all or get in a hole so deep he can't see the sky. A man's very likely to pull something out of joint reaching so far." He got up and refilled the coffee cup. "You do make good coffee. How are you at fixing breakfast?"

"Why do you want to know?"

He smiled. "Someday I might ask you to marry me, and I wouldn't want to get up first morning and find you couldn't fry an egg." He came over and sat on the edge of her desk and studied her intently. "Amy, you go on being a big business tycoon. I'll wait."

"What will you wait for, Ben?"

"That day when you'd rather be a woman." He put the cup aside and gingerly got into his coat. "I'm going out to the Vale place."

"You don't see anything in her," Amy said.

"Now, I never said I did." He smiled again and went out and got into the saddle and rode out of town.

By his figuring, he should make the house around dark, and he felt sure he could spend the night in the bunkhouse and come back the next morning. He rode easily across miles of open, wind-brushed prairie, staying when he could to the crests of the low rolling hills.

He was three hours southwest of town when he saw twenty or thirty men—he couldn't be exact at that distance—rounding up cattle, hitting them on the head with sledgehammers while Mexican skinners got the hides. There were two wagons being loaded, and as he rode on, in a direction that would have passed him near them, one man mounted up and came to meet him.

Ben Talon stopped and sat his horse while the man came up, a dirty-faced man in bloody buckskin pants and cotton shirt. He carried a rifle across the saddle and kept his finger in the trigger guard as he stopped.

"What you snoopin' around for?" the man asked.

"Is that what I was doing?"

"I asked you a question, mister." He looked at Talon's chevrons and smiled. "I know you. You're the Yankee major's dog robber."

"And I'll bet everyone knows you because you've got the biggest mouth in Texas," Talon said frankly. "You want something? Tell me about it then, and I'll be on my way."

"You alone out here?"

"No, there's a whole company behind me. You can't see 'em because they painted themselves the color of the grass."

"Mister, it's been some time since I've killed a Yankee, but I ain't forgot how."

"That so?" Talon asked. "What's your name? I ask because I want to see that it gets put on your grave marker if you so much as curl a finger around that trigger."

The man stiffened and stared, then said, "You ain't seen anything out here." He wheeled his horse and rode back, and when he was out of rifle shot, Talon went on.

He rode for another two and a half hours, then saw the ranch buildings off slightly to the right and cut that way. When he rode into the yard, a dozen men appeared, all carrying firearms.

They circled him as he dismounted, and he looked at each of them and said, "Ain't you heard? The police have passed a law against you owning guns."

One spat tobacco and said, "This ain't mine. I took the loan of it from him." He nodded to another man.

And he said, "I borrowed this from a friend."

"I'll bet you all did," Talon said and stepped onto the porch.

George Vale came out with his fierce mane of hair and his scowl. "I offered no Yankee an invite to this place," he said.

"Your daughter did."

The old man turned his head and bellowed and a moment later Emily came out. She put her hands to her mouth when she saw who it was, and George Vale took her by the arm. "Did you invite him here?"

"Yes, Papa."

He sighed and nodded. "Come in then. I still remember my manners." His glance touched Emily. "This is somethin' I mean to discuss with you."

"She didn't mean the invitation," Ben Talon said, and the old man looked around. "I'm imposing, that's for sure, but you'd be interested to know that there's some skinning going on about eight miles north of here. About thirty men and two wagons."

George Vale swore and clenched his teeth until knots of muscle stood out along his jaw. "Someday I'm going to have to take my gun and kill a few men," he said. "Come in, sergeant. Supper's on soon." He opened the door and held it open. "My son Jonas is out, but he'll be back. He's a bitter man, sergeant. I'd thank you to let me handle any matter that comes up."

He went on down the hall, and Emily spoke in a whisper. "Oh, why did you come here?"

"To see you," Talon said. "Isn't that a good reason?"

"But I don't want to see you."

"Are you sure?"

"Yes, I'm su—oh, I don't know. I've got to see to supper." She turned and ran down the hall. Ben Talon watched her go, then he went on down and stepped into the parlor, where George Vale was taxing his hospitality and pouring a drink for his Yankee guest.

6

THE TABLE had been set for seven: George Vale, his housekeeper—a small-boned woman with gray hair and a shy smile—and Emily and her two younger sisters and brother Jonas, who had not yet returned to the house.

And Sgt. Ben Talon, who did not seem ill at ease at all, not even when George Vale asked him to say grace.

The meal was simple in the extreme—meat, potatoes, and cabbage—but Vale made no apology for it. There was very little talk; the women remained silent because it was their place, and Vale had nothing to say.

Finally Ben Talon said, "I've been over on the Brazos. The carpetbaggers are really moving in around Palestine."

George Vale raised his head quickly and looked at him. "What did you say?"

"I said I'd been over on the——"

"You used a word, sir——"

"Carpetbagger?" Talon laughed. "That's what you people call 'em, isn't it? I don't know a name that fits better. They're buying up land. No one wants to sell, but a lot of people are in the fix you're in—lots of land and cattle but no cash—so rather than lose it all, they sell some and hope to keep going on the cash." He shook his head. "It just doesn't work, Mr. Vale. There's still no market, and then you have farmer troubles on top of it."

"You don't like farmers, sergeant?"

"Sure, they're all right, but this isn't farming country. Not enough water. A man who was blind in one eye and couldn't see out of the other could tell that." He sighed and pushed back his empty plate. "Well, the carpetbaggers are like an army of ants; they'll be coming this way soon. If everyone holds out, they'll leave. It's the quick profit they're after."

"Like Taylor Blaine?" Vale asked. He leaned his elbows on the table and looked steadily at Talon. "Let me ask you a blunt question, sergeant. Is it true that a Yankee who didn't want to fight could pay someone else to take his place in the draft?"

"Yes. Two of my brothers did it."

Vale seemed stunned into a moment of silence. "You can admit this?"

Talon laughed softly. "Sir, how can I deny it when it's the truth?"

"It's a thing I would never admit," George Vale said softly. "I just don't think I could bring myself to it. I'd feel something. Shame, anger, something."

"I feel something," Ben Talon said. "But I don't pretend my way through life, Mr. Vale. I don't think I like people who do."

There was a stamping of boots in the hall, and a man's rough voice, then Jonas Vale stepped to the archway of the dining room and stopped there. He was twenty-one or -two, and his face was still boyishly smooth. His clothes were dusty from long riding, and he carried a pair of heavy pistols, although one sleeve was pinned back at the elbow.

He strode into the room and stopped by Ben Talon's chair. "I saw his horse, and I couldn't believe it." His voice was tight with anger, and he looked at the women. "Please leave the room."

"There'll be no trouble here," George Vale said. "Sit down, boy. Your supper's cold."

Jonas Vale put his hand on Ben Talon's shoulder, fisting a bit of his shirt. "I took an oath to kill any Yankee who stepped into this house," he said.

Without exerting himself, Talon knocked Jonas Vale's hand away and watched him go white around the mouth. "Then after that you'll kill any who step in the yard or on the property or in the county. Where's it going to end, friend? You want to be paid back for your arm? How many men do you figure it's worth?"

George Vale pushed his heavy voice between them. "I gave you an order, boy. Sit and eat or leave the room."

"Let him settle it," Talon said. "I'd as soon he did it now as to have to watch my back later." He slid his chair back and stood up. "As you can see, I left my sidearms to come to the table. That's a custom with me; I don't need a pistol to eat."

"I shoot no man in the back," Jonas Vale said. "And I won't stand and have any man say that I would."

"There doesn't seem to be much anyone says that you like too well, does there? Your father invites you to sit and eat, and you don't like that. You don't want your sisters to sit here. You don't like me or what I say. Now why don't you tell us what you do like, and then we'll try real hard to do it, and tonight you won't have to cry yourself to sleep because the mean old world hasn't been nice to you." He saw Jonas Vale tense, and the blood seemed to drain from his face; the urge to reach for one of his pistols was strong in his eyes, but he held himself back.

"You just can't do it, can you? Just can't draw a gun on an unarmed man." Ben let his expression soften. "It's hell to want to fight and not have anything to fight against. Now you know taking me on isn't going to help you one bit. You know I'm not scared of you. So you stop for ten seconds and think of just what you can win. You might give a thought to what you can lose. You're not dumb, friend. Two and two makes four to you the same as it does to me. So what about it?"

George Vale spoke quietly. "Your supper is getting cold, Jonas. And you're keeping our guest standing."

"I'll get you some fresh coffee," Emily said and got up from the table.

Jonas Vale let out a long breath and pulled back his chair and sat down. "As long as you're a guest here," he said, "I'll cause no trouble, but don't count on it another time, in another place."

"All right," Talon said. "I notice blood on your boots. You found where the hide hunters were working."

Jonas Vale nodded. "More than three hundred head skinned out." He looked at his father. "I want ten men and your permission to ride."

"Denied," George Vale said. "We'll start no war. That's my final word. You start it, Jonas, and you're through on this ranch."

Emily came back with another pot of coffee and poured a cup for her brother before sitting down. George Vale went on, "It's a rotten feeling for a man to have—to know that he can't do anything and that no one else will do anything, either."

"If they took one branded hide," Talon said, "the Army would move in. You could brand, Mr. Vale. At least you'd establish ownership."

"I've got twelve men on this place," he said, shaking his head. "I should have eighty. And I can't pay the twelve I have. They stay because they have no place else to go, and as long as I manage to feed 'em and give 'em a roof over their heads, they'll stay."

"I'd round up and brand," Ben Talon said again. "You don't have any choice, the way I see it. And after I'd made my gather, I'd hunt up this fella Goodnight, and I'd drive to market."

"Where is the market?" Jonas Vale asked. "I've talked to Goodnight, and even he doesn't know where the railhead really is. He heard it was in Kansas, but he's not sure. It's too big a risk."

"Risk what?" Talon asked. "Sit here and you'll lose cattle to the hide hunters. Drive and you may lose 'em on the trail, but that way you'll at least lose while doing something." He hunched his shoulders and put his elbows on the table. "First off, no one has any money, so hiring men to round up and brand is foolish to talk about. So don't talk about it. Talk survival to 'em. Make 'em understand that if you win and make it to market, then they'll get paid. Put it on the jawbone, as we say in the Army. Mr. Vale, when it comes down to it, you're forced to drive whether you like it or not and whether you believe it or not, and it doesn't make any difference if Goodnight knows what he's talking about. You sit here and you'll lose everything, a piece at a time maybe, but you'll lose it all just the same."

Jonas Vale said, "Yankee, I'm glad I didn't shoot you. That's what I've been sayin' for months now."

"Yes, it all sounds like the right thing to do," George Vale admitted. "And I've discussed it with the others, but we always run into a wall. Who's going to pay for the grub for so many men?"

"I'd eat beef three times a day if I had to," Talon said. "I'd collect potatoes and greens and flour from everyone who could spare a bushel or a cupful. I wouldn't sit on my—I wouldn't just sit."

"You're a tough man," Vale admitted, "but it's easier to be tough when you have money in your pocket."

"That's so," Talon said, reaching into his shirt for a small leather purse. He dumped about ninety dollars in coins on the table. "That's what's left of three months' pay. With beans at four dollars a bag and flour selling for two and a half, that ought to take a hundred men nearly a hundred miles."

"We don't take charity," Jonas Vale snapped.

Ben Talon looked at him steadily, and the young man grew nervous. "Now don't show me how stupid you can be," Talon said. He bowed to the housekeeper. "I enjoyed the meal and the company; thank you." Then he looked at Emily. "Would you care for a walk? It's early."

"Now see here—" Jonas said, then closed his mouth and looked at the tablecloth.

Color was high in Emily Vale's face, but she stepped outside with him, and they walked slowly away from the porch. "My," she said, "you're as bold as brass. I do declare, I think Jonas nearly choked." Then she looked at him and laughed. "It's been three years since a man called on me. I do think I like it."

"Three years? That's not easy to believe."

"Three years since a gentleman called," she said. "Does your arm bother you?"

"Only if I bump it," Talon said. He stopped by the horse corral and leaned against it so he could face her, look at her. There was a quarter moon and a bit of a chill to the wind. "Cold?"

"No. Ben, you didn't come out here because I dared you, did you?"

"I came to see you," he said. "You don't believe that?"

"I don't think you ever do anything for just one reason. What does it matter to you what happens to the Vales?"

"Don't you want it to matter to someone?" He took out his pocket watch and popped the case. "I was going to stay the night, but I think I'll make a long ride of it back." He put his watch away and touched her face; then he bent and gently kissed her. "Good-bye, Emily."

"Good-bye?"

"For a while," he said. "Just for a while."

"I don't understand you, Ben. I just don't."

"There's not much to understand. Come on, I'll walk you back to the house." He took her arm and turned her; he said good-bye again at the porch, then got his horse and rode out.

Major Bolton was napping in his office when Ben Talon returned; Ben had camped the night on the prairie and reached the post in midafternoon. There was a drizzling rain smearing the windows of Bolton's headquarters building, and Talon stoked the fire, and the noise woke the major. He yawned and stretched and scratched his stomach.

"Any trouble?" Bolton asked.

Talon shook his head; he went to the door to throw out the old coffee and grounds and make some new. "Vale may spend the fall and winter rounding up and branding; I think I've convinced him of that."

"Well, that's something," Bolton said. He lit a cigar and puffed it gently so the smoke wouldn't bite his tongue. "Did you mention the drive?"

"Yes. He may throw in with Goodnight. The boy wants to. I think he has more influence on the old man than meets the eye. I ran across the hide hunters. Young Vale said they got nearly three hundred head."

Harry Bolton nodded. "That's about the count that was brought to me late last night when Scully and Field brought the hides to Blaine's place." He got up and walked to the window and stared out at the gray day. "How did Blaine make his connection with the renegades? Scully? Field?"

Ben Talon shrugged. "I don't know, sir. I don't think Amy Leland had anything to do with it."

"Is that a fact or a guess?"

"Hunch," Talon said. "There's nothing wrong with hauling Blaine's hides, major. Hell, it's pure business with her. Just freight, that's all."

"Maybe that's right," Bolton admitted. "But with the police on the lookout for the renegades, they've made themselves mighty scarce, and I know they wouldn't have let Taylor Blaine get near enough to make them a proposition. If he had a friend, someone local here the renegades trusted —" He clamped his teeth into the cigar and left the sentence unfinished. "There's talk going around that Blaine is willing to pay a dollar a hide. It's only a matter of time before these ranchers like Vale and Early and Kirby take him up on it. A man can stay broke just so long—then he's got to do something about it, steal if he has to." He turned his head and looked at Ben Talon. "How does George Vale feel about the hide hunters?"

"He's holding himself back, but it's an effort. The boy wants to ride on the hunters, but the old man's put his foot down. How long, though, is a big question."

"I don't want to see it start," Bolton said softly. "I dread it, Ben."

Scully and Field were in back of Blaine's place, backed up by the warehouse door, their wagons staggering under a load of baled hides. Two of Blaine's men were counting and inspecting the hides while a crew of Mexicans unloaded and four hunters lounged against the wall of the building, enjoying a common jug of whiskey.

The going and coming of the hide wagons was so common a thing now that no one in town paid any attention, and if they noticed that a few of the renegades came in for liquor and supplies, they made a point of not talking about it. After all, they were really good Texans, just unfortunate in getting off on the wrong foot a few years back during the war when their raids in the name of the Confederacy began to lose patriotic fervor and become outright looting for profit. But they were all good men now, working for a living, and many in town envied them for the money they made—those good Yankee dollars.

The arrival of Owen Kirby, along with three wagons burdened with hides and flanked by ten of his men, did cause a stir along the street, and when it turned into the alley, everyone stopped working and watched them pull up and stop.

This ceasing of effort was immediately detected by Taylor Blaine, and he left his office and walked to the back loading platform. Owen Kirby was there, sitting his horse.

"I've brought you some hides," he said. "A hundred and fifty."

"And I'll buy them," Blaine said, his manner friendly. He did some mental arithmetic. "That comes to thirty-seven dollars and fifty cents."

Color climbed into Kirby's face. "It was my understandin' that you'd go a dollar a hide."

"That's a rumor," Blaine said. "I gave you my price the day I met with you in the office."

Owen Kirby stared at the man, and his temper, long strained without relief, broke completely. "I came for a dollar, and I'll get it!" he yelled and reached for his rifle.

One of the renegades, the one with the jug, dropped it and it broke; then he had his .44 Starr in hand, and it boomed. Owen Kirby dropped the rifle half drawn from the scabbard, clutched his chest, and rolled from the saddle.

He had barely hit the ground before his riders, weapons in hand now, opened fire. The renegades scattered, and bullets thudded into the wall where they had stood. One cried out and went into a tumble, legs and arms flailing; he fell loosely and lay still, staring at the sky.

The Mexicans dove under the wagons, and Blaine dashed inside and closed the door. Scully had his rifle into play now and shot one of Kirby's riders from the saddle before he was cut down himself and fell off the wagon.

The firing suddenly stopped, for the renegades had vanished, and the mounted men milled around, looking for targets, reloading their guns while two quickly dismounted and looked to Owen Kirby.

He was alive, and a cry went up, and they tore off a wagon seat and carried him down the street to the doctor's home. The doctor made them wait outside, on the lawn, while he had his look, and a half hour later he came out.

"The bullet's out," he said. "He may live. If he makes it

through the night—" He shrugged and went back in and closed the door.

The men decided to wait it out at the saloon, but it was boarded up; they walked on down to Dan Canby's store and filed in and bellied up to the counter.

Canby waited on them, setting out two bottles and tin cups. "I heard shootin'," he said. "Then I saw you carrying Owen Kirby—"

"Yeah, yeah," one man said. "So you saw it. You've got good eyes."

Canby stared at him. "Now don't get sore at me, friend."

"Then mind your damned store," the man snapped. "If Owen makes it, we'll be leaving town, no fuss. But if he don't, we're going to burn that Yankee carpetbagger to the ground."

"Now that doesn't sound very sensible," Canby said cautiously.

"Who the hell said it did?" another man asked.

Canby knew the extent of their temper. He said, "Help yourself to cheese. I've got some books to tend to." He smiled and went back, stopping and turning when he reached his door. "Sorry about Owen. He was a nice man. Tough, but nice." Then he stepped into his room and closed the door.

Taylor Blaine whirled, his expression slack with fear. "Pull yourself together," Dan Canby advised. "Keep your voice down. The walls are thin."

"My God, why did they come here?"

"To drink," Canby said. "You're safe enough if you keep quiet." He looked intently at Blaine. "You know, if you hadn't tried to rub Kirby's nose in it and make him sell for a quarter, none of this would have happened. Do you really know what it cost that man to slaughter cattle for the hides just to get enough money to feed his family? No, you don't know, and you don't give a damn."

"I didn't think he'd go wild," Blaine said. He sat down and clasped and unclasped his hands. "If he dies, will they burn my place?"

"To the ground."

"You've got to stop them. Where's the law?"

"What law?"

"The police."

"By the time they got here, it would be too late."

"The Army then," Blaine suggested. "I have a right to protection."

"Sure, but you'll have to do it yourself."

Blaine shook his head. "Canby, this means as much to you as it does to me."

"No it doesn't. I take my profit when I can, and I'm happy with what I get. If it ends, it won't mean a damned thing to me."

"But you're my partner, and—"

"I'm not your damned partner," Canby snapped. "And you say it again and I'll open that door and call Kirby's men. Now shut up. I'm going back out there."

When he came up to the counter, he put out another bottle. The men looked at it, and Canby said, "On the house." He counted noses. "Did someone leave?"

"Smoky. He went back to the doc's house to see how Owen was coming along."

Canby said nothing; he knew it was best to leave them alone. They remained in the store the rest of the afternoon and on into the evening. It was getting close to his closing time, but he held off saying anything about it.

Then Smoky came back, a runt of a man with no upper teeth. He simply shook his head, and all of them straightened up and stepped back from the bar.

One said, "I guess we know what to do now."

"Boys," Canby warned, "you're being fools."

"Then you better stay out of it," he was told, and the riders filed outside.

Dan Canby went to his front porch and stood there and watched them cross over and walk down to Blaine's place. They smashed the front windows and got in that way and broke the base of the lamps to get coal oil, and within a few minutes they had a half dozen fires going. Mounting flame began to brighten the street, and someone saw it and ran and rang the firebell. Then Smoky dashed out of the burning building and ran across toward Canby's store, carrying a large tin box.

He set it down on the porch and said, "There's the carpetbagger's money box." He pointed to the lock; it had been pried open. "We took a hundred and fifty dollars."

"You shouldn't have done that, Smoky."

"A man gets what he comes after, or he shouldn't bother with it," he said. The other riders were bringing up the horses, and they waited until Smoky mounted up. People were out on the street now, but they hung back, not sure of what was happening. Then when the men rode out of town, the fire brigades were formed, and they tried to save the adjoining buildings.

It was too late to save Taylor Blaine's place.

Canby went inside and locked his store, blowing out the lamps.

Blaine was pacing back and forth; when Canby opened the door he wheeled and pointed a small pepperbox pistol at him. "Put that stupid thing away," Canby said. "Well, they've burned your place. That was the fire bell you heard."

"Why? Because I wouldn't pay a dollar?"

"Blaine, don't you understand anything? I'd get out if I were you."

"No. I'm going to fight. I can, you know. And I will."

Canby shook his head. "That would be the wrong thing to do." He nodded toward the front of his store. "One of them came over with your money box. They took out the hundred and fifty for the hides."

"So they robbed me, too."

"No, they didn't. Let it go. You got off cheap. And lucky."

Taylor Blaine was over his fright. "Let me tell you something, horse trader. They've started something with me they'll wish they'd never thought of. When I'm finished, they'll be sorry they didn't give me the hides."

7

AMY LELAND slapped her hand down hard on the desk top. "I will not haul one more bale of hides, and that is final!" Then she put her hands on her hips and looked at Dan Canby. He sat in an easy chair, one leg crossed over the other, a cigar drifting smoke past his fingers.

"Now why don't you be reasonable?" he asked. "Look, let me put it another way. You're in the stage business. A passenger puts down his money and is hauled from point A to point B and there are no questions asked. If the passenger turns out to be a bank robber, no one blames you because he got to town. Now it's the same with freight. A man pays his money and he's entitled to have freight hauled. It's not up to you to say what's hauled and what's not."

"How many men have you thrown out of your store and told never to come back?"

"Now, Amy, that's different. Those were always personal reasons. I still didn't stop selling food to his family."

"Owen Kirby is dead, and Scully is dead, and there's a full-scale war brewing, and I don't want to get caught in the middle of it." She waver her hand and sat down at her desk and leaned her elbow on it. "Dan, how did Taylor Blaine ever contact the renegades in the first place?"

"I did," he said frankly. "Blaine and I had a deal. I got a dollar a hide."

For a long moment she stared at him, then she slapped the desk again. "You're completely unscrupulous, aren't you?"

"Yes."

"You did it for money."

"Yes, and because someone was bound to do it. Even Kirby broke down and butchered for hides. It just had to happen sooner or later."

"Shooting? A war?" She shook her head. "Dan, you've got to take some of the blame for it. And so do I, for hauling Blaine's hides. I could have said no and put him out of business."

"But you didn't say no, and neither did I." He got up slowly. "We're partners, Amy. Let's not fight over this. Some time ago I came to the conclusion that I just couldn't keep everyone from sinking, so I've tried to save myself. Someone has to come out of this in halfway decent shape, and I figured that it might as well be me. I'd rather it was me than some Yankee. At least this money is staying in Texas."

"Oh, for Heaven's sake, Dan, stop moralizing!" She got up and walked up and down the room. "I feel like a vulture waiting for something to die. What's going to hold the Kirby place together now? If the farmers hear about it, they'll be swarming here, cutting it up with their fences and plows and—"

"You see? You know it's going to happen," Canby said. "Amy, sit down. Sit down and listen to me. If it's going to happen, then why don't *we* do something about it? At least have some control over it."

"What do you mean?"

"It would be better to pick the people who came here rather than take what comes." He gave his cigar butt a brief survey, then mashed it out. "Land development is a part of banking, and I own the bank. It only makes good sense to bring in farmers before squatters arrive."

"I can't believe I heard you right," Amy said. "Dan, I don't want any part of it!"

He shrugged. "I've made up my mind; it's an opportunity a man just can't pass up. I'll make loans, with their proved-up sections as security. It's just good business."

"Then let someone else have it," she snapped.

"That's not very realistic at all," Canby told her. "Amy, you've always had a lot of vision, and you weren't afraid to gamble. Go with me on this."

"Why? You don't need me. I've served my purpose, Dan."

"Amy, don't talk like that. I've always wanted to think that someday we'd be more than business partners. In a few years I'd like to go into politics; we're going to need influential men with money in this state. I want you with me all the way, Amy."

She watched him a moment, then said, "Do you want to buy me out, Dan?"

"No, I'd rather marry the business. I thought you'd guessed that."

"Of course; I'm not a fool, Dan. But what do you want? What are you after? I just don't know." She clasped her hands together and seemed very disturbed about it.

"My father left a peddler's wagon and two very tired horses when he died," Canby said. "I used to ride around the country with him while he sold pots and cloth and trinkets. That was my education, Amy, to add and work figures in my head. I learned how to horse-trade and always make a profit, because if I didn't, I'd go hungry. One day near Jefferson I got a wagonload of green peaches cheap. So I loaded the wagon with straw, wet it down, and covered my peaches; then I drove west, hardly stopping, keeping the straw damp during the hot days, and I sold those fresh ripe peaches for ten times what I'd paid for 'em. That's where I got the money to rent my store." He shrugged. "I made it pay by hiring no one, just working it myself, sixteen hours a day, seven days a week. When I enlarged it, I did most of the work myself to save the money. Some men spend their time looking for a woman or at the sunset or over the next hill. I've searched for opportunity, Amy I've wooed it more steadfastly than a man ever wooed a woman. I don't know what I'm after. Not just a pile of money. Hell, I don't hoard it, Amy. I use it. Build with it. And I'm not saying that I know what's good for Texas or what's bad. But I do know that we just can't sit here in grinding poverty. Someone has to move, to change, to do something, and it takes money. Either my money or some Yankee's money." He shook his head. "No, I don't want you to buy me out, Amy, and I don't want to buy you out."

"I'm not going to haul hides," Amy Leland said.

"Yes, you are, because you're in the freight business. All

right, so the money isn't as clean as you'd like it, but it's still money, good Yankee gold, and you pay your teamsters with it, and they raise their families with it, and you buy harness and equipment. That may not be ideal or even what you want, but it's money, a living where there isn't any other."

"Don't you think I've thought about it?"

"If you have, then I know you'll do the right thing," Dan Canby said. "I've got to get back to the store. Blaine's gone out to see the major this morning. He wants protection so he can rebuild his warehouse."

"Why, the fool! They're apt to burn it down again."

Canby laughed. "Sure, but it'll take lumber and labor, and he'll support a payroll for three weeks while he's building. That's what I'm thinking of—work and wages. We need a lot of that, Amy. A man has to have work and the pay for it, or pretty soon he loses sight of the fact that he's a man."

"Dan, I don't think I'll ever understand what you really are, saint or sinner."

"I can give you one squad and no more," Major Bolton said firmly. He sat behind his desk, erect in the chair, hands wide apart on the desk top. "Blaine, I'm not at all in sympathy with what's been stirred up."

"Major, I'm in a legitimate business, and I have a right to protection under the law. Since there are no locally constituted authorities—"

"Yes, yes." The major waved his hand. "You'll get protection. I'll have a squad escort you back to town." He sighed and put a match to his dead cigar. "Now, about this letter. Surely you don't want to push this matter."

"My property was destroyed and money taken from me," Blaine said. "I certainly do wish the matter pursued. I've learned the identity of the men involved, and I want them posted and arrested as soon as possible."

"Mr. Blaine, I cannot stop you from this course of action, but I can appeal to your good sense and hope you will be persuaded to change your mind. I'm here to establish government and some stability of economy. You're here to make money for your company. Let me point out that employing the renegades to gather hides was not exactly a moral thing to do."

"But perfectly legal," Blaine insisted. "The cattle were unbranded and on open range. The fact that these men are ruffians who spent the war raiding their own people is no concern of mine."

"Mr. Blaine, these men are all kin of someone around here; they have families and brothers and parents still living here, kin who have turned them out, disowned them. To have employed them as you did aroused a good deal of resentment. Did you know that one of Owen Kirby's sons was in the renegade bunch? That's right. Kirby had turned him out some three and a half years ago because the boy wouldn't go and fight for the South; he'd rather remain in Texas and raise hell." He held up his hand when Blaine tried to speak. "I believe I can persuade the Kirby riders not to molest you further. But to prevent any further occurrence you will have to offer these ranchers a fair price for hides in the event they want to sell."

"And who pays for my building? And the hides I had stored there?"

"Kirby paid with his life. Can't you let it go at that?"

"No, I can't. Major, I'm responsible to my father and brothers. They would, I assure you, definitely not understand my doing nothing. Now, I've lodged a formal complaint with the military government. I expect that it will be processed and these men put on the wanted criminal list."

"All right," Harry Bolton said. "But I believe you're making a very big mistake."

"It's my decision. Now, if your soldiers are ready, I'd like to return to town and begin a new structure. This time I'm going to build out of adobe and fortify it. A man has the right to protect his property."

They met at George Vale's place because it was more centrally located than Fred Early's or Owen Kirby's. Nearly a hundred and fifty men crowded the yard while Vale and Early and their kin sat on the wide veranda.

Jonas Vale seemed to head up the younger men, and when he acted as their spokesman, no one objected. "I don't like to blame a dead man for anything, but Kirby played a fool's hand when he went for a shoot-out with Blaine's bunch. Those renegades wouldn't be cleaning the range now if we'd sold to Blaine in the first place."

"Not at twenty-five cents a hide," Fred Early said. "He doesn't need our hides now. That's why he offered Kirby a quarter."

"He'd need us if the renegades were driven out," Jonas said, waving his hand to include those standing in the yard. "And they'd ride with me."

One of the men standing in the front row nodded; he was dressed in faded, patched jeans, and the heels of his boots were run over. "Mr. Vale, I've got a cousin on my wife's side ridin' with the renegades, and their kids wear new jeans, and they put somethin' on their table 'sides beef and grits. It kind of makes a man think twice."

"He's right," another said. "Mr. Vale, we all know there ain't goin' to be any cattle drive till spring. So we're all in for a cold, lean winter. If them renegades was out of here, Blaine would have to pay a decent price or he just wouldn't buy any hides. Me'n my wife already lost one young un this summer when her milk dried up, and—well, I'm with Jonas. We all are, Mr. Vale. We just can't wait, 'cause we can't hang on."

"Have you thought what this can cost you?" George Vale asked. "A lot of you are going to get hurt. Some killed."

They knew that, and he knew that they knew it, but as the man had said, they were about used up, and when a man gets that way, even the big chances seem small. They weren't weak; they could take nearly anything, but it got to them when their wives and children suffered.

Fred Early said, "I've got sixty men who're ready to ride. How many do you have, George?"

"About that," Vale said.

"And there's thirty from Kirby's outfit," Jonas put in. "Why do we want to waste time?"

"Yes," the old man said, "now that we've decided, I think it's best that we move. Early will lead his men. How many are here from the Kirby outfit?" There was a forest of hands raised. "Will you men accept the leadership of my son Jonas?" They nodded, and the matter was done. "You can remain here for the night. Camp by the well and in the grove. We'll try to feed you." He got up. "Fred, Jonas, come inside. I have a map there, and we can work out the details."

They followed him into his parlor, and he spread the map on the table. "Most of the renegades camp in the vicinity of Oak Creek; they can roam unmolested in that area and on north fifteen or twenty miles. Some of them have settled down on small parcels of land there. Early, I suggest that you leave around dawn with your men. Strike in a northerly direction and make a day of it, then around sundown swing west and continue until it's dark. Camp the night there. Jonas, remain here until noon or a little after, then move west and see if you can find where their main camp is. Remain under cover and wait until well after dawn before striking. By that time I'll have taken my men around to the south, and we'll catch them no matter which way they run."

It sounded agreeable to them; they nodded, and Vale put his map away. "I'd as soon leave them alone; time and the law are going to break them up. But at a time like this, a man just can't think of himself. Now if you'll excuse me, I'll see if the help can come up with a meal for everyone."

Three soldiers and a sergeant got into an argument in Dan Canby's store, which ended when Canby threw them out, but not before they had broken a showcase and ruined some merchandise. Major Bolton, wishing to settle these matters justly and quickly, sent Sgt. Ben Talon in to make an estimate and sign a voucher so Canby could be paid.

It was a little after seven when Talon reached town and tied up in front of the store. Canby was alone, getting ready to close the store, when Talon walked in.

There was still some glass on the floor, small shards that crackled dryly beneath Talon's boots. "The major sent me to adjust the damages," Talon said. "If you could give me some idea—"

"Two table lamps, a case of chimneys, and a bolt of cotton print that got coal-oil-soaked. And the showcase."

"How much?"

"About a hundred dollars," Canby said.

"That sounds about right," Talon said and began to fill out the pay voucher.

"What do you know about storekeeping or prices?" Canby asked.

"Nothing. But I've got a good ear for what sounds right." He signed it and handed it over. "Any time you're at the post, present that and you'll be paid."

"Suppose I rode out tonight?"

Talon shrugged. "The sergeant of the guard would wake the officer of the day, who'd wake Major Bolton, who'd pay you and mumble at the inconvenience."

"The stuff wasn't broken at my convenience," Canby said. "I'll go out tonight before someone changes his mind."

"That's not very likely," Talon said.

"Just your word for that," Canby said and began to snuff out the lamps. Talon waited on the porch, and Canby went out and down the street to get his horse. A few minutes later he left town, taking the post road.

Ben Talon's first thought was to catch up with Canby, then he decided to walk down to the freight office and see what Amy Leland was doing. He saw the lights in her quarters and knocked, and she came to the door with a shotgun in her hand.

"Oh, it's you," she said.

"Now there's a greeting to stir a man's soul," Talon said, stepping in so she could close and lock the door.

"How was your visit to the Vales'?"

"Very nice," he admitted. "Did I detect a note in your voice—"

"Don't be ridiculous. I don't care what you do."

"Are we going to stand here or go sit in your parlor?" He watched her, and when she turned, he followed her and settled himself in a large horsehide-covered chair. With his good hand he lifted his arm from the sling and placed the elbow on the chair arm. "The major tells me that Blaine is going to rebuild. Adobe this time."

"Does the major tell you everything, Ben?"

"Just about. We've known each other a long time, and he knows that when I lost my commission, I didn't lose my brains at the same time. You knew that Blaine has had Kirby's men posted on the wanted list. The police are going out there tomorrow to see who they can arrest."

"I didn't know that," she said. "What a shame! He ought to know better."

"He does, but he wants to stay in business. A good way to do it is to scare trouble away."

"That won't work here. Everyone has had too much trouble to be afraid of a little more. Can I get you some coffee?"

"If it's already made. Don't go to any trouble for me."

"That's a strange thing to say." She poured a cupful and gave it to him. Then she sat down across from him and folded her hands over a raised knee. "I was thinking the other day that I'd like to go horse hunting or something."

"Alone?"

"Now you know I didn't mean that."

He shook his head. "Those days are gone for you, Amy. You're in a position to hire it done now. It's only when you're struggling hard that you really have any fun. Unfortunately, too few people realize that until it's too late. I knew a fella once, a miner. Hunted for eighteen years before he hit it rich. He always cooked his own meals, washed his own clothes, hunted his own food. Then he hired it done. Servants did everything. Finally he got disgusted and bought a boat, figuring he'd just sail away from it all, but he even had to have someone sail it for him. Got to the point where he couldn't do anything for himself, and he kept getting unhappier until finally he shot himself."

"Ben Talon, that whole story is a lie."

"Well, but it does illustrate a point, doesn't it?"

"I still cook for myself," Amy said. "I still run things."

"But it's slippin' away from you. Two bookkeepers now. Next month a manager, then a servant. Remember what I told you."

She let the gaiety leave her face. "Ben, what are you saying I should do?"

"Be happy, I guess. You're not."

"Yes, I am."

"Happy with the way things are going? Happy with Dan Canby?" He shook his head. "You don't fool me, Amy. You don't like what happened in back of Blaine's place. You don't like what Blaine is doing. But how do you pull in your oar, Amy?"

She let out a long breath. "I don't know, Ben. Do you?"

"Not unless it's buying or selling to Canby. He's the only one who has the money. But I don't think he—" He stopped talking and cocked his head to one side. "Was that someone at the door?" He got up and took a lamp with him and went to the door. Then he opened it and shined the light in Emily Vale's face; she quickly pushed it aside and stepped in where she couldn't be seen.

"Is Amy Leland here?" she asked.

Hearing her name, Amy came from her room. She looked at Emily Vale for a moment, then said, "What is it, Emily? What do you want here?"

"I was looking for Dan Canby."

"Why would you think he was here?"

"Why, I—" Emily Vale looked at Ben Talon, then shook her head; she didn't want to answer. "I've got to see Dan Canby right away. His store was locked, and no one seemed to know where he went, so I came here. You're his partner. Perhaps you'll give him a message."

"What is the message?" Amy asked.

"My father and brother and Fred Early are going to go into the Oak Creek country after the renegades. Dan knows how to reach them. They've got to be warned." She looked from Ben Talon to Amy Leland. "Please help me. Give Dan the message as quickly as you can. I've got to get back before I'm missed."

"I'll ride with you," Talon said.

"Oh, no, it's too far. It'll be near dawn before—"

"That's all right," he said. "I'll get my hat." He went back into Amy Leland's parlor and got his hat. When he came back, Amy was alone.

"She certainly doesn't have to whistle very loud, does she?" Amy said dryly.

"Do you really think it's that way?"

"You don't show me differently," Amy said.

He had no intention of arguing with her; he nodded and went outside for his horse. Emily Vale was waiting in the thick shadows, and they left town together, and for better than a mile there was no talking.

They they walked and led the horses. Talon said, "What does it matter to you what happens to the renegades?"

"Tom is with them—my younger brother. I don't want him dead."

"Do you think your dad or Jonas does?"

"I don't really know, and because of that, I'd rather see the whole bunch get away than run the risk." She turned her head and looked at him. "You think that's wrong?"

"Who am I to say? What relationship does Dan Canby have with—"

"He's always helped them when he could, even during the war. Some say that Dan Canby made his first big money when he'd sell a barrel of flour to a man, then tell the renegades so they could steal it back, and he'd sell it over."

"Somehow that sounds like him," Ben Talon admitted. "Yet you went to him."

"There was no one else. Tom and I have met on the prairie. He's told me about Canby, bringing them supplies and working with them. It was Canby who got them to work for Blaine. The two of them have some kind of deal."

"That sounds like Dan, running after a dollar." He stopped and boosted her on her horse, then mounted his own. "How did you sneak out of the house without waking your sisters or the housekeeper?"

"Oh, the housekeeper left three days ago to visit her sister who lives over by Fort Graham. My sisters went with her, and they won't be back for a month."

"If you get tired, we can stop awhile, Emily."

"I—don't think I should, Ben. It wouldn't be right, us alone like this."

"Are you afraid?"

"Kind of. But I don't know what of. I don't know my feelings, Ben. I just don't."

"I kissed you once, and you didn't mind."

"You think I've forgotten? Let's go on."

8

BECAUSE SHE was really too tired to go on and wouldn't admit it, Ben Talon made Emily Vale dismount, and he built a fire and made her roll up in his blankets and sleep for a while. Her protest was a token; she was worn to a frazzle, and she went to sleep immediately while he sat by the fire and kept his rifle handy. Aside from not wanting to have her ride this lonely distance alone, Ben Talon hoped to reach the Vale place in time to keep the men from riding on the renegades.

It just wouldn't do to start a fight that would get brother firing on brother and the whole country in an uproar. They had more trouble than they could handle, but it was the way with people to always ask for more. It seemed like the more trouble they had, the more they wanted. Trouble addled the mind, it seemed. It made a sensible man foolish, so that he compounded his mistakes until something brought him up short and forced him to think again.

Talon didn't doubt that George Vale wanted to do the right thing, but once the shooting began, the cowboys would get wild—not much at first, but wild—and the day would come when other law-abiding people would ride on them, for they'd become as bad as the renegades.

After letting her sleep for nearly two hours, Talon woke her, rolled his blankets, helped her on her horse. Then they rode on, reaching the Vale place a bit before dawn.

George Vale and his men were gone.

So was Fred Early.

Kirby's men were in the cook shack having their breakfast,

and Emily dismounted and went around to the side of the house without anyone noticing her. As soon as she was out of sight, Ben Talon started whistling as he tied up, and Jonas Vale came out.

"What are you doin' here?" he asked.

"Happened to be in the vicinity." He turned his head and looked at the cook shack. "Gettin' an early start, ain't you?" He looked at Jonas. "The sky's just turning gray. You already eaten?"

"I didn't feel like it this morning," Jonas said. "Fact is, I don't feel none too good. Come on in, now that you're here. I'll have the help bring you breakfast."

"Coffee will be fine," Talon said, stepping inside. "Early and your father have already gone, huh?"

Jonas Vale looked at him. "How did you know about it?"

Talon shrugged. "Told you I was just riding around. You pick up things that way. Nothing people say, but what they don't—it all added up to a raid on the outlaws." He followed Jonas into the kitchen. "It's a damned-fool move, you know."

"But we're going to make it," Jonas said. His eyes were bright, and there was a pronounced flush to his cheeks; Talon noticed this as he sat down.

"You'll do better for yourself and for all of you if you ride back to see Goodnight and tell him you'll throw in with him in the spring."

"We'll be there," Jonas said. "You can bet on it. But now there's this business at hand." He cocked his head to listen to any sound in the other part of the house. "Wonder where Emily is. She's usually up about this time."

"What do you want her to do? Wave good-bye to you?"

Jonas Vale didn't get offended. "When I leave, Talon, you stay here."

"I thought I'd go along. When you get through with this fool's play, someone ought to be around who has the straight of it and whose judgment wasn't colored by bad temper." He studied Jonas carefully. "You know, you don't look well. What's the matter?"

The young man shook his head. "It came on me last night; I threw up my supper. Toward morning I was running a little fever. Probably something I picked up in Goodnight's camp. The damned fools over there don't know enough to wash pots and pans. But I'll be all right."

"Why don't you call it off? You've got an excuse."

Jonas Vale laughed. "Mister, if I was leaking blood, I'd ride when the time came."

There was no use arguing with him, and Talon knew it; Jonas was determined to go through with this. Talon wondered where Early and the old man were, then decided that they were riding in a circular direction, meaning to close in from the sides while Jonas and his men made the actual attack. There really couldn't be any other reason.

Talon finished his coffee and said, "When are we leaving?"

"Later. Around noon. Do you want a fresh horse?"

"No, I'll do with my own."

He went out under the shade trees and slept for several hours; then the cold wind cut him deeply, and he got up and walked around the yard. There wasn't going to be much of a sun; the sky was solid overcast, and the temperature was down in the forties, pushed by wind.

It was his intention to take his noon meal in the cook shack, but Emily came to the porch and motioned for him to come inside, and he went with her to the kitchen. Jonas Vale was not around, and before he could comment on it, she said, "He's not feeling well, so he went to his room to sleep." She pulled back a chair and put a plate of eggs and potatoes before him. "I wish we had more, Ben."

"Why, this is just fine." He waited while she sat down across from him.

"I was thinking of what I said to you the first time I saw you, and I'm ashamed."

He shook his head. "Now don't be. People have to get to know each other, Emily."

Someone came in the house and stopped in the kitchen doorway; he was one of Kirby's men. "Jonas ready to ride?"

"He's in his room," Emily said. "Down the hall and on the right at the end." The man left, and she looked at Ben Talon. "You're going, too?"

"Yes."

"You won't be able to stop it, Ben."

"Well, I've got to try."

"Don't get hurt doing it. None of them are worth it, really."

Jonas Vale came into the kitchen and filled a sack with biscuits and cold meat; he was sweating slightly, and his face was flushed. To Ben Talon he said, "If you're going, let's go," and then went out, the Kirby man following him.

"I guess it's time," Talon said, rising. Emily came around the table and put her arms around him and kissed him, and he held her for a moment, then stepped back. "Now that was sure nice," he said.

"Ben, will you watch over Jonas for me?"

"Why, sure." He patted her cheek, then picked up his hat and coat and went outside where the others were getting ready to mount up. He untied his horse, swung up, and sided Jonas Vale as they left the yard.

All the rest of that day they moved southwest across rolling land with the grass bent down by the wind, and come sundown the cold was biting through their coats, and now and then a man would blow on his hands and wish he'd brought gloves along. They made cold camp along a timbered creek, and Jonas Vale's teeth were chattering, and he wouldn't eat anything at all.

It was a miserable night, and they remained until nearly midnight, then got ready to move on. One of Kirby's riders tried to get Jonas Vale out of his blankets, but the young man was too sick to move.

Ben Talon went over to see what he could do; he felt of Vale's face and found him burning with a high fever. To one of the Kirby men he said, "Get a fire going."

"It might be seen."

"What the hell does it matter? He's not going on. He can't."

"Guess you're right there," the man said, and they began to gather brush. Soon they had a fire blazing, throwing out a wide circle of light.

The man named Smoky seemed to be in charge of the Kirby men; he came over and looked at Jonas Vale for a long time. "If I didn't know better, I'd say it was smallpox." Then he laughed at the hush this brought. " 'Course it can't be. There's no smallpox around here."

"He ain't always been around here," another man said. "He's been over in the next county and then some, with that fella Goodnight."

That was enough to make them back up, but Ben Talon remained by Jonas Vale. "A couple of you men make a travois, and I'll take him into town to the doctor."

"If he's got smallpox, I wouldn't go takin' him into town," Smoky said. He turned to several men. "Cut some poles and fix a blanket for him." He stood with his lips pursed. "We've got to be gettin' on if we're to hit them renegades come dawn. It's another twenty miles."

"Then go," Talon said. "I'll manage alone."

"Hate to leave you," Smoky said.

"Like hell," Talon said. "There ain't anybody man enough here to touch him." He looked around. "Go on. Lift him off his blankets. You? No? Go on then. Shoot yourself some renegades."

"Get the horses," Smoky said. Then he turned back to Ben. "Look, you already touched him. Ain't no sense to anyone else taking the chance of handling him. Besides, we got a job to do. Good luck there, Yankee."

"Oh, sure," Talon said and checked the travois that had been lashed together. They rode out, not wasting any time about it, and he managed to get Jonas Vale tied on. Then he mounted and swung east, dragging the travois behind him.

He couldn't really blame these men for deserting him. Smallpox was a thing that would drive fear into the bravest man, if that was what Jonas Vale had. And only a doctor could tell for sure.

To Talon's way of thinking, the stage station was the nearest, but there was no doctor there, and none within twenty miles. Town was his only bet, and there was a lot of open country yet to travel, and he couldn't go very fast; Vale was too sick for that.

So he turned almost due north and rode for better than two hours without stopping. The wind seemed to die down a little; he thought it was his imagination, but finally the night was still, and it grew warmer, so much so that he took off his coat and rode in his shirt sleeves.

He smelled the rain before it came, and this gave him time

to stop and dismount and untie his poncho. He covered Vale
with it just as the rain began. It fell heavily, straight down,
drumming the grass and soaking him thoroughly before he
got mounted again.

The rain held steady until dawn, then when it grew daylight, it seemed to slack off a little, falling in a steady drizzle.
It was nearly ten by his pocket watch when he saw Abilene
off a bit to the right, and he changed course, riding on for
another forty minutes before he reached the outskirts.

He saw a boy throwing rocks into a puddle near the end of
the street. Talon whistled, and the boy came over. "Sonny,
go fetch the doctor. This man's been hurt."

"Did you shoot him, mister?"

"Yes," Talon said. "Now will you get the doctor?"

The boy ran off down the street, and Talon got down from
his horse, muscles in his back protesting. He waited for ten
minutes, then the doctor came down the street, the small
boy tagging behind.

"Why the hell couldn't you bring him into town?" the doctor
asked as he came up.

"You take a look and you'll know," Talon said. "Go on
home, sonny. And thanks."

"I want to stay," the boy said.

"You git on home," Talon said. "Go on now."

The boy turned and walked away, and Ben Talon stepped
near the travois. "Do you know what ails him?" the doctor
asked, looking up.

"Smallpox, I guess."

"That's right. Lord knows where he got it, but if word gets
around—" He straightened. "There's an empty shack on the
other side of town, near the stable. Take him there. Get him
inside, then come to my office right away." He measured
Talon with his eye. "Have you any money, sergeant?" He
held out his hand. "I'll send someone for a complete change
of clothes for you. I'll burn everything you're wearing."

Talon gave him thirty dollars in gold. Then he mounted and
circled the town, coming in on the east side. He found the
shack, opened the door, unlashed the travois, and dragged
Jonas Vale inside. The bunk wasn't in good enough repair,

so Talon left him on the floor and went out, closing the door the best he could.

The doctor was waiting for him at his office; he had a bath ready and gave Talon orders to scrub thoroughly with strong soap and disinfectant. By the time Talon was finished, the doctor was back with a bundle of clothes, and Talon began to dress.

"I'm going over to the shack," the doctor said. "I don't suppose there's any real hope of keeping this quiet."

"I guess you can't keep a thing like this quiet," Talon said. "Is he going to make it?"

The doctor shrugged. "Some do, but most don't. But if he dies, it will have to be alone. Everything he's touched will have to be burned. Where did you find him?"

Ben Talon told him the whole thing, and the doctor listened, his expression going more grave as Talon talked. "All right, sergeant, here's what you'll have to do. You'll have to burn that place."

"Vale's ranch house?"

"That's right. Get everyone who's been in there to burn their clothes and bathe as you did. But you've got to put a torch to that place and every other building he's been in. This spreads like a prairie fire, sergeant. I don't have to tell you that." He clapped Talon on the arm. "You look pretty frazzled, but you can't stop now. Get a belt of whiskey and a fresh horse and get going."

The rain had stopped by the time Ben Talon reached the Vale place; it was late afternoon, and Emily ran out as he got down. "Where's Jonas and the others?"

"The others went on," he said, leading her toward the porch. Then he told her where Jonas was and that he had smallpox. He thought she was going to cry, but he shook her, and she listened carefully to him. "I want you to think back. Remember if you've been in a room where Jonas was since you've come home."

She thought, then shook her head. "No. I went back to sleep after you left. No, I haven't, Ben."

"Jonas couldn't really have started being contagious until his fever climbed high," he said. "That was about the time we started out; I remember that he was sweating. Emily, we've got to burn the house and the bunkhouse if he's been there."

"Burn it? Oh, Ben, no!"

"I'm sorry, but it has to be. The doctor explained it to me. All of you who've been in the house will have to scrub good with strong soap and burn the clothes you had on. I've got to do that, Emily. Now will you help me?"

"Do I have to?"

"No, I can do it myself, but you've got to understand that I don't want to."

She thought about it, then nodded. "There's a cook and a servant; I'll tell them. What can we take, Ben? Anything?"

"Whatever you're positive Jonas has not touched. If he sat in a certain chair, you'll have to leave it. All right?"

"Yes."

Darkness seemed to come early because the day had been so gray. George Vale and the men following him stopped on the prairie because there was a glow ahead where his house should be, and he studied this a moment before he could accept the fact that his place was afire.

He was not in a position to travel fast for he had wounded with him, a dozen men on litters and twice that many riding, some lying on the horse's neck because they could no longer sit erect.

The renegades had hit them well after dawn, well after the time when Vale had expected them, and they had come on in a rush, shooting their way clear—not many, no more than forty or fifty. Vale's men had thinned them out considerably before the renegades broke into the clear and vanished in the gray vastness of the prairie.

Some of the bodies they buried in shallow graves, then the ground, muddy and hard to dig, discouraged them, and they left some on the prairie and rode toward home, winners, but having won nothing.

When Vale made out the fire, he and a half dozen men rode on ahead, punishing their tired horses, and they stormed into the yard as the beams smashed down and the heat-dried adobe cracked, letting part of one wall settle in a shower of sparks.

Talon and Emily and the few who had been left behind stood by the well, and Vale flung himself off his horse, roughly demanding, "What started it? In the name of God, what caused it?"

"I burned it," Ben Talon said, and the old man flung himself on him and would have struck him if Emily had not rushed in and grabbed his arms.

"Papa, listen! Papa, we had to ! Jonas has smallpox!"

The old man was instantly calm, instantly grave. "Where is my boy?"

"I took him to town," Talon explained and told him what happened at the night camp.

"So they went off and left him," Vale said. "I'll kill them all!"

He didn't mean it; Talon understood and ignored it. "Likely some of them are working up a fever or starting one, Mr. Vale. But I think we've checked it here. Emily, the cook, and the servant have thought about it real good, and we don't figure that Jonas has been any place but the house. If the men from the Kirby place didn't drink from his cup, they may have missed it." He looked at the men who had ridden in with George Vale and noticed that one of them had a bloody bandage on his upper arm. "So you found the renegades."

"They found us," Vale said. "They made one bolt through and left a lot of dead. They left half of their own, too." He wiped a hand across his mouth. "Smallpox. I wonder where he got it."

"The doctor thinks maybe over in the next county. Smoky thought so, too. Did you see any of Smoky's men?"

Vale shook his head. "Early, either. I don't know whether or not they reached the renegade camp. When the renegades hit us, they seemed just as surprised as we were. None of us expected 'em so early. More like midafternoon." He sat down and put his hands on his knees and looked at the ruins of his house and the furniture and piled goods out near the tool shed. "God, what else can go wrong?" He looked at Ben Talon. "Will you tell me that? What else can go wrong?"

When Hank Swain saw Barney Ryder fall as he tried to climb aboard the coach, Swain figured that Barney had forsaken the pledge, and he went out into the yard to fire him on the spot. But when he got near, he saw that Barney wasn't drunk; he was sick. The passengers got out of the coach and stared at the fallen man, and finally one of them thought to go fetch the doctor.

That afternoon three more took sick, and nearly everyone in town knew that it was smallpox.

Ben Talon returned to the post and brought Emily Vale with him; he saw that she was comfortable in one of the officers' vacant quarters, then went to post headquarters to see Major Bolton. Talon had been away for a week because he hadn't wanted to leave Emily until he was certain that she had not contracted the disease, and when he'd known for sure, he'd insisted that she come back with him.

Bolton was signing some papers when Talon came in; he sat down when Bolton waved him into a chair. Then the major finished and rubbed his palm against his unshaven cheek. "Three days since I've shaved. Not very military, is it?" He offered Talon a cigar. "Well, we've got a good one on our hands, haven't we? Six dead in town and half the population in isolation. I've sent both of the contract surgeons in to do what they can and sent a courier to fetch three more. How are things out on the prairie?"

"You wouldn't believe it, major. Smoky and the Kirby men raided the renegade camp after they'd pulled out. Helped themselves to what they wanted. The renegades were all sick with smallpox; some had already died."

"Good Lord!" Bolton said. "How did it start, Ben?"

"Well, I've been trying to put it together," Talon said. "I figure I have all the pieces by now. First off, I thought that Jonas Vale brought it in, but then he wasn't the first that took sick. Old man Vale found where his young son Tom had been buried, and from the condition of the grave at the renegade camp, he figures that he died ten days ago. That means that the renegades had it before Jonas did." He shook his head. "Now a couple of the stage drivers have it. That really confuses things. I'd like to know if Jonas ever rode the stage."

"Ask him," Bolton said. "He made it. Fever broke, and he's staying at the doctor's house. Weak, but he made it."

"Would you ride in with me, sir?"

"Yes. I could do with the change." He got up and told the orderly to have his horse brought around. "I've declared the town off limits; we'll try to keep the post clean. What are you thinking about, Ben?"

"If Jonas rode the stage, and any of the renegades rode the stage—"

"That's been my thought, too. The coaches could be carrying the damned stuff all up and down the line."

"Major, have you heard any word about whether or not the Indians have it?"

"To tell you the truth, my patrols haven't reported seeing Indians for a month." The orderly came in to say that the horse had been brought around, and the major and Talon went out together and mounted.

After they cleared the guard at the gate and rode on toward town, Bolton said, "I've been very reluctant to order property burned, but the doctor, backed by Dan Canby, has been setting fire to several buildings. Both the surgeons agree that this is the best way to halt it." He turned his head and looked at Ben Talon. "I'd hate to have to tell Miss Leland to burn her coaches and stations."

"It may come to that," Talon said. "And Blaine's new place, too. If the renegades had it and brought in hides to Blaine's place—"

"That's right; I've forgotten about him since I pulled the squad back to the post. We'll check on it before we leave town." He licked a cigar into shape, then cupped his hands around the match. "I've heard where whole towns went up in smoke before an epidemic was stopped. Hate to see it come to that. These people have lost a war, sons, money; they can take only so much, Ben."

9

Amy Leland stared at them. "You want to burn my stages?"

Harry Bolton nodded gravely. "I'm sorry, but I see no other way. We've talked to Jonas Vale—he caught one of your stages near Cameron several weeks ago. At that time he noticed two men riding in the coach who were known to be part of the renegade gang. Now it's most likely that the two men Vale recognized were coming down with smallpox then and passed it on. Two of your drivers are down with it now, and there'll be more, and passengers who rode in those coaches."

"But to burn all of them—why, I'm out of business!"

Ben Talon said, "The stations, too, Amy." He took the cigar stub out of his pocket and threw it into the potbellied stove. "I've asked Dan Canby to come over here, since he's your partner. Amy, if there was any other way, don't you think we'd be glad to do it?"

"At any rate you're closed down for the time being," Major Bolton said. "I've already dispatched couriers south and north with orders for the police to stop the stages. At my surgeon's suggestion, I'm having notices sent to doctors from Fort Smith to Matamoras, asking them to contact anyone who has ridden on the line within the past ten days and isolate them for possible smallpox infection."

"You've just put me out of business," Amy Leland said flatly. Then she let out a long breath. "What does it matter? I'd have stopped the stages anyway."

Dan Canby came in and closed the door against the cold weather. He opened his coat and shook some heat inside.

"Just what's going on? I hear you're going to close up the town."

"A rumor without foundation," Bolton said, "but we are stopping everyone who tries to leave. And we're not allowing anyone to enter. I've just told Miss Leland that we'll have to burn her coaches and stations. We're certain that her stages transmitted the infection."

Canby looked steadily at him, then laughed. Ben Talon said, "You find this funny?"

"Burning the coaches and stations? You bet I think that's funny. Now you just try it, soldier, and you'll get hurt. We've got a fortune tied up—"

"We're talking about people's lives," Bolton said sternly.

"So what? They take a chance when they get on a horse. It's the same riding the stage." He shook his head. "Don't try to burn anything, major. I hope you've got sense enough to heed that warning."

"We'll start with the stages here in the yard," Bolton said. "Sergeant Talon, will you see that they are fired within the hour?"

"Yes, sir." Ben Talon brought his heels together and saluted with his left hand; his right, still bandaged, was tucked into his shirt because he still could not use it.

"Talon, don't put a torch to my property," Canby said. "I'll kill you if you do."

Amy Leland said, "Dan, the money can't be more important than—"

"It is!" he snapped. "I've got half the say around here, and there'll be no burning. No destruction of my property." He buttoned his coat and turned to the door. "I'm going to get my pistol, Ben. I'll use it on you if I have to."

He slammed the door on the way out. Bolton said, "You have the order, sergeant. Carry it out, using any means you find necessary."

"Yes, sir."

"Ben," Amy said, "God knows what's gotten into Dan. Be careful. And don't kill him."

"Not unless he makes me," Talon said and went out, tipping his head down against the rising wind. He went around the building to the wagon yard. Hank Swain was there as though he had a notion something bad was going to happen. Talon told him what had to be done, then he told Swain that, once the stages were wheeled close together, he was to get out of the yard.

"I seen Canby storm out," Swain said and turned, calling to a pair of Mexicans.

There was a five-gallon can of coal oil in the barn, and Talon got it. The coaches were being parked hub to hub, and he climbed up and began to pour coal oil over them, splashing it around. He emptied the can and threw it down; then he saw Dan Canby standing by the pole arch entrance, a pistol thrust into his waistband. Canby wore no coat or hat; he stood spraddle-legged, braced against the breeze.

"That's going far enough," he called against the wind. "Climb down or get shot off there, Ben."

Talon straightened. His pistol was tucked underneath his coat in a flap holster, and he knew that Canby would get off the first shot and that it would likely be a fatal one because Canby was what the Mexicans called a *pistolero,* a shooter with two gunfights behind him.

"I'm too good a target up here," Talon said and grinned and started to climb down, making a clumsy job of it. By the time he hit the ground, hidden by part of the coach, he had his coat open and the flap unfastened on his holster. He glanced at the barn and saw Hank Swain there. "Bring me a torch, Hank."

Then he waited while Swain wrapped a rag around a stick, soaked it in coal oil, and lit it. Swain carried it across the yard, all the time watching Dan Canby. Swain handed the torch to Talon, then ran for the barn. Talon held the torch away from him so that the heat and smoke didn't get into his eyes.

"If you throw that," Canby said, "you're a dead man, Ben. I don't want to kill you, but I will. You can't take this much from a man and not have him fight."

"We do what we have to do," Talon said and arched the torch on top of the nearest stage. He didn't wait to hear it land, but dropped and rolled. Dan Canby's bullet slivered wood near the driver's boot, and Talon was out of sight, his own .44 drawn now.

The coaches were beginning to burn; the flames spread quickly with great noise and a pall of dark smoke that billowed away between himself and Dan Canby.

Talon dashed across the yard and almost reached the barn door before Canby saw him and fired again. The range was more than sixty yards, and the bullet went a bit wide. Kneeling down, Talon raised his injured arm and planted it against the door frame. Then he laid the muzzle of his gun across his forearm, sighted, and squeezed off.

Dan Canby staggered, and one leg bent; he quickly clutched the upper thigh. He started to hop, stopping when Ben Talon yelled. "I could have put that one in your brisket, Dan! If I have to shoot again, I will!" He cocked the Remington and waited, squinting over the sights. Canby, hobbling, couldn't make cover ahead of another shot, and the man knew it. He hesitated only an instant, then dropped his Colt on the ground and sat down to try to stem the bleeding.

Talon left the barn, and Hank Swain and several others followed him over to where Canby sat. The wind husked dust and blew Canby's hair, and he looked at Talon, his expression tight because he was beginning to hurt a little now.

"Give him a hand there, Hank," Talon said. "Is this the end of it, Dan?"

"I don't know." He turned his head and looked at the coaches kind of melting together, collapsing, throwing out a strong heat. "If you only knew how hard they were to get and what they cost."

"Hell, man, I know."

Swain helped Canby stand; they started off down the street, Canby hopping along, throwing his weight onto Swain. Ben Talon picked up Canby's gun and stuck the long barrel in his waistband. One shot gone; that was really Canby's way: one shot, hoping to make the first one count.

Then he saw Amy Leland and the major standing in the back doorway; she was watching her coaches char to ruin. A hot rim, free from a burned-out wheel, rolled around the yard in ever smaller circles, then stopped, wobbling, in the dust, like some strange wounded bird in a death dance.

She turned and went inside, and Ben Talon went in, too. She was pouring coffee when he closed the door, and her eyes were red, but she wasn't crying, and he didn't think she would.

"I suppose I should be happy you didn't burn my freight wagons, too." She stared at her coffee cup a moment, then looked at Ben Talon. "When Dan went out there with his gun, I wasn't sure whether I wanted him to stop you or wanted you to not kill him. Do you understand how that could be?"

"Yes," he said and drank his coffee.

Presently she sighed and murmured, "I guess Dan's a strong-minded man, all right. I just didn't really believe he'd actually shoot at the Army to protect his property."

Ben Talon studied her a moment. The he said gently, "There's different ways of being strong-minded, Amy." And left it at that.

Bolton looked at his watch. "I think we'd better get over to Blaine's place." He sighed and put his watch away. "This is miserable work, Miss Leland. Just miserable." He put out his hand and touched her shoulder. "Perhaps, someway, somehow, we can replace part of the equipment you've lost. I don't know, but it's something we can hope for."

They left her building and walked toward town and Blaine's nearly finished building. His office was in front, but he was not there. He occupied a room for housekeeping, and Talon went toward the back of the building and found the door open.

One look was all he needed; Blaine was on his cot, his face broken out in pustules, and his eyes were glazed with fever. Talon closed the door and found Major Bolton waiting in front. "I'll go fetch the doctor," he said, nodding toward the back. "He's got it good."

"Well, that rather settles that, doesn't it?" Bolton said. "I'll wait here and make sure no one enters."

The first thaw came in March, and the weather turned mild for a change, and some of the more optimistic opined that a very bad winter was coming to an end.

For more than three weeks no one had come down with smallpox, and the doctor, who had aged five years in the past two and a half months, decided that it was possible that the epidemic had been checked.

But not without cost. The stages had been stopped for a

little over four months, and traffic in and out of town had come to a standstill. Smallpox had done what the police could not do, what Vale and Early and the others could not do; it had wiped out the renegades. All of them took sick, and those who survived took their scars and went home, hunting relatives who had once ousted them. Now there were no more renegades, just men back with families and having no more desire to go it alone, living alone, dying alone.

The smallpox killed the hide buying because, once recovered, Taylor Blaine hitched a ride on a northbound freight wagon and didn't bother to say good-bye to anyone.

Canby limped around for a while, but the bullet wound in his leg healed, and he stayed in town, stayed close to his bank. Once, when Ben Talon rode in, Canby stayed on one side of the street while Talon walked the length of the other; they were like fighting cocks, each unafraid but respectful of the spurs of the other.

Everyone in town knew that the smallpox had come in on Amy Leland's stages. Most understood that she wasn't responsible for that, but others who had lost loved ones felt that just burning her wagons wasn't enough, and there was talk going around that someone ought to burn her out instead of stopping with the stages.

But they never got around to it. News of the big cattle drive going north seemed to be on everyone's mind, and since Vale and Early were hiring hands, most of the young men in town left to join the drive. Amy Leland let them have four wagons, and these were loaded from Canby's store. Many people said that it was a real generous thing to do, while others thought that it was just Canby & Leland sticking their fingers into another money-making pie.

Some Army men came onto the post, having ridden down from Kansas, and they soon spread the word that the railroad was in Ellsworth and that the town was chock-full of cattle buyers just praying for a herd to come north and that the market was up to about thirty dollars a head. Of course, this was too late to pass on to Vale or Early or the others; they were already on the trail and didn't know exactly what to expect in Kansas.

But it didn't keep the people in town from doing some multiplication and figuring out that jointly Vale and Early were worth seven hundred and fifty thousand dollars, by the Ellsworth market. There was a lot of hand rubbing and lip smacking and talk about getting their credit extended at the bank and stores.

Spring brought new people to town, people with wagons and straw hats; the men wore overalls, and the wagons had a plow lashed onto the side, and these people had money. They stopped at Canby's and deposited their money and talked about land for sale, or land to homestead, or land to squat on.

They were all stern-faced, determined people who spoke in hard, Midwestern accents, stomping hard on the r's, pushing them into their noses so they twanged. They all had many children, and wives who didn't seem to like anything about Texas, and on Sundays they got together and prayed and sang loudly, and afterward they had a big feed, while the men sneaked off to nip at their jugs.

These people owned no cattle, just cows to be milked and pigs to root up the barnyard, and they fenced everything. The children immediately were put to work digging postholes and stringing single-strand wire and driving staples, and when they had fenced in the land they had bought or rented or squatted on, they fenced the barnyard, using wood, and then fenced the front yard and the back yard and put another fence up so they could keep chickens.

Ben Talon, who had been out of the county since late January, didn't get back until mid-May; he had been south, to Victoria, on special assignment, helping to reactivate the Texas Rangers. When he returned, he was surprised to find soddies and frame houses going up on creeks and around springs on George Vale's land.

As he approached one of these houses, the family came out to watch him, and he saw no display of weapons, but he noticed that the man stayed close to the open door, and Talon surmised there was a shotgun leaning there.

Talon's uniform was a help; it was blue, and Yankee, and these people expected no trouble from Yankees. He stopped and gave his horse some water, then tied him and walked toward the house. He introduced himself and shook hands with the man, who ignored his wife and seven children.

"It ain't much now," the man was saying, "but in another two or three years it'll be a nice farm."

"Guess you knew this land was all part of the Vale ranch," Talon said matter-of-factly.

"According to Mr. Canby, it's open range. It suits us fine. We'll be good neighbors to the Vales, although they ain't come around to bid us howdy."

"The old man and his boy and all of his riders are on a cattle drive to Kansas. But he'll be around when he comes back and hears you're here."

"Cattle drive to Kansas?" the farmer said. Then he laughed. "I never heard of such a thing. Why, it's too far. Any fool knows that." He let his laughter die to a chuckle. "How many head do they own, anyway?"

Talon thought a moment; he wanted to be honest. "About eighteen thousand head."

The man stared at him, his brow furrowed. "Don't lie to me, soldier. I'm not an idiot."

"Well, they left here in the spring, two outfits, with twenty-five thousand head between them," Talon said. "About two hundred riders, eight hundred head of horses, and four wagons. Believe it if you want to, but I'll tell you one thing you'd better believe: George Vale fought for this land, and he won't like to see you cut it up with a plow and muddy his creek. And if he calls on you to tell you to leave, he'll have seventy men riding with him, and I wouldn't stop to argue. I'd pack my things and get out."

"This land is as much mine as it is his," the farmer said.

"Well, that's your opinion," Talon said. "Hope you don't take it to the grave with you." He bowed to the wife and smiled at the children, then got on his horse and rode on.

Before he reached the Vale place, he saw three more farms.

It was dusk when he rode into Vale's yard. Another house had been built, a much smaller house, and as he tied his horse, Emily came out, then ran to him and flung her arms around his neck. A crippled horse wrangler, one of the five men who remained behind, found this too much to take—a fair Southern woman hugging a Yankee—and retreated to brood about it.

They went into the house; Emily had been fixing supper,

and she put on another plate and fixed a place for him at the table. She was full of chatter, and she was happy, and he let her ramble on through the meal, and afterward he insisted on helping her with the dishes.

Then they sat on the skimpy porch, and the air was full of summer flavor, the scent of flowers and dust and grass. "Papa and the others ought to be two-thirds there by now," Emily said. "It's hard to wait, Ben. Waiting's lonesome." She laced her arm through his and put her head against his shoulder. "And you've been gone a long time. Forever, it seemed."

"Oh, it wasn't that long. There have been some changes around here. I stopped at one of the farms. Saw some others. Dan Canby's name was mentioned."

"Sure, he's behind it all. Loans and giving them a discount at his store. He never gave anyone else a discount, Ben."

"Amy Leland ever get any more coaches?"

"The major found her three, but that's all. I heard talk that Canby wanted to buy her out, but she wouldn't sell. I know she turned him down when he offered her a loan so she could buy coaches." She turned her head and looked at him. "Ben, if anyone besides you had burned her out, I don't think she would have taken it. I think she'd have gone to Canby and fought with him. I'm sure she loves you, Ben."

He laughed. "You're having smoke dreams, Emily. Why, there's never been—"

"There doesn't have to be," she said. "Ben, a woman knows. She won't even speak to me, and that's because of you. Because you took me home and kept me at the post after the fire. I know what the talk is."

"Just what is it?"

She shook her head. "Ask Dan Canby."

"Why, I'll surely do that," he said, rising.

She took his arm to pull him back. "You're not leaving now?"

"I figured to ride on tonight, Emily."

"Ben, you don't have to do that. You can stay here."

He shook his head. "That might not sound so good if it was mentioned." Then he pulled her to her feet and put his arms around her. "I'll be around awhile now. I'll be back." He kissed her, not gently; he wanted her to know the hungers he had. Then he released her and went to his horse.

When he arrived in town, it was late, and the only lamps burning were in Blaine's building, and he wondered who occupied it now. The answer came to him when a colored police sergeant stepped out into the street and pointed a pistol at him. "Halt there," the sergeant said. "It way aftah curfew. Come in de light."

Talon eased his horse over, and the sergeant saw the uniform, and he grinned and put his pistol away. "Ah didn't recognize you, saagint. Would you care to step inside, suh?"

It was a question, and technically a choice, only Talon knew that it wasn't. He tied his horse and stepped inside; the place had been turned into a police barracks, with cells and squad room in back and Blaine's office now occupied by a pink-cheeked lieutenant who resented being wakened.

He rubbed his eyes and looked at Ben Talon and said, "Don't you know you can get shot for being out after curfew, sergeant?"

"I didn't know there was a curfew, sir. There's never been a need for one."

"My decision on that," the officer said. "You're Sergeant Talon, I take it. Been south with some sort of detached duty. I'm Lieutenant Ballard. For your information, sergeant, no one is allowed on the streets after ten o'clock. At sunrise the curfew is lifted."

"Why?"

"Because it's daylight, of course!"

"I meant, sir, why have a curfew at all? Has there been any trouble in town?"

"No, but Mr. Canby thought that a police barracks here would discourage any prospect of it," Ballard said. He was young, in his middle twenties, a man with no military experience and, Talon guessed, much less training. These commissions were political appointments, and although Ballard wore an Army uniform, his rank was only a token and he had no genuine status among military men. He knew it, and he was stiff with resentment.

Ben Talon said gently, "Well, now, I'll tell you something. Dan Canby is getting too damned big for his own britches.

Can't you see the man's out to feather his own nest?" He sat on the edge of the lieutenant's desk and ticked the points off on his fingers. "First, we have Canby picking out land for the farmers and catering to them through the bank and the store. Now suppose these men don't make it. Not all of them, but some of them. So what happens to the land when it goes bust? Canby has a lien on it. Can you see what's coming next? He's got a toehold, and he'll push until he's backed Vale or anyone else into the corner. Hell, he has the money to do it."

"These farmers have rights, Talon."

"Certainly. But is it really their rights Canby wants you to protect?" He shook his head. "Think about it and you'll see that it isn't. Lieutenant, you seem like a nice fella. Do yourself a favor and think about this before you throw all the force at your command on Dan Canby's side."

"Is there something personal between you and this Canby, sergeant?"

"No, I like him. And you might say that we're friends. But I can see what's happening, and I don't like it. Just look carefully before you jump, will you?"

Ballard gnawed his lip. "I should be offended, but somehow I'm not, sergeant. In time I may even thank you for the advice." He smiled and offered his hand. "Good night. Come and go as you please—I'll tell my men."

10

AMY LELAND was sitting in Major Harry Bolton's quarters by invitation. Ben Talon was there, and the orderly was clearing the table and setting out the coffee; he asked the major if there was anything else, and there wasn't, so he left.

Bolton settled in an easy chair and crossed his legs. "Miss Leland, as military governor of this sector, I have a great deal of power, and because of that, I must be very careful to exercise it wisely. It just wouldn't do, you see, to place restrictions on this and that and hope for the best; the police do that, and it doesn't get them very far. Every time they run up against something they don't like, they pass a law against it. So in the year I've been here, I may seem to have done nothing in particular for the welfare of Texas. I believe I have accomplished a great deal because in that year I am sure I have isolated one of the major handicaps you have to recovery." He glanced at Talon, then at Amy Leland. "Your partner, Dan Canby. This man can and will, in the space of another year, strip this country and put the profit in his pocket."

He put it out to her as though he expected her to argue, to disagree, and he was mildly surprised when she nodded and said, "Yes, I have to agree with you, major. For a long time I thought Dan was a sharp man who wanted to do very well in business. But it's more than that. He wants to do everything his way and wants everyone to do it his way, and he just can't settle for any less than that."

Bolton said, "I believe my primary function is to stop

Canby from gaining further control. I'm not after the man. I don't want to deprive him of his enterprises, but I believe that Canby would encourage trouble to the point of one man shooting another if he could profit by it. This was demonstrated to me when we burned the coaches."

"He was sore and lost his head," Ben Talon put in.

"Ben, this habit of yours of giving the other man the benefit of the doubt may do you in one of these days," Bolton said. "No, Dan Canby wasn't displaying his temper. He was displaying a greed that I find dangerous." He brought out a cigar and licked it before putting a match to it. "I've been thinking about this for a long time, and I think I have something, but it will require your cooperation."

"Major, I'll do what I have to do. You've been more than fair with me. If nothing more, it'll be a favor repaid."

"Fine," Bolton said. "As a military man I'd like to say that one way to defeat the enemy is to spread him thin, and generally this is accomplished by stretching his supply lines. Dan Canby needs your wagons, Miss Leland. Perhaps he was thinking of that when you and he became partners. It's a certainty that he'd have difficulty stocking his store if he didn't have a way to haul goods from Galveston. There are two ways to put a crimp in him. One is to sell out to him; this would require a large amount of cash. The second is to refuse to haul for him, thereby causing him to split the company, take half the wagons and men, and—"

"He doesn't have half the wagons," she said. "And I don't have half of his store. He has a third interest in the freight line, and I have a third interest in the store."

"Suppose he offered to buy you out," Talon said. "How much are you worth, Amy?"

She considered it. "Twenty-five thousand. With the three coaches running we still have the mail to carry and the way open to build up again. Yes, twenty-five thousand would be a very reasonable price."

Ben Talon raised an eyebrow. "That ought to hit his cash pretty hard."

"I don't think he'd buy," Amy maintained. "Dan wouldn't be fool enough to strap himself like that."

"Yes, I rather thought it would be like that," Bolton said.

"I've prepared an order for you, Miss Leland. With the Texas Rangers being reactivated under military assistance, I'll need every wagon you have available to haul on Army contract. The Comanches are beginning to cause a bit of a stir around Fredericksburg, and we think it advisable to erect a series of posts with the quickest dispatch." He smiled around his cigar. "This will keep you from losing money and at the same time force Dan Canby to spend a lot of money going into the freighting business, or close his store. It will also save you the trouble of fighting this out with Canby; he'll have to come to me with his complaint."

"Oh, he will," Amy said. "You can bet on it."

Bolton frowned and pulled at his mustache. "I don't like what Canby is doing with these farmers. The cattlemen are gone, and those who have been left behind won't do anything until the owners get back. And when they do, these farmers will think all hell broke loose."

Ben Talon said, "Care for an opinion, sir?"

"Sure."

"The farmers are here to stay."

They looked at him a moment, then Amy Leland laughed. "Ben, that's ridiculous. This has always been open range."

"It won't stay that way," he said. "It'll change. We all change every day, a little bit, and maybe we don't notice it until one day we look into a mirror and find that we're old." He shook his head. "I've been thinking about it, major, and I've made up my mind. The farmers will stay. Not all of them, but some will, and more will come. The Indians saw this happening, wagon after wagon, and they killed off some and more came. It's the same here now. Vale and Early and the others, they'll just have to learn to accept it. The land *is* open range, and any of it can be homesteaded."

The reasoning was not lost on Bolton or on Amy Leland; they sat quietly for several minutes, then Amy said, "Ben, instead of getting the farmers out, you'd rather work to keep them and the cattlemen from fighting. Is that it?"

"Well, in a roundabout way, Amy. The way I see it, Dan Canby wants them to fight. He wants to see men riding with rifle and torch. Eventually the farmer has to give in or get killed, and he pulls out. Then Canby forecloses on the place and either sells it again to another farmer or hangs onto it as a wedge to split up the range."

"Now I just don't believe he's going to do that," Amy said quickly. "You're both forgetting one thing: Dan's a Texan. He wouldn't—'

"He would," Ben Talon said so definitely that she closed her mouth and argued no further.

Later he drove her to town in a military ambulance and helped her down. She started to go in, then stopped and said, "Ben, I feel that we're no longer on the same side anymore, and it bothers me."

"We can't always agree, Amy."

She leaned against her door and crossed her arms. "I didn't think it was going to be like this when the war was over. Win or lose, I believed it would be different."

"What did you think it would be like?"

"Oh, people coming back and working, as they always did, with everybody pretty much the same. I just didn't think that while men were gone, others, myself included, would be —gathering together all the good things so that there wasn't anything left."

"War or no war, opportunities went on," Talon said. "You took them as they came along. It's not bad to take, Amy. It's bad when you hug a thing so tight it chokes."

"And that's what Dan's doing?"

"You know he is. You know the first thing on Dan's mind has always been money—money to use, money to build with, money to expand and build more with. Not just money for its own sake, on any terms whatever. In his own way he's a realist, and he's taken care of Dan Canby, and he's helped this country to make a recovery in the process. The same way you have. But somewhere Dan's gone over the edge. Maybe it happened when the wagons were burned, but I think it started long before that. But he's going to be stopped, and stopped hard. He'll need a lot of help when it happens, Amy." He touched the beak of his forager cap. "Good night."

She reached out and touched his arm. "Ben, are you and Emily Vale going to get married?"

"We've never spoke of it."

"Are you going to tell me it's none of my business?"

He shook his head. "Not you, Amy. Someone else maybe, but not you. We've been friends, haven't we?"

"Good night," she said and quickly turned and went inside.

He waited a moment, then mounted the rig and drove back to the post.

Dan Canby stormed and fumed and swore at Major Bolton, and none of it did him any good; the major assured him that he had a right to commandeer anything he needed, and that included banks and stores, in case Canby wanted to make trouble, and if that wasn't enough, he could move the troops into town and Canby could conduct his business with a lieutenant looking over his shoulder.

Canby left the post, still yelling about damned Yankees, but he had to look elsewhere for wagons.

Fred Early was the first to return home; it was in September, and Jonas Vale and what remained of the hands rode in a week later. Border bandits, Indians, stampedes, and trouble in Kansas had wiped more than twenty men off the payroll, and George Vale had never reached Ellsworth. A storm had stampeded the cattle, and he'd been unlucky. They found his watch and part of his slicker and his pistol some distance away, but nothing more.

Jonas Vale sent word around the country that he was paying off, and the families of the dead men came and stood in line with the cowboys, and Jonas paid the families a full share. Some of the men had no families, and Jonas split this money and gave it to the women who had no men now.

Ben Talon was there when Jonas Vale paid off, and afterward there was a barbecue in the yard, and it was dark before everyone had left. Jonas Vale watched them leave, said good-bye to them, then walked around the empty yard as though he wished they hadn't gone and left him with all this. He was an older man now, a hard-used man; the responsibility of all of this was his.

Ben Talon sat on the step smoking a cigar, and finally Jonas came over and sat down. "You don't know how often I thought of home," Jonas said. "Man, it gets to be an ache inside you after a while." He glanced at Talon and smiled. "You've done a lot for the Vales. I guess you've got your reasons."

"I've always steered clear of men who did things without reasons."

"Yeah, even a bad one's better than none," Jonas said. "Funny thing, though, when Pa was alive, I'd as soon go off half-cocked as not. But when he died, it all changed. After the stampede, when he was found—or what we could find—the fellas gathered around and just looked at the ground; then they looked at me, and I just couldn't make any more mistakes, Ben. Every decision I made had to be a good one. I guess that's the reason I'm not having my horse saddled to ride on the farmers tonight."

"Expect you saw a couple of their places on the way in."

"Yeah, and the wranglers told me as soon as I dismounted. Is it Canby's doing?"

"I think it is. It's an opinion that's not completely popular." He brought out two cigars and offered one to Jonas. "You're a rich man now, Jonas. You can put on men, pay regular wages, and make next year's drive from your front porch, with a hired trail boss doing the hard work. But as I see it, you and Early can pull power away from Canby because you have money."

"Well, I sure as hell won't be using his bank," Jonas Vale said. "I've got to settle with Amy Leland, pay my bill at Canby's, and then I'm clear with the world."

"A man can't ask for much more, can he?" Ben got up and stretched. "Guess I'll say good night to Emily and ride back. Tomorrow I'm supposed to go to Wichita Falls for a month."

"Ben, am I going to have you for a brother-in-law?"

"Why? Does the idea bother you?"

"No. I just wondered if it bothered you."

"What made you stop fighting the war?" Talon asked.

"I don't know. Somewhere between here and Kansas I got it through my head that it was over. And I've stopped being ashamed because we lost it."

Dan Canby shot Jonas Vale on a Saturday afternoon. The argument started over two barrels of flour; Vale insisted that he had taken three barrels, and Canby stood pat that he had loaded five in the wagons, and the upshot of it was that

Canby called Vale a damned liar and a cheapskate who was trying to weasel out of paying his bill in full.

There was no argument that Jonas Vale reached for his gun first; he fired first, the bullet missing Canby by a bare fraction, then Canby shot him through the body, and Jonas Vale staggered out of the store and into the street.

Vale was still alive when several men hurriedly carried him to the doctor's office, but it didn't look as though he'd last long.

Before the police could arrest Dan Canby, he got on his horse and rode out to the post and turned himself over to Major Bolton, who held him until two of his officers could conduct a complete investigation.

Lieutenant Ballard of the police force had already rounded up witnesses—the two clerks in the store and some onlookers on the street who had seen the tag end of it—and when Bolton was finished, he released Canby, having nothing to hold him on or charge him with.

Ben Talon was up on the Sweetwater with a company of engineers, building Fort Elliott, when a courier coming north with dispatches brought him the news, along with an order from Major Bolton to return as soon as possible.

It was almost four days before Ben Talon returned on a jaded horse; he turned it over to one of the stable detail and went immediately to Bolton's office and was told that he was in town. Catching up a fresh horse, Talon rode into town, and as he approached Amy Leland's stable yard, he saw Bolton's horse tied outside. He stopped, tied up, and went in.

Amy was cleaning out her desk, packing everything into wooden boxes. She looked up, saw him, and said, "Hello, stranger."

Bolton turned around, shook Talon's hand, then said, "Canby bought her out. Cash on the barrel head."

"Your price, Amy?"

"Yes, twenty-five thousand." She sat down on one of the boxes and folded her hands. "I was wrong, Ben. He wants it all."

"Canby wants to negotiate a new contract with the Army," Bolton said. "I may have to move troops in, but I don't want to do that, and Canby knows it." He blew out a long breath.

"Emily Vale wants to see you, Ben. Jonas has made it, but he's going to be a very sick man for quite a while. And there's talk around town that the farmers will take Vales' place over. I even suspect that Fred Early is eying that range. It's for the grabbing, you know." He glanced briefly at Amy Leland. "Ben, I can arrange a discharge for you any time if you want it. But we can't have any shooting or the start of anything like that. If factions get to potting at one another, I don't think there are enough troops in Texas to stop it."

"I'll ride out there," Talon said. "What are you going to do now, Amy?"

"Fight," she said. "Dan Canby has overlooked one thing: I'm a woman, and he couldn't shoot me in an argument. And he's given me a weapon. Twenty-five thousand dollars."

"Compared to what Dan is worth—"

"I know, but I think it's enough. Ben, you tell Emily how sorry we've all been about Jonas and all this trouble."

"All right," he said and went out to his horse.

He pushed on the ride south, fast march, dismounting at regular intervals to rest the horse, then swinging up and riding fast. By midafternoon he reached the Vale place and swung down near the well, tying up there. A dozen men loafed near the corral, talking and smoking. Talon was not a rancher, but he knew that there was little idleness on a ranch that made money.

Emily came out and started toward him, but he waved her back, and she stopped by the porch, not understanding this. Talon unbuckled his pistol belt and hung it over the saddle, then walked across the yard to where the men stood.

"Who's the foreman around here?" he asked.

One man took his time, saying finally, "He quit. Day before yesterday."

"Don't you men have anything to do?"

They looked at each other, then one man eased out in front. "I guess we do, but no one's give us any orders." He nodded toward Emily Vale standing across the yard. "She told us to do somethin', but she don't really know what it's all about."

"Try to remember what it was," Talon suggested.

"Can't," the man said.

He grinned just a split instant before Talon hit him, slamming him back into his friends with enough force to bowl two over and send the man back against the corral post. Blood ran from the man's face, and he slowly, carefully pushed himself erect.

"Remember now?" Talon asked.

"I remember less," the man said, and because he was Texan and not afraid of anything, he made his rush, arms flailing unskillfully. Talon met him, weathered a rain of fists, then grappled with the man. He locked his head in the crook of his arm and brought his hard cavalryman's boots down on the cowboy's toes and repeatedly hit him in the face, bloodying his nose and cutting him about the eyes.

Then he spun him away, caught him by the front of the vest, and sledgehammered him on the jaw. The man turned into a rag and fell, and Talon dragged him to the horse trough and dumped him in, ducking him twice before he hauled him out.

He propped the man up against the corral and shook him until his eyes focused. "Can you hear me? My name is SIR, and when I speak, you jump. I'll give orders around here, and I want to see head down and ass up. UNDERSTAND!"

The man nodded, and Talon let him go; he would have fallen again if two friends hadn't rushed in to support him. He looked at each of them. "Do I have to repeat myself with any of you? If I do, just step up and start swinging."

They looked around, exchanged glances, then another man shifted his tobacco and said, "I guess we heah you cleah, sur. An' ah remember what it was we was to do."

If they expected him to move, they guessed wrong; he stood there, and they left, moving as if they had someplace to go now, and when they'd caught up their horses and ridden out, he walked over to the porch.

Emily came to him; he folded his arms around her, and she began to cry, and he let it go this way for several minutes; then with his arm around her he took her into the house. She needed something to do, so he told her to fix him something to eat, and this calmed her, let her focus on something besides trouble.

He said, "I'm staying, Emily."

For a moment she seemed not to hear him; then she turned around and looked at him, not saying anything; she seemed almost afraid to speak.

"For good, Emily. Major Bolton said I could have my discharge. Will you marry me, Emily?"

"Ben—"

"I love you, Emily. I guess from the first time in Canby's store I knew there wasn't going to be anyone else. You knew it, too, didn't you?"

"Yes, Ben."

"I was a fool to wait this long. Hadn't intended to. Jonas asked me before I rode north if I was going to be his brother-in-law. He seemed to like the idea." He got up and came around the table and put his arms around her. "You don't have to answer now if you want to think about it."

"I don't have to think about it," she said softly. "I want to marry you, Ben. Whenever you want."

"Soon," he said. "We'll go to town tomorrow."

A wagon came into the yard, and he stepped back, looked out the kitchen window, then stepped outside. The wagon stopped near the porch. A heavy man in overalls sat on the seat; he had two strapping boys with him.

"Howdy there," the man said. "Name's Miller. My boys." He looked around. "This the Vale place? It don't look like much. Have a fire? Bad, fires." He finally got around to studying Ben Talon, then Emily stepped out and stood by Ben, her hand lightly on his arm. "Hear in town that this place is on the die-up."

"You heard wrong," Ben Talon said.

The man turned this over in his head, then said, "I got the banker's say-so on it. Likely he'd know." He looked around again. "Crossed a creek a mile back. Figure I'll build there, near the road."

"My advice is not to, because if you do, we'll move you out." Ben Talon pointed. "There's land to the south, some farmers living there. Go there if you want, but stay away from that creek."

"I like to make up my own mind," Miller said. "The land looks good, and it suits me. My boys and I will each take a section."

It was an alarming thing to hear, and Talon suddenly understood what made cattlemen grab their rifles and start shooting. But he kept his voice down and his temper in place. "Mr. Miller, this ranch is not going to fight with the farmers. There's a place for each of us. If you want a section, take it to the south. There's water there and your kind of people. But don't cut up this ranch to suit-your fancy. And not three sections. You'll have trouble, and I don't think you can handle it."

"The land's free."

"Yes, it is, but not free to make a hog of yourself."

"That's kind of insulting," Miller said. "Wouldn't you say so, Milo, Kyle?"

"It did sound that way," the older son said. He kept looking at Emily and smiling. "You belong to anybody, or are you free, too?"

Ben Talon turned, took one long step, picked up the Spencer repeater resting just inside the door, levered one into the chamber, and pointed it at the father. "Now turn your wagon south, friend. I won't bother to tell you again."

"The land's free," Miller said, lifting the reins. "You're only one man. We can fight, too."

"I don't want to fight, you damned fool! Are you so blind you can't see that?" He waved the muzzle of the gun. "Go on, you've overstayed your welcome."

They drove out and did not turn south; he had not expected Miller to, for the man was a mule bent on having his own way. Talon feared him, feared the relentless stubbornness in the man, for Miller was the very kind that would have to be pushed off, the very kind that would start what none of them really wanted started.

11

In Dan Canby's mind, the brightest day came in late February when Maj. Harry Bolton got his orders; the Army was pulling out, ending the governmental duties, and uniting to put down the Comanche trouble, which was growing more dangerous each day.

The police would be withdrawn from counties that went ahead with elections and created an office of sheriff to maintain law and order; it was the very thing Canby wanted, and he immediately had a stack of posters printed, announcing Pete Field as candidate. Field hadn't been doing much since the hide business collapsed; he worked for Canby, doing as he was told, and ran his blacksmith business when he felt like it or the work piled up.

Dan Canby felt that he was the best choice for sheriff.

Amy Leland did not.

As soon as she heard about it, she rented a buggy and drove south to the Vale place. Jonas Vale, partially recovered, had been sent East for further treatment. Meantime Ben had spent the winter rebuilding the house; it stood on the old site, broad and rambling, with a porch running around all four sides. When she stopped in the yard, a man came from the barn and took the rig, and Emily came out of the house.

Talon was out and wouldn't return until evening, but Emily insisted that Amy come inside and wait; she could spend the night and return to town in the morning.

It was almost dark when Talon returned with a crew of twenty men. He paused on the porch to remove his spurs and chaps and pistol belt, then stepped into the warm kitchen.

Emily was fixing supper, and Amy was helping her, and Talon smiled, surprised, but pleased. "Well, Amy, I haven't seen you all winter. What have you been doing with yourself?"

"Sitting on my money and watching Dan Canby grow," she said. "Ben, did you know that the Army has pulled out?"

He shook his head. "I've been on the range for nearly six weeks now. We're rounding up for another drive in a month."

"Pete Field is running for sheriff. Canby's candidate." She showed him one of the posters that were being put up everywhere.

He read it and laughed. "Honest? Hard-working? People's choice?" He threw it down. "Why doesn't Canby run himself? Pete's been a solid Canby man since he got a taste of easy money."

"He can't run unopposed," Amy Leland said, then explained the conditions of police withdrawal. "Of course, Canby will pay some fool to run against Field, someone who's bound to lose. I'm not going to sit by and see that happen, Ben."

"Get a good man who can beat Field."

"That's why I came to see you."

He looked at her, then shook his head. "You don't want me to run. Oh, no, I've got enough to do. Sodbusters moving in on us, putting up fences, and cattle to get to market. Amy, you're out of your mind."

"Ben, people know you. They trust you. I think you'd get a large share of the farmers' vote, too, because you've been fair to them. Ben, I want you to think about it."

"There's nothing to think about," he said. "I don't want it. Get someone else."

"Ben, there isn't anyone else."

"That's ridiculous. Are you telling me there isn't one man in this whole county who's better than Pete Field?" He sat down and kept shaking his head. "Amy, I'm thirty-four years old, and I've got a wife who's going to have a baby in another six months. I've got cattle to get to market in Kansas, and farmers trying to cut up our land and just looking for an excuse to take a shot at our riders. Now I just don't need the added responsibility of being sheriff. So forget it."

"Is that your final word, Ben?"

"It has to be." He leaned forward and braced his forearms

on the table top. "Amy, I'm just like any other man, willing to coast along until he's pushed into doing something to take care of himself. We don't fence range because no one is chipping at our boundary, and George Vale never put a brand on a steer until the hide hunters started stripping the range; an earmark had always been enough between friends. But the hide hunters were going blind, it seemed, so he had to hot-iron a slash across the flank. One of these days I'll probably have to paint 'em blue because we've already lost a few head to the farmers who just can't understand how an animal that isn't tied or fenced can be someone's property. And I figured the only way to stop these farmers from cutting Vale land to pieces was to legally own the land, so this winter sixty riders have filed on a section apiece with the land office in Austin; they've built cabins and are batching it or have moved their families in. When they prove up on it, Jonas and I will buy the land from them, and then we'll divide it between us. There isn't any more land on this range to be had." He shook his head. "No, I'm not going to run for sheriff or anything else."

"Ben, someone has to do something."

"You do it."

She looked at him oddly. "Me?"

"Why not? You ought to do something for yourself. The Army set you up in business with mules and stages. You're still a partner in Canby's store, and, like it or not, he has to give you a cut of the profits. You do something." He leaned forward and tapped her on the arm. "But understand something, Amy—this brand is not afraid of Dan Canby. I have the men and the money to fight him, and if he starts to squeeze me, we'll just have to take him apart to protect ourselves. We're not going to hog land or drive the farmers out; the ones who are here can stay. But we'll take care of ourselves."

"Ben, this isn't like you."

"What is it like? I have new responsibilities now, and I'll take care of them. If you want to stop Canby from grabbing it all, then you do it."

"How?"

"Think of something. You're not stupid. How much is it worth to you?"

"What do you mean?"

"I mean, is it worth enough for you to risk your money on? You don't have any hesitation in asking someone else to put everything on the block." He leaned back in his chair and studied her.

"Ben, it's easy for you to say, but there are limits to what a woman can do." She looked at Emily. "You're not helping me much."

"You always gave me the impression that you could take care of yourself. So go ahead."

"That's an easy way to push it off onto someone else."

"Amy, I'm not pushing anything," Talon said. "I'm just telling you as plain as I can that I have plenty of trouble of my own. Hell, just last week the Comanches cut right across my place to the north of here. It scared the devil out of Miller and his family."

She frowned a moment. "Is he the one who moved in on your creek?" He nodded. "I heard you threatened to run him off, give him a place to the south. But he called your bluff and moved in anyway."

"Miller is my business," Talon told her. "It's going to stay that way. And in case Dan Canby asks my intentions, tell him I leave people alone and like to be left alone. Don't send any more farmers out here."

She sighed and got up. "I wish you'd change your mind, Ben."

"Can't," he said. "It isn't that I don't want to—it's just that this is my most urgent responsibility."

"But sometimes a man takes on more because he has to."

"Not this man," he said, and that ended it.

Dan Canby liked to spend his idle hours thinking of all the money he was going to make if the Army cleaned up the Indian trouble and if the cattlemen let the farmers alone so they could bring in crops and pay back all the money they had borrowed from him. This was, Canby knew, the biggest gamble he had ever taken; he was spread so thin that it hurt to think about it, but he kept telling himself that if he hadn't grabbed when he had the chance, Yankees would have snatched at the opportunity.

He firmly believed that it was the Canby nerve and Canby money that kept them out of the county. He knew what was going on in Texas, the Yankee money pouring in and Yankees moving in along with it to run things to suit themselves and putting ninety cents of every dollar into their own pockets.

There were times when he wished he hadn't bought the freight line; it was paying its own way, even making a little money, but he needed stages running on regular schedules to show the kind of profit he liked. Yet he just didn't have the capital now to build it up again, and there was no chance at all of getting Army equipment.

Canby's office in the bank was the mecca of all his business activities; when a man wanted credit at the store, or something hauled, or a loan, he came to the office, passed through a clerk who screened him, and then Canby made his judgments.

Amos Miller sprawled in his chair; he seemed incapable of sitting upright. He was a rough-mannered man with an eternal sulk on his face. "Simple," he said. "I need more money. Some of my seed spoiled."

There was manure on his boots and dirt under his fingernails, and he kept spitting tobacco, missing the spittoon half the time. Dan Canby looked at the records a moment. "Miller, I've loaned you seven hundred in cash, and you've run up a three-hundred-dollar bill at the store. You owe others in town."

"A man has to live. You told me I could get a start here. Told me you'd back me."

"Are you going to get a crop in this year, Miller?"

"Some. What do you expect of a man in his first year? He's got to get settled, don't he?" He shifted in his chair and scraped the soles of his boots together, dropping pieces of dried manure on Canby's floor. Then he made small sweeping motions with his feet, pushing the pieces away from him. "I don't trust them cowboys. That Talon fella, either. Indians passed my place awhile back. A man's got to take care of himself first, then worry about plantin'." He scratched his unshaven cheek and smiled. "I figure you'll loan me the money, Mr. Canby. If I don't get it, I'll pull up stakes. Done it before. Do it again if I have to."

"Is that the kind of responsibility you feel toward people who've helped you?" Canby asked.

"Said a man's got to take care of himself first, didn't I?"

Dan Canby studied him a moment, then got up and opened his office door. He spoke to a clerk. "Adam, will you open the front door and hold it open?"

"Certainly, Mr. Canby."

Turning back to Amos Miller, Canby pounced on him, grabbed him by the shirt front, and jerked him out of the chair. Miller, surprised by this violence, offered no resistance for a moment, but the handling bumped his vast pride and his temper took control. He bellowed like a gored bull, struck Canby a mighty but clumsy blow that lifted Canby clean over the desk, and deposited him on the floor.

His swivel chair upset and kited into the corner, the back broken cleanly off, and then Canby scrambled to his feet and charged Amos Miller, weathering a flurry of wild swings in order to get into the man. He flailed Miller in the face, stomped on his toes, hit him in the stomach, and propelled him backward to escape this punishment.

They passed through the door of Canby's office, and Miller, to halt the retreat, grabbed the door frame with both hands and left himself wide open. Canby laid a sledgehammer fist against the farmer's face, bringing blood and cutting him to the bone, and the blow broke Miller's grip, sailed him flat on his back into the main room of the bank.

Customers gawked, and Canby grabbed Miller, dragged him to the front door, and pitched him headfirst into the street. The farmer tried to get up, but his strength was gone, and he rolled over and looked at Canby.

"You want to pull stakes, Miller? Then, by God, you pull 'em and be quick about it. Day after tomorrow I'll be riding to your place, and if you're not gone, you'll sure as hell wish you were." He turned back inside the bank, speaking to the clerk. "Close the door, Adam; we're letting flies in."

A quickly gathered crowd watched Miller get to his feet and paw at the blood on his face. He looked around and said, "Somebody give me a gun."

"Now you don't want to do that, mister," a man said. "Why don't you go home?"

Miller thought of an angry reply to this but realized that he'd made a fool of himself, and his only desire was to get away from them.

His wagon was down the street; he went to it, climbed aboard, and drove slowly out of town. His head was beginning to ache badly, and each jolt of the wagon sent pain around his skull to settle behind his eyes. His lips, puffed now so that he could not close them naturally, had stopped bleeding, and a large swelling began under his left eye. By the time he reached his own place, the eye was closed completely.

His sons were full of questions when they helped him down, and he grew angry at them and cuffed them and went into the house, where his wife made him go to bed. She got a pan of water and bathed his face and kept up a running chirp of sympathy, while his daughters hung back, waiting to see which way his temper would swing.

"Let Canby come to me," he said. "I'll kill him!"

His wife didn't ask if he'd gotten the money; she knew that he hadn't and that somehow it had led to this. She did what she could for him, then left him alone.

The boys stayed close to the house, for they had learned that he was an unpredictable man in defeat, and when his temper was up, they could expect the worst.

Milo, the older one, saw Indians in the late afternoon and told his brother. Together they went into the house to tell their mother, but since their father was sleeping and hated to be disturbed, they decided to say nothing and handle it themselves.

The two boys, armed with shotguns, went outside and saw nearly a hundred Indians topping a slight rise a half mile from the creek; they sat their ponies and watched, then they broke and came down off the hill, running, yelling. The boys stupidly fired their shotguns, although the range was still too long for a good rifle.

Kyle managed to reload his shotgun as the Indians reached the yard. Amos Miller, startled by the noise, bowled out of the door just as Kyle fired again, bringing down an Indian, the only one killed that day. The Indians overran them, and Kyle was driven through with a Comanche lance.

The other boy, starting to run, died with his father by the door. Then the Indians stormed about the yard, destroying everything, while a few dismounted and broke into the house.

Mrs. Miller hit one on the head with a skillet and was promptly killed with a knife. The two girls, locking themselves in a bedroom, were brought out, stripped, and dragged outside and held to the ground while the bravest of the young warriors raped them.

They were not strong girls; they cried and screamed, and finally the Indians grew tired of it, pinned them with lances where they lay, mounted up, and rode off in a southerly direction.

Lt. Joseph Ballard, late commandant of the State Police and now on active duty with the Army, brought a patrol close to the Miller place shortly before sundown, and his scouts reported to him that they had found what remained of the homestead.

Ballard's troop had been nine days in the field now, and the Comanches had led them on a wild chase, always managing to stay ahead of him. They'd run in a wide circle, and he was no nearer to them now than he had been when he'd picked up the trail near the San Saba. He only knew that he was beat and his men were beat and the horses were about through, so he ordered the command to camp the night, build squad fires, set up guards and pickets, and get a burial detail organized.

Ballard walked around while the light lasted and saw everything and wrote it down in a small book for his report, and it was grisly work, especially putting it down about the women. He had the married men take care of them; the bodies were wrapped in blankets and placed in deep graves. It was dark now, and he read the service with the help of a lantern held by the company bugler.

The guards challenged approaching horsemen, then they were let through, and Ben Talon came over and flung off; he had twenty-five men with him, all heavily armed.

"One of my riders saw the fires," Talon said. He had his

look and knew without asking what had happened. He also looked at the soldiers, their dirty clothes and beards, and he knew they had been long on the march.

Ballard was finished; he turned the detail over to the sergeant, and the graves were filled. "One Indian dead," he said, sitting down near a cook fire. "No, we didn't find him, but we found his shield. I understand that a Comanche wouldn't give up his shield while he was alive."

"You're learning," Talon said. "Different from the police, isn't it?"

Ballard smiled and shook his head. "Damn it, I just couldn't catch them!"

"You weren't about to," Talon said. "Any day of the week they can outride you, outfight you, and if you ever do catch them, you'll know it's because they want it and have a trick up their sleeve."

"There was no reason for this attack on this farmer," Ballard said.

"Yes, there was. What started all this, Ballard?"

"Nothing. They just went on the rampage last year."

Ben Talon took off his hat and scratched his head. "We both know better than that. Something happened. Somewhere along the line the Indians figure they've been mistreated. It's enough to set 'em off."

"Well, I don't know." He thought a moment. "Of course, there was that affair around Fredericksburg—some farmers caught an Indian woman and a boy stealing hogs, and before it was over, they'd lost their heads and hung them."

"Now you've got an Indian war."

"Over that? The farmers were tried and sent to prison, Ben."

"That's not enough to satisfy the Comanches," Talon pointed out. "When they speak of justice, they're talking about an eye-for-an-eye sort of thing. Jail, a fine—that's not justice. Just how come they decided to run in this neck of the woods?"

"They were pushed. Colonel Bolton has his troops in the field constantly."

"Colonel?"

"Yes, he got his promotion."

The sergeant came over, saluted, and said, "Burial detail complete, sir. Shall I dismiss the men?"

"Thank you, yes. I want a full guard detail tonight, and pay special watch over the horses. The Comanches may try to raid."

"Not before morning if they do," Talon said.

"I'm just following the book," Ballard said. "You heard the order, sergeant." He waited until the man left before going on. "Ben, I've got an awful lot to learn and not much time in which to learn it. It seems to me that Bolton has a damned small force to put down this kind of trouble. We never have enough men, and we've lost some, too. The Comanches do get tired of running, and the two engagements the Army has had with them didn't turn out well for the Army." He picked up the coffeepot and two cups, filled them, and handed one to Ben Talon. "The farmers have been hit—Miller isn't the only one. His is the fourth place to go. Everyone is raising hell, yelling for the Army to get busy, and the newspapers are printing some nasty stories about military incompetents." He shook his head. "It's getting so that when you take a troop in town people just line the streets to stare and cuss at you."

"The buffalo are going to be thin this year," Ben Talon said. "My men who made the trip north last year told me that hundreds of outfits were cleaning the plains of Kansas of buffalo. I hear there's a camp near the Nations called Adobe Walls."

"Who gives a God-damn about the buffalo?"

"If I was you, I'd care a lot, Joe. The Comanches live off the buffalo. So do the Arapaho and Kiowa. When the buffalo stop migrating and the Indians start to starve and freeze, you'll see a war from one end of Texas clear to the Canadian border. They can't live without the buffalo, and they'll do their damnedest to take two white men with every one of them that dies." He stood up and quickly drank the rest of his coffee. "I'm going back to my place. Likely there won't be trouble."

"I wouldn't count on it."

"Well, I do," Ben Talon said, "and I'll tell you why. We've got men and they're armed. They're full of Indian savvy. The

Comanches know what it'll cost to raid a Texas ranch. We'd fight on their terms, and they don't want that. Joe, remember this: they're trying to kill as many of us as they can and lose as few as they can in doing it. You come up with an idea that'll change that around, and the Comanches won't be long in suing for peace."

12

THAT SPRING eleven major herds were driven north to market, with the Early-Vale brand sixth largest. They followed old trails to new towns: Wichita, Abilene, and a place at the end of track called Dodge City. They left Texas, cattle and men and horses, and Texas would not see them again for eight and a half months, and she would never see some of these men again, for the news was common that the Comanche and the Kiowa and the Arapaho were united now for the big war to drive the white man out and bring the buffalo back.

There had been much singing and dancing and making of medicine.

And there was constant raiding.

Before the heat of summer came, Indians had leveled a dozen small ranches, killed half a hundred men, and had taken more than ten girls as prisoners.

They struck in the vicinity of Fredericksburg, ran north to Sherman, ducked up into the Indian Nations for a breather, then moved southwest as far as Coleman, burning, killing, while the Army ran after them and couldn't stop them.

Most of the time they couldn't even catch them.

It had all started as Texas business, but it didn't stay that way for long. Eastern newspapers began to pick up the story, and when it grew big enough, they sent a flood of reporters and correspondents to cover the news.

The farmers, who had come to Texas in response to the promotion of land speculators, were the primary target of the Indians. It was farmers who plowed under the grass, and this drove the Indians to a fury.

To Dan Canby's way of thinking, this could ruin him. The Indians and the Texas cattlemen didn't get along, but they didn't fight all the time, and since he had put his money into backing the farmers, trouble to them was deep trouble for him.

Many of them were packing up, leaving.

Many had already gone, leaving dead unburied and the place a burned ruin.

And more than a few never lived long enough to leave.

Which left Dan Canby sitting in his bank, holding a lot of paper on land that he couldn't readily sell.

Heavily armed and mounted on a fast horse, he rode alone to Fort Griffin to see Colonel Bolton about getting the Army to increase their patrol activity.

Bolton assured him that this was impossible; the Army was spread much too thin now. The meeting began to strain their tempers, so that in the end nothing was accomplished and a lot of harsh words had been passed back and forth.

Dan Canby returned to Abilene. He arrived late in the evening, but went to the hotel in spite of that and knocked on Amy Leland's door. He woke her; he could tell by the way she spoke, and he identified himself, and she opened the door for him.

He paused in the hall long enough to beat dust from his clothes, then stepped inside while she adjusted the table lamp.

"Dan, it's after eleven o'clock."

"Yes, yes," he said impatiently. "I've been to see that fool Bolton. He says he can't send a company here."

"Well, you really didn't expect him to, did you?" She belted her robe and sat down in a deep chair. "What do you want, Dan?"

He lit a cigar and rolled it from one side of his mouth to the other. "I've made up my mind that if the Army can't stop this Indian trouble, then it's up to me."

"You're going out and fight them all by yourself. How brave."

"Don't be funny," he suggested. "Amy, I want to recruit a private army, say two hundred men. That's all I'll need, two hundred men and thirty days. After that, there won't be any more Indian trouble."

"I don't think the Army will let you do that, Dan."

"How can they stop me? By the time they find me, I'll have solved their problems for them. Hell, Amy, it takes a Texan to fight Indians. Not these Yankee cavalrymen with their pack horses and sabers." He rubbed his hands together. "I figure I can get the men. Pay them one hundred dollars."

She did some mental arithmetic. "Twenty thousand dollars?"

He nodded. "You'd have to loan it to me, Amy. I just don't have that kind of cash now."

For a moment she studied him carefully, then said, "Dan, is there anything—anything at all that you don't figure you can do better than anyone else?"

"Now that you mention it, no."

"If you do this, you're going to get some good men killed. Maybe yourself, too. If you lose, Dan, you're going to lose it all. Do you understand that? You'll be broke, because the farmers will be gone and you'll be holding a lot of notes you can't collect on, and you'll have to pay back the twenty thousand you want to borrow from me, and I'll take the store in satisfaction of it."

"You wouldn't do that to me, would you, Amy?"

"Yes, if it means cutting you back to size. I liked the old honest, optimistic Dan Canby, but I can't stand the greedy, too-big-for-his-britches Dan Canby. If you want to come downstairs to the hotel safe, I'll get your money. But you'll sign a note for it and put up your store for security."

"That's drawing blood, Amy."

"It's business, the way you've taught it. A deal?"

He laughed. "What choice do I have? I've got to save these farmers to save myself."

The simple way to gather men, Canby knew, was to put on a barbecue and roll out six barrels of beer and a keg of whiskey; he hired three men to ride around the county, passing the word.

The affair was scheduled for Sunday on the courthouse lawn, and the crowd was large, as he'd expected it to be, for social gatherings were few and far between and a person couldn't beat free barbecue and beer.

There were games and sack races and dancing until early evening, and after everyone had eaten, the men gathered on the south side to hear what Canby had to say. They sat on the grass and drank and smoked, and he made his speech, made it carefully, playing on their native prejudice against Indians, and on their fears that what was happening to the farmers could just as easily be happening to them.

Canby was careful not to say anything that these men could really disagree with, and after he had made certain they shared his view that the Army just wasn't doing the job, he gave them his offer: a hundred dollars for one month's work; they would furnish their own horse, gear, gun, and ammunition.

They would, under his command, and the Confederate flag if it made them feel better, wipe out this Indian menace once and for all.

He listened to a lot of opinions. Some liked it, and some didn't, and a lot of men didn't know, but he kept on talking, kept on selling, and when he had sold enough, he began recruiting. He got out a book, and the men formed two lines to sign names or put down their mark, and when this was going well, he turned the recruitment over to one of his bank clerks and came over to where Ben Talon leaned against a tree.

"I didn't see you step up there, Ben," Canby said.

"You're not about to. Dan, this is the dumbest stunt you're ever liable to pull. Leave the Army alone. They'll get the job done."

"Not fast enough."

"You're going to get these men killed."

"They're grown men. They know the risks." He grinned and clamped his teeth firmly into his cigar. "I may surprise you, Ben. The laugh will be on the other end if I do the job and don't get a lot of them killed."

"My opinion stands; this is stupid."

Canby let his pleasure fade. "Ben, some people might say that you're scared."

"You're entitled to an opinion," Talon admitted. "Good luck, Dan." He turned and walked around the stone building and found his wife in the buggy. Amy Leland was there, and they stopped talking when he came up. "Where did Canby get the money to hire men?"

"I loaned it to him," Amy said casually.

"You know, he's apt to get himself killed."

"Yes, I've thought about that, but it's a gamble I'll have to take. Dan doesn't think anyone can lick him, Ben. I think he can be licked. The point is, it can't be a little licking. It's got to be a whopper, something that'll drive him down so hard he'll hurt his knees and have to take the slow way up. It's got to be a licking that will drive sense back into him."

"He stands to lose everything, Amy. Money, his life maybe."

"Yes, I know that. And that's why I want him to do this. He's got to learn that there really is more trouble in this world than he can handle. You won't ride with him?"

"Not a chance," Ben Talon said. "Ready to go home, Emily?"

"Yes, I'm getting tired." She slid over in the seat and he climbed aboard. "Come out if you can, Amy." She adjusted her bonnet, and Talon clucked the team into motion, turning out onto the street.

As soon as Ben Talon reached home, he went into the study and wrote a letter to Col. Harry Bolton and sealed it. He gave it to the horse wrangler and sent him on his way to Fort Griffin, warning him to stay awake and not to loaf along the way.

He didn't like to be the one to tell Bolton about Canby's plan, but someone had to, and Bolton would be sure to hear about it, anyway, and warned this way, he might be able to stop Canby. The Army did not need another force in the field, a force that was ragtag to begin with and possibly at cross purposes with military policy.

The cook went into town with the wagon for supplies and brought back the word that Dan Canby and a hundred men had ridden out the day before, heading northwest toward the Red River, the last known location of the Comanches.

In a sense, Ben Talon was relieved, for he believed that the Comanche bands had already cut back and were running south, regrouping there. If this was correct, then Canby was going to ride his men out, cover a lot of dry Texas real estate and get nothing for his trouble except saddle gall.

What Canby had no way of knowing, and Talon certainly could not know, was that Colonel Bolton and four companies of cavalry had managed to cut the Comanche-Kiowa trail near Palo Duro Creek, just a few miles from the Indian Nations. In a flanking movement Bolton and his force began to run the Indians south, making no contact with them, but keeping them in sight.

The Indians didn't want to fight; they weren't ready because the moon wasn't right and they didn't have the medicine for it, or some other reason; they were in the mood to run, but not too fast, for they wanted to wear the cavalry out, then cut about and kill them.

After four days the Indians stopped at one of Amy Leland's old abandoned relay stations, drank from the well, filled their water bags, and moved on. The cavalry, in close pursuit, did not stop, feeling that their supplies and water would hold out, and they had never before been so close to the enemy.

There was some fighting, sporadic sniping, a delaying action with light casualties on both sides, but the Indians moved on, turning west as though meaning to make a raid on Tascosa, and the Army pursued them, pushing hard to catch them.

For sixteen days the Indians led the Army by the nose, always avoiding contact except for isolated scout activity where a few shots were fired back and forth. Bolton, worn thin by this time, riding a very tired horse, knew that his command could not continue without a rest; he ordered a camp established on the Red River, planning to get on the move again soon enough to keep the Indians running.

But when day came, a thin gray light, the prairie was empty. Each rise was studied carefully through field glasses, and scouts bellied out and had a better look and came back and reported that the Indians were gone.

Dan Canby's citizen army made contact with the Indians on one of the Red's uncharted forks. The Indians were camped when Canby's scouts found them and reported back, and a mood of jubilation swept through the ranks, and Canby was hard put to it to keep them from attacking recklessly right away.

He managed to impose his will on them by threatening not to pay them if they disobeyed his orders, and then he made plans. Splitting the force in three parts, twenty men on each flank and sixty to make the frontal assault, he intended to attack at night. He had already selected several men as lieutenants; they were to be in command of the flanking force and move in when the assault took place.

There was a mass checking and oiling of weapons and a lot of bragging about how many dead Comanches would be left on the prairie come morning.

Canby was careful to keep up an optimistic front, but he knew that he had bought twenty thousand dollars worth of trouble; the scouts had estimated the Indian force at around a hundred and fifty, all fighting men; no squaws or children. Canby's original intention of taking two hundred men had never sounded better, and he was sorry that he had been eager and settled for less. But it was too late to retreat now. A man had to do with what he had, and surprise would help even the odds.

He had them mount up around midnight, and they moved out, splitting into three segments. The night swallowed them, for there was no moon and the stars gave next to no light at all. Yet a man could see, could make out the lay of the land, and Canby moved his men forward with great care; there was no talking or smoking, and the riders tried not to make the saddle leather squeak.

Finally he topped a rise and saw fires in the Indian camp, and this made him pause, for it was a foolish thing to build fires with an army on the prowl, but then he supposed it was like an Indian to do a stupid thing, and thought no more of it.

He led the charge because it was the thing to do, and they went into the camp, shooting and yelling, and a lot of Indians shot back, but it wasn't half as bad as Canby had imagined it would be. He lost a few men, then the flanking force struck with a fury, taking the horse herd in one fell swoop.

Canby led his men through, wheeled, and came back, and

the Indians were a little better organized now, although he supposed that no more than fifty or sixty put up much of a fight.

Some buck put a bullet into Canby's horse and it fell; he pitched off, rolled, and came up shooting, killing a Kiowa who was leveling a rifle at him. Dust was thick now; the horses were milling around, and the air had a dense stench of powder smoke, and bullets were flying about in a fashion he felt most dangerous, so he went belly down on the ground and let the fighting swirl around him.

From his place he could see that the Texans were winning, but it didn't seem that the Comanches were putting up the kind of a fight their reputation called for. Half of them were not fighting at all but crawling around, trying to find someplace to hide.

And the Texans kept riding in and out, shooting at everything that moved, and Canby wondered how the hell he was going to signal them to stop. In that moment he wished that he'd never gotten himself into this at all, but it was too late to think about that.

It seemed that many of the Indians were breaking away, losing themselves in the darkness. He yelled for men to go after them, but no one paid a bit of attention to him, and he gave up and stretched back down on the ground and let the fight die out of its own spent energy.

For more than thirty minutes riders pounded back and forth, their blood up, shooting at Indians on the ground, Indians running, and at themselves. But it stopped as he'd known it would, and he supposed they had used up all their ammunition, and he felt like swearing at them, but this wasn't the Army; there was no discipline, and losing his temper would only start a fight.

Finally he gathered about him those men he had placed in charge. Six Texans were dead and eleven more were wounded, two of these badly, and no one expected them to live out the night.

He was faced now with things he hadn't even thought of, like medical supplies and a doctor to do what he could. They had nothing, and they made camp there until morning. None of them got much sleep, with the wounded moaning in pain and the bad ones screaming until they died.

Canby thought the damned dawn would never come, but it did, and as soon as it was light, he had fires built and walked around, taking stock of things. The Texans were all through with fighting; you could see it in their eyes. Some of them spoke of mounting up and going home, but Canby wouldn't have it, and they stayed because they didn't want to get into a gunfight with him.

By his estimation, there were seventy dead Indians, and thirty of those had died from gunshot wounds. The others had just died, and when the daylight finally grew stronger, he could see why they had died.

They were covered with running sores, and the word went through the camp like a brush fire: smallpox.

There would have been an instant exodus if the Army had not arrived, the bugler sounding his horn in bright, ripping tones, and the point arriving with the main body coming over a rise.

A young second lieutenant and a sergeant approached first, and Canby was envious of this beardless youth, so efficient, so sure of himself; the lieutenant immediately appraised the situation correctly, ordered the Army to stay out of the camp, but to surround it completely.

The sergeant relayed these orders, and the young officer reported to Colonel Bolton, who, joined by three others, approached Canby. The colonel was in a foul frame of mind; Canby could gather that much from the man's expression.

"Are you the imbecile in charge, Canby?" Bolton asked, stripping off his gloves. "You've done a fine job here. Left alone, the Indians would have camped here and died of smallpox or recovered from it, but now you've scattered them, and it'll spread like the wind." He looked around at the Texans. "And all of these fine citizens have been exposed to it. You've done well, Canby. You ought to get a medal for stupidity."

"How in hell was I to know?" Canby said, then wished he hadn't.

"That's a bright question. In the first place, the Army would have taken care of the Indians, but you wanted it done yesterday. When the hostiles failed to attack us and the surgeon examined a dead Indian we found, he diagnosed smallpox, and we knew what to expect. Then do you know what we did, Mr. Canby? Instead of going off half-cocked, we sat down and thought about it. We started dealing with facts, not emotion, and because we did that, we believe we managed to learn the truth and act wisely. It came to our immediate attention that the hostiles were getting sick, and all at the same time. This could only mean that they contracted the disease at the same time, and since we have been following them for some time now, we reasoned that they got it at the well where the old relay station used to be. One of our doctors is there now taking a sample for examination." He put his hands on his hips and looked around the camp. "You and your men will remain here, under constant guard for three weeks at the least. When my surgeons are satisfied that you are not carrying the disease, you will be permitted to leave. Now I suggest that you take your ragtag outfit away from here, move upstream a hundred yards, and establish a camp. A military detail will burn this one. Any questions?"

"Colonel, we don't have enough rations to last—"

"Oh, I suspected as much," Bolton said. "Canby, you're not bright. Not bright at all."

"You don't have to rub it in."

"I guess I don't. Look around, Canby. Look at their faces. They know when they've been led by a fool."

"Hell, we can all make mistakes!"

"This big?" Bolton asked, then turned to one of his officers without waiting for an answer. "Send in a squad for a wagon and supplies. I want two companies to remain here on guard duty. The rest will form in the morning for the march back."

"Yes, sir."

"Dismissed," Bolton said and turned back to Dan Canby. "For your information, I gave orders before I left to have the farmers moved out of this locality. In fact, I'm cleaning out the county at least until the Indians are on the reservation. The farmers stir the Indians up, and we can't have that, can we?"

"What the hell am I supposed to do about the notes I hold?"

"Why don't you make a fire of them?"

"I'll have to close my bank, colonel!"

"Yes, we'll miss it," Bolton said dryly. "Don't look for sympathy from me. You can always go to farming. After all, you're sitting on a section here and a section there right smack dab in Ben Talon's range. If you know how to plant potatoes, you won't starve."

"You're the funniest thing I've ever heard," Canby snapped. "I lose my shirt and you make jokes." He pawed his mouth out of shape. "And I went and signed a note and put my store up for security so I could pay these men to—" He dropped his hand and fell silent, shaking his head. "How am I going to pay that back now?"

"Now you did get yourself in the hole, didn't you?" Colonel Bolton sighed and pulled on his gloves. "Well, I've got to get a burial detail organized here. You just can't leave dead Indians scattered around the prairie; it isn't tidy."

He walked away and Canby stood there. Several Texans came over, and one said, "If those Indians hadn't of took sick, the Army'd still be chasing its own tail. They've got a helluva nerve telling us what to do. Damned if I'm goin' to stay here under guard."

"The soldiers will shoot if you try to break away," Canby said. "Can't you see that?"

"I can shoot back."

This angered Canby because in this man's hardheaded stubbornness he saw much of his own, and he'd had enough of it. Taking the man by the collar, Canby shook him a little and said, "Don't give me any trouble, Mushy. Don't give anyone else any, either. I can get enough dumb ideas of my own without you coming up with any. Now go on and do as you're told. When a soldier tells you to jump, you just ask how far."

They left him alone, and he sat down on the ground and added it all up and didn't come up with much. There was no doubt in Dan Canby's mind that Amy would take the store; she was that kind of woman, tough enough to stick to her bargains, and she'd see that he stuck to his. The bank was finished; he had no cash reserves, and as soon as word of this got around, depositors would make a run on it, wipe him right out of business.

He had the freight line, and that was all, and right then he was sorry he had that; without it he could just pack up and move someplace else and get another start.

The fact that he could think of such a thing shocked him, angered him anew. Quit, hell! He'd rather take a job sweeping out the saloon. No one was ever going to say that he had quit because he'd been beaten.

He felt better, having decided this, and got up and went over to where the Texans were setting up camp.

13

NONE OF Dan Canby's men returned home until late June. Nearly twenty never came back at all, for some had died in the fighting and the smallpox took the rest.

Colonel Bolton managed to visit the Vale place for a talk with Ben Talon; he related in detail what had happened on the fork of the Red, and this was the first accurate account any of them had, which made it bad news, yet good news, for it ended the worry of many.

Bolton lived with his Indian trouble; they were to the south now, spreading sickness among themselves, and there was little fight in them because they believed their medicine had turned bad and their leaders had lost control.

He also had a new second in command, a Colonel MacKenzie who had a great grasp of situation and a lot of fire and ambition, which gave Bolton some free time to worry about civilians and mule-headed Texans like Dan Canby. Bolton talked and Talon listened, then argued, and Bolton kept talking, and Talon's arguments grew weaker, and finally he agreed that Bolton was right and promised to talk to Fred Early.

Early was sitting on the profits from last year's drive, and he had nine thousand steers on the trail when Talon rode into his yard and joined him on the porch.

"Going to be a hot summer," Early said, pointing to a vacant chair.

"Aren't they all?" He sat down and fanned his face with his hat. "I suppose you heard what happened to Canby?"

Early nodded. "Serves him right. Lucky for him the Indians took the smallpox or his whole bunch might have been wiped out."

"I don't know about that," Ben said. "Canby went off half-cocked, but nobody can say he isn't a good fighter. The Indians' getting sick was just as lucky for the Army as it was for Dan."

Early looked at Talon carefully. "What are you selling, Ben?"

Talon laughed. "Now why would I be selling—"

"You are. I can feel it. And I know I won't like it."

"You're right, Fred." He mopped sweat from his face. "As soon as Dan gets back, the depositors will make a run on his bank. We just can't let that happen."

"I can. I ain't got a dime in there."

"That's what I came to see you about. I'm depositing ten thousand. On my way now and stopped in to see if you'd care to ride in with me and make a deposit." He held up his hand to keep Early from protesting. "Fred, the county needs Canby's bank. However wrongheaded he may have been in the way he went about it, Canby's bank and Canby's gambles and Canby's guts have kept the carpetbagger crew out of our immediate neighborhood. It's either Canby or some Yankee moving in. I'm convinced that we've got to save him."

"You do that and Canby will be right back where he was, selling parcels of land out from under us all."

Ben Talon shook his head. "Not this time, Fred. Before we deposit the money, we'll go into partnership with Canby. You and I can outvote him on any loan. Keep the lid on him."

The notion appealed to Early, and he smiled. "By golly now, I never thought of that. I've always wanted to do a little banking; that's a fact." He heaved his bulk out of the chair. "Ten thousand you say? Give me a few minutes."

Early and Ben Talon rode into town together and immediately saw the crowd in front of the bank. The door was closed, and the shades were drawn, and Talon stopped and spoke to a man. "Canby inside?"

"He's at the hotel. But we're waitin'."

Talon nodded to Early, and they rode on and tied up in front of Canby's store. They crossed the porch and went inside. Amy Leland was behind the counter, and she smiled at them.

"I trust you gentlemen have come in to buy?"

"Came in to see Dan," Talon said. He glanced at one of the clerks. "Go over to the hotel and roll him out."

The man glanced at Amy, and she nodded slightly, and the man peeled off his apron and left. Early turned his head to watch him leave, then said, "You the boss now, Miss Leland?"

"I called my note when it was due," she said. "The place is mine, lock, stock, and barrel. Good merchandise but no bargains. Help yourself to the crackers, though."

"Dan knows this?" Talon asked.

Amy nodded. "He came here first thing. I offered him a job —twelve dollars a week. He stomped out, went to the hotel, and I haven't seen him since."

"See him now," Early said softly and nodded toward the open door. Canby was stalking across the street, and he stomped onto the porch, then stopped just inside the door. He was much thinner, and he wore scars on his face and neck that would never fade.

"Hello, Ben. You want to offer me something, too? Everybody's feeling so damned generous. Amy offered me a job, so let's hear what you have up your sleeve."

"Fred and I came in to make a deposit," Talon said. "Ten thousand apiece. We figure it will be enough to stop a run on your bank."

Dan Canby looked from one to the other. "What's the catch, Ben?"

"Fred and I are full partners. Each with a third of the business."

"And each with a third of the say on how to run it?"

"You catch on fast for a fella who's been sick," Early said. "Take it or leave it. I don't feel like bargaining."

"Neither do I," Canby said wearily. He walked over and leaned against the counter and folded his arms. "My foolishness caused some good men to die. I've put the depositors' money into unsound speculation, and I'm stuck with parcels of land I can't sell. I've lost my store. Frankly, I've lost a lot of pride, and I've come to realize that maybe I wasn't big enough to be a big shot. I believe I need some partners who have more sense than I have."

"All right, it's done then," Talon said, handing his saddle-bag to Fred Early. "Go find the cashier and get him to open the bank. See that everyone in town knows about the deposit. Get those people to go home and leave their money alone."

Early nodded. "Be careful if he starts to horse-trade," he said, nodding toward Canby. Then he went out and down the street.

"He sounds like he doesn't trust me," Canby said.

"Do you blame him? Dan, there's a few things to settle before we go any further. First, sell the freight line. You can find a Yankee speculator who'll pay more than it's worth."

"Why should I? It's making money."

"Damn it, man, we're just saving the bank. We're not pulling you out of anything. You played loose with the depositors' money, and now you've got to dig down in your pocket and make up the difference. The only thing you have left to sell is the freight line. Now about those sections the farmers started to plow up—we may sit down and do some across-the-board trading so that the bank's property is in one lump. We might be able to sell it as a ranch to one of the partners—for instance, you—and have the bank break even on it. But the difference comes out of your pocket."

Canby pursed his lips. "You know, I just thought of something: you turned out to be a better Texan than me, and you're a Yankee."

"You damned fool, I was never in a contest with you!" Talon snapped. Then he blew out his temper in a long breath. "Why in hell don't you get some sense, Dan, and ask Amy to marry you?"

"A man wants to be a success before—" He stopped talking and looked at Amy Leland. "I've wanted to ask you, Amy, but somehow all my ideas got in the way. There ain't much left of me now."

"I was thinking," she said, "that what's left is the only part that's worth anything. You told me once you didn't climb high just to fall, but sometimes we do anyway. Nobody cares how far the drop is, but they watch to see how you get up. I'm watching, Dan. And I don't think you're going to disappoint me."

Dan grinned. "Amy, one thing I always liked about you. You were ready to take a gamble whenever you were pretty sure it would turn out right. But I think you're about to take the biggest one yet."

Ben Talon quietly eased himself out the door.

BULLETS FOR THE DOCTOR

WHEN I sat down to write about Walter Judson Ivy, I realized instantly that it just wouldn't do to catch up the story at the point where I met him. There was too much to the man for that and too much had gone on before to firm the mold.

He was from a good Baltimore family; his father had been in the manufacturing business, and was certainly well off financially. Young Ivy had been sent to the best private schools where he was taught what a young gentleman was required to learn and he learned it well; indifferent students are not tolerated, either by the parents or the school.

At the age of fourteen, Walter Judson Ivy shocked his parents by running away from home and signing on a vessel bound for the China trade. He returned four years later, taller, heavier, quite sober and he had an enormous tattoo on his right forearm, which caused his mother to swoon and his father to swear profoundly, and then cast him out of the house.

All of which bothered Walter J. Ivy not at all.

He surprised his father by enrolling in a medical school, paying for it out of his own pocket from savings. His graduation three years later so stirred the pride of Ivy's parents that the Baltimore home was now open to him.

But fathers are always making plans for their sons and sons are always disappointing their fathers; it seems a role each is destined to play. Walter Ivy's father expected him to take up residency in one of the Baltimore hospitals, but young Ivy had a cantankerous streak in him and hied off to Texas. He set up practice in Goliad, which so incensed Ivy senior that he wouldn't even look up the location in his atlas.

And Walter Ivy fanned these fires of disappointment by sending home newspaper accounts of Goliad's wild and lawless development. Ivy's office was a two-room affair over the bank and he set broken bones and delivered babies and plucked cap-and-ball lead out of various and sundry lawless persons who could not seem to keep out of trouble.

Texas, in 1858, was not a land of tranquillity.

Walter J. Ivy was twenty-five when the War between the States broke out and he returned east immediately and took a commission as captain in the medical department. He served tirelessly and well and emerged a lieutenant-colonel, which of course softened his father's heart and the Baltimore home was again open.

A man of commanding presence, Walter J. Ivy was tall and strongly built, with a high forehead and rather thin, tawny hair. He had dense eyebrows and the habit, when vexed or troubled, of shooting them upward so that they seemed in danger of colliding with his hair. His eyes were rather gray with flecks of gold in them and his manner of steadily watching a person could be disconcerting, especially if one was bothered by a feeling of guilt or inadequacy. He always wore a mustache, but kept it trimmed as a concession to hygiene more than to style.

The war's end was many things to many men. To Walter Ivy it was a tiring horror and he was glad to be rid of it, but to his father, who had grown wealthy manufacturing needed goods, it was the termination of large profits. This is not to say that he was a heartless man who enjoyed war; he loathed it and prayed for a quick end to it, yet he was a business man who could not ignore the profit of it.

Walter J. Ivy was twenty-nine years old when he returned to Baltimore, and in his father's conservative mind, this was time to enter the institution of marriage and he went about the business of finding a suitable wife.

As Walter tells it, parties and dances and teas and social affairs were arranged so that he was flung headlong into this cultural pit of dry-mannered, predatory females who batted their eyes and promised pleasures and comforts after the church bells stopped pealing and finally he had a craw full and packed up and left, neglecting, as usual, to announce his intentions.

The world was turning and Walter Ivy felt that he was being left out and the next word his parents received of his whereabouts was a postcard from Fort Reno; Ivy had returned to the army and the Indian campaigns were getting

160

under way and he was simply a man who couldn't miss any of it.

Two years later, in 1867, he was at Fort Grant, Arizona Territory, a post reactivated to do battle with the war-like Apaches, and here I enter, Ted Bodry, nineteen years and two months, a corpsman in the medical department and attached to Colonel Ivy's staff.

I was one of those who resented being born too late for the war and as soon as I finished high school, I enlisted. At nineteen one has few choices and I rejected being a bugler because I have a poor ear for music, so I took what was left, the medical department.

It is hard to say what attracted Colonel Ivy's attention to me; I would like to flatter myself and think that it was because I tried very hard to do my duty well. Whatever it was, I became his orderly and this was the pivotal point in my life.

It was Walter Ivy's urging that led me to accept an early discharge, and it was Walter Ivy who put me on the eastbound stage and it was Walter Ivy who handed me my letter of introduction and recommendation to the dean of the medical school.

I didn't see him again until 1869 when he came home on leave. He was very pale and drawn and he carried a heavy cane and walked with a pronounced limp. Knowing him, it was needless for me to ask how he had been wounded, for he was a selfless man who often risked much to help someone.

I first knew he was back when I was summoned to the dean's office; Walter Ivy sat in a big leather chair by the dean's desk and he got up when I came in and we shook hands. He looked at me, noted the changes two years had made, then smiled and waved his hand for me to sit down.

"I've been looking at your scholastic record, Ted. It seems that one day you'll be a doctor."

"Yes, sir. Next year."

"I'll be in the east for a year," he said, "and I'd take it kindly if you'd spend the holidays with me. Perhaps I could drop in on you from time to time."

"I'd be very flattered, sir."

"Good," he said, feeling that the matter was settled. He smiled and got up slowly and offered his hand again. "I don't want to keep you from your classes, Ted. And I must get home and gird myself to resist the attempts being made to see me married. Father believes that a woman makes a lamb of any man."

I saw him three times after that, then the wild goose called and in 1870 he returned west, to Camp Apache, Arizona Territory and he remained there nearly a year.

My term of study was finished with surprisingly high marks. Graduation approached and all along I expected a letter from Walter Ivy, offering his congratulations, or something.

But there wasn't anything, and. this struck me as odd because I knew he had paid my tuition for three years.

I sat on the platform with my graduating class and looked at the sea of faces and wished that my own parents had lived to see this, then I caught a movement in the back of the hall and Walter J. Ivy walked down the aisle and took a seat near the front. He looked at me and smiled and put everything right with me.

Afterward we went for a walk, Theodore Bodry, M.D. and Walter J. Ivy, M.D. and we fed the birds in the park and watched the swans in the lake and listened to some young fellow serenade his girl with a banjo and an unstable tenor. We could hear her squeals of delighted terror as he rocked the boat, then he would play and she would say, "Oh, Herman, you play divinely." Which he didn't, but then love can make a masterpiece of any tawdry canvas.

We talked about what I would do and I expressed a desire to remain in the east for perhaps a year and intern at some hospital to gain surgical experience. Even as I said it, I knew that I had disappointed him and I was sorry to do that, but I kept repeating that I felt unqualified to establish a practice alone.

The position I finally got was in a small over-worked charity hospital and the pay was only two dollars a week, with long hours, poor meals, and a small room of my own.

Walter Ivy and I did not see each other for four months, but I knew that he was still in Baltimore. He was being seen everywhere with Dorsey Pribble, the only daughter of *the* Pribbles, who everyone figured were about as high as you could go with money and good blood.

She was a beauty of the first water, in her early twenties,

162

an intensely courted young woman who had yet to find a man who suited her. Yet she found Walter Ivy attractive enough and there was little doubt in anyone's mind that Ivy had at last fallen in love. But if he had, it wasn't enough to keep him home.

Leaving the army, he went to Victoria, Texas, and established a practice there; I learned this when he wrote and asked me to join him and it took me two hours to pack my bags, buy my ticket and board the westbound train.

Of course this upset Ivy's family and Ivy senior was furious. Mr. and Mrs. Pribble forbade Dorsey ever to speak his name, and when Walter Ivy wrote her, the loyal maid promptly gave the letter to Mr. Pribble, who threw it in the fireplace.

Mr. Pribble believed it was his duty to shield his daughter from cads and irresponsible bounders.

Several letters followed the first into the fire and I arrived in Victoria just in time to take over Walter's practice while he carried out some important private business.

He appeared suddenly at the Pribble house and had some violent words with Mr. Pribble, who just wasn't used to being talked to that way. Mrs. Pribble went into a swoon over the whole affair, which didn't last long because Walter left on the two o'clock train.

Taking Dorsey Pribble with him, of course.

They were married when the train stopped to take on fuel and additional coaches and in the years that followed I always wondered if he went back because he realized that he could not live without her or whether she came west with him because she knew he'd never come back east to stay.

I would say that the entire town turned out to greet them when they got off the stage coach. (In 1873 the trains did not probe that far south and every traveler had to ride the stages.)

Victoria in 1873 was the kind of town that took on a completely different complexion on Saturday night, when everyone for miles around came in to shop and talk and play cards and drink and see the professional girls who kept houses in the back of the main street. Quarrels that began on the range over water or graze were settled in Victoria, and no Saturday evenings ever passed without the sound of pistol fire. And now and then the bullets were directed at objects other than the moon.

Curiosity drew a crowd to Pringer's Hotel, where the stage line kept a passenger office. Walter Ivy was a popular man and it was only good manners to pay respects to the new bride.

I was on a call at the time and couldn't be there, but Aaron Stiles ran a vivid account of it in his paper. She was, according to Stiles, beautiful, young, and a bit alarmed but she had breeding and pride and seemed to accept the hooraw with friendliness. For Victoria, Texas, of the quick-trigger, quick-judgment school, this was more than enough and to all appearances, at least according to Stiles's fulsome article, the town had instantly accepted Dorsey Ivy.

Long before Walter Ivy went east to claim his bride, he had begun construction of a house and offices at the west edge of town. He selected a shady spot and the house was still full of sawed pine and paint flavors when he carried the lady across the threshold. Furniture had been wagoned in from Austin, the terminus of the railroad in those days, and a deep carpet covered the parlor floor and drapes hung heavy over the windows.

His offices were in the east wing of the house, five rooms, one serving as a five-bed hospital. I shared these offices with Walter Ivy and the night he got home it was well after dark when I put my horse in the barn and walked toward the house, not realizing until I reached the porch that he was back.

The housekeeper let me in, took my bag and coat and pistol—any man, even a doctor, would indeed be foolish to travel without a firearm with Indians about—then she said, "Dr. Ivy has returned with his bride."

"Well I'll be go to the devil," I said.

He must have heard me, heard our voices; anyway he came to stand in the kitchen doorway. "Ted," he said, laughing. "Come in here now."

When I came up to him he took my arm and steered me into the kitchen. "Dorsey, this is Dr. Ted Bodry, whom I've spoken of so often."

She turned from the stove where she had been making coffee and she looked directly at me with the brownest eyes

164

I have ever seen. In my opinion she was taller than average; I would judge near five-foot-eight, but she had a magnificent figure. Her face was inclined to the square side, but well-proportioned, with fine bones and a good jaw.

When she took my hand I was surprised to find it warm; most women have cold hands. I liked her, and perhaps I was instantly on guard against her, if you can understand how it can be proper to feel so about another man's wife. "Ted, I really have heard much about you. Walter is very proud of you."

But she looked at my youth and inexperience and rather made me feel as though I should apologize for it. I let go of her hand and said, "I won't ask you how you like Texas because most people who come here don't. But I can promise that it has a certain charm although I haven't yet discovered what it is."

"I'm sure I will," she said. "Women are very adaptable. Would you like some coffee?"

"Did you make it or did Mrs. Hempstead?"

"Why, I did." She laughed. "Does it matter?"

"After you drink it awhile, it does," Walter said and sat down at the table. She brought cups and sugar and cream. I rubbed my eyes because I'd been on the go since a quarter to six that morning. Walter said, "Did Mrs. Lovering come to her time?"

"Delivered day before yesterday. A girl. Everything is fine. I took a shoat and six layers. Is that all right?"

Dorsey frowned. "Shoat? Isn't that a pig?"

"A pig it is. And six laying hens. I'd say we were well paid, doctor." He lifted his wife's hand and kissed it. "My dear, sometimes we even get money for our services. Isn't that right, Ted?"

"Yes," I agreed. I glanced at Dorsey, then said, "I picked up a new patient while you were gone. One of Dirty Esther's girls came to me with symptoms that I diagnosed as gonorrheal urethritis. Naturally it's advanced, as you'd expect it to be. Chronic bilateral salpingitis."

Dorsey touched Walter Ivy on the arm. "Is he talking about what I think he's talking about? At the table? In mixed company?"

"Yes, he's talking about a woman of easy virtue who has

165

a social disease," Walter Ivy said. "Not a delicate subject, my dear, but,"—and he sighed over this—"we treat the sick without judging them, or asking for credentials."

"The poor woman," Dorsey said, genuinely touched. She reached out and patted my arm. "You go right ahead and discuss your cases, Ted. I will simply have to learn to be a doctor's wife. And I will."

And she did, but it took a long time.

2

THAT SUMMER stands out in my mind, not because it was a particularly good summer, but because it was an eventful one. The two biggest cow outfits were the Spindle and the T-Cross; they each carried a hundred men on the payroll and since they both made cattle drives north each spring, they both had money and a lot of it.

Of the two outfits, Spindle was a little better situated; they had the best water because Old Man Brittles got his crew to dam up some reservoirs. This cost him a good bit of money and Beachamp of the T-Cross thought it was a great foolishness and a waste. And a lot of people sided with Beachamp because he'd been there ten years and the summers were blessed with thunder showers which kept the creeks up and the grass green.

But that summer the last rain came on the seventeenth of April, and it wasn't much of a rain, lasting barely the afternoon. Of course, at the time none of us knew it was going to be the last rain and as a matter of fact no one paid any attention to it, except me.

An emergency call to a small ranch eight miles out of town got me out of bed around dawn; the father was highly agitated so when I went out to hitch up the buckboard, I took a look at the cloudless sky and left town with nothing more than my medical bag, a shotgun and a rolled raincoat.

Walter Ivy had delivered the Stiles' baby four days before and at the time I was in the northern part of the county officiating as coroner. (Walter and I had agreed to rotate this civic duty on a yearly basis.) So the Stiles' baby was really Walter Ivy's patient, but he was in Austin trying to increase his usual purchase of medical supplies and I was on my way to Pete Stiles' place.

Because we hurried, we made the distance in a shade under two hours and I went in to see what I could do. Stiles was a poor man, twenty-some, a hard worker trying to make a go on one section. His wife was young, about fifteen, and this was her first child.

They lived in one big room and she was holding the baby when I came in. Stiles stood awkwardly as fathers do when they are helpless and I put down my hat, shotgun and bag and asked a few questions.

"What seems to be wrong?"

"He pukes all the time," Mrs. Stiles said.

I took the baby from her and laid him on the table and examined him. He was obviously not gaining weight and he had thin, dry, loose skin. It was apparent that he was getting little nourishment and I turned to ask her if her breasts were drying up, but the question was needless. She was swollen and in discomfort and the front of her dress was damp from leakage.

After examining the infant's eyes, I listened to his heart, thumped him front and back, then said, "Mrs. Stiles, will you please nurse the child?"

Already I was reaching a conclusion, but I wanted to make sure.

Stiles started to make a fuss about, "My wife ain't goin' to show her tits— "

I ran him out of the house.

Mrs. Stiles nursed the baby for a moment or two; he was very weak and could barely nurse, then he was seized with a fit of projectile vomiting.

"I'll have to take the baby into town," I said and went to the door to call Stiles. He came in and stood there, not knowing what to do. "The child has pyloric stenosis." He didn't understand and to keep it from sounding dreadful, I tried to explain what the matter was all about. "This is a spasm of the pyloris muscle which acts as a valve and closes off the discharge end of the stomach. However I believe this is congenital. That is, I believe he was born with a restriction."

"Is he goin' to die?" Stiles asked.

"I'll have to perform an operation. Usually it is quite simple and safe. That's why I want you to put some straw in the back of the buckboard and ride into town with me."

He jawed and argued and didn't want his child cut into and cut up a fuss, but there's no need to go into that because

168

I won out and took the child to town. And it rained on the way and because Stiles owned no slicker, we wrapped the baby in mine, and I got soaked to the skin.

I operated that afternoon and the child showed immediate signs of recovery while I showed signs of coming down with a good cold. The child returned home in three days and Walter Ivy came back in time to let me go to bed with a roaring fever.

In his absence I had made nearly thirty house calls, plucked two bullets out of the stage driver after a brief brush with Comanches, delivered the Wringle baby which came ten days earlier than either of us expected—but you run into those things when a wife insists on plowing in that condition—and performed the abdominal surgery on the Stiles' infant, for which I had collected the sum of nineteen dollars, some poultry, a calf, a gold watch which I was holding in trust, and many words of thanks.

Over the years I've clung to the firm belief that few, if any, modern doctors can comprehend the demands made on a physician and surgeon in frontier practice. San Antonio, nearly a hundred miles to the northwest, boasted three doctors, and Goliad, a little more than half that distance to the southwest, had one doctor, for Walter Ivy had once practiced there and he never left a town unless he could get a doctor and a druggist to establish themselves there.

Still we served an immense country, three counties really and often we would ride for two days to tend a person too ill to be brought to us. It was a dangerous time with the Indians and all, and all men, save perhaps the boy boxing groceries in the store, performed dangerous work. And even that was not without risk because Linus Cohill's horse kicked him one afternoon, broke three ribs, then dragged the iron-shod rim of the wagon wheel over his foot and broke two toes.

Add to this the firearms-supported arguments, the broken bones from horse wrangling and the gorings from wild Texas cattle and it added up to a lively practice because all these things were in addition to the child bearing and the fevers and diseases which plague the innocent.

Since Walter Ivy and myself were considered well educated, we had other responsibilities. As I mentioned, we took turns being county coroner. This was not an attempt to evade responsibility, but since we served two counties, I was coroner in one while Walter Ivy served the other. Each year we swapped, running unopposed, and I suppose, being elected unanimously. At least I never talked to a man who had voted against us.

Walter was a Free Mason and was one of the Worthy-something-or-other; I was an Odd Fellow myself and pretty deeply entrenched in that. I'll never understand how I got on the school board and town council, and Walter to this day swears that his being a deacon in the Baptist Church was an accident since he had been an Episcopalian all his life.

So I was in bed with a fever when Walter got back from Austin and Dorsey was nursing me and all day long bringing in a steady stream of people who wanted to know what "Causes this terrible pain in my back, doctor?"

Yes, that was the summer all right, with a scalding sun and heat like a blanket every day. It was a summer exactly suited to a young man when the juices ran strong and he could go to bed exhausted and wake up with a bounce.

That was the summer when everyone watched the sky for the rain that never came and finally, around August, the creeks were down to a trickle and Beachamp started looking hate at those watersheds on Spindle land and watching Spindle steers fatten, for Brittles was going to weather it out and Beachamp knew that he couldn't.

I don't think there was anyone who didn't know that trouble was coming, but none of us knew what to do to head it off. Now and then, when we were lucky enough to get to sit down to a meal together we'd talk about it. Tempers, especially between the two spreads, were growing wire tight, and to keep things from coming to a head, Brittles had taken to bringing his crew in on Friday night and leaving the town to T-Cross on Saturday.

We all hoped that this would work and complimented Brittles on his consideration; the old man had fought for his land and knew what range war meant. Brittles knew that there was nothing wrong that a good rain wouldn't cure.

But come September it hadn't rained a drop.

There weren't even any clouds in the sky.

I was in my office at mid-afternoon, trying to rest because I had a patient eleven miles out of town who would be starting labor any time and since it was her first child, I was a bit concerned that it would take some time.

Dorsey knocked on my door, which was odd because she didn't do that unless I had a patient, and she knew that I was alone. She wore a thin cotton dress, trying to defend herself against the heat, but sweat darkened the shoulders and ran in small rivulets down her neck.

She sat down and said, "Dr. Bodry, I'd like to discuss pregnancy."

This brought my eyes open and she laughed softly. "Does Walter—"

"I don't think doctors like to attend their wives unless they have to," she said. "I've missed two periods."

We discussed the situation briefly and an examination confirmed her suspicions. I placed the birth somewhere in the middle of April and she seemed very pleased with herself. "He'll be wonderful with children," she said. "Of course, I'll have to write mother. Perhaps this—"

It wasn't my place to pry, but we were good friends, so I asked, "Dorsey, are you happy here?"

"Yes, Ted, happier than I've ever been."

"But you'd be happier if your mother would answer your letters," I said. "It's a rotten shame, that's what it is! People have to understand."

"It takes time," she said and got up from her chair. "Walter will be home tonight. While you're at lodge I'll tell him."

"You're young and strong and have good bones," I said, "and there are no reasons for concern or complications."

"I'm not afraid, Ted."

"Well, no, I didn't mean that." I said. "If Walter begins to act like a typical father—"

She shook her head. "Walter has never been a typical anything. It's part of his charm." Then she smiled again and went out and I was very pleased; Walter Ivy deserved a child and I hoped that it would be a boy.

Since it was my lodge night, I ate at the hotel, played a few games of pool, bought several cigars and walked three blocks east to the Odd Fellows hall. Afterward I had a drink at the bar, talked about the heat and the damned rain that kept holding off, then went home.

Since Walter had returned with his wife, I used a small side

171

room behind my office for sleeping quarters; it was ample for a bachelor and my comings and goings would not disturb them in the least.

I intended to travel at night to avoid the heat and I was in the barn, hitching up the buckboard when Walter Ivy came out. He leaned against a post for a moment, then said, "Ted, when you examined Dorsey, did you notice anything that—"

"She's very healthy," I said, "and I predict a normal delivery. Didn't she tell you that?"

"Yes, but I thought she was setting my mind at ease." He rubbed the back of his neck. "You have no idea how this pleases me, Ted, but we must take care. Nothing must happen to her."

"Nothing will, Walter."

"Yes, yes, I'm sure, still I wish you'd examine urine specimens frequently. If there's any toxemia or a possible diabetes mellitus—" He pawed his mouth out of shape and busied himself with the lighting of a cigar. "Pyelitis takes so many woman in childbirth that—"

"Walter, you know I'll take every precaution," I said. "And Dorsey said you wouldn't act like a typical father."

"Did she say that?" He smiled. "Well, I'm not typical. I'm a doctor and can keep my worry specific."

"Keep this up and you'll turn into an old fud," I said and checked my shotgun before getting into the buggy. Then I made sure my bag was complete, got in and backed out of the barn.

"When can I expect you back?" Walter asked.

I counted the days in my mind. "Try Saturday late, if the Indians don't get me."

"That's not very funny. You have your pistol?"

"Put it on with my pants," I said and drove out of the yard, taking the south road toward the Espirito Santo Mission, ruins now, but a landmark still.

Night traveling had the advantage of minimizing worry about the Indians for they were governed largely by superstition and would not sally forth at night. Still it was no time for a man to doze and I drove with the shotgun across my knee, keeping to a pace that would cover miles and yet save the team.

I cut across T-Cross land and after midnight I raised a line shack.

Three men melted out of the darkness, all heavily armed and I identified myself. Then a lamp was lighted and someone stirred up the fire and put on coffee.

No one thought it strange that I'd be about late at night; a doctor goes all the time, everywhere. I went into the shack and had my coffee, mentioning casually my destination and they nodded, taking note of this; they weren't a gabby bunch at all.

Refreshed, I got into the rig again and rode out, not stopping until the first flush of dawn brightened the sky and pushed back the darkness across the land. My destination was not far, a scant eight or nine miles and I reckoned to make it before the morning heat grew too intense.

The land was quiet. That sounds strange to say, upon reflection, but that was the way it was. Quiet. And land isn't quiet for there are birds hawking and wheeling and animals in the grass rustling about and there is a living, pulsating sound to the land that was now totally absent.

This alerted me and I shifted my pistol holster around to where it was handier and cocked my shotgun and kept one hand on it always. The country was rolling, grassy, with trees dotting the hillsides and I kept an eye on the ridges for there the trouble would come, if it came.

For miles I rode through this vast silence, seeing nothing at all, and then I came to the fork in the road that would lead me to Carl Rowan's place and I followed the path; it was hardly more than that, a bit of grass trampled by the infrequent passage of his wagon.

Finally I could smell smoke. Not fresh smoke, but that strong, rank flavor left by a dead fire and I lashed my team to a quicker pace. Topping a slight rise, I saw the Rowan place, ashes now, with the stone chimney partially crumbled and the fences down and the cattle slaughtered and Rowan, fire-blackened, in the yard where the Comanches had left him.

I knew they would have never taken Mrs. Rowan, not heavy with child, so I got out of the buggy and began to cut a circle around the place until I found her. She was dead,

173

and from the terrible hatchet wound in her head, it had come mercifully quick.

The Indians leave destruction that boggles the mind of man and makes him wonder what possesses them to break every breakable thing they can get their hands on. Rowan's plow was reduced to rubble and I rummaged around what was left of his tool shed and selected a shovel whose handle, although broken, was longer than the others.

I spent the rest of the morning digging graves, and sometimes that was a doctor's duty too.

3

WHEN I returned to town and made my report to the sheriff, it did not cause any alarm; rather it made everyone gloomy, as though with the heat and drought they had to have Indian trouble too. Rowan had some kin over Fort Duncan way and I wrote them a letter, explaining the circumstances, as I knew them, and offered my sympathy and the assurance that they were buried in a Christian manner and that suitable markers had been placed over the graves.

The sheriff and a party of four well-armed men rode out to see if they could pick up the Indians' trail, but I didn't think much would come of that and I expect they didn't either, but they were going to try. Now and then the Indians grew bold and careless and were caught.

A lot of good it did.

Walter Ivy had a case that he thought would be interesting to me and after a lunch at his home, we got into his buggy and drove across town to what was Victoria's better section; the people with the most money seemed to settle there: the banker and the storekeepers and two retired Confederate army officers, if you can consider any Confederate officer 'retired.' Many thought that Dr. Ivy ought to live in that section, but he wouldn't hear of it and I suppose it was because he had been raised in a proper house on a proper street and naturally rebelled against the idea of conformity.

As we drove along he discussed the case: "Yesterday, I got a call from Butram Cardine at the bank. His son, Lunsford, had been taken ill and he wanted me to look in on him. I went to the home and found the young man in bed. He complained of feeling poorly for over a week now, having a sore throat, general malaise, and a low fever."

"Have you examined a blood sample under the microscope?"

Walter Ivy smiled. "Of course. Do you think I'm one of those backward country doctors? The blood spread shows large numbers of mononuclear cells."

"Sounds like virus hepatitis," I said quickly.

"Possibly," Ivy agreed. "But I'd like to have you examine him. I would hate to make a hasty diagnosis of the case and be wrong."

I laughed. "Yes, Cardine is a man of influence."

"To hell with that," Ivy snapped. "I don't like to be wrong with any patient."

We stopped in front of the banker's home; it was a huge white house crouched among huge trees and a colored servant hastened out to take our horses around in back.

A maid opened the front door and we stepped inside. Sunlight through the stained glass foyer windows spread color into the deep green rug. Mrs. Cardine was a rather frail, flighty woman who kept wringing her hands and making puckers with her lips. Lunsford was upstairs, in his room and as we went up the stairs I kept thinking that I didn't like him much. He was near my age and as arrogant as wealth and position could make him, and the damned man was out-right handsome, tall and broad through the shoulders; he was everything I wasn't and I know it was childish, but I resented him no end.

The curtains were drawn to protect his eyes and I opened one near his bed to conduct an examination. His complexion was rather jaundiced, which pretty much confirmed my opinion that he had hepatitis. Really, I could have concluded my examination quickly, but I could not resist taking his temperature. Normally an oral temperature will suffice, and I know that Walter, in dealing with sensitive women, became very Continental and took the temperature under the arm pit.

This would not satisfy me and I put Lundsford Cardine through the position and took a rectal temperature, and knew when I did it that I was making a lifelong enemy.

He had a good fever all right, which cinched things in my mind.

Walter Ivy looked at his watch and said, "Lunsford, you're going to get better in no time. Didn't I see you at the dance two weeks ago?"

He nodded and Ivy patted his arm in a patronizing manner. "Well, you'll be dancing again soon."

We went out and Ivy remained a moment to offer Mrs.

Cardine words of encouragement, and to give her instructions. When he got into the buggy, he said, "What do you think?"

"Virus hepatitis."

"Sure?"

"Yes, I'm sure."

He clucked to the team, turned them and drove down a block and a half and stopped at Rolle Dollar's house. I said, "Is Angeline ill?"

"Feeling poorly," Ivy said and took his bag and we walked to the front door.

Let me say now that I had a special interest in Angeline Dollar; she was eighteen and quite lovely and because her father was very religious, she led an extremely sheltered life, so much so that my desire to call on her socially was constantly being put off by her parents' rigid conformity to manners and morals.

Her mother met us at the door and we went to Angeline's room; it was a dainty place with lace curtains over the windows and a wallpaper designed to reflect the feminine mood.

Angeline was in bed, as I expected her to be and Ivy smiled and sat down and felt her pulse. "You know Dr. Bodry, of course. How are you feeling? I thought I'd bring Dr. Bodry along to examine you. We want to find out just what kind of a bug has bitten you."

"That's nice of you, Dr. Walter," she said and smiled at me with devastating effect. Ivy got up and I sat on the edge of her bed. Examing a woman generally bothered me not at all, but to place my stethoscope against the round bareness of her breast was an experience nigh onto unnerving. When I wiped my thermometer with alcohol and shook it, Walter Ivy watched me carefully, and when I had her tuck it under her armpit, he said, "That's not your accustomed procedure, is it, doctor?"

I had never been so embarrassed.

And it was difficult to think properly with her blue eyes constantly on me, watching my every expression. She had a fever, not very high, but one of those steady burners that promised to mount dangerously.

Her mother stood by the door, her expression drawn with worry. "Is it serious, doctor?"

177

Walter Ivy shook his head. "I really don't think so."

This rather angered me for I had concluded that she had a good virus going and Ivy was making light of it; I consider it an error to delude patients or their families. Still, she was his patient and I held my tongue.

Walter Ivy said, "Angeline, did you go to the dance a few weeks ago?"

"She's not allowed to carry on," Mrs. Dollar snapped. "It was rude of you to ask."

"Of course," Ivy said, mollified. "Do you have any coffee, Mrs. Dollar? A cup would certainly be refreshing. Don't you agree, doctor?"

"Yes," I said, wondering what he was getting at; he was not a man easily molded by suggestion or force.

"I'll put it on," Mrs. Dollar said and left the room.

When her step faded on the stairs, Ivy looked at Angeline and said, "I know you went to the dance with young Cardine. I'm afraid it'll have to come out, my dear."

The beast made her cry and then he stood there, insensitive to her tears. "Come along, doctor," he said dryly.

"Really, Walter, this is highly irregular!" Her tears and his manner riled me.

"Try to be clinical, doctor. She has infectious mononucleosis, commonly called kissing disease. If you read your medical journals more carefully you would have seen my paper on it. It is a virus infection in which the lymph nodes and blood cells are attacked by pathogens." He opened the door to go down stairs. "Dry her eyes if you must but don't kiss her. Not yet at least!"

I thought that last barb totally unwarranted and I patted Angeline's hand, assured her that everything would be all right in spite of this uncouth horse doctor and then followed Ivy to the parlor where Mrs. Dollar was setting out the coffee cups. Walter Ivy was the soul of grace and politeness; he chatted a moment, clearly avoiding the subject of Angeline's illness.

But Mrs. Dollar wouldn't be put off, as I knew she couldn't, and as Walter Ivy knew she wouldn't. "Angeline complained of feeling poorly several days ago but I thought nothing of it."

"A sore throat?" Ivy asked.

178

"Why—yes."

"And a feeling of uneasiness? Perhaps a suggestion of upset stomach?"

"Why—that's it exactly!"

"And of course the fever and the swollen lymph nodes throughout the body," Ivy said, looking at me. "Do you still think it's—"

I waved my hand and drank my coffee; I'd made a big enough fool of myself and it was another Walter Ivy lesson ground in properly.

"Mrs. Dollar, Angeline is suffering from what we call infectious mononucleosis, commonly called, 'kissing disease.'"

I'm positive anyone down the street heard her gasp in shock and dismay. "DoooocTORIIIvy!" she said. "This is unthinkable!"

"Well, that well may be but this disease generally breaks out into an epidemic following dances and general social events where partners of the opposite sex exchange 'soul kisses.'"

I thought she was going to faint; she sagged into a chair, one hand to her breast, her eyes rolling heavenward and I reached for my bag and the smelling salts but Walter Ivy waved me motionless.

"Now, now, Mrs. Dollar, we mustn't let our narrow little minds run away with us. Your daughter, I'm happy to say, is a young girl with strong natural impulses, and young Cardine suffers from the same illness, only in a more advanced stage. When I first examined him, I was misled as Dr. Bodry was, then I began to suspect that he had picked it up from someone, although not in this community. Then when your husband asked me to look in on—"

"Please! Please spare me the horror of it all!" Mrs. Dollar cried.

"Madam, you're dramatizing this entirely out of proportion," Ivy said flatly. Then he did a thing that shocked me; he took her by both arms and shook her until her head bobbed violently and her eyes rolled. "Now listen carefully to me, madam! Your daughter will recover quite naturally in a week or ten days; I'll have Dr. Bodry check on her daily." He looked at me and there was a twinkle in his eyes. "I'm sure he can find time in his schedule."

"Yes," I said and let it go at that. Mrs. Dollar was staring transfixed at Walter Ivy; she had probably never been spoken to quite like that.

"Now I have a few instructions that you will follow to the letter," Ivy said. "Is that clearly understood?" She nodded meekly. "Personal hygiene is very important with the patient; she will take a tub bath daily and wash her hands after voiding. Each morning, immediately after breakfast, she will evacuate the bowels." Again that shocked gasp, but Ivy went on. "To encourage this, give her two glasses of hot fluid upon awakening. Add one teaspoon of bicarbonate of soda and flavor it with tea or lemon juice. Persuade her to remain up as long as possible and to walk around the porch or sit in front of an open window. Fresh air is important. Do not fuss with her diet; allow her to eat and drink what she pleases, but see that she gets lots of fluids." He released his grip and allowed her to relax in the chair. "I'll write out these instructions so you'll make no mistake. Pull yourself together, Mrs. Dollar. This disease is common enough—"

"Common?" She pressed her knuckles to her mouth, turned her head away and cried.

Ivy motioned for me to go upstairs and I was eager enough to do that for Angeline was in a bit of trouble and she should be prepared for it. I knocked lightly and went in and sat on the edge of her bed. "I suppose you heard the wailing downstairs? Well, it'll soon blow over and be forgotten." I took her hand and held it. "Do you think it was worth it?"

She knew what I meant and blushed and turned her face away. "You must think I'm terrible."

"I don't think that at all, and I'll be in to see you every day."

Walter Ivy was waiting for me in the buggy and when I got in, he said, "She'll catch the devil for this all right. Well, into each life a little rain must fall."

"Oh, damn your platitudes," I said and sulked a bit, and felt a little frustrated.

Walter Ivy said, "Just can't make up your mind, can you, Ted?"

"About what?"

"What irritates you more, being wrong in your diagnosis or because Lunsford Cardine had the fun of soul kissin—"

"All right, Walter. Never mind!"

That evening, Dorsey insisted that I have supper with them and since I had no house calls until seven-thirty, I accepted the invitation; I tire quickly of hotel meals for the cooking is not always the best and the diet is very limited: beef, beans, potatoes, tomatoes and greens when in season, bad pie and worse coffee. Travelers, pausing briefly in their journey really have no time to complain, but local people like myself, who haven't the time to prepare meals, have to suffer along with the soda bottle handy and indigestion right around the corner.

As a doctor, it is easy for me to spot a patient who is a bachelor and habitué of hotels and Mexican restaurants; they are over weight from greasy foods, suffer chronic indigestion and constipation, and have foul dispositions.

Mrs. Hempstead, the housekeeper, could pan broil a chicken such as you have never tasted and her pot roast was the talk of south Texas long before the Comanches wiped out her family and she came to work for Walter Ivy.

The thought of one of her meals was a delight and I over ate, as usual, especially when it came to the peach pie. With my call I had to excuse myself early and Walter agreed to meet me in Sharniki's pool hall for a game around nine o'clock, and I was positive I'd be through by then.

I had two calls, both in town. The blacksmith, in shoeing an ox—and they are devils at best—sustained a fractured arm, and since Walter and I had been toying with the plaster of paris and cloth cast, I wanted to check and see if swelling was binding it anywhere and causing him pain. Fortunately it was not; we had a beer, talked a bit and I went across town where I had an elderly patient with an unoperable tumor.

So it was about fifteen minutes to nine when I reached the pool hall. A sultry, dense heat lay over the town and the temperature was still in the nineties. To the south, heat lightning split the sky in ragged streaks; it seemed to be almost a nightly occurrence, but it held no promise of rain although they were getting it around Refuge and San Patricio.

The heat and the lightning only made us envious of those who enjoyed the cooling benefits of rain.

181

Most of Buford Brittles' riders were in town, you could hear them down the street, whooping it up in the saloon and Buford was in the pool hall, playing solitaire. Since Walter Ivy hadn't arrived, I played two hands of double with Brittles; we didn't talk much. Everyone lost their taste for conversation in this heat.

Then Walter Ivy came in and I finished my game and selected a pool cue. He took the break and was pretty decent about it, scattering the balls all over the table. I ran a seven ball in the corner pocket and was lining up the nine ball when my attention was distracted.

Rolle Dollar came in and laid a blacksnake whip on Sharniki's cigar counter, looked intently at Walter Ivy, then said, "I've not laid a whip on a man since I left Georgia." He spoke softly, slowly, drawling the words out, like they do all the time, and suddenly it was very quiet in the place.

A bit of cigar ash fell from Mike Sharniki's smoke and I swear I heard it hit the floor.

Walter Ivy laid his pool cue aside, but kept his hand on it. "You're not going to whip anybody, Rolle," he said.

4

ROLLE DOLLAR was a very tall man and extremely thin as though he were wasted by some undefinable disease. Yet he was a strong man; we all knew that, for he had bodily thrown rowdy cowboys out of his hardware store from time to time. I had never liked the man; his eyes were set close together and bracketed a long, bony nose and he always gave me the impression that his opinion was more valuable than anyone else's.

"There was no call to talk to Mrs. Dollar the way you did," Rolle said. "I won't have any man speaking lies to my wife. Sinful lies. I'll pray to God to wipe out this sin on your soul, Walter Ivy." He slid the whip off the cigar counter and spread ten foot of it out behind him.

There wasn't anyone there who didn't know what a black-snake could do; an average man skilled in handling one was more than a match for a proficient gunman and could cut a man to the bone before he could unlimber his pistol.

Walter Ivy was unarmed and Rolle Dollar knew it, but as I said, it wouldn't have made any difference. Mike Sharniki put both hands on the counter and said, "Rolle, I wouldn't start nothin' was I you."

"I'm the hand of God," Dollar said. "No man need tell me what to do." He watched Walter Ivy with his narrow-eyed stare and Buford Brittles got up and slid back his chair. "Keep out of this, old man."

"Intend to," Brittles said and put both hands on the back of his vacated chair and stood that way. He was a grizzled bear of a man with massive shoulders and drooping waterfall mustaches and jaws that worked unceasingly on his chewing tobacco.

I thought it was a muscle twitch in Dollar's shoulder that tipped Buford Brittles off, or it could have been the instinct born of past bad trouble. Anyway he moved faster than I ever thought a man his age could move and he flung the chair, not at Dollar, but up and where the whip would catch into it, tangle around the rungs.

The chair, caught in the whip, crashed into Sharniki's showcase and brought it down in splinters, showering cigars and pipe tobacco and cut plug all over the floor. And before Rolle Dollar could free his whip and set it again, Walter Ivy bounded for him.

He grabbed Dollar and flung him back against the wall where he hit a rack of pool cues. He lost his whip and bounced off the cues and he half fell in his attempt to get out of Ivy's way.

But there was no getting out of the way for Ivy snatched up the whip and raked it out behind him. With a bleat of fear, Rolle Dollar made for the front door and his feet just passed over the threshold when Ivy caught him around the ankles and sprawled him headlong across the boardwalk.

The noise was attracting a crowd and men boiled out of Mulligan's saloon, eager for anything to break the monotony of a dull, hot night. Rolle was on his hands and knees, trying to get up in a hurry but then Walter Ivy gave him the whip on the cracker-thin buttocks, renting Dollar's trousers and drawing blood.

His yell could be heard all over town and he went flat on the walk and Ivy hauled back and dusted the other buttock, again ripping the cloth and inflicting a deep wound.

Dollar, like most merciless men, was pleading for what he had always denied others.

Yet I felt sorry for him and said, "That's enough, Walter!"

"Just a couple more," he said coldly and made it good. Then he threw the whip into the street and said, "Go sew the sonofabitch up, and if you use anything but a dull needle we'll have words over it."

With that he turned and walked back into the poolhall as calmly as though he had just stepped out to take the night air.

He had, I'm sure, exhibited a side of his nature that none knew and few suspected. But it was something they all understood, a man sticking up for his rights and defending himself when he had to.

But there wasn't time for me to ponder the mores of Texas justice; there was a badly hurt man sprawled and crying on the boardwalk. I helped him to his feet, wishing that he had been injured some other place so he could have ridden the six blocks to his house.

Blood was running down the backs of his legs and soaking his shredded trousers and the sight of Rolle Dollar, buttocks exposed, excited sympathy in me and I looked around.

"Won't one of you loan me a vest? Anything to wrap around him."

One of the T-Cross cowboys laughed and said, "Goin' bare-assed won't hurt him none, 'cept his damned pride and he's got too much of that already."

They weren't going to help any; I could see that, so I went on down the street with Rolle Dollar, thankful that it was dark and that there were but a few people downtown. We had to go past the hotel and the newspaper and the store was across the street and the ladies turned away as we passed and spared Dollar that.

When I got him to his house, his wife did just what you'd expect her to do; she gave one unholy cry and fainted. The commotion got Angeline out of bed and she came down as I was stretching Rolle face down on the horsehair sofa and opening my bag.

She saw his distress and rushed to him. "Papa!"

Then he hit her. "Jezebel!" he shouted. "Harlot!"

It was a thing that could make a man's best intentions go out the window and out of mind; I had been uncorking the ether bottle and then I put the cork back in it, slipped it back into the bottle pocket of my bag and put eighteen sutures in his bottom, each one done right, and each one a separate agony. Then I dressed him and turned to his wife, who was stirring and trying to sit up; she certainly had missed the bad part. Getting Rolle up the stairs to his bed was no problem; he was angry enough to make it under his own steam and his wife went with him, heaping solicitude on him, and Rolle kept shoving her away.

I made Angeline sit down and put a cold pack on her cheekbone; she'd have a nice bruise all right. Upstairs Rolle was ranting and quoting Scripture; it was a frightful din, and with the windows open the neighbors must have heard everything.

"Sometimes I'm so ashamed," Angeline said softly and

made a study of her fingers laced together. "Why? That's what I keep asking myself. Why do people want others to live in fear of them?"

In one of those flashes of insight, I said, "I suppose it's because they are so afraid themselves that they can't trust others to be kind or thoughtful or fair." Then I told her what had happened; it was better that I tell her than to let her get it from gossip, and surely the whole town would be talking about it. Perhaps it was just the thing to take their minds off the drought and let tempers cool a bit.

"I'm ashamed of myself because this was all my fault," Angeline said. "But I—I didn't want to fight Lunsford Cardine. That's sinful isn't it? I mean, one thing leads to another, doesn't it? I suppose it'll get all over town, what I did."

"Now I don't think it'll come to that," I said, not too sure myself, but I was sure I should convince her if I could. "Lunsford is a gentleman, isn't he?"

I didn't get an answer and that left me with a little worry of my own; her mother came down the stairs, her eyes red from crying.

"Barbaric," she said, "that's what it is. Barbaric!"

"If you're talking about Mr. Dollar's conduct," I said, I would have to agree. Good night, madam. I'll drop in day after tomorrow and check his condition. He may run a slight fever, but I wouldn't concern myself about it. Also his appetite may subside, but I'd try to get some broth in him anyway." I gave her four pills; my oath overcoming my personal feelings. "These, taken as directed, will help ease his pain and allow him to sleep."

She took the pills, then said, "I'm going to have a warrant sworn out, mark my words!"

"That would be ill-advised," I said, smiled at Angeline, and walked out, trying to visualize what it would be like to have Rolle Dollar for a father-in-law.

And I just couldn't. Some things are too horrible to contemplate.

*   *   *

I was sleeping when the sheriff and his posse came back and woke me; it was a quarter to four in the morning and I fumbled for the lamp and then Walter Ivy came in, his eyes puffed with sleep. "I'd like to use your examining room, Ted." Without waiting for an answer he opened the door and went in and lit the lamps, then called to the sheriff, who was outside: "Bring her in here, Ben. Handle her gentle there. Right there on the table."

I stepped in and the men with the sheriff put the girl on the examination table. She was incredibly dirty, as though she had never known a bath. Her dress was torn and she was barefoot.

Ben Titus shooed his deputies outside and Walter Ivy looked at me. "Why don't you and Ben wait outside? Get the gist of this if you can, Ted."

I resented it a little, being pushed out of my own examining room, but I didn't want to make an untidy issue of it so I stepped outside with Sheriff Titus. He found the stub of a cigar in his pocket and lit it. Dust lay heavy in the creases of his clothing and he was unshaven and tired.

"Cut Comanche sign day before yesterday," he said softly, running the words together. "Followed 'em north but never caught up with 'em until dawn this mornin'. Found a camp somewhere west of Gonzales. We hit 'em hard and sudden. When the dust settled there was five dead and the girl."

"She's white," I said.

Ben Titus nodded. "Yep. White all right. Some buck took her in a raid, probably north of where we found 'em. From their looks I'd say they'd been travelin' some, and movin' fast. Figured that when we caught 'em camped in the open that way. Indians don't take chances unless they're about run out."

He turned to his deputies who stood idle nearby. "Why don't you go home now and get some sleep? And I don't think any of this is worth a lot of talk now, if you understand what I mean."

"Sure, Ben."

"We understand, Ben."

They walked off, leading their horses, dragging themselves because they were tired. Ben Titus puffed on his cigar and waited and then Walter Ivy stepped outside.

"Well, doc?" Titus asked.

"She's resting under sedation," Ivy said. "Ted, do you have a cigar? Thank you." He cupped his hands around mine when I offered a match and his face was drawn and angry. "I think I can draw a few safe conclusions for you, sheriff. She's perhaps nineteen and she was taken just a few days ago. I deduce that from the condition of her feet; they're bruised and cut and not yet healed. It's my opinion that she's German, probably from the colony up around Fredericksburg."

Titus nodded. "I guess there ain't no sense in me askin'—Comanches only take a woman for one thing."

"Yes, but the less said about it the better," Walter Ivy said. "Do you think you can locate her family, Ben?"

"Don't seem like much sense to try, Walter. I used to deputy up in that part of the country and them Germans are strange ones. From her clothes I'd say she was a bound girl to begin with."

"Sheriff, that's ridiculous!" I put in. "We don't have bound girls in this day and age."

He smiled at my ignorance. "They're furriners, doc. Got their own ways of doin' things. Yep, she's bound. And now that she's been used they ain't likely to take her back, fearin' of course that she'll up and fetch a breed in time. Them furriners are funny."

"The possibility of pregnancy exists," Ivy said, "although I think it unlikely in this case. Well, Ben, we've got to do something with her."

"Figured you'd know what," Titus said. "Goodnight."

"Wait now," Ivy said, but Ben Titus was walking away with no intention of stopping or turning back.

Walter Ivy slapped the back of his neck and said, "Now isn't that a hell of a note?" He blew out a long breath and made a decision. "Go and wake Mrs. Hempstead and while you're at it, heat a couple of kettles of water. Mrs. Hempstead can help me bathe her and we'll get her into a spare bed." He looked at me and suddenly flung out his hands in a helpless gesture. "Well, what the hell do you expect me to do with her?"

Her name was Christina Heidler and I am to this day

unsure just how she became my patient, but Walter Ivy, with his vast cleverness, managed to arrange it. She remained for a week in our small hospital while her feet healed and her spirit repaired the damage of the barbaric assault.

She spoke good English, although with some accent and she was a bright girl, rather pretty in a large-boned way, but not heavy fleshed as I thought most German girls were.

I felt it was Ivy's duty to give her a complete physical examination but he fended it off to me, saying that he had a call to make north on the Guadalupe and that was the last I saw of him for three days.

Christina Heidler had her mind pretty set on 'that other doctor' and it looked for a time as though the examination would have to be postponed. She felt that I was too young to be a doctor and of course this annoyed me to no end, and aroused my determination to carry this thing through.

I could see that we weren't going to get along at all; she argued, balked, protested, and argued some more and I rapidly lost patience to the point where I told her that if she had hurt her hand she would expect the doctor to examine it, and since she had been injured—she grasped my point immediately.

People can be cooperative when they want to.

Still, with Walter gone and Christina quite able to leave, I was faced with a decision, one that Walter really should have made. But I was still smarting a little and decided to arbitrarily take this on myself and I offered her a job as nurse, two dollars a week and room and board. Certainly it seemed a logical solution for in the past we had had to tend our hospitalized patients ourselves, or foist it off on Mrs. Hempstead, who was a little cross at times.

I felt that we needed a nurse and Christina was intelligent and strong and we could teach her and before long she would be quite capable of tending bed-ridden patients while we went our rounds.

It all sounded very brilliant and I was sure Walter Ivy would approve.

This decision was made on Friday, October 25, and it turned out to be one of the hottest days we had had, and one of the most tragic. I don't think anyone ever figured out why it happened, and only a few knew how, but it was Spindle's day in town and everything seemed normal, or as normal as could be expected with the tension between the brands.

Then Bob Scourby, who was the ramrod for T-Cross, got it into his noggin that he could ride into town any day he pleased and he got seven men who agreed with him. So, bolstered by a bottle of whiskey, Scourby took his men and this desire for independent expression and rode into Victoria, just looking for trouble.

They tied up at Mulligan's saloon, and since Spindle horses crowded the hitchrack, they solved this untidy parking problem by turning all the Spindle horses loose. Then they paraded inside, ordered in loud voices, and declared that any man who wasn't a hog with his water was welcome to drink.

Tennessee Frank, who ran Spindle, was a man of proud and sensitive stock and immediately took umbrage at the remark and demanded to know what Scourby meant.

Mulligan swears Scourby reached for his starboard pistol first and Tennessee Frank, proving once and for all that his reputation was more than talk, promptly drew and shot Scourby dead, then seriously wounded a cowboy standing next to him.

At the precise time the first shots were fired, I was in Angeline Dollar's parlor, inquiring about the state of her health and thinking unprofessional things.

The walls of the house muffled the shooting somewhat, but I knew it was more than some wrangler letting off steam and I grabbed my bag and tore out of the house.

5

THE SHOOTING continued as I ran for the main street; it sounded like a squad practicing at the rifle butts, and as I rounded the last corner, the swamper from Mulligan's was out in the street yelling for a doctor.

I'm not sure what I expected when I barged into the saloon, but certainly not what I found. Bob Scourby was dead and so were three of his men. Another lay against the brass footrail, one hand draped inelegantly in the spittoon; he had a horrible wound in his neck. Two lay in the bloody sawdust and one blew pink froth past his lips when he breathed; a lung wound for sure.

Tennessee Frank was down with three bullets in him, but he was alive. A dead man was sprawled across his legs and Mulligan helped me get him off. Two Spindle men were beyond help and another sat against an upended table top, his empty pistol in his lap; both hands clutched a stomach wound.

"Go get some help," I said to Mulligan. "A dozen men! Tear down some doors to carry these men! Get a wagon!" I had perhaps a dozen other instructions but he dashed out and cut me off.

There were at least thirty Spindle riders standing in the saloon, staring dumbly at the sudden destruction; many of them had not fired a shot and later I decided that only a few —the dead and wounded—had been quick enough to get into the fight before it was all over.

But they were the men I needed and I shouted them into action; they tore off the tops of Mulligan's poker tables and we began to carry the wounded outside. Ben Titus was running down the street toward us; he took it all in at a glance and saved his questions for later.

"There's dead men inside," I said and Ben Titus nodded.

"That's my department," he said and I hurried on toward my office.

Christina Heidler was making up some beds in the hospital

room when I rushed in. "There's been a shooting," I said, then further qualified that. "Get four beds ready. You'll have to help me the best you can. It's all we can do."

All we can do; I'll never forget that phrase.

There is no use in trying to describe what happened in its natural sequence, or to relate what the sheriff did, or others did, because they had their work and I had mine and I just had to stop and gather myself and fight down the instinct to do everything at once.

A doctor can't do that. He has to take things one at a time, make up his mind as to who needs help the worst and then do what he can.

That damned phrase again.

I had Tennessee Frank brought into the operating room. One bullet had broken his thigh six inches above the knee but I gave that only a passing attention. He was also wounded high in the chest, a serious enough thing, but not something likely to cost him his life.

Frank was unconscious and I incised his lower abdomen, knowing as I did so that his chances were slim; abdominal wounds of this nature carried high risks and while I had Christina spraying carbolic acid to kill bacteria, the terror of peritonitis lurked like a shadow behind us.

The bullet had perforated the lower intestine, and with artery forceps to control hemorrhaging, I sutured and hoped for a little luck. Tennessee Frank's other wounds were serious enough and I probed and found the bullet in his chest; it was a .36 caliber from a Navy cap and ball pistol and had not penetrated deeply enough to be fatal.

The bullet in his thigh was removed and once he was in traction, Christina and I wheeled him into the hospital room and transferred him to a bed.

By my watch an hour and fifty-one minutes had passed.

Buford Brittles was outside, and all of his men and at least twenty-five people from town. He looked immeasurably sad and said, "How's Tennessee, doc?"

"He may make it, if he's lucky."

Someone had thoughtfully pulled a blanket over the other Spindle rider and Buford said, "He died not ten minutes after he was brought here. I guess you've done all you could for us."

His tone, hard, unrelenting, the tone of a man pushed to the limits of his control made me say, "Buford, I don't want any more patients, you understand?"

"A man's got to take things as they come," he said and turned away, pushing through the crowd and taking his riders with him.

I had the T-Cross man with the lung wound brought in, and when I was through and he was resting in bed under sedation, I tended to the last of the living participants in this madness.

Once cleaned, his neck wound was more ugly than serious and after cleaning it and staunching the bloodflow, I bandaged him with a compress and got him into bed with a pain killer. He wanted whiskey but I held out for an injection.

Somehow I had lost track of the passage of time and then I noticed sunlight slanting through the west windows and realized that the day was about gone and there would be a long night ahead of me. The operating room was a mess and I went outside, got two pails of water and fixed a fire to heat them. Christina came from the adjoining room and eased the door closed. Her dress was bloody and so were her hands and perspiration soaked her shoulders and bosom.

"You don't rattle easily, do you?" I said.

"What is this, 'rattle?' "

"Faint. Get frightened."

She shook her head. "Nothing can frighten me." Then she sighed. "You rest. I'll clean."

"We'll both clean," I said and got the mop.

It was almost dark by the time we were through and each had bathed and changed clothes. When I stepped outside my room I noticed that a slight breeze had sprung up; it stirred the trees and the dead, sun-killed grass and swirled flavors of the earth into the air.

Ben Titus came down the street, his gait plodding. When he saw me sitting on the stoop, he stopped and said, "Three alive. Nine dead. God, that's a waste! Good men too. A couple had families."

"Tennessee is in bad shape," I said. "Whether he pulls through or not is up to God. I did all I could, but—" I shrugged. "The infection is what he'll have to fight off, and I can't help him."

"When's Doc Ivy coming back?"

"Tonight, maybe, if the stage gets in on time." Christina came out and nodded politely, then sat down beside me. She had changed to a clean cotton dress and her tawny hair, damp from her bath, was tied back with a ribbon.

"Feelin' all right there, girl?" Ben Titus asked. She looked up quickly, knowing what he meant, then Titus smiled. "One thing you got to understand about my deputies is that they're good for nothin' except possein' now and then and they get three dollars a day, which is about all the honest money they'll ever earn. Of a consequence they do what I say, and say what I tell 'em to say. Folks around here have come to understand that you came here hired by Doc Ivy and Doc Bodry here. We can let it go at that if it's all the same to you."

I was watching her face and her eyes and she gave no indication that she was going to cry. The tears just spilled over and ran down her cheeks and she nodded her head and kept nodding for a moment, then Ben Titus cleared his throat, turned, and walked back toward the center of town.

"Old Ben now, after spending half his life chasing rustlers and such, you wouldn't think—" I stopped talking because Christina grabbed my hand and pressed it against her cheek then kissed it and quickly got up and ran inside, leaving me wondering what it was all about.

Since Dorsey wasn't feeling well and Mrs. Hempstead was in one of her grumpy moods, I decided to go up town and have supper in the hotel. But I first went to the back where Christina had her room and knocked lightly. I heard her speak and pushed the door open. She had been stretched out on the bed but she sat up quickly.

"I'm going up town for perhaps an hour. Look in on the patients and if anyone stirs, come and get me right away. All right?" She nodded and I winked and closed the door.

When I reached the main street I found Buford Brittles and all the Spindle riders mounted and clogging the street. Ben Titus was there, and Aaron Stiles from the paper; they had been talking to Buford and stopped when they saw me come up.

The wind was picking up in strength and it seemed to sway him a little as he sat his horse. "Ted," he said, "I'll

194

tell you what I've already told the others: I've had enough. Tonight I ride on T-Cross."

"Buford," Titus said, "there's no call to do that." He reached up as though to touch Brittles' horse, then let his hand drop. "There are dead men on both sides. It should end there."

"I've worked as hard as any man for what I've got," Brittles said. "Fought for it too. I won't be set upon by another brand, Ben. I won't be made to apologize because I had the foresight Scully Beachamp lacks."

"You can't ride a man down," I said. "Buford, I've known you to be a fair man. Rough, granted, but as fair as I've seen. If I could, I'd stop you."

"Man, I've toasted under this cursed sun as much as any man and I've stepped backward to keep T-Cross and Spindle apart. But tonight tears all, by God. I can no longer trust Beachamp because he can't control his men." He made a motion with his knees and his horse backed, then he turned and his men turned with him and rode slowly from town.

I took Ben Titus by the arm. "Aren't you going to stop him?"

"How?" Titus asked and went down the street to his office.

I would have gone back too, only I remembered what I had come to town for and decided there was no need starving. So I went to the hotel and ate pot roast, then had the cook box a supper, which I took back to Christina. She was sitting on the stoop when I came down the street; I could see around the corner of the building and there were lights on in the Ivy parlor and I could hear the soft strains of the pump organ.

"I know you didn't get any supper so I brought you this," I said, handing her the cardboard box. She broke the string and opened it and began to eat.

"The wind's coming up strong, isn't it?"

"It's certainly a break in the heat," I admitted. There didn't seem to be any point in my telling her that there would be more killing before morning; she'd had enough to put up with. "In my spare time I want to teach you what you must know to be a good nurse. And I have a number of books I want you to read." I let a little silence run on.

"Christina, are your parents both gone?"

"Yes. Nine years ago."

"Any brothers or sisters?"

"Many, but they have families of their own and were poor. I lived with a friend of my father's but he could no longer keep me. His children were growing and could do my work, so I was bound to a man named Stutzmann. The Comanches killed him and his wife."

"Do you want to go back to Fredericksburg? That's where you're from, isn't it?"

"I don't want to go anywhere," she said. "I'd rather stay here. If it's all right. I don't think Mrs. Hempstead likes me. She is German and another woman around—well, she thinks I will take her place. That's not so."

"I'll reassure Mrs. Hempstead," I promised. "She's a nice woman and I know you'll get along once she understands that you're only helping in the hospital." I patted her hand. "You get some sleep. I'll stay up and wake you when I get tired."

"You should sleep," she said, but got up because obedience was a strong habit with her. I thought she was going inside, but she paused with the door open. "Will you promise me something?"

"If I can."

"If I have a child, promise you'll kill it."

It is hard to put into words how much this shocked me. "I can't do that, Christina. And you don't know you're—well, Dr. Ivy doesn't think so."

"How can I bear to wait until I know?" she asked, then went inside before I could attempt to answer.

Sitting alone there on the step, I realized how well she had hidden her inner anguish and her shame although no blame for it could be laid on her. She was a calm girl and her trouble ran deep, held back, hidden; it would have been better if she had broken down and wept and given vent to the emotion bottled up within her.

But I didn't think she would do that, and it was too bad. It occured to me then that if Ben Titus and the posse hadn't found her she would have killed herself at the first opportunity. Many white women taken by Indians did just that, and many a Texan, before being killed himself, put a bullet into his woman's head to keep her from being taken to the blanket by a Comanche or Kiowa buck.

I stayed up until a little after two, then went to Christina's room and gently shook her awake, then went outside to wait while she dressed. There was really not much for her to do; I had done most of it, and nursing is a messy business. The cowboy with the bullet wound in the neck was restless and I had to tie him in bed, then he had an involuntary urination and I had to untie him and change the bed clothes.

Tennessee Frank rested as well as could be expected and the T-Cross rider with the lung wound seemed to be holding his own. My instructions were simple, to keep them covered, for the night was turning off chilly, and to watch the lung wound and wipe away any blood that appeared on the nose and lips.

Hemorrhage there was my big worry for if he started to thrash about and bleed internally, he was a dead man and I couldn't help him. Opening the chest surgically almost always proved fatal; the shock of the operation could not be counteracted due to the length of the procedure.

It wasn't until I stretched out on my bed that I realized how exhausted I was and for a time it seemed that I just couldn't sleep. But I did, and slept soundly. So much so that when I woke, it was with a snap; I sat up in bed, certain that someone had called me. Then I heard it again, Christina's voice and I went out, not bothering to pull on a shirt.

As I went through the examining room I became conscious of another sound, like the beating of a thousand small bird wings, then I saw her standing outside by the open door and the rain was pouring down, sheets of it, hammering at the parched ground until it rained a mist.

She was soaked to the skin and holding up her arms to let it run down the length of them, then I stepped out and let it beat against my face.

There is something glorious in a rain after a long dry spell; it seems to soak into the skin and fill the body with strength and renewed hope. The sky was melting, draining torrents and then I put my arms around her and brought her inside and closed the door. She leaned her back against it and pulled her shoulders up until she had no neck and water dripped off the hem of her dress and she closed her eyes and smiled and it was the first time I had ever seen her do that.

The first time she had shown genuine happiness, and it was then that I stopped worrying about her.

6

AT DAWN the rain stopped and the sun came out, bright through the clouds, and water dripped from eaves and muddied the ground and the streets and no one minded at all.

I went uptown early to have my breakfast and to inquire at the hotel about the stage, which was a good fourteen hours overdue now. The agent had heard nothing, so I walked four blocks down to the telegraph office, thinking there might be a message. Ben Titus was there writing out a message; he handed it to the telegrapher.

"You get an answer to that, Curley, I'll be in my office or at home." He smiled and took my arm, saying, "Want a word with you, doc."

"This came for you a half hour ago," Curley said, handing me a telegram.

Dr. T. Bodry
Victoria, Texas

Make apologies to Dorsey . . . affairs have taken me to Abilene . . . will return in week or ten days . . . know you can carry through. . . .

Walter

"Hope that ain't bad news," Ben Titus said.

"No, Walter's just chasing rabbits again."

He frowned. "What does that mean?"

"Never mind. What did you want to see me about, Ben?" We left the telegrapher's place and walked slowly along The boardwalks were swollen and as we stepped along, mois ture oozed up around the nails.

"I was goin' to come to your office," Titus said, "but I knew you had enough problems of your own. Buford Brittles rode into town not fifteen minutes ago. He was alone. Came to my office. Just walked in, said nothin,' took his gun and laid it on my desk and told me he would never touch a firearm again."

"My God, he didn't go through with it?"

Titus shook his head. "Nope. He was in the yard and he'd called Scully Beachamp and his family out, announced his intentions and lit the torch." He looked sideways at me. "Then it started to rain. I guess it was the coincidence, the knowledge of what he was going to do, and the rain, but anyway Buford just up and figured that God had reached out and spared him. He's over at the church now, talkin' to the parson and Rolle Dollar." He shook his head again. "I looked in there on my way to the telegraph office. Buford is kneelin' and prayin'. He up and took religion real serious."

"I wouldn't dispute that the rain was Providential, Ben. Too bad it couldn't have come a day earlier."

"How's Tennessee and the others comin', doc?"

"A day or two will tell one way or another." We had come to my turn off; I stopped a moment and we talked about generalities, then I walked on back to my office.

I was disappointed that the stage hadn't arrived because I was expecting some medical journals and some books. Doctors ruin their eyes reading, then ruin their health staying out at odd hours in all kinds of weather putting into practice what they've read.

Being a doctor was, to many, some kind of a pinnacle reserved for a special kind of man, and I suspect they were right; it takes a special kind of man who can bear the eternal burden of helplessness, for with every cure a doctor could effect there were a dozen instances where he had to stand back and watch his patient die. My large interest was surgery, and the strides being made in that field; it seemed to me to offer the most hope for the suffering, and each day, each year, hitherto unbreachable barriers were scaled, and in my own brief career, I had seen new skills added. During my first year at medical school, tumors were nearly always terminal, but in five years antiseptics and sepsis had made possible prolonged operations; personally I had excised tumors of the neck, ovarian tumors, vesico-vaginal fistula, and amputation of the cervix uteri, and in all cases saved patients from a terminal condition.

None of these things were without risk to be sure, but with cocaine and digitalis and chloroform, and the success in most instances of blood transfusion—although some patients died

200

unexplainably—it was possible for me to perform a tracheotomy, or gall bladder operation, or the removal of the spleen, and Ceasarean section did not automatically mean the death of the mother.

This was, in my own mind, the large difference in thinking between Walter Ivy and myself; he was a doctor who believed that surgery was the last resort and much of his reading concerned drugs and treatment medicinally. Walter had a great interest in bacteriology and it was his everlasting interest in microscopic examination of specimens that broadened my own powers of diagnosis and firmly wedded in my own mind the association of scalpel and microscope.

*　*　*

Walter Ivy's sudden decision to remain away caused all of us to make some adjustments. Dorsey's temper was strained considerably, due more I think to her condition and the fact that she was feeling poorly much of the time.

I was a bit put out myself because I had to take on the added load of Walter's patients, but then I had done this before and it merely meant a little less sleep for me. All this meant that I had to sit down and devise some kind of a schedule in order to get everything done.

My patients in the hospital were recovering nicely and within ten days they were sitting up and eating so heartily that I had to call on Buford Brittles and Scully Beachamp for some kind of financial assistance.

They were again the best of friends, both sorry for their hard words and they both understood the delicacy of my mission, which was in essence, presenting a bill before the patients were discharged from my care.

The upshot of it was that both Beachamp and Brittles settled with me in full and I walked rather light-headed to the bank with a little over three hundred dollars in cash in my pocket.

Lunsford Cardine was minding the window; I presented my bank book and the money, holding out twenty dollars to pay the grocery bill. He made his entries, handed the book to me and said, "I want a word with you, Bodry."

His tone was the same as always and I still didn't like it.

"What about?" I knew that he was still seeing Angeline Dollar on the sly.

"It's come to my attention that you've been paying a good deal of attention to Miss Dollar."

"So?"

"So I don't like it," Lunsford said. "And I like it less since that frump came to live with you. The whole town's talking about it."

I could feel my temper deep in the bowels, building, rumbling, rising to escape and I placed both hands firmly on the counter. "Lunsford, let me tell you something educational: Do not ever repeat that, to me or anyone else. If you do I'll pound your stupid head off."

Then I picked up my bag and walked out; I was afraid to remain longer and as I walked toward the store to pay my bill, I wondered what made me so angry, the insult to Christina or the implication that I was hopelessly in love with Angeline Dollar. Although I had seen a good deal of her since her illness, I had to admit that there were facets of her personality that I disliked. She had a coyness that was irritating and she had the habit of always speaking depreciatingly about herself in the hope that I would leap to her defense.

That can get tiresome after a time.

And her mother was an abomination, conversationally anyway, and her father I would as soon not discuss; I simply disliked him as a man and abhorred him as a patient.

The rain came again, in the middle of the next week, a nice sprinkle that convinced everyone that the dry spell was really over. Grass was perking up and the creeks were partially full and the town settled down again and even the Indians stopped raiding, a blessing if there ever was one.

November came with colder mornings and I kept busy with my patients and my reading and two hours each day I taught Christina Heidler the rudiments of nursing.

It is amazing what you can learn about a person without half trying. She had a good education, having completed the first eight grades of school and two of high school, an unusual thing for a girl in those days. Her ability to read German made some of my old textbooks quite useful to her, and with a mentality that was far above average, she soon be-

202

came increasingly valuable to me, and patients whom I had never dared bring to my office and hospital were promptly popped into bed and cared for properly.

I got a letter from Walter; he raved about Abilene and during his stay he had been deluged with patients. He ended with a promise to return, but I knew Walter and didn't put too much stock in it.

Dorsey was pretty put out about it, and one evening when I came in from a call in the country, she came to my office before I could hang up my coat and wash my hands.

And she came right to the point. "I've written Walter all about the German girl.".

"You mean, Christina?"

"You know exactly who I mean, Ted Bodry."

"Yes, I do," I said, sitting down. "What have you written Walter?"

"Don't pretend you don't know."

"I'm not pretending anything," I said, getting a little angry.

"I can't keep that girl here any longer," Dorsey said flatly. "I mean it, Ted. She has to go."

"Dorsey, you've never kept her at all. Her room and board is paid for out of my own pocket." I waved my hand to include the office and operating room and the three rooms behind, Christina's and mine, with the storeroom between. "I've always paid Walter rent on these rooms, Dorsey. None of it ever came out of his pocket. And Christina's no burden to Mrs. Hempstead; she cooks in her own room and washes her own clothes. As a matter of fact, Dorsey, I don't think Christina's ever once been inside your house. She wouldn't intrude on your privacy. And neither would I. So don't say that I have."

"Oh, you're so damned righteous!"

"Not intentionally. But I'm not guilty of anything either. Look, you're pretty upset with Walter gone so long and—"

"Don't patronize me!"

I drew in a deep breath and let it out slowly. "Just what is it you want me to do, Dorsey?"

"Get rid of that girl."

"I can't do that," I said. "She's a valuable pair of hands to me. Since she's been here I've been able to extend my practice, as well as take care of Walter's practice. And I've also performed three operations." I shook my head. "She's becoming too valuable to lose, Dorsey." I was tired of discussing it, justifying what needed no justification in my mind; I got up and went to the door and opened it. "I don't think there's anything more to be said, Dorsey. If you want, take it up with Walter. He can decide."

Her manner changed—perhaps she saw that I was adamant. "Oh, I hate him!" she said and began to cry, and I understood what her trouble was. So I made her sit down and gave her a shot of medical brandy and fifteen minutes later her attitude had brightened and she went back to the house and I walked down town to the telegraph office. I wrote out what I wanted to say and handed it to the telegrapher, who read it, then looked at me sharply.

"You sure you want to say that, Doc?"

"Exactly that. How much?"

He read it, counting the words: Get . . . the . . . hell . . . home . . . where . . . you . . . belong . . . and . . . stop . . . acting . . . like . . . a . . . damned . . . underwear . . . salesman. . . . "Fifteen words, Doc; that'll be two-eighty."

I paid him and walked out while the telegrapher was clearing the line. Walter would be furious when he got that, perhaps furious enough to get on the next stage for Victoria! He wasn't fooling me any; a new town beckoned to him and he looked at the grass and was deciding whether or not it was really greener and unless I was mistaken, he had already wired friends in the east and offered to sell his Victoria practice.

He'd done it before and what a man will do once, he'll do again.

Tennessee Frank came in to see me the next day; his wounds were healing splendidly and I took the cast off his leg. We talked about the shooting and he acted as though he could hardly remember the sharper details of it and I suppose it was really that way, a bit of a blur in his mind, just a few shocking seconds of complete violence.

The two T-Cross riders were completely recovered and working again and I considered them completely discharged.

The next day, when the stage arrived, I went to pick up my mail and another package of journals. Walter and I were both fairly prolific correspondents, especially with other doctors, and Walter was always working on some paper to be submitted to the medical journals. I never bothered with it myself, but I had a friend practicing in Cincinnati who had been operating for tubal pregnancy and I was very interested in his technique and successes.

Of all the burdens of woman, tubal pregnancy stands in my mind as the most terrible. It sometimes happens that the embryo develops in the tube leading to the uterus and as it grows it ruptures the wall of this tube. Serious hemorrhage follows and the doctor is forced to watch the life ebb as a torrent of blood pours into the abdominal cavity and could not until now lift a hand to help her.

This misplaced pregnancy is uniformly fatal and even while I was in medical school, learned doctors discussed opening the abdomen and correcting the situation surgically, but no one was bold enough to risk the hazards. But it was inevitable that someone would; my friend from Cincinnati, who had been kind enough to diagram his technique and report his results to me.

Walter returned that night, riding all the way from San Antonio on a livery stable horse and I suppose it did his old cavalry soldier soul good to do so. He had the good sense to spend a couple of hours with his wife before coming to my office; it was after ten o'clock but I was there reading, waiting for him, certain that he would show up.

He came in, tanned and robust and he flopped in a chair and looked at me for a moment. "You know, I should be sore at you, Ted. What would people think if they read that wire?" Then he waved his hand and laughed and lit a cigar. "I was ready to come home anyway. That's a lively place, Abilene. People have money and they need a doctor. The nearest is the contract surgeon at Fort Phantom Hill."

"Decided to move?"

He looked at me a moment. "Would you mind, Ted?"

"Why should I mind?"

He seemed very surprised. "Why, because you'd be going with me. Wouldn't you?"

"I don't think so, Walter. I have a good practice here and I like it here."

"You'd like it there," he said quickly. "Come on now,

think it over. I can get three thousand in cash for your practice."

"You've had offers?"

"Well, it doesn't hurt to try."

"What does Dorsey say?"

He laughed. "Dorsey goes where I go. One place is the same as another to her."

"She ought to get out more, make friends," I said. "Walter, I think it would be a mistake to move. We're established. It would only mean doing a lot of work all over again, like building a hospital. Besides, I've been meaning to ask you, if I can ever get you to light long enough, about buying some new equipment."

He laughed and waved his hand. "Ted, let's face it, you're a gadget man. I'm from the old school that believes what a doctor can't carry in his bag isn't worth having." He got up and stretched. "In the morning suppose we get together for an hour and you can bring me up to date on the general state of health. Want to talk to you about that German girl too." He winked and went out and it was a few minutes before I could get back to concentrating on my books.

7

IN THE DAYS that followed I kept waiting for Walter Ivy to say something about 'that German girl' but he never did and I concluded that he had talked to Dorsey and she had told him of my firm stand on the matter.

Walter knew when to let well enough alone.

He resumed his rounds as though he had never been away at all and I slacked off a bit, catching up on some of my rest.

Or trying to.

Mrs. Dollar sent a boy with a note and asked me to call and I went to her house in the early afternoon. She was in the parlor; it was her throne room and of course we had tea and small cakes, which made me immediately suspicious because it just wasn't her nature to be generous.

"I would like you to recommend a good doctor," she said.

You learn not to get offended; I said, "Walter J. Ivy."

"Mr. Dollar would never permit him in the house; it would be useless to ask. I was referring to a doctor in some other town."

"Well, there's Dr. Radcliff in Goliad. And Dr. Baker and Dr. Kyle in San Antone. Are you ill, Mrs. Dollar?" I waited a decent interval for her to answer, and when she didn't, I said, "Really, whatever you tell a doctor is in strictest confidence, and you must eventually confide in someone."

"The matter is much too delicate," she said flatly.

It was the kind of a thing that made a doctor sigh, this damned female modesty; it had fettered the progress of obstetrics for four hundred years.

"Madam, forgive my bluntness, but does this matter concern a pregnancy?" I watched her face, her expression, her eyes, and they told more than I had guessed. "Madam, does this concern Angeline?"

I had not suspected that she was so near the breaking point, but suddenly she fell to weeping and I could not stop her. So I went outside and saw some boys playing across the street and one came over at my whistle. I pressed a nickle in his hand and told him to run up town and fetch Rolle Dollar, then went back into the house. Mrs. Dollar was sobbing and pressing a handkerchief to her mouth and I sat down and let her weep; she was a woman who felt sorry for herself most of the time and this likely did her a lot of good.

Rolle Dollar didn't waste any time getting home; he rushed into the house and sat down beside his wife and put his arms around her. He dried her tears and patted her shoulder and then he looked at me as though I were to blame for it all.

"God frowns on this shameful house," he said. "She is in the hands of the Devil."

I didn't want to get involved in that, so I steered another course. "Mr. Dollar, trouble always *seems* worse than it is. Since neither of you have taken me into your confidence, I would like to excuse myself from the matter. I've already recommended to Mrs. Dollar several fine doctors, and I take it from her inquiry that you plan to take Angeline to another town."

"My mortification and shame is too—"

"Damn *your* feelings," I snapped. "Man, your concern should be for the girl!" I forced myself to be calm, clinical. "She should be examined and placed under a doctor's care. The moral issues do not enter into the picture at all. The circumstances that produced this state may be regrettable, and entirely repugnant to you, but nevertheless she should have competent medical help. Now, do you wish me to withdraw from the case?"

"It'll be the talk of the town," Rolle Dollar said.

"Not from me," I assured him.

He was a man completely at a loss as to which way to turn. "Dr. Bodry, what do you advise? I don't know. On my soul, I just don't. For ten days now I've been in a daze, half out of my mind. I've always led a pure, Christian life, and now this—" He seemed too overcome to continue.

"I think, since you've asked, that we ought to face the facts. And fact one is that Angeline is pregnant. Fact two is that barring a miscarriage or complications, she will bear a child. It isn't something you can hide, Mr. Dollar. If you feel the shame is too great, then sell out and move to another town and tell everyone that her husband died. But at best that's risky. Texas is big, and yet it's small and soon the truth will come out. Someone will see you, or her; it's a thing that can't be hidden." I paused to let this sink in. "Point three is that you're going to have to have a doctor. Either myself or Dr. Ivy or some other physician. Your personal feelings don't matter, Mr. Dollar, and I sincerely suggest you consult Walter Ivy as soon as possible so that he can examine her."

"I've had words with the man," Dollar said, "and when I've had words with a man, I want no more to do with—"

"Mr. Dollar, you're not asking for treatment. It's Angeline we should be concerned with. Besides, neither Dr. Ivy nor myself have any choice, for by our sworn oath we can not refuse to treat anyone, any more than a priest can deny a man the right to confession." I picked up my hat and bag. "I would like for you to give what I've said serious thought. Please let me know."

Rolle Dollar nodded. "I talked to Butram Cardine and there'll be a wedding this Sunday. He's given me his word."

Since it's never a good policy to offer personal advice, I let myself out and went back to my office. By the time I reached the head of the block I knew something was wrong because four horses were tied up in front and there was a spring wagon there too, the bed full of straw, which meant that someone had been hauled in it.

I ran the rest of the way and met one of the Hulse boys; their father had a place about four miles out. He grabbed me and nearly towed me through my office and into the operating room. Guy Hulse, the youngest, lay like a dead man on the operating table and Christina was putting cold packs on his abdomen, which was badly lacerated and swollen. Old Peter Hulse and his other three boys crowded around and got in her way and I rudely pushed them aside.

"Pete, you stay. The rest of you wait outside. Git!" Then I looked at the old man and turned to examine the boy. He was young, eighteen or so, a big, healthy boy with a wrestler's shoulders. "What happened to him?"

"Horse fell and rolled on him," the old man said. "Is he gonna die, Doc?" He shifted his feet, making scraping sounds on the floor. "What makes him swell up like that? Is he busted up inside?"

There was no doubt in my mind that young Hulse was hemorrhaging badly internally, and I strongly suspected that he had a ruptured spleen. I turned and immediately began to scrub up, giving rapid orders to Christina to prepare Guy Hulse for an immediate operation. His complexion was bad and I knew that I'd have to give him a transfusion.

"Pete, get out now, but send in your oldest boy. Alfy? Isn't that his name?"

"You going to cut my boy?"

"I'm going to try like hell to save his life, and I need Alfy. Now move. Every second counts."

Pete went out and Alfy came in; Christine had already brought a table close by and parallel to the operating table. "Lay down on that and strip to the waist, Alfy."

"Not in front of no woman I ain't," he said.

So I hit him in the mouth and it stung him and he blinked his eyes at me and did as he was told. Christina made ready to give the transfusion and I got the antiseptic sprayer hooked up and filled with diluted carbolic acid and began operating it with the foot pump. It was an untidy procedure, but it saved lives and that was all I cared about.

Alfy's eyes grew round when I found the vein in his arm and inserted the needle, but he didn't wince, and I adjusted the mixture of sodium phosphate which acted as an anticoagulant.

Christina acted as my anaesthesiologist, although the term was unknown in those days, and I made my first incision. She counted the patient's pulse and reported it to me in a calm, steady voice and I gave my complete attention to my work. I could have used another nurse or a doctor to hand me instruments, but there was no one and I hated the seconds I wasted looking up at the tray beside me.

Alfy, whose blood ran from his arm into his brother's veins, started to say something, but Christina said, "Don't interrupt the doctor, Alfy."

Then she went on counting Guy Hulse's pulse and at the same time watching the chloroform breather very carefully, while I tied off the ruptures with forceps until I could tie off all the vessels. Working fast but carefully, I was ready

210

to close in twenty minutes and I ordered the transfusion stopped.

Walter Ivy came in and I looked up. "Don't come in here without a scrub up," I said.

"Oh, for Christ's sake," he said and started to step.

"Damn it, Walter, I mean it!"

He looked at me steadily, then shrugged and walked out, closing the door. I discontinued anaesthetic and Christina helped me bandage the patient and we transferred him to a homemade gurney and moved him into the hospital room and into a bed.

I heard a thump in the other room and went back. Alfy was sitting on the floor, both arms outspread to brace himself. "I fell," he said.

"Let me get you some brandy," I said and stepped out into my office. The Hulse family was there, with Walter Ivy. "He's no longer bleeding and his pulse is good. With luck now he'll be on his feet in two weeks."

The old man looked at the bottle in my hand. "If'n you're gonna get drunk, Doc, we'll go along with you."

"It's for Alfy," I said and went back in.

I just let him swig and he took three good swallows and it rooted color into his cheeks. He reluctantly handed the bottle to me. "That's good stuff, Doc."

"Why don't you take a couple of more swigs and get your strength back?"

"You sure know what you're doin,'" he said and tipped the bottle again. I went into the hospital and Christina was making Guy Hulse comfortable, tucking the sheets in on each side so he wouldn't roll out.

"He'll be good and sick when he comes out of the chloroform."

She smiled. "I'll stay with him."

"Good," I said and went back to my office. The Hulses were outside with Walter Ivy; they were talking softly and quit when I stepped out. Alfy was tucking in his shirt tail and looking very bright eyed.

Old Pete Hulse shifted his feet and said, "He was bad hurt, huh, Doc?"

"Another hour and you'd have buried him," I told him

frankly. "The spleen was ruptured and filling the abdominal cavity with blood."

Old Pete nodded as though he really understood, and perhaps he did understand. "Alfy says you went and took his blood and run it into Guy's arm. Can you do that, Doc?"

"Yes, it's been done," I said. "Guy had lost too much blood by the time he got here and he wouldn't have survived an operation."

"How much of my blood did you take, Doc?" Alfy asked.

I shook my head. "I have no way of telling, Alfy. That's something we just haven't worked out yet."

The old man nodded; his son was alive and he was satisfied. "Doc, I only got eighty dollars in the bank, but I could give you fifty prime steers if that'd—"

"My fee is ten dollars, Pete. Pay me when you take Guy home."

He nodded once, and then turned to his wagon. His boys mounted up and turned out and I watched them go, feeling that this was one damned good day after all.

Walter Ivy stood there and when I started to go back into my office he said, "You got kind of short there, didn't you, Ted?" He followed me inside and perched on the edge of my desk. "I don't think I had that coming."

"Yes, I know that, Walter, and I apologize. It was just that I'm on needles and pins when it comes to surgical sepsis. Perhaps even a little afraid. After all, the abdominal cavity was beyond the reach of surgery for so long that I still can't believe I'm being careful enough. The introduction of bacteria—" I waved my hand, terminating the explanation.

"I would have never given him a transfusion," Walter said. "Too many risks. Too many unknowns, Ted. There have been deaths."

"Yes, and they'll find out why. But he was going to die if I didn't get blood into him. I just couldn't stand by and watch that."

He sighed. "What are his chances?"

"Good, I believe. As good as Mrs. Miller after I removed her spleen." I couldn't hold back a smug smile. "And the last time I rode past her place I saw her hoeing weeds in the garden." The whiskey bottle was sitting on my desk, down considerable since Alfy had helped himself; I got two glasses and poured. "Walter, I'll tell you what I want to do. I'd like for us to get out of this building and put up another, a regular hospital."

"That would be a pretty big investment," he said, pursing his lips. "Now a lying-in hospital I can see. There's an advantage to that, Ted. Isolation for contagious diseases and care of the bed-ridden; there's a good revenue from that, Ted."

I looked at him. "And a small surgical room?"

"Well, yes. I don't think we should go overboard on surgery, Ted."

"Doctor," I said, "I would like to point out a thing or two. When a man has the bellyache or the croup he goes to his family doctor, but when he develops a cancer of the bowel, he goes to see a surgeon or an undertaker."

"Your point escapes me, Ted."

"The point is, they come to see the surgeon, traveling for miles, a hundred miles perhaps, if they know he can help them and has the facilities." I raised my hands and spread them out as though I were framing words chiseled in marble.

"Can't you see it? The WALTER J. IVY MERCY HOSPITAL?"

That got him off his butt and off my desk and he walked about, trailing cigar smoke, his eyelids pulled close together, his eyebrows shot up there in the vicinity of his hair. "I suppose you've looked into the cost of the building and equipment?"

"Yes, Walter, I have. A two storey building of brick would cost eight thousand dollars. Equipment, another ten. Expenses for operation for the first year, six more. That's twenty-four thousand dollars. I have a little over four saved. The rest would have to be borrowed, providing you matched me dollar for dollar."

He stopped pacing and looked at me. "Where would you put it?"

"On that three acre plot on the west edge of town, near the river."

"Who owns it?"

"Butram Cardine."

Walter Ivy smiled. "You've really put some thought into this, haven't you, Ted?"

"Would you like to see my sketches?" I got them out of a

bottom drawer and he studied them at length, rocking back and forth on his heels.

"I like it," he said. "Ted, I really like it."

"As well as Abilene?"

He looked at me. "Where the hell's Abilene?" Then he laughed heartily.

8

ON SUNDAY, Lunsford Cardine, being a stinker with enough money to travel, left Angeline Dollar at the church, sobbing into her mother's bosom, and Rolle Dollar stalked the streets with a repeating rifle, looking for Cardine.

Fortunately, Ben Titus and three other men disarmed him and bore him, struggling and calling for vengeance, to his home.

And then I was summoned.

Titus felt that Dollar was making a big fuss over nothing; after all, Angeline wasn't the first woman jilted at the church, but then Titus didn't know the truth of the matter and no one was going to tell him either. I gave Rolle a sedative to quiet him and when he was resting, I went back to my office, in a way glad that he hadn't found Lunsford Cardine; Dollar would have killed him for certain and then Angeline would have been in a fine pickle.

On Monday I got on the stage for Austin. Since Walter wanted to get started on the hospital right away, I had to see an architect and have building plans made. Had we been building a hotel I wouldn't have bothered, but a hospital was different.

I remained in Austin for ten days and it was a relief; I hadn't realized how much I needed some time to myself and a little relaxation. Austin was quite a city and I went to the band concerts and the theatre and the music hall, figuring that it does a man good to watch pretty girls kick up their legs.

As it was good to get away, I found it equally good to get back and as the stage approached Victoria I wished the driver would let out the horses a little instead of poking along.

Ben Titus met me when I got off the coach; we drew aside to let other passengers and baggage unload. "Got a line on young Cardine," Ben said. "He's in El Paso. I ain't told Dollar yet."

"I wouldn't," I told him.

215

"Kind of thought I ought to keep it to myself," he said.

"Thanks anyway, Ben." My bags were on the porch and I got them and walked the few blocks over to my office and room in back. I changed to a clean suit, washed, and went into my office to look through my mail.

Christina Heidler heard me and opened the door of the operating room; her smile was a bright, spontaneous thing, and I said, "How is my patient?"

"Walking about. Not much, but a little." She held the door open for me and I stepped into the operating room and passed through to the ward. Guy Hulse had been moved to a corner bed and a screen set up, the reason being that there were two women patients. Mrs. Clayborn had slipped on a frosty porch and hurt her back and Walter Ivy had her in traction, which made her feel so much better. And Mrs. Huddleston had a badly fractured arm; a chunk of wood had flipped up while she had been chopping.

They were Walter's patients and I was cheerful and friendly but kept my nose out of their business. Guy Hulse was the picture of health regained; he sat up in bed, propped by pillows and he grinned when Christina and I stepped behind the screen.

"Pa says you whittled on me proper, Doc."

"Well, we did carve you a little. Sewed a little too." I felt his pulse, strong and steady. "Been having visitors?"

"Sure 'nuff," Guy said. "But I can't fight with Alfy no more, Doc. With his blood running in me, it'd be like hittin' myself. And we used to have some real set-tos."

"Let me look at your scar." I examined him carefully; the healing was pink and firm, then I dropped the tail of his nightshirt. "Guy, I'm going to send you home tomorrow. But you stay off horses and no heavy work until I tell you. Don't carry wood or water. Understand?"

"Whatever you say, Doc."

"That's what I say." I motioned for Christina to follow me and we went back to my office. "Close the door." I waved her into a chair. "I've been thinking a lot about you, Christina. You're not pregnant, you know."

She looked steadily at me. "Yes, I know."

"You're young and pretty and healthy and some day a man is going to come along and you'll fall in love and get

216

married. But until then you have a life of your own to lead. I want you to stay with Dr. Ivy and myself."

"Isn't it more you than Dr. Ivy that wants me to stay?"

"It may be now, but that can change. It will change, if it hasn't already. You've been taking care of his patients, you know. He can't sidestep that even if he wanted to." Then I told her of our plans to build a hospital, providing we could get the land and the financial backing. "Christina, I've grown fond of you, and I'm afraid in many ways, dependent on you. I want you to stay."

"Then I'll stay," she said.

I frowned and got up and walked around the small office. "Christina, I know you'll stay, but I keep getting the feeling that somehow I'm making you stay. That isn't what I want."

"I suppose that's true, but I'm the one at fault, not you." She waited until I looked at her. "Lying doesn't come easy to me, and pretending is something I never had time for, and I don't want to embarrass you, but I've done something I haven't a right to do. I've fallen in love with you."

I opened my mouth to tell her that she didn't know what she was saying, that she was mistaking gratitude for love; in short, all the stupid, vapid things men say when they are caught completely by surprise.

But I didn't say anything because she shook her head, asking me to be silent. "Please sit down," she said, and clasped her hands tightly together. "I'm sorry I said that. I thought it would be easier, but now I can see that it isn't. You'll remember that I said it and—" She acted close to tears. "Please, I would like to go away after all."

"Where would you go?"

She shook her head again, then said, "I don't know. Anywhere. It would be better, I know that."

I put my head in my hands for a moment, trying to organize my thoughts. "This is a devil of a mess—you know that? If I said anything at all you'd construe it as pity. If I told you that I was fond of you and needed you here, you'd think I was saying it to spare your feelings." I paused to light a cigar. "Damn it, Christina, give a man time to sort out his feelings, will you? Now that it's come down to it, I wonder

217

why I was so set on your staying. Because I wanted a nurse or—"

"What else could it be?" she said quickly.

I studied her carefully. "Christina, don't be a *dummkopf!* Your experience may have stained you in the eyes of fools like Rolle Dollar, but not a man like me. Do you think for one second that I—" There was no sense getting into that. "You are going to stay. Clear?"

A lifetime of obeying commands was strong in her; she nodded her head. "Whatever you say." Then she turned and left my office and closed the door and I decided that I had accomplished absolutely nothing, and perhaps fogged up my own emotions good and proper. Now I wasn't sure how I felt and this made me unsure of myself, a status I didn't enjoy.

Butram Cardine fit my mental image of a banker, a rather smallish man who always wore conservative suits and sat behind his large walnut desk in a squeaky swivel chair.

All along I had thought that Walter would handle the negotiations, but he was called into the country and I went to the bank in his place. Cardine sat in his chair, tipping it back, squeaking it continually while I displayed the building plans and quoted figures. I noticed that when he had something to say he always stopped squeaking the chair, and he had a lot to say.

Nothing really suited him. The building was too large. There was too much equipment. He wanted to cut this and that and finally he had it pared down to practically nothing and he enjoyed every minute of it.

It was one of those times when you want very badly to tell a man where to put his money, but you dare not because you need him and he knows it and enjoys playing his games. The fact that both Walter and I were prepared to sink our total savings meant nothing to Cardine, and the meeting terminated dismally, with nothing at all being solved, or even close to being settled.

When I told Walter he was very disturbed about it and I got the impression that he felt I had lost my temper and botched it, although he didn't come right out and say so. A good thing too for I'd had just about enough for one day.

The only benefits derived from the meeting was that word soon got around town that we were planning a hospital; many spoke to me about it but I could promise them nothing.

It was all very discouraging.

At least until Thursday afternoon. I'd been out to the Stover place; the boy had fallen from a pear tree and hurt himself, but it turned out to be little more than severe bruises and when I tied up my rig in front of my office I noticed that Scully Beachamp's matched bays and buggy was soaking up the shade next to Buford Brittles' rig.

They were waiting in my office, smoking, talking softly, the best of friends now; they got up when I came in and we shook hands. I said, "Now neither of you looks a bit sick."

"Best of health," Beachamp said. "We heard talk about the hospital you and Doc Ivy want to build."

"That's about all it is, talk."

Buford Brittles said, "Heard you had plans drawn and everything. Wondered if we could take a look."

"I'd be happy to," I said and cleared the desk so I could spread the plans. I showed them the front and side elevation, then the first floor plan. "This is the entrance hall and Dr. Ivy's office and examining rooms are to the right. Mine are right across the hallway. On each side is a storeroom for drugs and dressings and general supplies. Directly in back is the emergency room, with surgery and recovery room right across the hall."

Brittles pointed. "Is that an elevator?"

"Yes, we'll need that for transporting bed-ridden patients to the second floor wards."

"That's going to be quite a place," Brittles said. "Take quite a few people to run it, won't it?"

I nodded. "In time, when it is operating to capacity, about sixty people."

Scully Beachamp whistled softly. "How much money do you need, Doc?"

"I—twenty thousand dollars," I said.

Brittles looked at Beachamp. "Halves?"

"Kind of figured that way." He offered his hand. "You want to go to the bank with us now?"

For a moment I was so stunned I couldn't speak. Then I said, "I think we need an attorney. Suppose I wire Austin?"

"All right," Brittles said, "but we shook on it. Let us know when he gets here." He put on his hat, ready to leave now. I got up and went out with them and watched them drive away. They were heading toward town when Walter Ivy came down another street in his buggy. When he pulled in and tied up, he said, "What did those two old war horses want?"

"They just loaned us twenty thousand dollars."

I enjoyed it, watching his eyebrows shoot upward, watching him swallow twice before speaking. "You're not joking?"

"About that much money?" I shook my head. "I'm going to wire a lawyer and have him draw up the papers. With luck, we should start building within a month."

"Still got your heart set on that piece of property west of town?"

I nodded. "There isn't a better spot around here, Walter."

"And Cardine owns it."

"Well, we'll just have to buy it from him."

"At his price?" Walter shook his head. "I think Mr. Cardine ought to donate that as a measure of his civic pride."

"Hell, he'll never do that!"

"Let me work on it," Walter said and walked around the house.

I didn't think any more about it until lodge meeting three nights later and then I noticed that Butram Cardine was getting the cold shoulder from Rolle Dollar and Mike Sharniki and a few of the other businessmen in town, but it wasn't until later that I found out just what was happening.

Walter had called at the bank and Cardine had quoted a firm asking price, which was plenty steep in any man's language, and Walter had told him he'd think it over.

Only Walter started talking it over with everyone in town and in a way that only Walter can talk. I could just hear him and see him by closing my eyes. He'd stand there with that bland, I'm-a-big-friendly-dog expression in his voice, saying, "Yes, sir, I wanted to put up the hospital on that land. Dr. Bodry picked it and you know how I feel about that young man. Salt of the earth. Give him my arm up to here. Bodry's done a lot for people around here and you'd think a man like Cardine would appreciate it, but does he? Just wants to make a dollar. Doesn't care how people have to suffer. It isn't *his* misery. It makes a man think about the money he keeps in that bank. For two cents I'd draw it out and do my business in Goliad."

Around town he'd go, making his rounds with cronies and friends and anyone who'd stop and listen, talking it up, never really saying anything bad but pretty much painting Cardine as a skinflint who'd take pennies from his mother's purse.

So Butram started getting the cold treatment at lodge and it kept up this way for nearly a week and I wondered when it would break. Cardine was a civic-minded man, with a finger in everything and I knew that he had the best interests of the community at heart. And because he was sincere, all this bothered him a lot and it was only a question of time before he broke down and sent a boy with a note, asking either or both of us to drop into the bank at our convenience.

We did, but I could see that the matter had already gone too far. I wasn't against paying a reasonable price for the land, but Walter Ivy had used his influence to the extent that Butram Cardine had to give it to us outright or be forever remembered as a money-grabber by the townspeople.

Walter Ivy thought this was a grand gesture and promised Cardine that he'd put a bronze plaque in the cornerstone to remember this generosity; it was the wrong thing to say and Cardine was furious when we left the office and his anger was at me as much as at Walter and I couldn't blame the man for that because we'd been tarred by the same brush.

I spoke to Walter about it when we got into his buggy. "Damn it, you didn't have to push his nose in it that way. Why make an enemy of the man?"

"Hell, he was never a friend."

"A neutral is sometimes as valuable as a friend."

"My boy, listen to old Walter for a minute. The day will come when Butram Cardine will thank me for wresting from him this generous contribution." He patted me on the knee and clucked to the team and from his expression I could tell that he was certain everything was all right.

But I still wondered.

9

ON WEDNESDAY, November 26th, I got a wire from Dr. Calendar in Cincinnati, inviting me to spend ten days with him in a new surgical clinic he and a partner had established. I should have turned it down, with the foundation work beginning on the new hospital and patients to see, but I didn't hesitate at all; I wired back that I was taking the first available transportation to Austin and the railroad, and bought two round trip tickets to the hotel.

Walter Ivy was having his midday lunch with his wife and I walked around to the front entrance, knocked, and Mrs. Hempstead let me in. As I went toward the kitchen I realized that I hadn't·been inside Walter's house for a long time.

He smiled and offered a chair when I came in. Dorsey was quite round now and her complexion was good although her disturbed body chemistry had given her a few pimples.

"I'm sorry to disturb you, Walter, but I want to go east for a few weeks." I explained the offer from Dr. Calendar. "It's something I can't afford to pass up, Walter, and you can handle my practice while I'm gone." I didn't remind him that I had handled his patients more than once.

"Well, I certainly don't begrudge you the opportunity," he said thoughtfully, "but with building going on and many details to look after, this could have come at a better time."

"Yes, I know. However I've made arrangements to go. I'm taking Christina Heidler with me."

Dorsey, who hadn't been paying too much attention, looked up quickly. "Really, Ted, together all that distance?" She looked at Walter, as though she expected him to say something. "You know how people talk."

"Yes, and isn't it a shame? However, I believe she can get some valuable training by observation," I said. "People are just going to have to go ahead and talk."

"Oh, they will," Walter said. He sighed and pushed back his empty plate. "Calendar, Calendar—oh, yes, he's that bright young man who's specializing in abdominal work. Risky business. He'll kill more than a few before he's through. Frankly, I'd rather they passed on in their own bed than on my operating table." He shook his head. "God, the war was bad enough. Died like flies the minute the stomach wall was punctured. Terrible risk, going in there. Broken bones are one thing, but I think a man's future lies in internal medicine. Correct the symptom before it develops, not surgery afterward." He sighed as though he argued a hopeless cause.

There was no sense of my staying; I got up and replaced my chair. "This afternoon, Walter, if you could drop around to my office, I want to discuss several cases with you. I have Bert Caslin on digitalis; his heart's very bad. And there's Mrs. Ryker over at the junction; she's terminal cancer I'm afraid and it's merely a matter of sedating her to make her as comfortable as possible."

"I have some time around three," Walter said, so I smiled at Dorsey and left the house, feeling that I was certainly putting Walter to a lot of trouble. When I got around to my side of the house I saw Rolle Dollar walking back and forth, hands in his pockets, head down as though he wanted to observe each step he took.

He looked up when I drew near, then took my arm before I could step inside. "Doc, can you come to my house? Angeline's pretty sick."

"Of course. I'll get my bag."

He waited and we walked together and he hurried; it was really the first time I had ever seen him do that. Mrs. Dollar was in her usual state, wringing her hands and puckering her lips.

I went upstairs, alone; I insisted upon that. Angeline was in bed, and her complexion was bad although her pulse was strong. I questioned her briefly; she complained of severe pain in the abdomen and my first thought was the appendix, a trouble area we couldn't do much about.

But I went on with my examination and when I detected vaginal bleeding I knew what was wrong and went downstairs. I washed in the kitchen then went to the parlor where Rolle Dollar and his wife waited.

I suppose my expression gave away the seriousness of it all; I said, "It's a tubal pregnancy."

Mrs. Dollar simply wailed and flung herself on the sofa. Rolle Dollar was slower to comprehend.

But before either of them could start talking about funeral arrangements, I said, "No I want you to listen carefully to me. Mrs. Dollar, straighten up and pay attention!" Few people ever talked to her with that tone and she sat up and ceased her blubbering. "This condition has always been fatal, but it is now within the realm of the surgeon to correct. I know a surgeon in Cincinnati who has operated successfully and I want to take Angeline there. Right away. Rolle, you'll have to make immediate arrangements for a closed wagon. I want a litter suspended by leather straps to take up the shocks. In Austin we'll put her in a private car—this will cost a lot of money, but we're talking about the girl's life."

"I'll take care of it," Dollar said solemnly. He looked at his wife, then left the house. I rolled down my sleeves and slipped into my coat, trying to think of something to say. There wasn't anything.

Mrs. Dollar said, "Lunsford Cardine should be killed."

"Do you think that matters now? I have a telegram to send. I'll be back this afternoon. We ought to be able to catch the night train out of Austin tomorrow evening and be in Cincinnati by early tomorrow afternoon. Try to get a grip on yourself now, Mrs. Dollar. Don't go to pieces on me."

"I'll try," she said. "Oh, what a cross to bear. What a curse!"

Rolle Dollar had the blacksmith build it to my instructions and I suppose that it was the first ambulance Victoria had ever seen. We took a spring wagon, made heavy top bows and erected wooden sides and covered them with canvas. Inside, the litter was suspended like a hammock and the patient would ride in relative comfort. Two jump seats were installed because both Christina Heidler and I intended to ride back there.

Quite a crowd gathered outside Rolle Dollar's house when we brought Angeline outside in a litter, swathed in blankets until only her head protruded. Rolle and another man hefted her into the ambulance; the luggage that Christina and I had brought along was stowed under the front seat and I went around to check it.

Guy Hulse sat on the seat and he grinned at me. "What the hell are you doing?" I said, surprised to see him.

"Why, I'm goin' to drive you to Austin, doc. Seen Rolle at the blacksmith shop and he told me you was takin' Angeline east, so I said I'd drive."

"You're a damned good man, Guy," I said and went back; Christina was inside and Aaron Stiles from the newspaper was there with his pad and pencil.

"Care to tell me anything, doc?"

"Bad appendix," I said, loud enough so that others heard. "I know a surgeon in Cincinnati who operates successfully for that. We're taking her there."

"Serious as that, huh?" Stiles said, writing away.

"Fatal if not operated on," I said and got into the back and closed the doors. Suddenly Mrs. Dollar came bowling out of the house; I guess it just hit her that we were actually taking Angeline away and I rapped on the front window, telling Guy Hulse to get going.

It would be simple to say that we reached Austin without incident and an hour later got on the train, which is what we did, yet what happened bears telling.

Guy Hulse and his brother, Alfy, had been in town when they got word we were going to make a night drive of it to Austin, and Guy volunteered to drive while Alfy, on a fast horse, rode on ahead on a mission that was not clear to me until later, around ten o'clock to be exact.

The weather was cold and windy, but the tight sides of the wagon helped hold it back. For a time I kept a kerosene lantern going, for heat more than light, but the fumes became strong and I had to put it out. Christina and I were bundled in heavy coats and mittens and we kept Angeline swathed in blankets, and I give her credit for having grit; she wasn't one for crying out in pain and I knew there was pain.

I could have given her a shot to ease the pain, but with the temperature near freezing, I felt it was better to wait until morning, until it warmed up a little.

Around ten o'clock I heard Guy Hulse whoa the team and stop and I opened the back door and got down to see what the trouble was. Some cowboys from the Rafter K outfit had built a huge fire alongside the road and they came around to the back with lanterns and torches. One toothless gnome of a man had a coffee pot and tin cups and another had a kettle of hot soup.

It was a thing that could al ost bring tears to a man's eyes, and nothing tasted better. Christina Heidler spooned coffee and soup into Angeline Dollar and then some cowboys came to the back of the wagon, carrying hot rocks in their chap legs, using them like slings. They dumped the rocks into the back of the ambulance, at least a dozen headsized, and immediately the heat began to radiate.

They had heated them for four or five hours and the heat would remain a long time. Up front, Guy Hulse and some of the Rafter K outfit hitched up a team of fresh horses and before I could express my thanks, we were moving again.

Now I could see what Alfy Hulse was doing, riding out a cold and blustery night, wearing out Lord knew how many horses, going ahead of us, telling whoever he met that we were on a mission of mercy.

By morning, I had hoped to reach Gonzales, but there was the river to cross and the freeze-thaw, see-saw kind of weather we'd been having would leave the river swollen and I expected trouble there.

There wasn't, really, because we were met by thirty riders from the T-On-A-Rail outfit. They'd spent hours cutting timber and roping together a raft and when we stopped, they had coffee and bacon and biscuits waiting for us, and another load of hot rocks.

The team was unhitched and the ambulance rolled onto the raft; it settled deeper into the water but the wheel rims did not get too wet. Then the cowboys made their ropes fast to the raft and to a man plunged their horses into the icy water and swam us across. A huge fire had been built up on the far bank; fresh horses were hitched and we moved on without delay.

Dawn brought a gray, cheerless sky, and with the inside of the ambulance kept reasonably warm by the rocks, I gave Angeline an injection and she slept.

At a stage station twenty miles south of Austin we ran into the first of the snow; it continued to snow from then on, light, drifting flakes, more powder than anything, but keeping up steadily it soon layered the land a brilliant white.

Alfy Hulse was at the stage station; he opened the back door and grinned at me as Christina and I stepped down. Alfy Hulse showed the effects of a sleepless night, and the hard riding.

The first thing he said was, "You all right, doc? Everything all right?"

I shook hands with him, too moved to speak, then we went inside briefly. The station agent and two Mexican hostlers carried heated rocks in the tin coal scuttle and placed them inside the ambulance and before they closed the door, the Mexicans crossed themselves.

Sedated, Angeline would sleep so I felt no sense of guilt when I backed up to the stove alongside Christina and toasted some heat into my backside.

Alfy and Guy Hulse brought us some coffee. I looked from one to the other and said, "Rolle Dollar owes you more than he can ever repay. Are you both going on to Austin?" I expected that perhaps Alfy would stay at the station and wait for Guy to come back.

"We're goin' on," Guy said. "Angeline, she's makin' it, ain't she, doc?" He looked at his brother and shifted his feet. "Doc, I know a telegram costs money, but after the operation, I'd appreciate it if you'd wire us and let us know how it came out."

"Why," I said, "I'd be glad to do that." I studied them briefly. "Say, have you got a personal interest in Angeline, boys?"

Alfy shrugged. "She don't know we're alive, doc. It don't matter none though."

I said, "But soft, what light thru yon window breaks? It is the east and Juliet is the sun."

"What's that mean?" Alfy asked.

I reached out both hands and encompassed two shoulders. "Boys, promise me one thing? When she comes home, comb your hair and bring her—well, don't bring her anything. Just come and see her!"

Alfy shook his head. "I don't know, doc. Rolle Dollar's got some set ideas and he knows that both Guy and me ain't above havin' a drink now and then."

"Rolle Dollar will be a changed man, believe me." I took a notebook and pencil from my pocket and wrote for several minutes, then I gave the page to Guy Hulse. "Will you see that the telegrapher gets this in Austin?" I gave him five dollars to pay for it. "Read it if you want."

"Neither of us can read, doc," Alfy said solemnly.

"Then I'll tell you what it says. I told Rolle what you two have done and what the men of the Rafter K and T-On-A-Rail have done. I suggested that he sit down at his desk, with pen in hand and humility in heart and write his letters of thanks."

"Aw," Guy said, "you didn't have to do that. The fellas were glad to do it."

What was there to say?

It was time to leave and we got into the ambulance. Alfy tied two fresh saddle horses on behind and we started off. I remained quiet, thinking about this night and how I probably would never forget any of it.

A man cannot practice medicine on the frontier without getting to know a lot of people, and in both the cow outfits I recognized men that were considered extremely dangerous by peace officers, some with pretty wide reputations as gun fighters and killers. In general they were an unwashed, profane lot, living dangerous, lonely lives and any of them would be lucky to live to the age of forty.

But that night, there were no kinder hearts, no gentler hands, no feeling more sincere than each of them felt. And everyone of them knowing that they were helping a girl whose station was above them, unjustly, perhaps, but there nevertheless.

It was a cruel paradox that could anger a man a little.

Christina Heidler spoke. "I love you, Ted Bodry."

I looked at her in the pale light filtering through the front window. She took off her mitten and slipped her warm firm hand into my mitten and her fingers were strong.

"Dr. Ivy helped me because he's a doctor. You helped me because you're kind. It doesn't bother me to tell you that I love you. I can live with it because it will be enough."

10

DR. HARRY CALENDAR met the train and I hardly recognized him, muffled so in a great fur coat. He had an ambulance waiting and Angeline Dollar was transferred immediately; Christina and I rode in Calendar's coach while hospital orderlies went in the ambulance.

The snow was deep, banked along the edges of the street and carriage wheels had been replaced by sled runners. Calendar produced a lap robe for our feet and on the way to the hospital I discussed Angeline's case with him. As I expected, he intended to operate immediately and he wanted me to assist, but I had to decline. I wanted to observe closely his technique before I was prepared to assist.

And he understood.

He had taken rooms for us in a small hotel three blocks from the hospital; we had only to register and get our key from the desk clerk. He was the same Harry Calendar, always in command, always thinking of everything.

At the hospital we separated and Harry gave us instructions as to how to get to the surgical amphitheatre. We walked down several long halls and found a gathering by a large double door. On the wall was a notice board, with a list of operations and surgeons scheduled; it rather boggled me, that more surgery was being performed in one day than I would do in six months.

We went in and took seats; they encircled the operating room, sharply tiered so that those observing got an unobstructed view directly over the operating table. There was, for me, a great excitement that I had not felt since my medical school days and I had forgotten how many were in attendance on the patient. Dr. Calendar was assisted by two surgeons, and there was a scrub nurse, a surgical nurse, and two nurses administering the anaesthetic. I was particularly interested in the equipment for spraying the instruments with antiseptics (boiling had not yet come into practice; I suppose it was so simple no one ever thought of it.)

I was impressed with the way the surgical nurse prepared the patient, first carefully washing and shaving the area to be incised. Later I learned that this was becoming more accepted as a method of introducing better sepsis; the minute hair follicles can hide bacteria and the policy of shaving pubic hair during normal delivery was encouraged in the better hospitals.

The first incision interested me because a dye was used to trace the exact location of the incision before any instrument was introduced. Abdominal entry had always concerned me because the abdominal wall contains important nerves and muscles and the surgeon cannot simply hack his way through them; the incision has to be made in such a way as to do the minimum of harm.

Dr. Calendar made his first incision some three inches long in a downward and inward slope, cutting between the muscles rather than across them and I was interested to note that his single cut was through the sheath of the main muscle, the rectus abdominis, one stroke, not a series of deeper cuts which always left the opening a bit ragged.

For thirty-seven minutes I watched, never once taking my eyes off his hands and it is difficult to say how I really felt about it all. He was like a grand musician playing a silent, magnificent organ, deft, certain, incredibly delicate. Without discussing the matter with him, I assumed that the operation would terminate in a complete hysterectomy, dangerous, with high mortality; I could have foreseen no other course.

And I could not have been more mistaken.

With a technique certainly advanced he meticulously closed, suturing carefully, minutely, and when he had finished and stripped off his gown, I left with Christina Heidler, feeling quite drained. We waited for him in the hallway and after a few minutes he came out, shrugging into his coat. He was a thick-set man, rather short, with rich dark hair and he wore gold-rimmed glasses. In age he was close to thirty and certainly already established in surgical fields.

We went into a cafeteria in the basement of the hospital and took a corner table. Harry Calendar said, "Prognosis, good, doctor. She should convalesce here for at least a month before making that long journey back. Traveling such distances alone—"

"Maybe we can work something out, Harry. I would like to have Miss Heidler remain here for some nurse's training, particularly in surgery." He looked at her. "If you don't mind, Christina, you could return with her."

"An excellent arrangement," Calendar said. Then he winked. "You've got a damned pretty nurse, doctor. Trade you."

"Thank you, no," I said. "But speaking of nurses, I was really impressed with your surgical assistants. I've always felt that I never had enough hands, Harry, and now I see that it's nearly impossible for a man to do competent surgery without proper assistance."

"Surgery is undergoing a tremendous upheaval," Calendar said. "For centuries it has been the by-product of medicine, almost sheer butchery. But of course anesthesia has removed the horror of it to a large degree and people no longer hold surgical practice in dread. Well, at least they are becoming educated to it. And surgery is just not suited to home laying-in, Ted. The patient must be hospitalized and post-operative care is often as important as the surgical procedure itself. When I went into residency here three years ago, the surgical facilities were rather inconsequential. I would say that they have expanded to ten times what they were then and plans are under advisement for building another wing." He took a slim cigar from his pocket, offered one to me, then lit both of them. "Are you still in practice with Dr. Walter Ivy?" I nodded. "Quite a fellow there. Very good, I understand. Tremendous bedside manner."

"I take it you don't approve."

Harry Calendar shrugged. "Ted, you just don't have the knack for telling a joke, passing on gossip, and handing the patient a pill. I detected that right away while you were a student. You were very intense. Very questioning. It takes that to be a surgeon."

"Well, I certainly feel inadequate enough," I admitted. "That's why I snapped at the chance to come back for a few weeks. I intend to spend a good deal of my time in the amphitheatre taking profuse notes."

Calendar laughed. "There'll be ample opportunity, Ted, because we have some men here who are doing very advanced work, particularly in vermiform appendix disease, or typhlitis

231

or perityphlitis, or whatever you happen to want to call it. These abdominal infections are often terminal and there's considerable research to determine cause and arrest."

"Yes, I lost four patients of typhlitis. As a matter of fact, I suspected that in the Dollar girl."

"It's none of my business," Harry Calendar said, "but her husband didn't come along?"

I glanced at Christina, then said, "He's, ah—"

"Of course," Calendar said, assuming the obvious. "I should have known. Well, it's a shame because the odds are that she could conceive again, normally." He drew deeply on his cigar. "We've got a man here from Vienna who's doing some interesting hernia work. He's just published an important paper on the removal of a cancerous larynx, but his real devotion is to gastric surgery. He's operating twice this week and once the next. You'll want to observe."

"I certainly will!"

Harry Calendar looked at his watch. "I'm due on the wards. Why don't you go to your hotel and rest up. I'll meet you in the dining room at seven and we'll have dinner. If possible, I'll bring along a man you'll find very interesting. He's doing some new work on kidney stones." He got up and smiled at Christina. "Beautiful, simply beautiful, doctor."

Then he hurried off; he never seemed to walk anywhere.

I looked at Christina and she was looking at me; we both laughed.

"He's an unusual man," I said.

"Oh, but *very* interesting," she said, in that way women use that arouses an instant jealousy.

* * * *

The hospital had a training program for nurses and Christina Heidler attended these daily, beginning early in the morning and not terminating until late evening and I would see her only at dinner and perhaps a hour or so afterward.

I was very busy, attending lectures, observing surgical technique, and digging into the business of operating a hospital because I intended to have one of my own; there was no doubt in my mind that the administrative work would fall to me and not be shared by Walter Ivy who was always very busy being the good country doctor.

Angeline Dollar was in the surgical ward and I paid a visit each day; after all, she was still my patient and her recovery was steady, each day releasing her a bit from pain, and finally on the tenth day she was allowed to walk around a bit, supported by two nurses. Of course today we get the surgical patient right out of bed and make them go to the bathroom, but then we believed in strict rest and quiet, and actually retarded their recovery.

It seemed inconceivable that my visit was at an end; the time had gone so rapidly. Since I had to catch a ten o'clock train, Harry Calendar dined with Christina and me in my hotel room, and professing a call, he left early.

Of course I wanted to be alone with her, and I said all the stupid things men say, like, "Are you sure you'll be all right? Do you have enough money? You will wire me so I can meet your train?"

None of it was any good, because I had once acted as though I couldn't love her and now I sat there like an oaf, actually in love with her and not knowing at all how the devil to say it.

It was a dismal situation.

Then she said, "You're not very good at small talk, are you, Ted?"

"Abominable."

"Then why try?"

"It's been a full, exciting ten days, hasn't it?" I fell quiet, brushing lightly at my mustache. "You know, Harry's right; you're a lovely girl. I've always thought so." Again that blasted silence. Finally I flung out of the chair and moved to her and pulled her to her feet. "In the name of God, Christina, marry me and settle once and for all this infernal ache inside me!"

"You only have an hour before train time," she reminded me.

"Blast the train! You're not being very romantic, you know."

She put her soft hands on my face and kissed me lightly. "Ted, go home. Think about it. When I come back you'll know if you really want that."

"Damn it, I know now!"

"No, you think about it. Please?"

"You're bound to get your way," I said. "All right, Christina, I'll go and I'll think about it but I won't change my mind."

"It's hard to tell these things, Ted. But if you do, I'll understand. Honestly."

I still had my hands on her arms and I gently drew her to me; she came willingly and I held her while I kissed her; it was the most satisfying experience of my life.

She wanted to go with me to the train but I wouldn't hear of it; it was almost zero out and I knew she had to get up early the next morning. So we didn't say goodbye; I just left with my bags, caught a carriage and arrived at the station just in time to get aboard.

Although it was more expensive, I had a compartment to myself and spent the long hours studying and recompiling my volumes of notes. At Austin there was a half a day lay over before I could catch the southbound coach; the weather was cold and windy and I wasn't looking forward to the stage ride.

Walter Ivy met me at the hotel and the weather was as balmy as a spring day, with a warming wind coming in off the gulf. He helped me with my luggage and bales of books and notes, then said, "How's your patient?"

"Recovering. Would you mind dropping me off at the Dollar house?"

"They got your wire. Can't it wait?" He saw that it couldn't and sighed and clucked to the team. When I got out of the buggy by Rolle Dollar's gate, Walter said, "I'll unload this stuff for you. Why don't you have supper with us?"

"Are you sure Dorsey won't mind?"

He smiled. "She's settled down in her pregnancy, and is feeling much better." He popped the lid on his watch. "Say an hour?"

I nodded and he drove on.

When I turned up the path, Rolle Dollar came to the front door and held it open for me. He seized my hand and nearly broke my knuckles. "Mrs. Dollar is in her room; I'll fetch her. Make yourself at home, doctor."

I sat down and she came in a moment later; Rolle had his arm around her and this display of affection surprised me. Mrs. Dollar wanted to shake my hand and she screwed up her face as though on the verge of tears but managed by supreme control not to cry.

Rolle said, "We got your wire. The first one, and the last one that you sent after the operation. It humbles a man. Indeed it does." He looked genuinely sorry. "I sat up all that night, reading the Word, and taking stock of myself, doctor. I've cast many a stone at the Hulse brothers and at old Pete. Shiftless, I've called them. And worse too. Not fit, I've said." He sniffed. "I went to 'em. Yessir, I did that. I went a humble man. They took me into their house, such as it is, gave me food and drink and we talked as friends. That Alfy is a straight-forward boy, that he is. Unlettered, to be sure, but straight in the eye and heart. And that's what matters, isn't it?"

"It's a pretty good world, Rolle. A little rough around the edges, but a good world. Your daughter will regain her health. Someday she'll marry and, well, she may even make you a grandfather."

"Praise God," Rolle said.

"Amen," said his wife.

He cleared his throat. "You know I hold drink to be one of man's greatest sins, doctor, but I ordered two cases of the best whiskey from Mulligan and sent a case to the men at the Rafter T and a case to T-On-A-Rail."

"You did the right thing, Rolle. It was something they'll understand and remember."

He nodded, feeling a little better about it, I suppose. Then he said, "I'd like to know that doctor's fee. Send him a check first thing in the morning."

I reached inside my coat. "I brought the bill, Rolle. With hospital care and surgeon's fees, it comes to two hundred and eight dollars."

He took the bill from me, not batting an eye, and this from a man who had fifty cents of the first dollar he ever earned.

"I expect you've got a bill for me."

"I'll tell you what, Rolle. You have an ambulance built for me to my specifications and I'll call it square. Cut any corners you want, but I mean to have a carriage that a person in pain can ride in without jolting their insides loose."

"By the Lord in Heaven," Rolle Dollar said, "you'll have it!"

11

GENERALLY, WHEN people say they'll do something it means when they get around to it, or in their own sweet time, so I was a little surprised when a week later, Rolle Dollar approached my table at the hotel and sat down across from me. He eyed my pushed-aside plate, the remaining pie crumbs and my almost finished cup of coffee.

"About through there, doc?"

"Except for a cigar and the expulsion of a little swallowed air."

"I want you to come down to Peerly's blacksmith shop."

"Now?"

He bobbed his head, so I laid fifty cents on the table, gathered up hat, coat, and bag and went out with him, putting them on as we went through the lobby.

We walked two blocks down and Rolle seemed almost on the verge of trotting ahead of me, he was that excited. He opened the door for me and I stepped inside the shop. Peerly's blacksmith shop was dirty; they all were, with a profusion of iron scattered about and horseshoes hanging from the rafters and the place was cozy from the forge fire. Rolle led the way back; Peerly was there, whistling away and we stepped through another door. There were lanterns hanging from the uprights and I stopped just inside the door, like a man will when his breath is a bit taken away.

Rolle Dollar rocked back and forth on his heels. "How do you like it, doc?"

He meant my ambulance. My beautiful ambulance. I walked around it examining it while Amos Peerly and Rolle Dollar stood there, pleased with it all. Peerly had taken a stage coach running gear and overhauled it; it was painted black with gilt striping, a gleaming, immaculate thing. And on this chassis he had constructed an ambulance body of solid oak with double doors in the back; the whole thing was suspended by broad leather straps which would give it the easy, rocking chair ride of a stage. The body was painted a glistening white and the driver sat outside, forward, on a high perch. Inside there was a suspended litter and two upholstered jump seats. A storm lantern had been fastened to the roof and, outside, two large coach lights with polished reflectors would brighten any dark avenue.

I went over to where they waited and waved my hands, wondering what I could say. "Rolle, I want the Hulse boys to take this to Austin to meet the train. We'll bring Angeline home in it."

"That's mighty nice, doc, but I told Alfy Hulse he could use my buggy. It's kinda that I want to see my little girl sittin' up."

"Sure," I said. "That'll do fine, Rolle." Then I looked at Amos Peerly. "How long have you been workin' on this, Amos?"

"I got started the day after you got back, doc. Ain't done nothin' else, really." He grinned. "But I enjoyed every minute of it. Even the undertaker ain't got a rig this fancy." He took me forward, towing me by the arm and showed me what he'd built under the front seat. It was a heavy metal box with a drawer that pulled forward. "You just fill this with coals on a cold night and the heat goes into the back to take the chill off. Ought to make it cozy as a kitchen, doc."

It was ingenious and I examined it in detail with the flue that carried the heated air into the back without introducing fumes. The fire box was surrounded by an air chamber which vented under the seat.

"It's the best coach I've ever seen, Amos!"

"Never built anything like it before," Peerly admitted. "Always wanted to build coaches. Started out that way back east, then I came here and took up blacksmithing."

"Tomorrow morning I'll drive it up and down the street so everybody can see it." We went back into the blacksmith shop. "Rolle, Amos, I thank you and a lot of people will thank you."

Peerly waved his hand and Rolle Dollar said, "Doc, I just want to see my little girl step out of that buggy under her own steam and smile. She's all the missus and I've got. Comes down to it, nothin' else really matters."

Alfy and Guy Hulse came to see me before they left for

237

Austin; they wanted to know if there was anything special they had to do, and I suggested that they make sure they had an extra lap robe and didn't try to make sixty miles a day. They grinned at this and poked each other on the arm and left my office.

I could understand their impatience; I was impatient myself, but not to have Angeline Dollar back. The last ten days had been lonesome ones for me, making my rounds and returning to an empty office.

It is still amazing to me how men can develop a specific blindness when it concerns a woman. From the first I had wanted Christina Heidler to stay, telling myself that she needed a place of her own, and I think I really believed that. And subsequently I encouraged her to remain, tying her, really, hoping she would become so dependent that she would dare not leave me; I suppose I had that subconscious fear that she would leave. And all the time I was talking one thing and feeling another.

A miserable situation for a professional man, and one I didn't enjoy.

As much time as possible was spent west of town where a crew of twenty workmen, mostly Mexican, were laboring to complete the foundations. The concrete had been hauled in from Port Lavaca and after fifteen days of forming, the basement and walls were finally poured.

Had the details been left to me I would have made a lot of mistakes and spent money needlessly; we were spared this through the efforts of Leland Burgess, the attorney from San Antonio. He had duplicates made of the plans and contractors were invited to submit bids, with the upshot being that a local firm would build the foundation, an Austin company would erect walls and structure, while a San Antonio company would install all plumbing and heating. Well drilling was done locally and a New England firm shipped the first windmill in south Texas; this unit pumped the water into a huge storage tank, highly elevated, and from there the water was piped throughout the building.

Indoor plumbing, novelty though it was, had finally come west.

Completion date was scheduled for early fall of 1874, and

then, with the building up, work would only begin for me, since the organization and administration were going to be my responsibility.

Walter Ivy and I spent three days out of town; we had a few outlying towns where we held clinics. This was Walter's idea and we had been doing it for some time, generally alternating office and home calls. He had set up a schedule so that we always arrived at the same time of the month and set up in a small place reserved for us. Each month we would make the rounds, stopping at two large ranches to the southwest, a small village populated mainly by Mexicans, and ending with a swing north that brought us back to Victoria.

And it seemed to me that people saved up all their aches and pains for our monthly visits. We worked together at the ranches and Walter remained there while I made a tour to some of the places owned by homesteaders; they would leave a message for me, saying they were feeling poorly or that this was bothering them, or something.

Always something.

And I noticed that during this last year more and more homesteaders were nibbling away at the lands preempted by the big ranches. Fences were going up and the plowed field was becoming more commonplace. Orchards were planted and wheat was being sown and cotton fields sprang up and the face of Texas was slowly, surely being changed.

The temper of Texas was changing too for I noticed that the cowboys all wore their pistols, even around the ranch house, and that talk was going around about fence cutting and pretty soon we'd have the Texas Rangers if the cattlemen didn't put away their snippers.

Homesteaders were watching carefully anyone who came near their places and there was not one house that I was able to approach without being covered by a rifle or shotgun. Weapons were only put away after I was identified.

On the way back Walter and I talked about this; he had a nose for trouble and suspected that pretty soon we'd be getting a rash of gunshot cases, and he figured it was only a matter of time before the law stepped in.

I suppose it was my youth, but I was more confident in the sound judgment of man, then I remembered the senseless shooting in Mulligan's place and didn't shrug off his opinion too lightly. After all, few men had the feel of the country like Walter Ivy had; he seemed to have a finger eternally on the pulse. And he knew these people, understood them better than I did, perhaps better than I ever would. Where I lost patience with them, he maintained his. Where I considered them backward, he thought of them as conservative. I thought they were too provincial; he felt that they were just set in their ways.

It was, I'm sure, this genuine compassion that made Walter Ivy so popular and influential. In the many meetings I had attended with him—the town council and the school board—I have watched him sit there, slumped in his chair, littering the front of his vest with fingernail scrapings, apparently removed from mounting arguments. Then he would clear his throat and everyone would stop talking and he'd sit there, his eyebrows bunched up, and put his knife away. When he stood up, everyone listened to him and I would hesitate to say how many foolish moves this procedure has halted.

It brought us a fire department, and a public park, and two new churches and a two storey school house, the only one south of Austin.

Many of Walter Ivy's medical views did not coincide with mine, but that he was a sensible man with both feet firmly rooted in Texas soil was beyond dispute; he seemed determined to do what was best for the most people and because of this he would have made a poor politician.

We arrived home late, as usual. Dorsey had retired and I was ready to collapse, but I heated water for a bath, soaked weariness away, then had a stiff drink of whiskey and went to bed.

The sun coming through my window woke me and I shaved before bundling into my coat and going up town. It was early, but I wanted to be early; this was the day the Hulse brothers should be coming back.

Rolle Dollar and his wife were at the hotel and there was a goodly crowd around, waiting for the ambulance to show up. My intentions had a short life when one of Ben Titus' deputies came up to me and drew me aside. "Hate to spoil this homecomin' doc, but I do wish you'd come over to the jail and have a look at Ben. We just can't seem to wake him at all."

All this was done quietly; no one else had heard him. I said, "All right, I'll go right over. But get Dr. Ivy too."

"Sure thing." He trotted off down the street and I unhurriedly left the hotel and walked a block and a half over to the jail. The other deputy was with Ben Titus; he was in the spare room where he slept when he was on duty.

Obviously he had gone to bed in a normal manner, or normal for a lawman; boots and gun off. His breathing was shallow and his pulse was extremely faint. I examined his eyes and had just about decided when Walter Ivy came in, quite out of breath.

"I think it's his heart," I said, stepping back so that Walter could attend him. Finally he motioned for me to help him remove Ben's shirt and vest and roll the sleeve of his underwear; I took out my knife and slit it to the shoulder and Walter prepared an injection.

He motioned for me to check his pulse and I did while he slowly pressed the plunger. Within seconds it seemed that Ben's pulse grew stronger and we watched him closely for a half hour. By then Walter was satisfied that Titus was resting easy.

"I don't think he dare be moved, Ted," Walter said gravely. He looked at the deputies; the other one had come in earlier but I hadn't noticed. "He's got a bad heart and he needs complete rest and quiet."

"Is he goin' to be all right, doc?"

Walter looked at the man, then said, "I honestly don't know. I would say for certain that if he recovers, it'll mean taking things very easy for the rest of his life."

The two deputies looked at each other, the question in their eyes. "We got to get a new sheriff, huh?" One scrubbed the back of his neck with his hands. "I don't want the job, doc. You, Herbie?"

Herbie shook his head, and Walter Ivy said, "Ted, stay here. I'll go see Aaron Stiles and Butram Cardine. I'll try not to be long."

I understood what he had to do for the mechanics of government had to go on and someone would have to be appointed sheriff until next election. And I believed him when he said he'd try not to be long, but I really wished he'd stayed in attendance and let me go back to the main street.

But I stayed and missed out on it all; Ivy was gone almost two hours and when he did come back I had to work at controlling my temper. And he knew it because he said, "I really am sorry, Ted."

"Forget it, Walter."

"I really am—"

"The patient comes first," I said. "Are you going to stay here now?"

"Yes, for a while." Then he smiled. "That was a pretty sight, that ambulance. I'd get over to your office right away, if I was you." Then he took my sleeve. "Ted, are you going to marry her?"

"If she'll have me."

He thought about it. "She's a strong woman, boy. She won't tame into a lap cat."

"Who wants one?" I said and went out, hurrying now.

I stopped in my office just long enough to fling my bag on the couch, then went through my room to the short hallway connecting the storeroom and Christina's.

Before I knocked I heard her moving about, then I heard her voice and opened the door. She had her luggage on the bed and was putting things away and when I stepped into the room she put the things down and watched me.

"Ben Titus had a heart attack and I had—"

The devil with the explanations. I went to her and put my arms around her and kissed her and she came full against me, warm and yielding and then she put her head against my shoulder and rested there.

"I told you it wouldn't matter if you'd changed your mind," she said softly. "But it did. When you weren't there—

"I wanted to be, Christina. I tried to be. But damn it all—"

"It's all right now," she said and laughed and pulled away from me. "Everything's all right now."

"And our patient?"

"Well. She stood the trip nicely."

I took her arm and brought her to me again; it was maddening to have her so near and yet not close enough. "Tomorrow morning I'm going to the courthouse and take out

242

a license. And in the afternoon we'll hitch up my buggy and see if we can't find a house for rent. I've missed you."

"It's been a long winter," she said softly. "But good."

I pulled my head back and looked at her. "Now what does that mean?"

She smiled. "It means I've waited a long time for you to put your arms around me, a long time for you to know that you could love me." She sighed and rested her head against me. "Ted, I will spend my life trying to make you happy."

12

CHRISTINA HEIDLER and I were married on Sunday, January 4, 1874, and Walter Ivy handled all the arrangements, renting the whole dining room of the hotel for the ceremony and I was quite stiff and nervous through the reception afterward. Reverend Loch Angevine performed the whole thing. Dorsey attended the ceremony and the reception, which surprised me because this was the first time she had left her house since she arrived. She was heavy with child and short of breath and Walter was very attentive, but then I suspect that he always had been.

I felt sure that things weren't going right between them although he never said anything and I didn't expect him to because he was a man who kept his personal business to himself. And Dorsey was not the wife he had expected or hoped for but Walter had made his bargain and would stick to it; he was that kind of a man. It must have been very difficult for a young woman, accustomed to servants and plenty of money and the comforts of a large eastern city to adjust to life in a Texas town. She surely must have missed the gay social life, but more I think she missed the gentle, mature surroundings of Maryland. Texas was a place of extremes. Even the weather was that way, hot as blazes or cold as the Klondike. Surely there was no one in town who was her equal, culturally, and she had made no friends at all. I'm sure ladies tried to call on her, and knowing Dorsey, I'm equally sure she rebuffed them.

And in Texas you only do that once.

Dorsey would never have admitted it, but she was a snob. In Baltimore, where the industrial climate was largely manufacturing, she circulated in a circle of mill owners and plant owners; I don't think she ever talked to a sweaty Polish worker or spoke to a tobacco-chewing Swede, or listened to the troubles of an Irish immigrant.

But in Victoria, Texas, she couldn't ignore the cowboys and cattle and rough men and rough country; it was always there, out her window, every time she looked. In the summer, dust settled over everything and a house was nigh impossible to keep clean; she must have fretted endlessly over this. Men swore and ladies pretended not to hear it and there was always the flavor of the cattle yard east of town when the wind was right, and it was, most of the time.

She was a very unhappy, very pregnant woman, and it was my thought that she wished there was some way to undo the whole thing.

However, I wasn't going to worry about Dorsey.

Christina and I had planned to go to Austin for ten days on our honeymoon; we intended to leave on the morning stage and I had my suitcases all packed. Our house wouldn't be vacant until then and we were going to stay the night in the hotel, and leave about ten in the morning.

I had considered all arrangements made, finalized, and finished.

But you never can tell.

Christina was the center of all attention and Walter Ivy took my arm and drew me out of the lobby to a small pantry off the kitchen. His manner was grave and he kept running his hands through his thinning hair. "Ted, I'm afraid something's come up that involves you. Wish to God it didn't, but it does and I can't help it." He looked at me steadily and I could see that it was an effort. "Dorsey has made up her mind to go back home, Ted." He nodded. "Yes, she's going to leave in the morning. It's been coming. I knew it but hoped that somehow—" He shrugged the rest of that away. "The thing is, Ted, I love that woman. Worship the ground she walks on. I'm going with her, Ted. What else can I do?"

I can't say that I was surprised, but I was shocked that it would happen at such an inopportune time. "Walter, don't give in to her! It's the worst thing you could do."

"I know it but I can't help myself."

"What about your practice here?"

"Give it up, I guess. I'd like to see you buy it, Ted."

"I can't. All my money is tied up in the hospital. And what about yours, Walter?"

"Have to withdraw it," he said.

I could feel my temper rising and not at the predicament this placed me in, but at Dorsey for doing this. "Walter, you

245

know I can't refuse, but get Dorsey and meet me upstairs in my room. Thirty-one at the near end of the hall."

Before he could object I left him and went up the stairs. I paced a bit and lit a cigar and then Walter knocked and opened the door for Dorsey. I could see by her expression that she was plenty put out about this, so I came right to the point. "Dorsey, I understand you're going home in the morning."

"Then you understand correctly," she said. "What of it?"

"Frankly," I said, "I don't care where you go, but since Walter is going with you, I have to take over his practice and we have to reach some kind of terms."

"Practice?" she said, making it into a dirty word. "You call that a practice? I want him to go back to where he can be a *real* doctor. Why he could make fifteen thousand a year in Baltimore without ever leaving his office."

"Dorsey, I'm not interested in your greed. It's of no interest to me that you're a willful snob. Texas doesn't need you. You don't have anything they want."

"Now just a minute—" Walter began, but closed his mouth when I stared at him.

"No, you listen to me! I know everything I am is due to you and I'm not forgetting that. But this isn't the time to think of you or me. I'm thinking of our patients, the people who look to us for the only help they're going to get. You want me to buy you out and you know the only way I could do that is to give up the hospital. It might be six or eight years before I could begin building again. How many people will die in the meantime because I wouldn't have the facilities to help them?"

"You're being ridiculous and dramatic," Dorsey said and I whirled on her.

"You shut your mouth! Since you've made no contribution, keep out of it." I looked at Walter Ivy. "This is what we're going to do, Walter. You'll pull out of the hospital; that's four thousand. But you sign a quit claim deed to your house. I'll turn *that* into a hospital until the other one is completed. At that time I'll put the house on the market and sell it for at least what it cost you to build it, plus an amount that would be reasonable rent for the time I've used it."

"Don't you do it, Walter!"

But he wasn't listening to her; he nodded and said, "All

right, Ted. I'll have the papers in order by evening." He took Dorsey by the arm and steered her to the door and she balked because she had something to say to me.

"Oh, you're a snot, Ted. You've milked Walter for all you're going to. It's over! The ride on the man's back is over. You won't last by yourself because you need Walter to stand up. And when you fall, I'll laugh!"

"Come along, Dorsey." He tugged at her arm and pulled her into the hall and found Christina standing there.

Dorsey stared at her and said, "Don't think a wedding ring changes anything for you." Then she started to cry uncontrollably and Walter Ivy shook his head and led her sobbing down the hall.

After they disappeared down the stairs, Christina came inside and I closed the door. She said, "Dorsey is so unhappy that she hates everything. She didn't mean a thing she said."

"You're a lovely bride," I said.

She smiled and took off her veil and carefully put it on the dresser. "I think I know what's the matter with Dorsey. For the first time in her life she doubts that she is woman enough for Walter, or woman enough to live here. All around her she sees people whom she always considered inferior and now she understands that here they are better than she is. It's a hard thing to know."

"We're not going to be able to go on a honeymoon, Mrs. Bodry."

She smiled and tilted her head to one side. "I have a feeling that it won't matter."

And then she came to me, my arms went around her, and I was pretty sure that she was right.

I'm not sure that I really became accustomed to having Walter Ivy gone; certainly it meant a heavier burden for me and there were days on end when I got up at sunrise and didn't sit down with my wife and have supper until ten o'clock at night.

Many of Walter's civic duties fell to me and I tried to dispatch them with the thoughtful attention that Walter had always given them. With Ben Titus recovering from his heart attack, the county supervisors asked my recommendation for sheriff, until next election. At that time and place, honesty and courage were attributes more important than education and knowledge of law, and I suggested Alfy Hulse. He was only twenty-four, but his reputation was well established and he had the respect of all who knew him.

He was sworn in in mid-February and it was a proud day for Old Pete.

Work continued on the hospital, with Rolle Dollar and Butram Cardine coming up with the money that Walter Ivy had withdrawn.

Spring came early with warming winds and a good sun and I noticed that new people were coming to town, some in wagons, and some on the stage. A land office opened up on main street and business took a turn upward and I noticed that Miller's store was stocking new items.

Rolle Dollar told me that his hardware business was growing for these farmers had money, and even though a lot of them were Yankees, they got along well, went quietly about their business, joined the churches and sent their children to school.

In May, I got a letter from Walter Ivy; he was in practice in Baltimore and Dorsey had had her baby, a boy. She seemed, according to Walter, quite happy now and spent a good deal of her time with her family. But a letter is many things; it is the words written and the words implied and judged against prior knowledge of the writer, it reveals things unspoken.

Walter's practice was substantially better paying than what he had in Victoria for he largely served only those who had money and he gave only a half day a week at the county hospital where the poor and the foreign-born went. He tried to convince me that he was happy and pleased, but I knew that he wasn't. Some doctors are content with token medicine while others are destined only to heal and suffer and die a little with each patient whose condition is terminal. I'd always known that Walter was that way. He'd doctor anyone, Mexican, Indian, poor, rich, anyone, and the money was the least of his worries, although he'd always made out that it meant a great deal to him.

But his words had never matched his deeds, and the deeds were what I judged him by.

He did not want me to write to him at his home and from that I gathered that Dorsey really held a grudge, so I wrote to him at his office and told him about Texas and the people he knew and how things were growing. And even as I did it I knew that it would get to him good because the man had roots here and even his wife couldn't tear them up.

I also wrote to several doctors, asking them whether or not they would be interested in coming to Victoria to establish themselves in my practice; my work load was getting very heavy and I knew that if it continued, I wouldn't be able to go it alone.

Christina was a tremendous help; she managed as high as eight bed patients at a time for we had converted half of Walter's house to additional hospital space. And my reputation as a surgeon was spreading so that by summer time I had operated on and discharged sixteen patients who had traveled quite a distance for help.

I also lost four and this depressed me although I knew it had to happen occasionally.

The feelings between cattlemen and homesteaders began to take on an explosive potential around June because the creeks were down and the cattlemen always reached for all the grazing land they could get, fattening up for the fall market, and of course the farmers had their fences up and their crops coming up and threats passed back and forth.

An Ohio man named Will Stang was the leader of the farmer element; he was a nice man, medium height, with a slow way of talking and a lot of sense to what he said.

Stang had a Mexican boy working for him and one day— no one is sure just what set it off—the Mexican boy hauled off and knocked down one of the Circle B riders, and by the time the cowboy hit the dirt he had his six-shooter out and had put a ball right in the middle of the Mexican's chest.

By the time I was notified and got up town, a huge crowd ringed the downed man and the priest was there, holding up his right hand and even as I knelt to make my examination I could hear him: "Si vivis, ego te absolvo a peccatis tuis. In nomine Patris et Filii et Spiritus Sancti. Amen."

Then the Mexican boy died with my finger on his pulse and I looked at the priest and at the cowboy who stood there, still holding his six-shooter; blood dripped from a split lip but he paid no attention to it.

The priest said, "He is gone?"

I nodded and he bent and took a small vial of holy oil from his pocket and put some on his thumb and made a cross on the dead man's forehead. Then he stood up and went through the crowd and they gave way for him.

Alfy Hulse pushed through, took it all in at a glance, then held out his hand. "I'll take that pistol, Scotty. Let's have no more trouble now."

The cowboy flipped it around and handed it over butt first. Hulse put it in his hip pocket and took the cowboy by the arm. "I'll have to lock you up, Scotty." The cowboy nodded and went with him, offering no resistance.

Three weeks later, after Alfy Hulse had investigated and the grand jury convened, Scott Breedon was bound over for trial.

It seemed like everyone turned out for it and the courtroom wasn't nearly big enough to hold a fifth of the crowd, so they lined up to the bar at Mulligan's and across the street at the hotel and waited it out, the cattlemen on one side and the farmers on the other.

And in all of it, Buford Brittles remained neutral. His cowboys always came to town unarmed or if they felt they could not, they were fired and hired on somewhere else. Scully Beachamp did not go this far, but he would not side with the other ranchers and join their fence cutting and trouble making. Brittles and Beachamp waited out the trial on the hotel porch, which was the unspoken domain of the farmers. Will Stang was there and he talked to Brittles and Beachamp; I don't know what about.

When the jury came in, I was on call and didn't hear about it until that evening when I sat down to my supper. Christina gave me the news.

"The cowboy was fined five hundred dollars and put in jail for ninety days," she said. "It was pretty well established that the Mexican boy went out of his way to pick the fight."

"That's what I understand. It seems that he followed Scott Breedon from store to store, ragging him on." I sighed and sliced my roast beef. "Well, I'm sure it hasn't ended with the trial."

13

THE MOST uneasy kind of peace settled over the county because Alfy Hulse, in an unprecedented move, had Judge Enright place the principals under a three hundred dollar peace bond, and that just about included every cattleman and farmer within a radius of fifty miles. It looked like voter registration day at the courthouse and they stood in silent knots, faction against faction, waiting to pay the county clerk.

Now no one wanted to start the trouble, lose the money, and go to jail on top of it.

The hospital was becoming an imposing building, bright brick; the walls were up and the roof was being tiled and workers were busy completing the interior details. Daily I spent some time there, looking it over and as equipment arrived, I saw that it was stored properly and not tampered with.

Dr. Calendar recommended to me a young man who wanted to practice somewhere in the west; we exchanged letters and he sent references and he was scheduled to arrive in July. I had been in contact with three other men, all recommended highly by Walter J. Ivy; they were asked to leave their practices as soon as possible.

All these matters I discussed thoroughly with Buford Brittles and Scully Beachamp and Butram Cardine, who, at my insistence, sat as the hospital board on non-medical matters, and all funds were spent on a voucher over their signature. This, I felt, was business-like and promoted good faith in all concerned.

They were not partners, for after Walter pulled out became the sole owner and the money advanced was a loan, on which interest would be paid and the principal amortized. My arrangements with the doctors were simple; they were in private practice at a central location, paying the hospital rent for their offices and using the hospital nursing staff.

Correspondence was a detail mercifully lifted from me by Christina, who wrote endless letters and inserted advertise-

...ments in many papers, including some in the eastern papers. Nursing, in those days, was really not a profession, at least in the United States, although Saint Thomas Hospital in London, England, turned out the finest nurses under the direction of Florence Nightingale.

All this correspondence resulted in the employment of six nurses, all trained to gently tend the sick, and they were to arrive in the early fall.

Two events occurred that I thought were of far-reaching effect; the Texas Rangers sent three men to Victoria to look into the fence cutting, which still continued in spite of the peace bond, and the Texas-Pacific Railroad was building trunk lines through Victoria to Port Lavaca.

To me this meant quicker, more reliable transportation and reconfirmed my belief that people would travel for many miles to undergo hospitalization and treatment. It also meant that I would get medical supplies from the east more quickly than by the present method of boat. Overland through the Indian country had never been good.

The army under MacKenzie was doing a job of keeping the Comanches and Kiowas contained in the central and north part of the state and we were enjoying some freedom from hostile raids, but no one was foolish enough to think this situation was permanent. There had always been times of peace, only to have it erupt into periods of intense fighting.

It just wasn't possible to convince a Texan that there was such a thing as a good, living Indian.

A social highlight occurred when Alfy Hulse and Angeline Dollar got married and Mrs. Dollar cried uncontrollably through the ceremony. I suppose it was because her dreams had been shattered and her hopes fulfilled, which left her at war with herself. She had always wanted Angeline to marry someone very important and events had made this impossible, at least in her mind. Then after Angeline came home, Mrs. Dollar hoped that someone would marry her; it didn't really matter who.

I thought it was wonderful because Alfy loved her and I could tell just by looking at her that she loved Alfy; it's the way a marriage should start anyway.

Being sheriff had changed Alfy Hulse somewhat; he was more serious-mannered now, taking his responsibilities with great solemnity. It was just about everyone's opinion that Alfy would be a shoo-in at the next election.

The wedding was a grand affair, even though it hurt Rolle Dollar to pay for it. I made the reception, got my cup of punch, kissed the bride, and found my wife, who had gone to the church for the ceremony.

We took our drinks and found a corner of the lobby away from the crowd. Alfy Hulse found us a few minutes later and came over, looking a bit stiff in a celluloid collar and ascot tie.

"Really a grand affair," I said. "My congratulations." I shifted my cup of punch to the other hand and shook his. "You're looking pretty solemn, Alfy. It wasn't that bad, was it?"

"Wish I could talk to you a minute, doc. In private."

I glanced at Christina. "Let's go in the kitchen. Will you excuse us, dear?"

We skirted the crowd and stepped into the kitchen; Alfy closed the door. A Mexican dishwasher labored away, humming softly to himself. Alfy said, "Doc, Angeline told me why you took her to Cincinnati, and it's all right with me. I've raised my hell and I'm none too proud of it. Some of Dirty Esther's girls got plenty of my money." He wiped a hand across his mouth. "But this doesn't matter at all, doc."

"Then what is the problem?"

"Lunsford Cardine came back to town last night."

"The hell you say!"

Alfy nodded. "Butram came to see me late last night at the jail. Lunsford was drunk and passed out, but the old man thinks he's huntin' trouble. Seems he's turned kind of wild. Wears a gun and a big mouth now. The old man claims Lunsford read the engagement announcement in the paper last month. He didn't come back for any good, doc."

"No, I guess he didn't," I said thoughtfully. "But what can I do about it?"

"I don't want trouble," Alfy said. "But I'm not going to have my wife's name on every dirty mouth in town. Doc, I'll kill him first."

He meant it and I didn't blame him.

So I stood there a moment, trying to figure out something that would save everyone a lot of trouble, then I said, "Alfy, you ought to take Angeline away now. I know it isn't what you planned, but if you both got out of town, it might give some of us a chance to cool Lunsford down and send him on his way."

"Kind of sounds like running."

"Alfy, think of your wife, not your pride."

He nodded. "You're right, doc. I'll do just that."

I started to open the door for him and heard the buzz of sound from the lobby change tempo; it was a subtle thing, a loss of gaiety. Then Angeline screamed, not loud; it was more an angry bleat than anything and I flung the door open as Alfy elbowed past me.

An avenue had opened up and Angeline was standing in the center of the lobby, trying to break free of Lunsford Cardine's arms.

"That'll do," Alfy said and Lunsford let her go; Angeline rushed sobbing into her father's arms.

Lunsford Cardine was not the same man who had left Victoria. Always as dandified as his father's money could make him, he had found being on his own less than grand. Now he wore range clothes, jeans and a tan brush jacket and a bone-handled pistol on his left hip in a cross-draw holster. A five-day beard stubble hid his cheeks and he looked at Alfy Hulse and laughed.

"You aren't the only man who's put his arms around her," Lunsford said, smiling.

"I said that'll do!"

"Sure. You've gone up in the world and I've gone down." He looked around the room. "Pretty nice wedding, huh? Pretty little bride, huh? She'll make a nice widow."

Then his hand dropped and scooped up his gun and he shot as the muzzle came hip high; the bullet struck Alfy Hulse in the chest and he staggered back but did not fall. His pistol was under his coat and I think he was reaching for it when Lunsford's bullet caught him, but that didn't stop him.

He fired as he fell and Lunsford grabbed his throat, screamed and whirled and took six stumbling steps outside before falling on the hotel porch.

A few men rushed to him but nearly everyone seemed to converge on Alfy. I was there first, kneeling, opening his vest and shirt and yelling for someone to get something to carry him on. It was a bad wound, very bad, missing the heart but so close that I was certain there was serious damage.

Angeline was nearly hysterical and Christina and some other woman took her away. Someone took down a door and they carefully placed Alfy on it and he was borne out.

Lunsford Cardine was still sprawled on the porch and I could see that he was dead and no one seemed to care about it at all. I ran on ahead to get ready and then a buggy came up behind me and stopped so I could get in; it was Rolle Dollar and Christina and we went on, Rolle lashing the team.

Alfy was brought into the operating room and I quickly shooed the others out. Christina was cutting away his clothes; he was unconscious, his breathing ragged and bloody and his pulse was weak and erratic.

Christina looked at me and said, "Help him." She had tears in her eyes.

"I can't," I said helplessly. "No one has successfully opened the chest." I wiped my face with a trembling hand. "The bullet's too close to the heart to try to probe."

"Try!" She shouted this.

"He may die if I make one mistake!"

"He's dying now, damn it!" She wasn't angry at me; she was angry at her helplessness and the senseless brutality that had put him there.

We worked frantically, desperately; she operated the sprayer and I scrubbed, then began to probe, carefully, almost with held breath. Christina wiped sweat off my face as I worked, then I felt the bullet, and I prayed fervently that for once I would be given a genuine healer's touch, for once be raised above the level of ignorant, bumbling country doctor appalled at his true lack of knowledge. I prayed for God to reach down and touch both myself and this dying man, to guide my hand and my instrument to a place where mortal eyes couldn't see and to bring out that which was causing him death.

Then I pulled out my probe and dropped the .44 into the pan Christina held waiting.

To describe the remainder of that day and that night is like trying to totally recall a childhood nightmare; I know that we kept carbolic-soaked compresses on the wound and that he somehow hung on, breathing, fighting for his life.

I didn't leave his side, but Christina went out and told the people gathered in front that he was still alive. When night came they were still there and they built a large fire in the street and kept it going through the night. Some people from the Baptist church came and the minister prayed, kneeling in the dust, and they sang hymns—*Jesus, my Lord, my God, my all—we pray to thee.*

Some of the ladies—I never knew who they were—brought coffee and sandwiches for those outside and Christina brought a cup inside to me.

"Tell them he still lives," I said and she went out again.

At dawn they were still there, coming and going, but always returning and I watched Alfy Hulse, watched his fever mount as he fought on, making no sound, no sign, no movement.

I was dreadfully tired, and slept in small increments, sometimes ten minutes, sometimes more, but rarely more than a half hour at a time. Through the day I kept him covered with blankets and kept changing his sterile dressing and in the afternoon I fired up the stove although it was summer and a bake-oven heat was heavy everywhere.

The crowd thinned somewhat during the day and once Christina came in and I think she said that Lunsford Cardine had been quietly buried; I didn't care about him.

Angeline had been outside all that night and finally her father carried her home; it was the only way he could get her to leave and she was too tired to resist.

That night, or perhaps it was early morning—I was too exhausted to look at my watch—Alfy Hulse's fever broke and he stirred and I gave him water immediately. From that moment on he began a slow, steady climb out of the pit, an inch at a time, and when the dawn came I stepped outside, wobbly, almost unable to stand. Fifteen or twenty people stood around, waiting for me to speak.

"He's pretty well out of danger," I said and my voice

sounded strange to me. "Go home now. Someone stop at Rolle Dollar's house and tell Alfy's wife."

Then I went back inside and closed the door.

Christina came a short time later; she had a large tin lunch pail and spread the first good meal I'd had in days on a small portable table. Alfy Hulse was breathing regularly and he was resting well. Tomorrow or the next day he would open his eyes and look around and know where he was, and from then on it would only be a matter of time.

"I think," I said, "that if I had put a knife to him he would have died, Christina. It just may be that no one will ever be able to open the chest and have the patient survive."

"You really can't believe that, Ted."

She was right; I didn't, but it all seemed so remote. "I believe that if we'd used an anesthetic he would have died. I'm certain of that. He didn't have the strength to fight off the effect, and any vomiting would have set off the bleeding." I scraped a hand across my bearded face. "When I probed for the bullet I prayed because I was reaching in and touching a man's life. A mistake—"

She smiled and took my hand. "You didn't make any mistakes, Dr. Bodry."

"I take no credit for it."

She got up and went into the room next to my office and turned down the covers of the bed there. Then she came back and helped me off with my vest and shirt and made me stretch out. She took off my shoes and trousers and I kept foolishly insisting that I could do these things for myself and she kept scolding me in that sweet, gentle way she had and that's all I remember because I fell asleep.

When I woke, it was daylight and I sat up and rubbed my eyes. There was a wash stand in the room and I splashed water over my face, towelled dry, then stepped out into the hallway. Christina was in the operating room; Alfy Hulse had not yet been moved to a bed, and when I looked in she was giving him water through a bent glass tube.

"What time is it?" I asked.

"A quarter to eleven," she said and smiled.

"It certainly is remarkable how a few hours sleep will refresh a man."

"Yes," she said. "Especially since you went to bed at a

quarter after eight yesterday." Then she came over and put her arms around my neck and gave me one of those soul kisses that could cause so much trouble.

Not with us though.

14

A PHYSICIAN on the frontier did not have to doctor everyone; a fair percentage of the people doctored themselves, or purchased all medical supplies from the snake oil salesmen who roamed about in their wagons, and although I thought they were an abomination and a pox on the healing arts, I rather enjoyed their shows.

Usually the show was given on the main street, or in the town square and there would be a colored man dressed as some savage from a dark and mysterious continent no one had ever heard of, and usually another man, or a young woman, dressed in veils and possessing all the mystic healing powers of the East.

The 'doctor' sold his medicine in bottles, usually a simple concoction largely made up of alcohol, spices, root herbs, and belladonna as a pain killer. Specifically it attacked no general complaint, but it sold for a dollar and up a bottle, depending upon the show, the skill of the barker, and how big a sucker the customer was.

Victoria had her share of medicine men shows; they came to the town long before I did and I suppose the barker felt that I had infringed upon his exclusive territory. But still they came, each year, with their show and bottles and a lot of people, who would never think to come to me with a complaint, bought the medicine.

The doctor got those who had tried these remedies and found them useless. He got trouble very far advanced and because of this his work was difficult, and then I began to see the value of Walter Ivy's 'preventive medicine', his continual effort to educate the patient and the family on the necessity of visiting the doctor when they felt only a bit poorly.

This was something I had never done, and didn't particularly believe in, never really understanding that the average man was slightly afraid of a doctor and lacked a doctor's faith in medicine.

And this was why I was particularly eager to welcome Dr. O'Brien and Dr. Strudley when they got off the southbound coach. O'Brien was a dumpy man, quite overweight; he had a round florid face eternally cracked into a smile and his hair was brick red. His hand-shake was firm enough to crush the knuckles of a blacksmith and his laugh was a smothered chuckle deep in his chest.

"Doctor Bodry, this is a pleasure," O'Brien said. "Could I get someone to handle the luggage? I have four bags and that large steamer trunk on top."

"The freight agent will bring them to the hospital," I said and turned to Dr. Strudly. He was as English as any man could be. Tall, very military, he wore a bowler and a Grenadier Guard mustache and he carried a silver-headed cane. His grip was firm, polite, reserved; I immediately judged him to be highly competent as well as efficient.

"An honor, sir," Strudley said. He used his cane to point to the other baggage on top of the coach. "Mine, I'm afraid."

With the promise that their luggage would be brought on, I invited them to crowd into my buggy and we drove west to the hospital. They had a good view of it at the end of the street; it was an imposing building and I was immensely proud of it. I parked in front and tied the horse and we went inside, stopping in the foyer. Sunlight reflected brightly from the polished marble and Dr. Strudley said, "Oh, I say!"

"May I show you to your offices and around the building?"

I led them down the hall and paused before a door. The sign said: ARCHIBALD STRUDLEY, M.D.

He looked at it a moment, then opened the door and stepped inside. A good rug muffled his step and he looked at the desk and bookcases and cabinets, all solid walnut, and he gently punched the leather chairs. "This is really quite grand," he said, smiling. "Quite unexpected, sir."

I moved past him and opened another door, then stepped to the other wall and opened one more. "You have two examination rooms, doctor, each separated by a storage and supply room that is accessible from either room. This assures privacy."

Then I took Dr. O'Brien by the arm. "Your room is just across the hall. If you'll step this way—"

I let them look around and waited in the hallway until

they both came out. Down the hall were two more offices and when they saw the names on the doors, I explained that they hadn't arrived yet but I expected both of them in three weeks.

Then I took them on a tour of the first floor—the second was still completely vacant—and we spent some time in the operating room; they wanted to look at the equipment. Personally I believed it to be the most complete this side of San Francisco, and there were two recovery rooms, and quarters for the surgical nurse or doctor to call.

As we walked deeper into the building, I explained: "At the present time we are using the rest of this floor for hospital facilities. The facilities, when conditions warrant, will be moved to the second floor. Then there is a full basement, which is actually segmented into comfortable quarters. The doctors have a front entrance and the nurses have two side entrances."

Christina stepped out of a door farther down the hall and stopped. "Gentlemen, may I present my wife, Christina. She is my sole nurse until the others arrive later this month." I presented them. "Dr. Strudley. Dr. O'Brien."

Dr. Strudley bowed over her hand and O'Brien held it a bit longer than I thought proper, but I couldn't blame him for that. Christina was a lovely woman, more so now than when we had been married. I knew she was happy. Not as happy as I, to be sure, for I really felt that I was a changed man. I had gained some weight and my disposition had improved one hundred per cent.

"Would you like to visit our patients, gentlemen?" She turned and held open the door and we stepped into Alfy Hulse's room. He was propped up in bed with a third grade reader; he had not been wasting his time and Christina, who taught him when she could, claimed that he was a good pupil.

I took his pulse; it was strong and steady. "How are you feeling, Alfy?"

"Fine, doc." He looked at Strudley and O'Brien but said nothing.

"Gentlemen, may I introduce our sheriff, Alfred Hulse. Dr. Strudley and Dr. O'Brien." They shook hands and I turned to Christina who had come in with us. "Dear, would you undo the bandage, please."

261

When she had exposed Alfy's healing wound, both Strudley and O'Brien examined him. "Ugly devil," Strudley said and looked questioningly at me.

"Made by a .44 pistol ball. It had come to rest touching the superior vena cava."

Dr. Strudley's imperturbability broke. "And you probed for that!" He looked at Dr. O'Brien. "Amazing, wouldn't you say, doctor?"

"Indeed," O'Brien said, thoughtfully. "Tell me, doctor, do you generally take such risks?"

Before I could answer the door opened and Angeline stepped in. "Oh!" she said, surprised to find us there. I quickly took her arm and hauled her into the room before she could leave. I introduced her and Christina replaced the bandage around Alfy's chest.

"Mrs. Hulse has been a constant companion and a great help these last few weeks," I said. Then I steered them out of the room, and turned them down the hallway.

There were five other patients: a gall stone, a laying-in after a difficult childbirth, a Caesarian section, and two cowboys who had had a fling in Georgia and come back with swamp fever. Fortunately they had been from Spindle and the minute Tennessee Frank found out they were sick he hauled them into town for me and I kept them from spreading it and causing a panic since the symptoms of swamp fever and Yellow Jack are the same.

The only difference being that with one you died and the other you recovered.

It took a few days before Dr. Strudley and Dr. O'Brien got settled in and I took them about town, introducing them to the mayor and the leading citizens and I hired Guy Hulse to drive them on their rounds; I didn't want them getting lost because there was a lot of Texas out there and all the Indians hadn't been run out by Colonel MacKenzie's soldiers.

Still I felt this was the best way to get to know the people, to get out for ten days and make the rounds of the farmers and ranches and see some of the country and sample home cooking and frontier hospitality. They'd learn about Texas politics and Texas troubles and they'd try to decide who was right, the cattlemen or the farmers and they wouldn't be able to make up their minds either.

The end of line of the Texas-Pacific was only twenty-six miles north of town now. We were beginning to feel the impact because some of the engineers stayed at the hotel and the survey crew used Victoria as a base because they were building a roundhouse to the east of town and business was booming like it had never boomed before.

And the last man I expected to see was Walter Ivy.

I was in my office, making up an order for medical supplies when someone knocked, opened the door, and there he was, a little heavier, his hair a little thinner, and certainly more solemn than I had ever seen him.

"Close your mouth, Ted," he said, smiling, flinging his hat in a chair. "This isn't a throat examination."

"What the hell are you doing back?" I asked, crudely, but to the point.

"Ted, do you have room for an older, wiser pill-pusher?" He sat down and crossed his legs, and looked at me as though he were cadging a drink.

"Did Dorsey come back with you?"

He shook his head. "No, I—ah—well, she's pregnant again, Ted. I couldn't persuade her."

I studied him for a moment. "Walter, you never asked her. Isn't that it?"

He tipped his head forward and nodded. "I just couldn't take it anymore, Ted. God, it seemed as though I lost touch with everyone except her parents; she was always over there. Or they were always over to our house." He wiped a hand across his mouth. "Ted, all my life I've had the feeling that I'd be easily smothered. Have you a place for me here?"

"Walter, it wouldn't be the old arrangement; things are too far along for that. I could rent office space to you and you could go back into practice, the same as O'Brien and Strudley are doing." I put my elbows on the desk and clasped my hands. "Walter, what's going to happen when Dorsey comes to her time? Will she come back here or will you pull up stakes and go east again?"

"I don't know," he said. "I hope I have the strength to make her come to me."

"Like the last time?"

263

"I wish you wouldn't throw that up to me, Ted. I let you down badly, I know."

"I managed."

"Yes, so it seems. Has your practice picked up?"

"Three times what it was seven months ago when you left."

"I suppose I'm still remembered?"

"You know the answer to that."

He got up. "Could you find someplace for me? A back room? A spare closet?"

"Now don't start that throw-me-a-bone-I'm-starving-to-death business, Walter. Your suit cost eighty dollars, at least, and from a private tailor. That watch charm is ruby, isn't it? About a hundred and ninety dollars?" I leaned back in my chair and regarded him carefully. "Walter, you've always managed to take care of yourself very nicely. Your office rent is one hundred dollars a month, just the same as the others. you pay for your own nurse."

"I don't want a nurse, Ted."

"Who's going to take care of your patients?"

"I always have," he said. "That hasn't changed."

"All right." I opened a drawer and gave him a folder. "This is a rate charge for hospitalization, surgery, etc. I think if you'll study that you'll find everything quite equitable."

"My, we certainly are all business, aren't we?" He winked and folded the papers and put them in an inner pocket. "Are you still living in my house?"

"Yes. We've closed off one wing, the old office wing."

"I'd like to move back into it," he said matter of factly. "As soon as possible. I'll set up my office there."

That was a surprise and it stung me; he was rejecting the hospital and I wasn't sure why. But my pride wouldn't let me argue with him. "All right, Walter. If it wouldn't inconvenience you, could you live in the wing as I used to and give Christina and me a chance to find another house and move out?"

He waved his hand; Walter could be really magnanimous at times.

When I told Christina that Walter was back and that he wanted to move into his house she just snorted through her nose and withheld her opinion, which wasn't very good at best and was getting steadily worse. And I wasn't sure what she disliked, the idea of Walter coming back or leaving a pregnant wife.

It is truly difficult to divine the mind of woman and wise men do not try.

In ten days, Christina and I found a small house on Pearl Street and it had a nice garden and back yard and a carriage shed, and since we were both partial to low, ranch-style adobe, I bought it for sixteen hundred dollars; we moved in immediately and since Mrs. Hempstead had always favored Dorsey and subtly reminded us that we would never have her kind of class, we let her go and she stayed on with Walter Ivy as his housekeeper.

Alfy Hulse was released from the hospital, as were my other patients, but somehow the beds never remained vacant long. Dr. Strudley and Dr. O'Brien were partially responsible for this because they had both practiced in large hospitals and understood the advantages of hospital care and urged their patients to forsake home treatment.

Thank God the nurses arrived. Five of them and they came south on the train; end of track was now the roundhouse while a new depot and freight shed was being built.

The one who immediately impressed me was Mrs. Murdock, a woman in her late forties, English, unbelievably proper, and as grim a person as I've ever seen. She inspected the hospital like a field commander looking over the sorriest troops ever to be inflicted upon his command. Nothing was right. The place was not nearly clean enough to suit her and there wasn't a decently made up bed in the place, or certainly not neat enough to suit her.

Hercules in the Augean stables was a doddering old swamper compared to a determined woman attacking dirt. Mrs. Murdock could bark orders like a top sergeant and there was no doubt in my mind, or in the minds of the other nurses, who was going to be head "cap" around there.

Mrs. Murdock, an amazing woman; she would even have been an amazing man. Married to a lieutenant in the Coldstream Guards who had fallen in 1856 in the Crimean War, she was left with two small children and only a small pittance from the Crown. She dedicated herself to helping the sick and bedridden, learned by practice, and soon advanced to formal nursing.

With her children grown and happily married, she came to America, and then she came to me, I'm happy to say.

In one week's time she knew every nook and cranny of the hospital, could recite from memory the inventory of my supply rooms, and at all times knew every detail of everything that went on.

The great stone face could instantly cow the roughest cowboy. Yet I noticed that no child ever showed the slightest fear of her, for she had the gentlest hands and it was not uncommon for a crying infant to stop when she brushed its forehead.

15

THE RAILROAD certainly brought prosperity to Victoria and the war-tattered economy of Texas was finally on a firm and independent footing. Cattlemen now drove to the loading pens and sold to the local buyers; the day of the big drives was nearing an end although in isolated parts of the state, they still went north with the herds each spring.

Most all the ranchers and farmers had put down wells and now the windmill salesmen came and before fall, you could see them, whirling landmarks where once there had been nothing but rolling land and grass.

If a man had the time it was pleasurable to go down to the depot and watch a freight train being unloaded. Shining John Deere plows and harrows and new buggies and wagons. Prices on many items in Rolle Dollar's store came down, especially the breakable items; the railroad was just not as rough as freight lines and items could be less expensively packed.

Then a flatcar came in and was put on the siding and it changed everyone's life in some way. In many cases it ended life.

The flatcar contained barbed-wire, the first any of us had ever seen.

At first everyone thought it was for Rolle Dollar, and an angry group of cattlemen converged on his store to have words with him. But the wire didn't belong to him; he had earlier thrown the salesman out of the place and refused to handle it.

So an independent store had opened up in a back room.

The salesman was a representative of a wire company from Peoria, Illinois, and he had four helpers, four of the toughest looking men I had ever seen. They all stood six foot four in their stocking feet and they wore derbies and high, turtle-necked sweaters and carried brass knuckles and the cowboys hated them.

But none of the cowboys wanted to fight with them.

These gentlemen made certain that the wire was safely

transported from the railroad siding to the warehouse in back of Bingham's saddle shop—and Bingham, who had only rented the barn because the money was good, was all but an outcast.

Farmers made their purchases there and the helpers loaded the wagons and escorted the farmers out of town, riding a sort of shotgun to the farm, and there unloading the wire.

The salesman made a lot of money because there was no doubt in anyone's mind that the barbed wire was superior to the old single-strand stuff. And any steer driven into the wire would be torn pretty badly.

So the veterinarian was bound to pick up a little business there.

George Thursday, a young El Paso lawyer who had moved to town six months before, handled all the books for the hospital—his practice was not yet so extensive that an outside job insulted him.

I mention this because people were paying their bills. Not only the current ones, but for services rendered up to two years before. These Texans had their pride and they knew that ten dollars wasn't the usual fee for delivering a baby, so they came in and paid me the other forty and went back home feeling square with the world.

And the Mercy Hospital's account at Cardine's bank crept into the black.

Well into the black.

But it seemed that the hospital routine would just never settle down, and then it dawned on me that it never would. Dr. Fred Ellsworth, a young surgeon from Chicago arrived. So did Dr. Linus McCaffe, a physician from Baltimore; he was a friend of Walter's, a robust out-going man not above talking about someone else's business.

It was obvious to me that we were going to have to furnish the second floor before winter, and that wasn't far off. Until now we had ordered all meals for the patients and staff from the hotel; they were brought to and fro in a dogcart, and Mrs. Murdock didn't like that at all.

Walter Ivy, I'm sure, would have immediately labeled her a meddler, a complainer, but I found that everything she said made sense, and Mrs. Murdock wanted a kitchen and dining room for the staff installed in the basement.

A little figuring soon pointed out that her argument would save us a good deal of money in the long run. So we consulted Rolle Dollar and sent to Kansas City for the equipment and Mrs. Murdock handled the hiring of personnel; she must have interviewed forty people carefully before selecting six, all negro.

This caused me a moment of concern, for although I had not picked up any southern prejudices, I knew how strongly the feelings of these people ran and little bothered them more than negroes running around and not belonging to anyone. Mrs. Murdock was firm as only she could be, and I let the matter go.

I was asked to attend a meeting of the county supervisors, not an unusual thing, so I had an early dinner with my wife and walked over to the courthouse. Walter Ivy was there, which didn't surprise me much; he had been getting back into the old swing again and I only saw him now and then since his practice kept him pretty busy.

When I came in he looked around and patted a chair near him so I went over and sat down. The small room was choking with cigar smoke and the supervisors were arguing over the cost of cement sidewalks along main street. I listened to the pros and cons of it and finally they had a vote; the sidewalks would go in as soon as bids could be let.

There was a man there I didn't know, and finally he was identified as Prentiss Chalmbers, of the Edison Electric Company. Mr. Chalmbers was an engineer and he wanted to sell the county board on having an electric light plant built and street lights installed. For better than forty minutes he displayed graphs and charts and explained that a power company could, in twenty years, amortize the investment through sale of electrical power to individual customers.

Walter thought all this was boring as hell, but I was interested.

But Mr. Chalmbers didn't make his sale; unanimously the board felt that people were perfectly satisfied with coal oil lamps and that seemed to be that.

He gathered his charts and briefcases and as he passed down the aisle, I touched his sleeve and he stopped. "I'm Dr.

Bodry. Would you meet me in the hotel bar, say in an hour, for a drink?"

"Delighted, doctor." He nodded and went out.

Came then the matter for which the supervisors felt that my presence was needed.

My bill for the care of Sheriff Alfred Hulse.

Mike Sharniki, who was the chairman said, "Doc, this here bill is a little steep, ain't it? Four hundred and seventy dollars?"

"I thought it was very clearly itemized," I said. "Alfy was in the hospital for thirty-two days, and for the first week he required almost constant day and night care. At ten dollars a day I think that's most reasonable. Your wife thought so when she had that miscarriage two months ago."

He wasn't going to argue about that I could see. "Well all right, doc. It says here your fee is a hundred and fifty dollars. As I recall it took you all of fifteen minutes to get the bullet out of him."

Walter J. Ivy cleared his throat and everyone looked at him. He said, "It seems to me that Dr. Bodry's error is not breaking the bill down to component parts. Now I would have charged a dollar for taking the bullet out."

There was an instant buzz of talk, which stopped instantly when he said, "However," and he waited for silence to run on a bit. "However, I would have charged you three hundred dollars for knowing where to dig for it. That's really not much for a good man's life, and I trust no one here is going to say that Alfy Hulse is not a good man. Best lawman we ever had!"

Someone moved that they pay the bill, and it was seconded and passed. Walter and I left right after that and as we walked across the lawn, he said, "You need someone to collect for you."

"Walter, I never once doubted your power of persuasion."

We reached the corner where he turned and he stopped to light a cigar. "Ted, thanks for turning some of the collections over to me. I'd have never known if—"

"I would have, Walter. Are you spending a good deal of time in the country?"

"You know me, the wandering pill peddler."

"What do you hear from Dorsey?"

It was a question he hadn't wanted me to ask, but I didn't care about that. He pursed his lips and shot up his eyebrows. "Not much. To be honest she hasn't answered my letters. Damn it, what kind of a wife is she anyway?"

"She's probably asking the same kind of question about you."

He laughed although it wasn't funny to him. "I heard that Dr. McCaffe arrived. He's a good man, if you can stand him. I think he came from a large Irish family of seventeen where no one had any privacy or secrets; he just can't mind his own business."

"Is he a trouble maker?"

"Oh, no, no, no, no, nothing like that."

He started to turn away and I took his sleeve. "Walter, why don't you ask him how Dorsey's getting along?"

"Perhaps," Walter said, "if I happen to run into him." Then he turned and walked slowly down the dark street and I thought: now there goes an unhappy man, and a damned fool.

At the hotel bar I found Prentiss Chalmbers and we took our drinks to a table. "I was very interested in what you had to say tonight."

He laughed. "It's too bad I can't say the same for the board. Ah, well, time is on my side. We're in the process of putting in electricity in San Antonio and Dallas. Other towns will follow. It's inevitable."

"I had some experience with electric lights in Baltimore." I said. "They impressed me as being highly superior to lamps, even with surgical reflectors." I leaned forward. "Mr. Chalmbers, I run a hospital and if you can spare the time before you leave, I would like you to look over the building and discuss the possibilities. We have a steam boiler in the basement now for heat and hot water. Perhaps—"

He smiled. "A small dynamo and steam engine just to furnish light for the hospital?"

"Yes."

He thought about it a moment. "Could I look at it now? I really would like to take the morning train because I have an afternoon appointment in Austin."

I paid for the drinks and we left the hotel together.

At the hospital I introduced him to Mrs. Murdock; I hadn't

thought for a moment that I could have escorted him through without her knowing about it. And she got a lamp and went on ahead of us into the basement.

Chalmbers inspected the furnace and the flue and made many calculations on a note pad; we spent thirty minutes while he poked around and asked questions about the walls and floors. Finally we went back to my office and Mrs. Murdock left us.

I gave Chalmbers a cigar and a light; he settled back in a chair and said, "I would say a little over four thousand dollars. Of course that includes shipping, installation, and an electric motor to convert your pull elevator to electric. Electricity is power, doctor, not just light. It does useful work."

I shook my head. "I just couldn't go that much money, Mr. Chalmbers. Perhaps in another year—"

"Your bank—"

"No, I'm in debt for twenty thousand dollars now. Private loan."

He laid one of his business cards on my desk. "Doctor, I must catch the train, but talk to your backers. Four thousand dollars is not a lot of money considering the investment you already have. Please exhaust a few possibilities before giving up the idea." He got up and buttoned his coat. "Wire me at the Senator in Austin. I'll be there three days." He drew deeply on his cigar. "Doctor, let me make you a proposition. It's been my observation that doctors are pretty influential people in a community. A doctor gets a new buggy and it isn't long before someone else buys one. I want to sell Victoria on electric lights. All right, I'll go through the back door if I must. I'll refigure this so that installation and equipment is at our cost, and run electric lights to your home from here." He winked, and smiled. "In a year, or less, my company will be back to install them for the town. I'd take that gamble."

"In round numbers, what would that figure be?"

"About three thousand dollars."

It set me to pacing around the office; the gamble was there, and it looked good to me, a risk that I believed would pay off. It meant that I wouldn't be able to buy one piece of equipment for eight months, and I'd have to talk Butram Cardine into a personal loan, but I believed I could swing

272

that. So I turned to Prentiss Chalmbers and said, "I'll wire you the money in Austin. Is that satisfactory?"

'Perfectly. And I'll come back, make up specifications, and sign the contracts. I want you to understand that this unit, boiler, engine, and dynamo, is not simply a basic unit. It should be ample to handle your needs and expanded applications for many years. It's not wise to try to get by. Never open up a possibility of overloading the equipment."

I saw him to the door and shook hands with him, and after he left I checked with Mrs. Murdock and went home.

Christina was in the parlor, wrapped in a wooly robe, curled in the big chair with a book. She put it down when I kissed her then she got up and went to the kitchen, bringing back a tray with coffee and peach pie.

"What's new and exciting with the county board?"

"They paid Alfy's bill," I said.

"Good."

"They also turned down a proposition from the Edison Electric company to put up electric lights."

She thought about it a moment. "It would be nice, wouldn't it? But I suppose it's expensive. Everything nice is."

"I talked to the representative," I said. "As a matter of fact, if I can get a loan from Cardine, I'm going to have a plant put in the basement of the hospital." Then I told her how much and took some of the joy out of it.

"Do you think you ought to—well, go deeper in debt?"

"That really doesn't worry me," I said. "Christina, all I've seen this country do is grow. Really. The railroad's come here and people have come here. Why, two years ago when I rode south and found that family killed by Indians, all the country there was prairie. Now there's eight farms out there, with houses and barns and fences up and crops growing. Look at the town. Why this spring alone there were eleven new houses built. Everything's growing, Christina. I've just got to grow with it."

"Ted, I wouldn't hold you back. You know that." She put her arms around me and kissed me, then raised an eyebrow. "Everything's growing, but we're not raising a family. Got something against kids?"

273

"I'm trying. I'm trying," I said, holding back a smile.
"Try harder."
"Oftener?"
She smiled. "That too."

16

IF I had known anything at all about railroads I would have realized that the roundhouse switch yards meant something, but my knowledge is limited to riding on the trains. So when Murray McCloud, the division superintendent, called on me, it was somewhat of a surprise and I wasn't sure exactly what he wanted.

McCloud was an eastern man and spoke with a real Yankee twang, but he was blunt and to the point, and he liked business first and his fun second. He wore corduroy pants and jacket and flat-heeled boots and he had dirt under his fingernails, which immediately impressed me for I am partial to supers who work.

He had a map and unrolled it on my desk, then placed his finger on Victoria. "This is going to be our terminal. As you know, end of track is now pushing southeast to Port Lavaca. The survey crew is working now in the vicinity of Goliad, to the southwest. By summer of next year we'll have a rail down to Gussettville and Laredo on the border. And from the Gussettville junction we'll have lines to Rio Grande City and Brownsville." He folded the map and put it on the floor. "That means we're talking about a crew of three thousand men, doctor. Quite naturally we have our own physicians and emergency facilities; they're always getting hurt. Railroad building is not a safe occupation. However, our facilities are limited. Always have been and always will be. We just cannot hospitalize the injured. No place to put them. Therefore, the railroad would like to enter into negotiation with you for the care of these men."

The possibilities of this rather staggered me, but I tried to act as though I discussed these things every day. "Mr. McCloud, what are the percentages? Your accident rate in ratio to the number of workers employed?"

"Around six and a quarter per cent," he said, drawing a notebook from an inner pocket. He consulted it. "Eighty per cent of those are fractures, abrasions, and crushing accidents. Eleven per cent are injuries due to strain. The rest, general failure of health through disease." His manner brightened. "We are not particularly bothered by social diseases, doctor, because we take care to clean up the towns we work near. A dirty red-light district can put half the crew down with runny peters, to put it bluntly."

I jotted these figures down on a pad. "Exactly how would you like for me to proceed, Mr. McCloud?"

"The railroad is not interested in bogging down further with more paperwork, doctor. That is to say, we're not in favor of a rate that is based on individual injuries or diseases. What we want is an overall, blanket charge that will cover everything." He leaned his forearms on my desk. "Understand, doctor, that every patient you get from us will require hospitalization. We understand this, so we expect to pay for it. But any railroad that wants to stay in business knows that to get good workers and keep them you have to feed well and take care of them."

"I'll discuss this with my colleagues immediately," I promised. "Where can I get in touch with you?"

"I'm just moving into my office near the roundhouse," McCloud said. He offered his hand. "Call on me there. And if I'm out, the chief clerk will know where to find me or get in touch with me."

I walked with him to the door, then went back to my office and worked for several hours, jotting down figures. Of necessity I had to work from the percentages of fracture cases, which predominated as to injury type. And then I had to compute on the most serious, leg and rib fractures, to arrive at a stable fee.

Finally I sent for Mrs. Murdock and she made certain the other doctors were notified of a four o'clock meeting; I requested that they all rearrange their schedules and be there.

I even invited Walter J. Ivy, although I didn't expect him to respond.

And I should have known better than to figure that because he came to my office ten minutes later. Fred Ellsworth arrived and Mrs. Murdock brought him an extra chair. Then McCaffe, O'Brien, and Strudley came in and sat down and I explained in detail the proposition offered by the railroad.

No one doubted that it was a good thing; it could be a

bonanza that would, for over a year, guarantee the hospital a substantial income. I gave them the figures I had come up with and then we broke them down carefully, taking first the fee for hospitalization.

Dr. Archibald Strudley had an opinion: "Our standard fee is ten dollars a day, and four more for a special night nurse if around the clock attendance is required. You've quoted ten dollars straight across the board, Ted, and I jolly well think that's a bit high. Eight would be more in line, you know. I was resident in Charing Cross and on the main the average nurse can quite capably handle eight average bed patients. And the more you have, old boy, the less expensive it is. Ten dollars a day wouldn't near cover the cost of home care, while in the hospital it's ample."

"I'm inclined to agree," O'Brien said. "Archie's figure of eight dollars seems most reasonable. Good for us and good for the railroad."

Walter Ivy cleared his throat but no one paid any attention to him.

"You have the averages working for you, old boy," Strudley said. "According to the figures you've outlined, we should have eighteen or twenty beds constantly occupied. That's two thirds of the second floor. That would average out to two hundred dollars a day."

"All right, eight dollars then."

We discussed in length the other facets, surgeon's fees, physician's fees, cost of the operating room, and once in a while Walter Ivy would clear his throat and finally Archibald turned and glared at him, his handlebar mustache bristling.

"Well, sir?" he demanded, with unnecessary emphasis.

Walter Ivy's head came up and he looked at Strudley for nearly a minute and I had never seen him with that expression; he was like a little boy who had been unruly in class.

He got up and said, "If you'll excuse me, I have calls to make."

"Walter," I said quickly, "I wish you wouldn't go."

"I can contribute nothing here," he said and walked out.

Strudley swiveled around in his seat to watch him, then said, "What a ruddy bore."

It was on the tip of my tongue to contradict him, but I

held back, suddenly realizing that Strudley was more right than wrong. Walter Ivy, in the presence of these men, did not come to the forefront, and this saddened me considerably.

Still there was business to get on with and it was a quarter to six before we hammered it all out, the blanket fee which would cover everything from a mashed toe to the most serious abdominal surgery.

Eighteen dollars and seventy-five cents a day.

George Thursday came to my house after supper that night and we sat in the parlor until quite late, preparing the first draft of the contracts; he intended to have them ready the next day and take them to Murray McCloud himself.

It was very late when he left and Christina had already gone to bed, but I wasn't ready to sleep, so I got my hat and coat and walked across town to Walter Ivy's house.

The lamps were still on in the parlor and I knocked; he came to the door a moment later and seemed surprised to see me. "Come in, Ted. I was reading."

As I stepped into the parlor I could see no book or paper and knew that he hadn't been reading, but it was none of my business. "May I offer you a drink, Ted?"

"Thanks, Walter. Whiskey and water." I sat down and put my hat on a side table. "How is Dorsey?"

"Well. I got a letter from her father. Not very friendly in tone, but informative. She's going abroad for two months with her parents. England and France." He came back and handed me my drink. "What brings you out tonight, Ted?"

"Just hungry for some talk, I guess. Old ties and all that."

He bunched his eyebrows. "It seems to me the old ties are pretty well broken, Ted."

"Walter, that sounds a little petulant. I do wish you'd forget that incident this afternoon. Strudley is a little crabby and gruff by nature, but he's a good man."

"I consider his an insufferable ass!" Walter said, with surprising vehemence. "It seems to be the pattern with a man who's been to Oxford, Leipzig, or Zurich. They know it all and anyone else's opinion isn't worth a tiddly-damn." He hoisted his drink and tossed it off, straight.

For a few moments the ticking of the hall clock was the only thing that broke the silence, then I said, "Walter, I wish

278

you'd reconsider and join the hospital staff. You'd find the arrangement quite satisfactory."

"Do you really think so? A man must be his own boss, Ted." He shook his head. "I wouldn't be worth anything in staff conference; you saw that this afternoon. I was an outsider and they damned well showed me my place." He splayed his fingers against the leather arms of the chair. "Ted, I believe in home care for my patients. I believe that a member of the family can offer the patient far more through love and devotion than any nurse, no matter how well she's trained. It is a gospel with me, Ted. The natural way for a woman to give birth is in her bed, in her own home, attended by a mid-wife or a friend, not some disinterested, sterile, hatchet-face who happened to go to school to learn how to carry a bedpan. It is just as simple as that."

"Walter, I've never for an instant considered you a foolish man. Please don't make me revise that opinion now."

"Revise what you damned please," he said. "I'm not like you, Ted; I don't automatically believe that every change, every step of progress is for the best. I love medicine, the country doctor, call-me-any-hour-of-the-day-or-night kind of medicine. I'm not dazzled by polished marble floors and a nurse in a starched uniform. Pomp and ceremony is for the military, Ted. You can't run the heart on a schedule."

I sighed and picked up my hat. "I'm sorry I disturbed you, Walter."

He smiled unexpectedly. "Walking out on an argument, Ted?"

"There doesn't seem to be much point in continuing it. But you're turning into a disappointed man, Walter. For God's sake, and your own, I wish you'd reach some reconciliation with your wife."

"That wouldn't be hard. I could go back to her."

"Can't you do that?"

He shook his head.

"Good night, Walter."

I let myself out and walked slowly back to my house. The hall lamp was still burning, although it sputtered, nearly out of kerosene; I blew it out and walked quietly up the stairs, trying not to wake my wife.

She was awake, propped up in bed, reading; she put the

magazine down when I came in and I undressed. "Did you go to see Walter?" I must have looked surprised, for she laughed. "After you left the house I wondered where you would go, then I guessed that it would be Walter's. And if you called this late, it meant that you were bothered by something serious. A disagreement?"

"The man needs his wife. If he had any sense he'd go back to her."

"If she had any sense she'd be here," Christina said. "Ted, it's the man that makes the woman happy and content, not the house or the place where the house is built." She grew thoughtful. "I think it's his son. He needs the boy. Walter's a natural-born father, Ted. He'd spoil the boy rotten, but he's that way. He's got to give love and when he's denied that, he turns sour."

"I never thought of it that way."

"Well, isn't it that way? The army for many years, that was his love. Then you. Why did he single you out, Ted?"

I thought about it, then smiled, "Because of my singular brilliance? No?"

"No."

"That's a crushing thing to say to a husband. Did you know that the top of your nightgown is unlaced?"

"Don't change the subject."

"That material is quite sheer, isn't it?" I sat on the edge of the bed and put my arms around her and she half tried to push me away.

"You are just not concentrating," she said.

"Oh, but I am!" I said and blew out the light.

She giggled when I slid under the covers.

A wire to Prentiss Chalmbers caught him at the hotel in Austin; my proposition was simple and put very straight forward: I wanted the electric dynamo and would buy it if the company would extend a line of credit. I would make my first payment, one third of the amount, ninety days after the plant was installed, and two equal payments one month apart.

Late in the afternoon I got an answer from Chalmbers; the equipment would be shipped from Buffalo, New York within ten days for he had wired in the order and recommended that the credit arrangement be approved. I could

280

expect the workmen in two weeks to install the base for the dynamo and steam engine, and put in the wiring and fixtures.

Perhaps I was taking a chance, counting my chickens before the eggs had been laid, but I felt completely confident that the Texas-Pacific Railroad would sign the contracts I had offered. If they didn't, then I'd try to negotiate a personal loan at the bank. Butram Cardine was not exactly a friend, but he wasn't an enemy either. The death of his son had made him very solemn, and he constantly wore a mantle of shame, as though his son's downfall was really his fault.

When a man feels that way, the best thing to do is to leave him alone.

The Texas Rangers had set up a tent camp about a half-mile north of town, and increased their number to seven, all gaunt, hard-eyed men who walked softly and made people jump when they spoke. The fence cutting went on, but it was not as wide-spread as it had been, mainly due to the rangers constantly patrolling, and Alfy Hulse's deputies on the move all the time.

And Alfy was back on the job, gaining weight now to where you could hardly know that he'd had both feet in death's door. I saw him now and then and twice I went to his house on Sycamore Street to see Angeline. Marriage agreed with her; she was getting plump and was constantly gay and hoping that she'd hurry up and get pregnant because she knew that Alfy would be a wonderful father.

Why do women always think that? In town alone I knew a hundred men who were terrible fathers.

And some women who were worse mothers.

But in the beginning they all thought they were going to be wonderful.

With Angeline and Alfy I had no doubt at all. All the giddy, little girl-teasing ways she had once had and which had irritated me so much were gone. She kept a neat house, cooked well, and knew how to make Alfy come home nights.

And it made me wonder if she hadn't really reduced the good things in life down to the basics and not cluttered them up as Dorsey cluttered her life. And Walter's.

Some people just couldn't remember that it was good to be alive.

17

SINCE IT is a general feeling in Texas to ignore Mexicans, I do not hold anyone at fault that the Mexican boy who had been shot down on Victoria's main street was quickly put out of mind, and once Scotty Breedon paid his fine and served his time in the jail, he went back to work as though it had never happened.

Only the Mexicans working for Will Stang didn't forget it and they paid pretty close attention to their fences, taking turns each night to guard them. The fence cutters were still pretty busy and you might wonder why all the fuss about a little cut wire. Perhaps it is best appreciated if one realizes that ten per cent of a farmer's total investment goes into his fences. Digging post holes is a tedious, slow job; they must be set straight and even and the job is usually laid out by a surveyor to make certain you're not on someone else's land. Then the wire has to be strung, stretched and stapled so that it does not sag. All this costs money and a good deal of it.

A cut wire means more than splicing; it means restringing for a hundred yards, and a little of this can soon run a farmer into the hole since he's working hard to get a foothold to begin with.

So with the two Mexicans alternating patrol on Will Stang's fence it was only natural that sooner or later they were going to meet up with the wire cutters.

It was one of those starry, black, moonless fall nights and the wire cutters, Scotty Breedon, his brother, Jonas, and a cousin called Jim-John bellied up to Will Stang's fence with cutters in hand. And the mysterious hand of fate which stirs us all gave a peculiar swirl to it then and brought Jesus Garcia and his double-barreled shotgun to that point as Scotty Breedon snipped the first wire. It sang when it parted and Jim-John swore when a barb cut the back of his hand.

Those two sounds were enough for Jesus Garcia; he was no more than twenty yards distant and he pointed his shotgun down toward the ground and fired: BAM! BAM! as quickly as he could pull the triggers.

The first charge of buckshot caught Scotty Breedon and his brother, Jonas. Scotty took most of the charge in the head and chest and died instantly, and Jonas, badly wounded and partially blinded, got up and ran stumbling across the prairie, searching for where he had left his horse.

Jim-John, badly frightened, jumped up and Garcia's second charge took him through the lower legs and he fell, screaming and rolling.

The unaccustomed violence and Jim-John's screaming frightened Jesus Garcia and he dropped the shotgun and ran toward the house about three-quarters of a mile away. Of course the shooting woke Stang and his wife and Garcia's cousin, but he reached the yard by the time they dressed and rolled out and lit lanterns.

It took a minute or two to calm Garcia and get the straight of it, but then Stang put him on a horse and sent him to town for the sheriff and doctor while he and Garcia's cousin took lanterns and a wagon and went out to find the wounded men.

Alfy Hulse woke me and told me quickly what had happened; he had a saddle horse waiting for me outside. When I came out, Sergeant Burkhauser and two other Texas Rangers were mounted up and ready to go; we left together and wasted no time getting to the Stang place. Mrs. Stang, a pretty woman in her thirties, was on the porch and she pointed as we rode up, indicating the south pasture and we went there, guided by the lanterns bobbing about.

"Thank God you got here," Stang said as we dismounted. Scotty Breedon lay pretty much as he had fallen, wire cutters still in hand. His brother was gone, but Jim-John lay ten yards away, dead now. His left leg had been nearly blown off at the knee and the right one would have been beyond saving; he had bled to death trying to drag himself back to where they had left the horses.

Sergeant Burkhauser, with a lantern and the instincts of a fine hunting dog, said, "There were three. The other one's wounded. Better come with us, doc. You goin' to stay here and get the straight of this, sheriff?"

"Yes," Hulse said.

"Where's Jesus Garcia?" Stang asked.

"He wanted to wait in town," Hulse said.

A ranger brought up our horses through the break in the fence and we swung up and started trailing the wounded man, Burkhauser leading the way. We found the place where the horses had been picketed, and blood on the grass; the horses, a bit frightened by the smell of blood, had reared and pulled their pins, but the trail ended so we assumed that the third man had caught up his horse and managed to haul himself aboard.

Burkhauser picked up the tracks of the horse and once a direction was established, Burkhauser blew out the lantern. He lit a cigar and said, "This is Circle B graze. Let's pay a call on Sam Usher."

I wondered why he had waited this long to identify the brand; we all knew who Scotty and Jonas Breedon worked for, but then I realized that Burkhauser had held open the possibility that the third man had worked for another brand.

Now that he was certain, he lifted his horse into a trot and two miles later we came into the dark yard; there was no light showing anywhere.

A voice from the vicinity of the porch said, "There's a dozen rifles trained on you so move easy!"

"This is Burkhauser, Texas Rangers! And you'd damned well better put those rifles up in a hurry and strike a light!"

He had a bull voice and there was a flurry on the porch, then several lanterns were lit and Sam Usher and his son stepped into the yard, holding the lantern up so he could see.

"What the hell you want here?" Usher asked. He was a typical Texas cattleman, as lean as a razor back hog, tough as a saddle, and he held little fear of man or beast.

"A little fence cuttin'," Finley Burkhauser said, stepping from the saddle. "Scotty and Jonas Breedon are dead, Sam. We think the third man made it back. Brought Doc Bodry along."

"No one here," Usher maintained.

"Don't be a fool now, Sam," Burkhauser advised. "We'll make the fence-cutting charge stick so why let a man die because you can't let go of a thing?"

Usher's son shifted his feet and moved his hand an inch closer to the butt of his pistol; Burkhauser said, "Sonny, it would grieve me to have to shoot a young fella like you, but things are a bit touchy right now and I'd have to figure any move you made was hostile. So if you get to jerkin' your hands I'll have to blow you plumb in half." He looked steadily at the boy, then switched his attention to Sam Usher. "Well, Sam, you don't have all night about this."

"He's in the bunkhouse," Usher said wearily. "The boys are with him but I don't think it's any use."

I didn't give a damn for his opinion; I turned and trotted across the yard and rushed into the bunkhouse, ignoring the pistols suddenly pointed my way. Then I saw the man, a blanket completely covering him.

One of the cowboys said, "You're ten minutes too late, doc."

"I didn't want to be," I said angrily. "Sam wanted to jaw in the yard."

"Well, he made it back," another said. "That's what he wanted, I guess." He looked at me. "Scotty and Jim-John?"

"Dead," I said and walked out.

Everyone was in Usher's house; his wife was making coffee and Burkhauser was asking questions and writing the answers down in a notebook. Then he snapped it shut and put it in his pocket. "Sam, I want you to come into town in the morning and turn yourself in to Alfy Hulse. We'll get the judge to hold a hearing and set bail. Now you understand I'm bein' reasonable about this. Don't make us come after you."

Sam Usher nodded. "All right, Burkhauser. I'll be there."

"I guess there's no more here," Burkhauser said and the two rangers with him went outside. "Sam, Sam, you damned fool. If you caught a man rustlin' your beef, you'd hang him. Don't you think this is just as serious? Or did you figure that it wasn't because he was a farmer?"

Usher's expression turned bleak. "I don't want to go to prison, Burkhauser!"

"You be in town in the morning or I'll have every law officer in the state of Texas after you," Burkhauser said and turned to the door. He stopped there. "Tell me something, Sam: do you think Scotty got what was coming to him for killing that Mexican?"

"It seemed a little stiff to me," Usher said. "The fine was enough; I had to borrow to pay it."

"Well that boy's cousin killed your men after they cut Stang's fence," Burkhauser said. "Now who the hell do you think the joke's on?"

He brushed past me and went out and I followed him and we mounted for the ride back. We rode along a way, then he said, "Sometimes I just don't understand a man's thinkin' at all, doc. Usher's a good man, but he just can't get things in the right perspective and believe that a farmer has the same rights he has."

"Sergeant, what do you think a jury will do?"

"It's hard to say, doc. People have been livin' under this threat of violence for some months now and they're gettin' tired of it. Could be that they'll hit Sam Usher hard and let that be a warnin'. Or they might let him go."

"They do that," I said, "and there'll be more fences cut and more men killed."

The jury deliberated for two hours; they did not let Sam Usher go. He was fined fifteen-hundred dollars and given two years in Huntsville prison, a verdict which outraged many of the cattlemen, yet impressed them that high-handed methods were going out of style in Texas.

It was the beginning of the end of a long reign for the man on horseback; the man on the street had a voice and he was using it and none of the cattlemen were stupid enough to think that they could swing an election and buy the law on their side.

So the wire cutters, like the illegal running iron, went into the bottom of feed bins and haymows and there was no more wire cutting. In November the Texas Rangers departed and the land settled down to the winter, which gave every indication of being mild.

The summer had been reasonably cool, with now and then thunder showers breaking up the hot spells and keeping the creeks up; it was what old timers would someday call a good summer, and I suppose, on the main, it was.

It was a good summer for me, both professionally and personally satisfying, since the hospital was increasingly becoming the Mecca for the sick and we had patients come from as far as Abilene and Jefferson for operations or treatment.

Certainly one of the sensations—and old timers still talk

about it—was the evening when Prentiss Chalmbers closed a switch in the basement of the hospital and the dynamo hummed and electric lights came on all over the building and pushed the night completely away. In front, over the main entrance, a cluster of frosted glass globes flooded the brick walk with light and the crowd gathered there gasped, then cheered.

I went home immediately; Christina was waiting for me and the house was dark. Inside the door I turned a porcelain switch and the parlor lights came on, brighter than fifteen lamps, and we went through the house, turning on the lights and marveling at the wonderful brightness of it all.

"I've never seen them before," she said softly, almost crying. "It's like the day never ends, isn't it?"

Aaron Stiles, who liked a bit of controversy anyway, wrote a lengthy article in the Victoria paper and chided the county board for being so short sighted that the town as the whole didn't enjoy this blessing.

It was a good article and Christina clipped it out and put it away.

Electric lights in the hospital opened new horizons for us and took much of the terror out of night emergency cases, if you can imagine what it is like performing a tracheotomy on a four year old choking on a button and nothing to illuminate your work but a kerosene lamp. Ward duty became easier for lamps are cumbersome and you either leave them on and waste kerosene or you're always lighting and blowing them out.

The lights pulsated slightly; you noticed this right away, but in fifteen minutes you forgot about it and could read without strain and operate without fear.

Everyone seemed very enthusiastic about the lights and most of the town council and county supervisors came around for their tour of the plant in the basement and they would stand there and watch the brass governor balls on the steam engine whir around and listen to the hum of the dynamo and shake their heads at the incomprehensible miracle of it all.

Guy Hulse, who worked full time as ambulance driver, janitor, and general handy man, was given an intensive course by Prentiss Chalmbers in the care and maintenance of the plant, and although it was beyond my understanding, Guy could shut the plant down in the daytime, change lightbulbs, rewire switches, rig extra lights for special use, and make repairs on the dynamo when they were needed. He didn't understand anything about electricity except that it was like water through pipes; if you kept the flow uninterrupted everything worked fine.

Mechanical aptitude, which Guy had in abundance, was a dark, mysterious tangle for me and I could not replace the nut on a buggy axle without cross threading it.

I rather expected Walter Ivy to say something to me about the lights, but he did not. He came around one evening, looked at the cluster of outside lights a moment, then walked to Mulligan's saloon and began his evening drinking. Alfy Hulse spoke to me about this because Walter was carrying this on a little too far and too steadily and once Alfy had had to escort him home while Walter sang old cavalry songs in a loud, off-key voice.

We didn't see much of one another; he still practiced in the county, keeping his office in the wing of the old house, and he never brought a patient to me. He lost a few; doctors have to learn to live with that, and I never heard anyone blame him because death is understood by all people.

He came to me one night when I was in my office, studying some journals; I looked up to see who had opened my door without knocking for no one on the hospital staff ever did that.

He stood there, hat in hand, then said, "May I sit down, Ted?"

I hastily waved him into a chair and he seemed relieved to find himself welcome. "A late call?" I said, trying to establish some level of conversation.

"No, just putting something off as long as I could," he said. "Ted, will you loan me the money to go back to her?"

"How much do you need?"

"Four hundred would do nicely."

I started to ask him about his practice but he waved his hand, cutting me off; he didn't want to talk about anything and I understood how much it had really cost him to come to me this way. I got a key and unlocked a cash box I kept in my bottom desk drawer and counted out the money.

He got up, pocketed it, then said, "I was hoping I could count on you, Ted."

"Why, Walter, you—"

He shook his head, turned to the door and walked out.

Alfy Hulse told me later that Walter Ivy remained sober that night and took the morning train.

18

TWO EVENTS of great importance to me happened in the summer of 1876: Angeline Hulse gave birth to a boy and he was named Harry Calender Hulse; I promptly dispatched a telegram to Harry in Cincinnati, knowing he would be immensely pleased and flattered.

On July 2nd, Christina went to the hospital and I paced up and down the hallway and decided then and there that every hospital ought to have a rubber room for prospective fathers. Dr. Strudley was the attending physician and Mrs. Murdock was really snapping orders to the nurses, and in due time, with no complications at all, I became the father of a girl, which was what I wanted all the time anyway.

And before you think that doctors get this attention for nothing, let me put in that I promptly paid the bill, a hundred and thirty-one dollars and took my wife and infant home three days later.

I hired a maid, a girl from Goliad who was half Spanish, half French, and had an addition built onto the back of the house to accommodate her. She was quite young, hardly more than a child, and each month she sent ten dollars to her mother because there were two younger sisters to support and no steady work except washings and the like.

Unfortunate people are really unfortunate.

That summer brought great news for Colonel Ranald Mac-Kenzie had moved all the Comanche and Kiowa Indians to a large reservation just north of the Red River in the Indian Nations, and Texas knew what it was to live for once without hostile threat.

Walter Ivy never wrote to me at all through the preceding winter and that summer and I wondered what he was doing, and how he was doing, and whether or not he had patched things up with Dorsey; a man can worry about things like that.

But I couldn't worry long because my position in the community had expanded with the population growth and the hospital required most of my attention and I was very happy with my wife and baby daughter, so I really didn't care what Walter J. Ivy was doing.

This may sound a bit heartless, considering what I owed Walter Ivy, but I lived in Texas, which was big and robust and growing like untended weeds, and of course it was Texas, the land of the paradox and the extremes. Towns like Victoria, with robust leadership, were sporting cement and brick sidewalks and afternoon tea for the ladies was a popular thing and every parent of any means made sure their daughter finished high school and the son went on to college. We had our churches and our community theatre and our hospitals and all the culture we could get or afford, and a lot we really couldn't afford.

Still Texas was the frontier, wild, with wild men and wild cattle and a man might wear a waistcoat and hard hat in town, but when he passed beyond the limits he wore a pair of .44 pistols and knew how to use them or he might not reach his destination.

Texas railroads were laying down new rails, but the stagecoach was still the way to travel if you wanted to hit any but the bigger cities. Farmers came in by the hundreds and settled and really it didn't change the complexion of the country much; Texas was cattle, with vast empires ruled by stern barons.

I really had no time to worry about Walter Ivy. Rather I put my faith in human nature, and knowing Walter Ivy's restless spirit, I rather looked for him to come back.

He would find Texas changed. We had law, grand juries, county attorneys, judges, small claims courts, and the largest outlaw and cattle rustler population in the entire west. And for boyhood heroes, Texas youth had the notorious Judge Roy Bean, John Wesley Hardin, and other popular gunfighters.

Doctors no longer pulled teeth as a sideline; we had bonafide dentists with degrees of such solid character that they no longer had to travel about in a wagon to escape the wrath of outraged patients.

We even organized a county medical society, of which I was elected secretary and treasurer, and it pleased me to have Dr. Strudley serve as the first president. We were a proud and dedicated part of the state medical society and now it was not possible for some half-trained charlatan to set up practice and bilk sick people with candy pills and snake oil.

The society examined credentials most carefully and any doctor wishing to practice had to be a member of the local society, or he just didn't get anywhere at all.

Monopolistic it may be, but we were protecting the health of our patients, and to each of us this was of the highest importance.

And Walter Ivy came back on Christmas Eve.

Christina and I were holding an open house; perhaps twenty people cluttered our parlor with laughter and talk and I was having such a good time that I didn't even hear anyone knock. Then I saw our housekeeper motion to me and I went up to her. "There's a gentleman here to see you, doctor."

Oh Lord, I thought, not a patient tonight. I went with her to the entrance foyer and she opened the door. Walter Ivy said, "If this is a bad time, Ted, I can come back."

"Well for gosh sake! Come on in, Walter." I started to take his arm then I saw someone standing down on the walk and I leaned forward to see and when I couldn't I switched on the porch light. "Dorsey!" I went to meet her; she had a child in each arm and I put my arm around her and led her to the porch. "What are you standing out here for? Go on in, Walter. René, fetch Mrs. Bodry." I was simply bubbling with words.

Dorsey said, "Ted, please, can we go to your study? I don't want to—well, to meet anyone just yet."

"Certainly," I said and went ahead and opened the door. When they stepped in I snapped on the light and closed the door. "Put the baby on the sofa there. Say, that's a husky looking boy." I took the oldest from her and he promptly grabbed my nose and pulled. Strong little devil.

I put the boy on the floor and he crawled about. "Sit down," I said. "When did you get in, Walter?"

He looked at his watch. "Eighteen minutes ago. The hotel was full-up. Damned unusual, isn't it?"

"Being the junction of the railroad brings a lot of travelers to town. I hope you've come back to stay."

I tried not to pointedly stare or to appear to be examining them, but it was difficult not to. Walter's suit was showing wear and Dorsey was not dressed in the fashionable way she always liked.

Walter seemed a bit nervous and kept running his hands through his thin hair and Dorsey made an elaborate study of her fingernails. Then he said, "I'd like to find a situation here, Ted. But I suppose now there isn't much for a man in private practice."

Christina knocked on the door and I stepped out into the hall quickly. "Will you give us a few minutes, honey?" I spoke softly.

"Is something the matter?"

"I'm not sure. All right?"

She kissed me lightly. "Sure, Ted."

Then I went back in; Walter and Dorsey had been whispering and they broke it off quickly. "Would you like a drink? The jolly season, you know."

Walter shook his head. "I'm on the wagon, Ted. You might as well know it straight; I hit bottom. Lost a patient. There was a suit. Took everything I had. Everything Dorsey's parents left her. You're looking at a man who got here on borrowed money, Ted." Then he gave a humorless laugh. "I left here that way too, didn't I?"

"Hell, that doesn't matter, Walter. Dorsey, can't I get you something?" She looked at me as though I had offered her charity, but she said nothing, just shook her head.

I sat down and looked at them. "What made you decide to come back here, Walter?"

"Where else could I go?"

It was a good question.

Dorsey stopped toying with her fingers and looked at me. "I know you don't have a very high opinion of me, Ted."

"I did until you taught me different," I said. This was no time to be subtle or polite.

"If I'd have stuck with Walter perhaps none of this would have happened; isn't that what you think?"

"I wouldn't care to speculate on that, Dorsey. But you made Walter reach for something he didn't want and stretch too far to get it. You can't tear a man apart, Dorsey, and expect him to come to much." I looked at Walter Ivy. "Did they revoke your license to practice?"

"No," he said. "There just wasn't any practice. Patients

simply switched to another doctor." He shifted his feet. "When I left here, I didn't have much of a practice. I guess I drank it away."

"You guess?"

"All right, I drank too much. But that's over now. I want to get started again. Small, of course. I have no equipment now. And no money."

"Well, I can ask the county medical board to meet after Christmas," I said. "It's their decision."

He looked at me steadily for a moment. "So you have that out here too now, huh? Who's the president? You?"

"No. Archibald Strudley."

Walter laughed again. "Hell, I might as well forget it."

"You're not giving the man any credit at all," I said. "He's not narrow-minded, Walter. Let the board convene. I can offer you a position at the hospital. It'll be salaried, but you can get along on it and in time build up enough savings to start again."

"How much time?" Dorsey asked.

I shrugged. "Depends on how much you can save."

"You're not answering my question," Dorsey said in that hard tone she could fetch up on a moment's notice.

"All right, Dorsey, the salary is forty dollars a week and office space. Walter will be my assistant. He will see the patients referred to him and that's all. He'll also be admitted to membership in the county medical society and in two or three years, when they find out he's not back on the bottle, he can go into private practice. Now that is the best I can do, Dorsey. It'll mean living in a small house and washing your own clothes, but there's nothing disgraceful in that."

I expected her to suck in her breath and go into an outraged tantrum, but she simply said, "Ted, I think that's generous. Don't you, Walter?"

"Yes, more than I'd hoped for."

"Now won't you please come and join the party?" I said. "René can bed the children down in the nursery and you can have the bedroom in the east wing for yourselves. Please accept it as something willingly offered."

"You're very kind, Ted. And thank you," Dorsey said.

I called René and Christina came in and Dorsey took the two children and went out with them.

After the door closed, Walter Ivy said, "They'll have a good cry. I wish to hell I could, Ted. It might make me feel better." He sighed and patted his pockets, but he was out of cigars and I offered him one of mine, and over his protest, shoved four more in his pockets. "Sixty thousand dollars, Ted, that's what it cost Dorsey. And I don't understand it. Not to this minute I don't."

"Don't understand what, Walter?"

"Why she did it. Took her money and bailed me out." He sighed and hid behind a wreath of cigar smoke. "I didn't know her parents had died, Ted. She was unbelievably angry at me for leaving her like I did. When I went back she wouldn't let me in the house. So I stayed at a men's club. Then my trouble came and it was a pretty lonely feeling, no wife, no one to turn to." He sighed. "It was what they're now calling appendicitis in some circles, but it's still perityphitis to me. She was a lovely girl, twelve years old with ringlets two foot long down her back. The attack came on suddenly and I prescribed a strong cathartic. She was dead in eleven hours and the autopsy showed pus throughout the abdominal cavity."

"Dreadful, Walter. But hardly grounds for a suit."

He smiled and shook his head. "When her father came to see me, I was drunk. The child's nurse also said that I smelled like a hot mince pie. The father was wealthy, a man of influence. It never got to court, of course. Dorsey heard about it and it was settled quietly in chambers."

"You didn't send for her?"

Walter shook his head. "No, she came to me. She paid the attorney in cash. Sold the house, everything, to do it. Then she looked at me and said, 'Well, Walter, we do have to go on living, don't we?' I haven't figured out what she meant by that. We talked. I knew it was impossible for me to continue any kind of practice, and we had to live. She had no home. I had none. A friend with a good deal of pity loaned me train fare for the four of us and forty dollars. I've got eleven left."

"I wish I could offer you more, Walter. Believe me."

"I'm glad to get this," he said. "It's more than I expected." He smiled. "I'd have been a poor risk for a loan but I'd have asked for one. The pride's gone, Ted. Dorsey's too, I'm afraid. And I'm sorry about it."

"Why?"

"Well, she's a proud woman."

"Too proud."

He shrugged. "I won't argue it. But it'll hurt me to see her wash clothes and scrub floors."

"It won't hurt her. It'll do her a lot of good, Walter."

"Well, you always were the optimistic one, Ted. She's a good woman, Ted. Stubborn, vain, and proud like you say, but I love her. God knows where I'd be today without her. It'll take a lifetime to pay her back."

"Don't do it."

He frowned. "But it was her money, Ted. All she had in the world. Her inheritance."

"Damn it, Walter, it was the only thing she ever gave to the marriage. Don't be an ass and take that away from her. Fact is, I think it might be the only thing she ever gave anyone. She did it because she loves you. Be thankful for that."

"I hope you're right."

"Walter, I feel sure I am. Live now. No fancy servants to wait on her. Let her be a woman. She may turn out better than you thought." Then I got up and took his arm. "Now come and join the party; I insist."

"This will be embarrassing for me, Ted."

"So what? What do you expect to do, pull a sack over your head and go around that way so no one will know you?" I opened the door and propelled him into the hall. Then we went in to join the others.

19

THE MEETING of the county medical board was in the supervisor's board room at the courthouse, and to facilitate business—and because our membership was small—these meetings were always jointly held with the societies of the neighboring counties.

On calling the roll, I found that representatives from the counties of Calhoun, Refugio, Goliad, Lavaca, and Jackson were there, as well as our own county, Victoria.

The agenda was quite long, but finally we got down to that singular item, membership, and Walter J. Ivy's name was offered. There was no immediate objection and I didn't think there would be, but the matter was open to discussion, and Dr. McCaffe, who had friends in the east and kept in touch, had something to say.

Everyone had something to say, and I would like to be able to claim that it was my brilliant argument that saved Walter Ivy's application, but it didn't turn out that way. Reason being that Dr. Strudley wished to debate the matter with Dr. McCaffe, and in order to legally do so he appointed me chairman pro-tem for the duration of the motion and I had to sit there and keep my mouth shut.

In the final analysis it was agreed that each of us was a good deal less than perfect and that each of us could clearly remember standing by and watching a patient die because we had been stupid, or ignorant, or smug enough to make a hasty diagnosis and find it wrong. Walter Ivy had been unfortunate in that the patient's parents were in a position to destroy him, but his misfortune was not a lifetime condemnation, and his application would receive a favorable vote from the society.

So Walter Ivy became an employee of the hospital, the doctor who was always there, on call throughout each day and all night two nights a week. It must have been humiliating for him, to have no patients of his own, and to be subject to the orders of every doctor in the place.

The most familiar sound in the hospital became, "Dr. Ivy, would you assist me, please?"

Within ten days I found a house that Walter could rent; it was a small place, just four rooms with a nice yard and a garden and Christina and I had mixed emotions when they left our house. We didn't want to see them go yet we were delirious with joy that they were going, for Dorsey had to work very hard to keep from being snappy and resentful.

She had made her decision, her bargain, yet she wasn't quite reconciled to living with it. It would take time and I'd just as soon she did it on her own, and in her own house.

The first day of 1877 was clear and cold and there was a rime of ice on the water bucket on the back porch when I woke and carried in wood for the kitchen stove. After breakfast I walked to the hospital and Mrs. Murdock was waiting with a report; every morning she did this, bringing me up to date on what had transpired during the night. We always had a dozen railroad men in the hospital; it seemed to be an average that did not vary much one way or the other, and as soon as one was discharged, another would be brought in.

I spent the morning checking records and hospital business, then I heard the whistle at the roundhouse and started to take out my watch, thinking that it couldn't be noon already. But the whistle kept blowing, short, strident blasts.

"Wreck!" I said to the empty room.

As I came out of my office, Mrs. Murdock hurried down the hall, a roster in her hand.

"Dr. Ellsworth and Dr. McCaffe are here. Dr. O'Brien and Dr. Ivy are on the second floor wards. Shall I summon them, doctor?"

"Yes, in my office. Tell them not to rush; it makes the patients apprehensive. Where is Dr. Strudley?"

"At home, sir. It's his day off."

"Have someone go for him."

I stepped back into the office and turned to the window that gave me a good view of the town and the main street. As I watched, a minute went by, then another, and then I saw the man running toward the hospital, mackinaw flapping, legs pumping.

He stormed in, panting, and I made him sit down and poured him a drink of whiskey, not that he needed it, but it would calm him. "Doc, some bandits blew the trestle on San Fernandez Creek south of Gussettville! They thought it was the payroll train, but it wasn't. It was the work train goin' to end of track!" He looked at the bottle. "Could I have another hook of that?" I poured and he downed it.

"It's bad then," I said. "How many were hurt?"

He shook his head. "The conductor shinnied up a pole, cut in to the telegraph wires and called back. The train's derailed. It's real bad, doc." He wiped his mouth. "There's a train leaving in fifteen minutes. Murray McCloud will hold it that long for you."

"You tell him that will be fine."

When I stepped out, Mrs. Murdock and the others were waiting in the hallway. I said, "Dr. Ellsworth, you're to remain here with Dr. Strudley when he arrives. The rest of you bring bandages, morphine, all the supplies you can carry. Mrs. Murdock, have Guy Hulse bring up litters, blankets and all that and load a wagon; we'll meet him at the train."

"Right away, doctor." She moved on down the hall.

"I'll meet you gentlemen at the train. Be quick and dress warmly; we may be out there all night and then some."

I gathered what I thought I would need, bundled in my heavy coat, put on overshoes and made sure that I had mittens and a wool scarf. Then I went to the railroad yard and Murray McCloud's office; it was a madhouse and he was barking rapid-fire orders. When he saw me he waved me inside and in a moment came in and closed the door.

"Goddamned bandits," he said. "Mexicans, the way I got it. There were a hundred men on that damned train, Ted. God knows how many of 'em are dead or crippled." He flapped his arms wildly. "The whole train went off, engine to caboose. The engine's in the creek. The boiler blew up. Scalded the engineer and fireman to death. Oh, Jesus, you don't know how a railroad man hates this!" He looked out the window where the work train was making up, a huge crane looked like a gigantic, gaunt bird, all neck and no beak. A string of caboose cars was being hooked up. Then he turned back to me. "The dispatcher has cleared the track and we'll keep it clear, because we're going to highball, doc." He turned again to the window. "Say, ain't that your man with a wagon?" He flung open the window and yelled down. "Hulse! Hey, Hulse! Take that over to the caboose where the rest of the stuff's being loaded!" Then he waved and slammed the window shut, closing out the inrush of cold air. Then he poured a drink for himself. "Someone coming with you?"

I nodded and he seemed relieved. "Murray, when we start to bring the injured back, I'll want two of your caboose cars. We'll spray the insides thoroughly with antiseptics and—"

"Christ, you can paint them sky-blue-pink for all I care. The railroad's yours, doc." He grabbed up his mittens and buttoned his coat. "It's time to go. I hope you told your wife you wouldn't be home for supper."

"Mrs. Murdock will take care of that," I said. "She takes care of all the details."

"Yeah," McCloud said. "You ever want to get shed of that wonderful old bitch, I'll make her division super. If I didn't have a wife and four kids I'd marry her myself. They just don't make 'em like that any more."

We left the building and walked across the confusing mass of the switch yard; everyone ran around, yelling orders and it was amazing to me that anything was done, but it was, quickly, and correctly. The train was made up, two engines hooked in tandem, huffing and breathing as though they just couldn't wait to let all out and get rolling.

Walter Ivy and the others were there, on the rear platform of the caboose. Guy Hulse had his wagon parked nearby; it had been unloaded.

I called out to him: "Guy, have the ambulance waiting when we get back. See if you can get the undertaker's hearse and any other carriage that's closed."

"How about Herman Muller's meat wagon?" he yelled.

The train lurched forward and I bobbed my head and he waved and turned the team around. With two engines pulling, the train picked up speed rapidly and it rocked along and the clack of the trucks over the rail joints picked up in tempo.

The pot-bellied stove was kicking out heat and McCloud passed coffee all around. "It's two hundred miles to the wreck," he said, glancing at his big railroad watch. "The engineer tells me he can hit seventy-five most of the way and eighty after he passes the Gussettville siding. That puts us about three hours out."

Linus McCaffe looked around nervously. "Seventy-five, by God that's pretty fast, ain't it?" He tried to sound as though he reached this velocity as a common occurrence, but he was thinking what we were all thinking, that that was a fair clip, and a little faster than we liked to go.

There wasn't much talk; we drank coffee and smoked and Murray McCloud took out his watch quite often and then he said, "Seventy-eight point three miles an hour. Old Ernie must have the throttle bent."

Dr. O'Brien said, "How can you tell?"

"Count the telegraph poles," McCloud said. "I know how far apart they are and I look at my watch. The rest is simple arithmetic."

"I wish you hadn't told me," John O'Brien said.

We slowed through Gollad and Aransas, to about fifty, and then built up speed again. And after slowing briefly for the Gussettville siding the engineers really opened it up.

We slowed finally and arrived at the scene of the wreck at two-thirty in the afternoon and all I can say is, thank God it wasn't night. Of course the trestle went up along with a case of dynamite and the engine and tender were flung up and over, landing upside down in the creek bed, where the engine's boiler exploded. The rest of the cars, about six flat cars and ten work cars, ran on over the horrible wreckage, spilling and tumbling and breaking and flinging themselves every which way.

The survivors—and there were at least forty men moving around—had organized into work crews, aided by a work train that had come out of the Gussettville siding and had gone back before we arrived. There must have been seventy-five men in the Gussettville crew and most of them were working furiously, laying down a temporary siding; the ties were in and the rails were being laid.

But understand that in dealing with such heavy equipment, nothing is done quickly; it all takes time, hours of time. Our concern was for the injured, and there were so many that it was difficult to know where to start.

Right away I had the last caboose unloaded; this would be

pushed onto the siding as soon as the switch was put into the main line, and in the meantime I had Dr. McCaffe set up a first aid station in the car to take care of the walking wounded and those only slightly hurt. In this category I placed broken arms and cracked ribs.

It is not possible to describe with words the sounds of such an accident. We arrived roughly four hours after it had happened and still there were men buried in the wreckage, men alive and screaming for help, or for someone to kill them and end their agony.

Blankets were used to wrap the living as they were gotten out. The dead—some of them anyway—were being moved to one side and laid on the bare ground. I counted sixteen and guessed that that number would double before we were through.

I told Dr. O'Brien to stay with one crew that was digging into a jungle of sheared lumber and bent steel, and Walter Ivy went with another.

Toward evening a company of Texas Rangers arrived; they reported briefly to McCloud that the Mexican bandits had been stopped before they reached the border and they were on their way now to a place north of Rio Grande City where the Mexicans were holed-up and making a fight of it.

As the mangled and maimed were being removed and our morphine supply dwindled, I made a decision. I found McCloud and drew him to one side. "Murray, I've got eight men, very bad. I suppose there's another twenty or thirty in there somewhere, alive. But I can't wait. If I do, some of these men will surely die. I've got four certain amputations, one both legs above the knee. I can't get enough morphine into them to kill the pain without killing them."

"Do you want to send the train back now?"

"That's six hours before it'll get back," I said. "That's too long, Murray. It's a case of waiting and having some of these men die or sending the train now and surely having others die." I scrubbed a hand across my mouth. "You have two engines. Can you get everything except one engine and a caboose on the siding?"

"Yes. Touchy, but it can be done."

"And can you get a man up the pole to cut into that telegraph line?"

"No trouble."

"Then what I want to do is put the worst cases in the caboose. I'll write out a wire to Dr. Halverson in Gussettville. He can do his best, which will be far better than we can do here now, and when we take the rest back we can stop and pick them up and then go on to Victoria and the hospital."

"Sounds good," Murray said. "Give me twenty minutes." He dashed off, yelling orders and I sat down and took a leaf from my notebook and composed a message.

Dr. Elmer Halverson
Gussettville, Texas

Placing in your care these desperately injured. No facilities here for operative measures. Do your best and accept my apologies for placing in your hands an impossible situation. However, it is much worse here. If possible, prepare patients to be moved when hospital train comes through late tonight or early morning.

Regards,
T. Bodry, M.D.

The work train was slowly backing; it had left one engine idle on the main line near the wreck and the rest of the train backed far down the track and there dropped off a caboose, then inched forward on the hastily laid siding. I could see it settle as the weight of the crane car moved onto it and there was a great deal of creaking as the rails took the weight. And as soon as the last car had cleared the switch and it could be thrown, the engine idling on the main line backed up, connected to the caboose and pulled forward again.

The injured were loaded and I sent Dr. McCaffe back with them; he would return as soon as possible. McCaffe's complexion was gray as I gave him instructions: "Remain with Dr. Halverson and assist him in any way. You'll likely be in surgery for two hours. Give him any supplies he needs, then return with the train."

He kept nodding his head and looking at me. "God," he said, "it's awful, isn't it?"

"I imagine it's like war," I said. "Good luck. Save who you can and don't weep for those you lose."

"I think I will anyway," he said and I jumped down as the train started to move backward, picking up speed.

20

IT WAS amazing how Murray McCloud could maneuver the train, sorting out what he wanted; I thought it was like a serious game of checkers on wheels, a series of clever moves that reversed the order of the engine and wrecking crane so that it could be backed up to the wreck and lift rubble and debris out of the tangle.

When night fell, lanterns were rigged on poles, and two men carried a wooden case of ammunition clear of the wreck scene and fired star shells into the air where they burst and cast a bright, unearthly light over the whole landscape. This was not continuous, only when someone wanted a moment of clear light to fasten a clevis, or when we were trying to bring a man out.

Some cowboys came to the wreck just before midnight and they had a chuck wagon and a large canvas tent and a huge cast iron stove that took eight men to unload. I later realized that this had come out of the ranch house when I saw the wall collar still on the pipe, a brightly painted circle of tin to match someone's wall paper.

They built a huge bonfire and lit the stove and cooked a meal, beef, potatoes, some string beans, and about fifteen apple pies. The coffee was made in twenty gallon pots, cowboy coffee, strong enough to float a horseshoe, and scalding hot.

It was the best food I ever tasted.

The cook made a large cauldron of soup for the injured men; hot soup or broth can give strength to a sick man better than a pound of beef steak. Murray McCloud had some of his men ladle it out and feed it to the injured.

Of all of us, Walter Ivy was more qualified here because of his military and wartime experiences. We all were shocked, stunned by the enormity of the wreck and the number of injured, but Walter had seen it before, not here, but he had seen it, dealt with it, and was less disturbed by it.

Around three o'clock in the morning we got all those out

who were still alive and Murray McCloud had the train on the main line, ready to roll. One of his men was atop the pole with his emergency key and when he shouted down the all clear the conductor waved his lantern and we started back.

Twenty-one dead men on a flat car and the two caboose cars jammed with badly wounded. The other men, most of them bandaged or broken somewhere, rode in another car.

Dr. O'Brien looked completely exhausted; we all were, red-eyed and dog tired. We drank coffee and smoked cigars; McCloud's cigars because we had given all of ours away. Finally O'Brien said, "I wonder how Linus made out in Gussettville?"

McCloud looked at his watch again. "You'll know in forty minutes, doc."

"Maybe I don't really want to know," O'Brien said. "What a mess. How long will it take you to clear that out of there, McCloud?"

"Three days. We'll work around the clock on it." He yawned and rubbed his eyes. "Hell of a way to start the new year, isn't it?"

"It's a hell of a way any time," Walter Ivy said.

We smoked our cigars awhile, then I said, "Walter, you've been to war. Does a man ever get used to seeing a thing like this?"

"Never," he said flatly. "If he does, he's no good to anyone." He took his cigar out of his mouth and looked at it. "Ted, a doctor has to be clinical as hell because he sees a lot of suffering and more than his share of dying, and he can't go to pieces over it. But in the privacy of his own soul he can cry over it. No, a doctor must be clinical all right, but he must also be the kind of a man who is so outraged by death that he will not rest until a cure has been found or a technique developed to arrest that which offends him." Then he looked up at each of us, seemingly embarrassed because he had made a speech.

John O'Brien butted out his cigar and said, "Dr. Ivy, I want you to know that I'm very happy to have you on the hospital staff."

"Why—thank you," Walter said and looked at the scuffed floor of the caboose.

The train finally reached Gussettville and I went to the

vestibule and leaned out as it slowed for the station. There was a large crowd and many lanterns and Dr. Halverson was there, and McCaffe; they had six of the men in a large wagon, bundled in blankets and these men were gently lifted into one of the cars.

Halverson and I met on the platform; he was a man in his forties, and a bit grim about the mouth now. He shook his head and said, "I couldn't save two, doctor. I'm sorry. Terribly sorry." He was very depressed about it.

McCaffe had been tending the loading and he came up, blowing on his hands. He shook Halverson's hand. "It was an honor to assist you, doctor. I took the liberty of making a list of the supplies we used. I'm sure Dr. Bodry will have them replaced on the next southbound." He looked at me. "I'd better get aboard." He clapped Halverson on the shoulder and left us.

"Would you be so kind as to send me your report and bill?" I asked. Then I took his arm firmly. "Doctor, I have three cars of injured men there. How many of them do you think are going to die before I can get them into surgery? Now go home and drink some whiskey and get some sleep. And accept my everlasting thanks for your work tonight."

The conductor was signalling and I hopped aboard as the train started to move. The engineer had the all clear and he bent the throttle again, but I was getting used to it, or beyond caring.

We arrived in Victoria just as dawn was breaking and Guy Hulse had the ambulance there and the hearse and several other wagons, including the meat wagon and the grocer's delivery van. I went on ahead to the hospital and Mrs. Murdock was waiting.

"Dr. Ellsworth and Dr. Strudley slept the night here," she said. "We've set up all the spare beds; everything is ready."

"Mrs. Murdock, we'll have them in the offices before we're through; there's that many."

She didn't turn a hair. "Doctor, we're ready for that too. Your wife is coming over and I've put on ten suitable women from town to assist in the nursing. Over your authority, I've cancelled all time off for the next forty-eight hours."

I shocked her immeasurably by kissing her cheek and saying, "You're a jewel."

"Oh, my!" She turned and scurried down the hall and that was the only time I ever saw her flustered.

Then the ambulances began to arrive and the gurneys ran up and down the hall and Mrs. Murdock supervised the whole thing like a foreman directing steers into the night pens. All surgery cases—and there were nineteen—went on the main floor where Dr. Ellsworth and Strudley examined them, taking the most desperate first. I joined them, scrubbed up and left the rest to Mrs. Murdock.

Seven amputations in a row; it was like a sterile slaughter yard. We were all slightly nauseous from the anesthetic but we could not stop. Dr. Ellsworth's gown became so sodden with blood that he finally tore it off and threw it in the corner and continued to operate in the top of his underwear.

I was conscious of people coming and going, of people helping me. Once I looked up and saw Christina assisting, and another time, at the head of the table, Dorsey. Was that Dorsey?

Seven amputations, and two men died on the table and they were taken quickly out. There was a crushed chest; we couldn't save him, and there were successions of horrible wounds caused by shredded timbers and splinters and steel.

Two nurses scrubbed the floor constantly and Dorsey got down on her hands and knees, like a man searching for a lost collar button and sponged and wiped the floor beneath our feet so we would not slip.

At a quarter after twelve there were no more patients being wheeled through the swinging door and we looked at each other as though we couldn't believe it. It was a nightmare finally closing and we stumbled out and into the hallway. Strudley, the indomitable Englishman, was looking a little peaked and trying not to hide it. We went through the back entrance and let the cold, fresh air clear our heads.

No one said anything. There wasn't anything to say. Ellsworth, always a good surgeon, had risen to new heights, overcoming fatigue and nausea. He had made no mistakes. If the man could be saved, he was saved on that table and we all knew it.

Mrs. Murdock came out and took me by the arm. "Come

along now, doctor. We'll clean up and then I have a nice pill for you so you'll get some rest. Come along like a good boy now?"

We went to my office; it was the only one not crowded with cots and she made me wash up and stretch out on the leather couch. There she was, glass of water in one hand and a pill in the other. Too tired to argue I took it, stretched out and remembered her smiling as she closed the door.

When I woke it was dark outside, but the light over my desk was on and I groggily sat up and looked at my watch.

Twelve-thirty.

She had ears like a cat and I must have made some noise; she was in the room with her stern face and spotless uniform. I said, "Mrs. Murdock, how many times a day do you change your uniform?"

"Six," she said dryly.

"And what do you do in your spare time?"

"Laundry," she said. "How are you feeling, doctor?"

"Like a mule kicked me. And the others?"

"They've all had some rest. We play no favorites around here, doctor."

I laughed. "Mrs Murdock, you're the kindest, most considerate woman I've ever known." Then I looked at her steadily. "And I would venture to say that your husband knew what a jewel he had."

"Adelbert and I were very happy," she said, her eyes suddenly smiling. "When he died, my grief was tempered by the knowledge that I was one of the few women who had ever known complete fulfillment." Then she turned starchy and proper again. "If you'd like, doctor, I'll fix you a cup of tea."

"Thank you, Mrs. Murdock. I'd like a cup. You might bring a pot and invite any of the others in. We might as well get on with the grisly business of statistics."

"I've already done that, doctor."

She went out and I sat down behind my desk and rubbed my hands over my face. I needed a shave badly, but that could come later. Tomorrow or the next day.

Aaron Stiles from the newspaper came in a few moments before Dr. McCaffe and O'Brien arrived. Then Walter Ivy came in with Dr. Strudley, who said, "Dr. Ellsworth is sleeping."

"Let the poor man have his rest," I said and waved them into chairs. "Gentlemen, you all know Mr. Stiles. He's looking for something to print." I glanced at Archibald Strudley. "How bad is it?"

"Well, of the total train crew, there are twenty-one dead, thirty-two with minor injuries, and fifteen on the critical list. We lost four here and Dr. Halverson lost two." He sighed. "It sounds appalling when you call them out like that, in numbers, but considering the seriousness—yes, the hopelessness of those six men, we've done a job of it. A bully good job."

I looked at the others. "Would any of you care to add to that?"

O'Brien shook his head; so did McCaffe.

"We'd have lost double that five years ago," Walter Ivy said softly. "And how many would be dead now if we didn't have this hospital?"

No one wanted to speculate, but they knew what he meant.

Without saying anything about it, I knew that we would all be on round the clock duty; I didn't thank them because they didn't expect it and wouldn't have wanted it.

The meeting was concluded and they left, except Walter Ivy and Aaron Stiles. He folded his notebook and turned to the door. "It was a bad thing all right. A real bad thing."

Then he went out and from the window I saw him hurry up the street.

Mrs. Murdock came in. "Two nurses would like to see you, doctor. Of course it's against the rules, but in this case—" She smiled and stepped aside and Christina and Dorsey came in.

Dorsey said, "You look very tired, Walter."

"I've never felt better," he said. "Never." Then he stepped to the window and looked out. A wan sun was shining but the wind husked cold and sharp around the building corner. "When a man finishes twenty-four hours like this he thinks to himself that nothing as bad can ever happen again. But it does, Dorsey. It's trouble. And it's out there, a flood, a typhoon, an earthquake, disease, pestilence; God knows what's really out there. But when it comes, I'm going to be here, Dorsey." He turned and banged his fist down on the desk. "HERE! That's where I'm going to be!"

"I know, Walter," she said softly. "We'll both be here. I'm not afraid." Then she took his arm and turned him to the door. "Why don't you come home and rest? Just for a few hours?"

"Yes," he said. "I'll do that. Will you excuse us, Ted?"

They went out together and I let the silence run; the wall clock ticked loudly and Christina watched me, her eyes warm and full of love.

"And you, doctor? Where will you be?"

I looked at her and laughed. "Here."

"Walter's going to be all right," I said. Then I sighed and closed my eyes for a moment. "I don't think I'm ever going to catch up on my sleep, Christina."

"Oh, you will. Why don't you come home and I'll fix you some ham and eggs. I don't have to go back on duty for four hours." She came over and put her arm around me. "Humor me, Ted. I'm pregnant again."

What a time to tell a husband! It struck me very funny and I laughed and she watched me, a half smile on her face.

Then she said, "I knew you'd be pleased but I didn't think it was that hilarious." She wasn't angry and I knew it so I got up and put my arms around her and kissed her resoundingly.

Then I put on my coat and we stepped out into the hall; Mrs. Murdock walked up. "I'm going home for a few hours, Mrs. Murdock. If you want me for anything—"

"Everything will be taken care of, doctor."

"I'm sure it will be," I said, turning toward the entrance. Then I stopped and turned back. "Tell me, Mrs. Murdock, where will you be when the next catastrophe strikes?"

"Why—here, of course. What did you think? This is my home."

Then she turned and stalked off as though she were going to give the troops a good dressing down. I took Christina's arm and we went out into the biting air. It was a day for walking and I breathed deeply of the flavors carried up from the gulf, a tangy freshness of the sea.

Out of the roundhouse yard a train huffed, loaded with timbers and a full crew, the trestle gang going to rebuild what had a few days before been destroyed. I heard the train whistle for a crossing and then the sound of it was gone, carried away by the wind. Overhead a bird wheeled and tossed, riding the currents, sailing about in great circles.

I stopped and looked at the town, then said, "You know, Christina, a man would be a little crazy if he ever missed any of this."

"Yes," she said, "I know."

Then we walked on to our house.

Will Cook is the author of numerous outstanding Western novels as well as historical frontier fiction. He was born in Richmond, Indiana, but was raised by an aunt and uncle in Cambridge, Illinois. He joined the U.S. Cavalry at the age of sixteen but was disillusioned because horses were being eliminated through mechanization. He transferred to the U.S. Army Air Force in which he served in the South Pacific during the Second World War. Cook turned to writing in 1951 and contributed a number of outstanding short stories to *Dime Western* and other pulp magazines as well as fiction for major smooth-paper magazines such as *The Saturday Evening Post*. It was in the *Post* that his best-known novel, *Comanche Captives,* was serialized. It was later filmed as *Two Rode Together* (Columbia, 1961), directed by John Ford and starring James Stewart and Richard Widmark. Sometimes in his short stories Cook would introduce characters who would later be featured in novels, such as Charlie Boomhauer who first appeared in ''Lawmen Die Sudden'' in *Big-Book Western* in 1953 and is later to be found in *Badman's Holiday* (1958) and *The Wind River Kid* (1958). Along with his steady productivity, Cook maintained an enviable quality. His novels range widely in time and place, from the Illinois frontier of 1811 to southwest Texas in 1905, but each is peopled with credible and interestering characters whose interactions form the backbone of the narrative. Most of his novels deal with more or less traditional Western themes—range wars, reformed outlaws, cattle rustling, Indian fighting—but there are also romantic novels such as *Sabrina Kane* (1956) and exercises in historical realism such as *Elizabeth, By Name* (1958). Indeed, his fiction is known for its strong heroines. Another common feature is Cook's compassion for his characters, who must be able to survive in a wild and violent land. His protagonists make mistakes, hurt people they care for, and sometimes succumb to ignoble impulses, but this all provides an added dimension to the artistry of his work.

America's Authentic Western Storyteller
T.V. Olsen
Two rip-roarin' Westerns for one low price!

High Lawless. The trail of the dry-gulcher who killed his partner lands Ed Channing smack in the middle of a seething range war. It will take a blazing shootout to settle all the scores—and one good man to bring justice to a lawless land. *And in the same low-priced volume...*

Savage Sierra. Even without the four bushwackers hunting him down, Angsman is going to have trouble staying alive with Apaches on his trail. But Angsman knows a man stays dead for a long time, long time, and he isn't ready to go to hell just yet.

__3524-3 **HIGH LAWLESS/SAVAGE SIERRA (two books in one)** for only $4.99

Canyon Of The Gun. His father shot dead, Calem Gault stands alone against the range king who pulled the trigger. He is just a green kid with fury in his blood, but before he is through, young Gault will have justice—even if it means a one-way ticket to boot hill. *And in the same volume...*

Haven of the Hunted. With the Civil War over, Lute Danning wants to gather outlaws like himself to sabotage the Union victors. Trouble comes with the arrival of a stranger—one who fought for the North and despises every Johnny Reb who ever battled to save Dixie.

__3545-6 **CANYON OF THE GUN/HAVEN OF THE HUNTED (two books in one)** for only $4.99

LEISURE BOOKS
ATTN: Order Department
276 5th Avenue, New York, NY 10001

Please add $1.50 for shipping and handling for the first book and $.35 for each book thereafter. PA., N.Y.S. and N.Y.C. residents, please add appropriate sales tax. No cash, stamps, or C.O.D.s. All orders shipped within 6 weeks via postal service book rate. Canadian orders require $2.00 extra postage and must be paid in U.S. dollars through a U.S. banking facility.

Name _____

Address _____

City _____ State _____ Zip _____

I have enclosed $_____ in payment for the checked book(s). Payment <u>must</u> accompany all orders. ☐ Please send a free catalog.

Two Classic Westerns
In One Rip-Roaring Volume!
A $7.00 Value For Only $4.50!

"These Westerns are written by the hand of a master!"
—*New York Times*

Shadow Valley. While searching for his brother's killer, Holt Cooper runs into a kill-happy mob trying to lynch an innocent man. Cooper's bullets will have to go a long way to fight off the gunslingers—and the last one will be for the real murderer.

And in the same action-packed volume...

Fort Vengeance. Major Dan Fayes has been sent to Fort Costain with one order: subdue the Apaches. What he doesn't expect is that the cunning Indians are armed with the new Henry rifles, and that there is a traitor in the ranks.

__3477-8 $4 50

Barranca. Matthew Dustin and Sheldon Burnett are wanted men, drifters dodging the armies of two countries. Behind them is certain death; ahead, the promise of enough silver to buy safety anywhere!

And in the same low-priced volume...

Jack of Spades. To the army of lawmen who scour the West for him, he is the elusive Jack of Spades, the most desperate gunman on the entire frontier. But the worthless sidewinders who killed his best friend will have a new name for him—death.

__3384-4 $4.50

LEISURE BOOKS
ATTN: Order Department
276 5th Avenue, New York, NY 10001

Please add $1.50 for shipping and handling for the first book and $.35 for each book thereafter. PA., N.Y.S. and N.Y.C. residents, please add appropriate sales tax. No cash, stamps, or C.O.D.s. All orders shipped within 6 weeks via postal service book rate. Canadian orders require $2.00 extra postage and must be paid in U.S. dollars through a U.S. banking facility.

Name _____

Address _____

City _____ State _____ Zip _____

I have enclosed $_____in payment for the checked book(s).
Payment <u>must</u> accompany all orders.☐ Please send a free catalog.